Squinting, he began to see shapes forming in the shadows.

There on a walkway ten feet above his head, he saw, quite clearly, a lithe black and yellow shape run along a rope stretched taught across the void, seeming to defy gravity with its inverted aerial run. It wasn't Sidney's missing companion, but another simian altogether.

And then there were more. As if he now knew what he was looking for, Ulysses could hardly miss them. There were rhesus monkeys dangling from ropes and walkways, gnawing nuts and bits of fruit; spider monkeys by the dozen, family groups gathered on shelf-like perches attached to the walls; mandrills scaling vertically suspended ropes. He even thought he could make out the squatting shape and orange fur of an orang-utan on one of the higher levels, half-hidden behind a balcony.

"Don't bother answering that," Ulysses said coldly, his hind-brain hot with alarm, his grip on the gun in his hand tightening to knuckle white. "Where's the Magpie?"

Preternatural awareness flashed through his brain like a migraine.

"Right here!" came a cackle from the rafters above them. "As is you, Mr Quicksilver, as is you. Right where I wants ya!"

An Abaddon Books™ Publication
www.abaddonbooks.com
abaddon@rebellion.co.uk

First published in 2008 by Abaddon Books™, Rebellion Intellectual
Property Limited, Riverside House, Osney Mead, Oxford, OX2 0ES, UK.

10 9 8 7 6 5 4 3 2 1

Editor: Jonathan Oliver
Cover: Mark Harrison
Design: Simon Parr & Luke Preece
Marketing and PR: Keith Richardson
Creative Director and CEO: Jason Kingsley
Chief Technical Officer: Chris Kingsley
Pax Britannia™ created by Jonathan Green

ISBN: 978-1-905437-86-3

Printed in Denmark by Norhaven A/S

PAX BRITANNIA

HUMAN NATURE

JONATHAN GREEN

Abaddon
Books

WWW.ABADDONBOOKS.COM

For Michelle – Congratulations!

PROLOGUE

Catch of the Day

The Reverend Nathaniel Creed gazed out across the oily black waves towards the impossible place where sky met sea, and considered what it meant to be a man.

In the unreal twilight that came just before dawn the North Sea appeared as an oily surge – an ocean of bleak blackness that mirrored the darkness slowly gnawing away at his heart.

To be a man was to be a thing divine, was it not?

The night was darkest just before dawn, or so they said. But what about the darkness that was slowly but surely eating away at his soul, that had consumed him from the inside out like the worm in the apple, like a rotten canker, for the last seventeen years? He felt himself tense, every fibre of his body tightening in impotent rage.

His soul had never been more steeped in darkness and malice. Did that mean that redemption was waiting just around the corner? Was it darkest just before the light of revelation showed itself too? Was he on the verge of his own epiphany?

The scales had fallen from Paul's eyes three days after he had been struck down on the road to Damascus. Nathaniel Creed had been struck down seventeen years ago. When would be his moment of enlightenment? When would his revelation come? How long did he have to serve like this before the Lord absolved him of his sins? How long?

"How long?" he demanded of the sky. "How long?"

His scream of frustration was snatched away by the

wind sweeping over the hilltops and out to sea, and then it was gone, his desperate plea swallowed up by the turgid polluted clouds, his anger made impotent by the hugeness of the vista before him.

The Reverend Creed's fists bunched in anger, knuckles whitening, nails digging painfully into the palms of his hands. The pain startled him, distracting him from his fury. He blinked, as if on waking from sleep, and looked down at his hands. He could feel that his palms were wet and in the near darkness his fingernails appeared glossily black. Without a moment's thought he wiped his hands on the material of his cassock, the coarse black cloth rough against his lacerated palms.

The Lord is my shepherd; I shall not want. He maketh me lie down in green pastures; He leadeth me beside still waters. He restores my soul. He leadeth me in the paths of righteousness for His name's sake.

What was it to be a man? he wondered. To be a man was to be a creature bound by emotions, at the mercy of one's appetites, to love, to hate, to feel. But he was a priest; he was supposed to be above such transitory, ephemeral concerns. And yet didn't the Bible demand that he love his Lord and Saviour – *Love the Lord your God with all your heart, and with all your soul, and with all your mind, and with all your strength* – hate the Enemy and feel with all the passion of Christ on the cross?

And did not the Bible teach that all men are sinners? Wasn't it Man's fallible nature that had forced God to take human form that he might die for the sins of all? So, then, to be a man was to be a sinner.

Behold, the hour is at hand, and the Son of Man is being betrayed into the hands of sinners.

Well, he was certainly one of those.

He had sinned – O how he had sinned – and he had

been repaid ten times over for it.

Eyes narrowed, he fixed the brooding firmament with a gaze as cold and hard as stone, as if he was trying to discern heaven there beyond the clouds.

"My Lord, why have you forsaken me?" he railed at the stormy sky. As if in response, the clouds broiled and distant thunder rumbled across the cold grey surge at the horizon.

How had it all come to this? He had had hopes, dreams, aspirations... once. But they were long gone. He had had to give them up long ago, exchanging them for his penance, for his transgressions of the flesh.

And it came to pass in an eveningtide, that David arose from off his bed, and walked upon the roof of the king's house: and from the roof he saw a woman washing herself; and the woman was very beautiful to look upon.

The surf sucked at the rugged rocks at the foot of the cliff, the greasy waters petroleum-black as an oil slick. As sunrise drew closer the pollutant cloud cover lightened, puffs of magenta and turquoise appearing amidst the otherwise interminable grey.

The Reverend Creed stared down at the exposed rocks one hundred feet below, made rough and ragged by the relentless attentions of the sea. He could end it all now, should he so choose. He had that much power at any rate – the power to end his own life. The Lord had seen fit to give Mankind the gift, and curse, of free will after all.

If any man defile the temple of God, him shall God destroy; for the temple of God is holy, which temple ye are.

The hungry surges roiled and broke to white water on the black rocks, the gaping maw of a sudden hollow in the waves, a whirlpool forming as the surge pulled back out to sea for a moment, beckoning to him. But he ignored its tempting summons, as he had on every other occasion.

He would not give the Lord his God the satisfaction of condemning him to an eternity in Hell for taking his own life. No, he would see out his penance to its end, all the while hiding his shame from his parishioners, until God chose to end his life, and release him from his perpetual torment.

To his flock he would ever be the genteel vicar of St Mary's, there to serve their every spiritual need. They would never know of the sin that stained his heart black, as black as the hungry sea.

Look like the innocent flower, but be the serpent under it.

Behind him, back along the cliff path, the squat church hugged the cliff top, as if it feared being uprooted from the exposed spot by the unrelenting wind. But it needn't have worried; behind it, on the wind-swept escarpment above the town stood the black skeletal remains of the Abbey that both raiders and kings had attempted to destroy in the past, and yet still it clung on, its stone pillars and buttresses seeming to grow out of the very ground.

Reverend Creed turned his attention towards the town. Lights were coming on in windows on the other side of the Esk as well as in the nearer buildings that clustered together on the slopes beneath the church in the parish of St Mary's. Whitby was waking up.

But while some were only just beginning their day, others – like the Reverend – had been up for hours already.

Creed was momentarily distracted by a bobbing shape out beyond the coast, riding the rolling waves like a skittish colt. It was a fishing boat, clinker built, nets slipping from its sides. Whoever was on board would doubtless be feeling every rolling surge and sucking tug of the sea. But then, the Reverend considered, it probably wouldn't bother the lone fisherman, when so many of the townsfolk made their living from the sea.

As he watched the fisherman hauling in the dragging nets, he was momentarily distracted from his melancholy as he considered that when it came to the fishermen of Whitby, what it meant to be a man was to be, in fact, half-fish, or so it seemed.

For the briefest moment something like a wry smile twisted the priest's lips, a mouth unused to smiling forming a gargoyle grimace in its place.

"Father?" a voice called from behind him, from the direction of the cramped graveyard.

In an instant the smile was gone and he turned to face the figure standing there amidst the weather-worn gravestones. His penance was still not done.

He closed his eyes and, with a harsh prayer, offered himself to God. *Take me now*, he willed, *if you are done with me.* He swayed there in the pre-dawn light, the wind tugging at the uncombed wisps of hair at the sides of his head.

"Father?"

He opened his eyes again. The Lord was not done with him yet.

God is jealous, and the Lord revengeth; the Lord revengeth, and is furious; the Lord will take vengeance on his adversaries, and He reserveth wrath for his enemies.

Reverend Creed turned back towards the church, preparing to face another day of dealing with past sins made flesh, and cursed inwardly, the cruel scowl now shaping his features looking much more at home there.

George Craven started, feeling his skin turn to gooseflesh beneath his weather-alls, despite the layers of linen, wool and rubberized fabric.

"Someone must've walked over me grave," he muttered to himself. Still pulling in the net, hand over hand, the hemp rough going unnoticed under the thick calluses covering fingers and palms, he looked back over his shoulder, back towards the black cliffs of Whitby.

He had that uncomfortable feeling that someone was watching him. For a moment, he thought he saw that someone, up there on the cliff, past the church of St Mary's, the squat building silhouetted against the torpid grey-green clouds.

Squinting to perceive any more through the pre-dawn twilight and across such a distance, the fisherman blinked. And then the figure was gone.

"Who was that, I wonder?" he muttered. "Who'd be out at this hour? Apart from you, George Craven," he laughed suddenly, the sensation of being observed passing, his goose pimples diminishing.

Further back, beyond the edge of the grass-tufted cliffs, the ancient, semi-skeletal silhouette of the Abbey rose black out of the gloom. George's goose bumps returned.

"Talking to yerself again, George," he said, hoping the sound of his own voice would shake the renewed feelings of unease, and then stopped, catching himself. "People'll say yer mad if yer not careful," he added.

But he wasn't going mad, not really, and George Craven knew it. Talking to himself while he was out in the *Mabel*, was just a habit of his, something he did to while away the monotonous hours. No, he wasn't mad, bored with the monotony of it all maybe, but not mad.

The fishing boat bobbed and rolled beneath his heavy booted feet, the fisherman bobbing and rolling with it, never losing his footing for a moment.

The Cravens had always been fishermen, for as long

as anyone in the family could remember. George had followed in his father's footsteps to the sea, like his grandfather before him, and his great-grandfather before that. It probably went all the way back down their family tree to the bottom, where it was rooted in the very sea bed itself.

George's grandmother would cackle like the fish wife she was, through cracked teeth and blistered gums, that Old Man Craven must have married a mermaid, and that their offspring had been trying to get back to the sea ever since.

George smiled as he remembered his grandmother, a cheery soul, and a dab hand with a net needle and a length of twine, as well as with a penknife and a piece of Whitby jet.

Distracted, George's gaze fell to the nets at his feet, now swamping the bottom of the boat. The haul hadn't been great and he would be making a pretty poor showing at the fish market later that morning. By the light of the swaying oil lamp hanging from the mast he could see that there were precious few fish of any worth, meaning he would be back out again tonight after precious little rest. Octopuses and cuttlefish writhed slimily over the wriggling fish as they all suffocated on the deck of the small boat now that they were in the open air. A spider crab or two crawled over the catch, not large specimens themselves, but worth a bob or two at least. He was almost surprised they weren't bigger though; with the increasing industrialisation of the North of England, the growth in unchecked pollution levels in the sea had gone hand-in-hand with the growth of some of its inhabitants.

"Yer not goin' t'make yer fortune with this little lot," he complained to the salt-sea air. "Yer not ever goin' t'make yer fortune out 'ere," he mused, pensively eyeing the shoreline again. No, he was never going to get rich this way.

And then there was something else... something else that by rights shouldn't even be amongst the catch.

The fisherman squinted again, this time peering at the glistening conglomeration of glistening creatures caught in the net. The catch looked like one grotesque amorphous creature as it pulsed and heaved, all misshapen tentacles, barbed fins, gasping gills, flicking tails, scales and sucker pods.

"Is that hair?" George gasped in surprise.

The catch seethed and moved and there it was again. If it hadn't been right there before his eyes, he wouldn't have believed it. Gasping and choking, the gills at its neck flapping uselessly, the creature was dying, but George just stood there in the rocking boat, staring in dumb amazement.

"Neptune's beard! I don't bloody believe it!" he exclaimed, and dropped the net.

ACT ONE

The Curious Case of the
Whitby Mermaid

November 1997

CHAPTER ONE

Gabriel Wraith Investigates

The waiting room was opulent to the point of over-extravagance, Miss Michelle Powell considered, grander and more grandiose than what she was used to certainly, even though her father's legacy had made her independently wealthy. London's foremost consulting detective was obviously doing very well for himself off the back of such a reputation. But then it was also patently clear that he was someone with money and breeding as well. A house in Bloomsbury, no less, only a stone's throw from Russell Square and the austere edifice of the British Museum.

Rising from the chair to which she had been guided on being admitted to the town house, Miss Powell began to pace the room, as one would if enjoying the works of the grand masters on show within the National Gallery.

She admired the Qing dynasty vase above the mantelpiece, the black ebony-wood pedestal bearing a marble bust of the Roman emperor Hadrian and a decorative screen from nineteenth century Japan. She paused before the portrait of a girl in seventeenth century Dutch dress. It was of the Flemish school, she believed, and as a result she strongly doubted that it depicted a distant family member of the house's owner. The oil painting was just another adornment, something of monetary value to be collected and then subsequently shown off.

There was something of the air of an art gallery to this room, in fact, as if everything were on show for appearance's sake, rather than it being there for any reason of emotional attachment or because it spoke to the soul of the house's owner. But then that, in its own way, spoke volumes about the mysterious Mr Wraith.

"Miss Powell?"

The young woman jumped, and gave an involuntary cry of alarm, startled by the sudden reappearance of the manservant. Where a moment before she had been alone, the hawkish butler had suddenly appeared in the doorway, as if he had miraculously materialized out of thin air.

"Are you all right, Miss Powell?" the butler asked, in that forbidding monotone drone of his. It was how she imagined the Grim Reaper would speak, which was an analogy that went well with the manservant's pallid features and hollow cheeks, their gauntness merely serving to highlight the underlying bone structure, giving his features a knife-edge sharpness.

"Y-Yes. Th-Thank you. I'm fine," she stammered, trying to regain her composure. Nervously she adjusted the purple velvet top hat that was already carefully positioned on top of her immaculately coiffeured hair, held in place with half a dozen hat pins, before straightening the bodice of her fitted crushed velvet jacket. She looked – and indeed was – the height of fashion. Only the brass-trimmed velocipede driver's goggles hanging around her neck seemed incongruous when put with the rest of the outfit. But then where was it written that chic young ladies couldn't be budding amateur engineers as well, in this more socially-enlightened Neo Victorian age?

"Very good, ma'am. Then, if you are quite ready, Mr Wraith will see you now."

"Very good," Miss Powell repeated unconsciously, her tone clipped – possibly over-severe she considered, her cheeks reddening at the thought – in an effort to regain her composure.

Why did she feel so intimidated by this place? There was no need to; she wasn't some silly working class girl applying for the position of scullery-maid. She was the client here after all. Then why did she feel so nervous?

"We'd best not keep your employer waiting," she went on. "I'm sure he must be a very busy man."

"Very well, ma'am. If you would like to follow me?"

The butler, dressed in the regulation black, as if he was going to a funeral, turned and marched out of the waiting room with carefully paced strides. Miss Powell followed, the skirts of her dress sweeping the floor as she kept pace with the man, who moved with all the precision of a fish-stalking heron.

He led her back into the just-as-opulent entrance hall of the Bloomsbury house and from there up a mahogany and marble staircase to the first floor. From there they crossed a landing and came to a halt by a pair of grand doors. Seizing the gleaming brass door handles in his white-gloved hands the butler opened the doors and entered the room.

"Miss Powell, sir," the butler announced before promptly backing out of the room again.

Michelle stepped forward, suddenly feeling self-conscious again. There, standing before an unnecessarily large marble fireplace was Maximum Londinium's foremost consulting detective, Gabriel Wraith. He was standing straight as a beanpole, staring disinterestedly out of one of the windows on the opposite side of the ballroom-styled chamber. His profile looked as sharp as a stiletto dagger – hawkish nose, jutting chin and pointed, vespertilian ears – accentuated by the way his boot black hair had been scraped back from a widow's peak and kept in place with so much hair lacquer that it gleamed in the light of the ostentatious crystal chandeliers that lit the room.

The room was almost bare of furniture, other than for a leather-topped desk in the far corner, on which stood a reading lamp and a carefully positioned copy of *The Times*, a large magnifying glass resting conspicuously on top of it. It certainly didn't look like the sort of room where a consulting detective could actually do any work, Michelle thought. Was all this ostentation really just for show, she wondered.

She cleared her throat nervously, even though she wasn't really sure that she should be so presumptuous as to speak first in the presence of the gentleman detective.

His head snapped round and he studied her with unblinking ophidian eyes. He appeared thin almost to the point of anorexia. Michelle caught her own curve-endowed figure in one of the tall mirrors that stood between the windows on the other side of the room and, unable to help herself, automatically found herself thinking that she was looking rather less than totally stunning that day, even though no right-thinking male would have ever agreed with her.

"You sent word, Mr Wraith," she said, trying to hide the anxious excitement from her voice. "You have, I take it, something to report?"

"I have news, Miss Powell, good news."

"You have recovered it?"

Gabriel Wraith put a tapering white finger to his lips and the young woman was almost surprised to find her words faltering into silence. He had hushed her without saying a word.

The thin man flicked aside a tail of his jacket and dipped long fingers into a waistcoat pocket, pulling out a glittering silver chain, and the pendant that dangled from it.

Wraith stared at the jewel as it spun and sparkled in its setting on the end of the chain. Michelle watched him intently. There was a hungry, almost lascivious, look in his snake-like eyes. She almost expected him to lick his lips in delight at any second, as if the jewel was good enough to eat.

"The Huntingdon Jewel," he said at last, his unblinking eyes never once leaving the faceted face of the gemstone which now swung only inches away from the end of his nose.

"Then I was right," Michelle said with unashamed relief. "You have it!"

"Yes, Miss Powell, I have it. I have it indeed." The consulting detective continued to stare at the gently turning jewel. "A black diamond is it not?"

"Yes... That's right," she replied, suddenly cautious. "Why do you mention it?"

"Oh, no reason, Miss Powell. No reason. Merely out of professional interest. Worth a fortune, is it not?"

"I told you, Mr Wraith, it is a family heirloom. Its value is beyond reckoning, as far as I am concerned."

"Come, come, Miss Powell, there is no need to be so suspicious," Wraith said, and smiled for the first time since he had begun his audience with Michelle, holding court as a university don might deign to entertain a group of first year students. She had preferred it when he hadn't been smiling. "It is a very rare piece, that is all, and one with a most fascinating history."

"Legend, that is all," Michelle was quick to point out.

"If you say so, Miss Powell, if you say so. Still, all those people who have met untimely and unusual deaths. Some might say it was cursed."

"There is no curse!" Michelle said pointedly, taken aback herself by the vehemence of her own retort.

"No, of course not, Miss Powell. Of course not. Perish the thought. But fascinating nonetheless."

"Mr Wraith," Michelle began, concentrating on controlling her growing anger and impatience – it was like the man was deliberately goading her – "I appreciate you recovering what I thought had been lost forever – nay, I am delighted – but I would be grateful if you would now fulfil the final part of our agreement by returning the Huntingdon Jewel to me."

Gabriel Wraith snatched the dangling pendant up into his hand again, clenching the piece tightly within his closed fist, and looked at Michelle directly. Once again, she had preferred it when he hadn't been looking at her. She could feel the hairs on the back of her neck standing on end, as her sense of unease grew.

This is getting ridiculous! she scolded herself silently. *Pull yourself together, woman; it is almost within your grasp. Only a minute more and it shall be yours!*

"Mr Wraith?"

The consulting detective smiled again and then, with a sudden movement, tossed the pendant the length of the room into Michelle's waiting hands. She immediately began to inspect the jewel in its setting, looking for any signs of damage, any clue that the original black diamond had been exchanged for a forgery, but there was nothing; as far as she could tell, it was the genuine article, and she should know.

"I'm sorry to say that the other items – the watch, the money, the jewellery – the rest of it had already been fenced on. I am truly very sorry," Wraith said, his words devoid of any real sentiment.

"But you managed to recover the pendant," she said,

possibly rather too quickly. "The rest doesn't matter."

"But it was worth a tidy sum, was it not, Miss Powell? A tidy sum indeed."

"The rest of it didn't have the same... sentimental value, Mr Wraith. Let us not speak of it again."

"As you wish, Miss Powell. As you wish."

"Then I believe that our business together is concluded."

The stick thin gentleman detective raised one supercilious eyebrow.

"There is just the small matter of the remainder of my fee, Miss Powell, or had you forgotten?"

"I had *not* forgotten," Michelle said, extracting a slip of paper from within the bosom of her bodice, and proffering it to him. "Your cheque, Mr Wraith."

"Carstairs will take it on your way out," he said, waving her away as if the concept of an exchange of funds for services filled him with disdain, and he hadn't been the one to suggest payment in the first place.

"Ma'am?" And then Carstairs was there at her shoulder again, without having apparently entered and crossed the room to get there.

Michelle could not help letting out an involuntary cry of surprise.

Having recovered herself, she placed the cheque onto the butler's outstretched porcelain palm.

"Good day, Miss Powell," Gabriel Wraith said from his position at the fireplace.

"Good day, Mr Wraith," she responded, and without waiting to be told twice, turned on her heel and strode out of the room, Carstairs swiftly taking his place ahead of her without even having had to speed up to overtake her. "And if I don't see you again, it will be too soon," she added barely under her breath. She didn't want to spend a minute longer than she had to in that house.

Turning back from observing his guest's hurried departure, Gabriel Wraith relaxed his affected pose of arrogant supremacy and moved gracefully from his place at the mantelpiece to the reading desk positioned so carefully in the corner of the room. Picking up the folded newspaper he returned to his perusal of its column inches.

Gabriel Wraith loved the smell of newsprint. It was the smell of information, of intrigue and of inscrutability. And he always found *The Times* to be satisfyingly abundant in both.

The front page was laden with pieces about Prime Minister Valentine's war on climate change. Even if their hoped for revolution had not come to pass, the Darwinian Dawn's campaign of terror had certainly raised awareness of ecological issues around the globe. And the new PM was not averse to using such concerns as a means of promoting himself. He had made the subject his own personal project, effectively killing two birds with one stone. On the one hand he was seen to be listening to the general populace's concerns, and thereby helping to avert any further terrorist activity from groups like the Darwinian Dawn, whilst, on the other hand, doing as much as he could to distance himself from his traitorous predecessor.

Much was being made of Prime Minister Valentine's efforts to make a stand on climate change and industrial pollution here at home, in the capital to be precise. Early next year would see the launch of the *Jupiter* Station, which the popular press had already dubbed the Weather Machine.

It was claimed that the *Jupiter* would be capable of controlling and influencing the weather over London, and ultimately the rest of the South East, the primary intention being to rid the capital of the worsening pall of smog that smothered its streets and clung to its towering skyscrapers with greasy perniciousness.

There were parts of the Upper City that were now almost permanently trapped within the Smog as it was commonly known. The *Jupiter* was being constructed by the factories of the philanthropist millionaire Halcyon Beaufort-Monsoon, apparently as an act of true altruism by the reclusive industrialist, for the paper reported that it wasn't going to cost the tax payer a single brass farthing. Whether this wondrous machine would actually work as was intended was yet to be seen.

Gabriel Wraith turned the page, and let out a disgruntled *harrumph*.

There, taking up a quarter of the page was an over-embellished advertisement for Doctor Feelgood's Tonic Stout.

What was becoming of one of Magna Britannia's greatest institutions, for it to sport such gutter press advertisements, the kind he would have expected to find plastered to the walls of East End slums?

Over-embellished with all manner of curlicues and ornamentations available to the typesetter, the advertisement made much of the supposedly beneficial properties of the fictional doctor's health drink. Wraith had seen their like before – he could hardly miss them and nor could anybody else – they were plastered all over brick walls and billboards from here to the suburbs, while animated, kinema-style versions ran on a loop on broadcast screens across the capital, and had done for some weeks now.

He moved on, scanning the tightly-printed columns, searching for any morsel, any titbit, that might lead him on to his next endeavour.

Apparently Professor Alexander Oddfellow, scientist, inventor and eccentric, who had been missing presumed dead for some months had turned up again at his Warwickshire home, while in another part of the country there were still concerns over the health of the industrialist Josiah Umbridge – a rival to the philanthropic Beaufort-Monsoon – who had now not been seen in public for over a year.

On page seven, as he scanned the lines of densely-printed text, Gabriel homed in on one name, mentioned almost in passing as part of an article about the re-building of the Amaranth House at Kew Gardens, destroyed before it was even officially opened by a terrible fire. Half the page was covered by a photograph of the re-building work in progress, the original exotic glasshouse having been razed to the ground by the blazing inferno.

The passage briefly mentioned that Ulysses Quicksilver had somehow been mixed up in the incident that had seen the glasshouse's destruction, the very morning of its intended opening, much to the chagrin of new Prime Minister Devlin Valentine, who was now focusing his energies on the *Jupiter* project and on building a better Londinium for all.

"Page seven," Wraith chuckled to himself. "He won't like that. He won't like that at all." He turned the page.

The first thing that caught his eye was the hideous photograph. At first he thought it was something from the Royal College of Surgeons Hall in Edinburgh; one of those inhuman aborted foetuses that morbidly curious pathologists seemed to delight in keeping around the place, preserving them in formaldehyde for posterity, as if it was Great Aunt

Maud's ashes they were hanging onto so proudly.

Then he looked more closely. The thing was humanoid, at least in part, but rather than being some partially-formed embryo it was in fact disfigured as a result of the chemical process that it had been subjected to, in a crude attempt to preserve the specimen.

The photographic reproduction wasn't the best either. What Gabriel had at first taken to be a malformation of the legs, limbs joined where they shouldn't be (as in cases of sirenomelia), he now realised was actually a fish's tail, rapidly losing its scales it appeared, and any doubts he might have still harboured were dispelled as soon as he read the suitably sensationalist headline that accompanied the piece: 'Mermaid stolen from Museum'.

Gabriel Wraith read on with interest, a wry smile spreading across his pinched lips.

A minute later he picked up a small brass bell from its place on the desk, next to the reading lamp, and gave it a short sharp ring. Only a moment later, the doors to the room opened and Wraith's butler returned.

"You rang, sir?"

"I am needed elsewhere, Carstairs. I am needed most urgently. A crime has been committed and an incisive mind will be needed to unravel the mystery."

"Very good, sir."

Wraith examined the photograph of the mermaid in its formaldehyde-flooded glass jar one more time before placing the paper carefully back on the desk.

"Fire up the Bentley, Carstairs. I cannot keep my public waiting. The game is afoot."

CHAPTER TWO

November in Mayfair

"Page seven? Is that all? I risk life and limb for queen and country, *again*, and that's all I get? A passing comment on page seven?"

Bartholomew Quicksilver looked up languidly from his breakfast plate and swallowed his mouthful of scrambled eggs.

"But Ully, big brother, you don't really want the press making a big fuss about your night time exploits do you?"

Ulysses Quicksilver fixed his younger sibling with an icy glare. Barty stabbed a piece of sausage on the tines of his fork and popped it in his mouth, giving Ulysses a broad grin. Ulysses' wintry expression melted a little.

"Well, no," he blustered, "but a little recognition wouldn't go amiss. It's been two months. *Two months*, and still no word of thanks!"

"From whom?" Barty asked distractedly eyeing what was left of his grilled tomato.

"The Ministry, of course, brother dear. Do try to keep up!"

"But I thought your contact at the Ministry was long gone," Barty managed through a mouthful of tomato.

"Of course he is! But that doesn't mean that Department Q has up and left!"

"Oh."

"Oh? Is that all you can say."

"Come on, Ulysses, you've hardly touched your breakfast, and it's one of Mrs Prufrock's finest."

Ulysses eyed Barty, looking him up and down. "Yes, I can see how much you've been enjoying Mrs Prufrock's cooking over the last couple of months. Eating me out of house and home, no doubt.

"You know I have an addictive personality," his brother countered.

"Is that what Doctor Armitage calls it? And better food than the gee-gees, eh?" Ulysses said pointedly. "I don't know, I risk life and limb –"

"Yes, you made that point already," Barty said, making a point himself, ignoring Ulysses' jibe about the few pounds he had put on since moving into the Mayfair residence, and effectively taking the wind out of Ulysses' sails.

"I don't know what's worse," Ulysses fumed, "your lack of interest or the Ministry's."

"Very well, assuming for a moment that I *am* interested, what's happened to Department Q then?"

Ulysses' annoyed expression didn't change but he realised that this was as good as he was going to get so he made the most of the opportunity.

"Word is there's been a shake-up. No more direct ministerial interference. And about time too."

"No more ministerial involvement?" Barty said, putting a piece of black pudding in his mouth and chewing it lugubriously.

"It's been brought in under the wire, along with Prime Minister Valentine's other reforms, in the wake of the terror attacks and Wormwood's attempted coup. About time too. Can't have politicians getting in the way when there are Magna Britannia's national interests to protect."

Barty swallowed and paused in his decimation of the breakfast plate in front of him. "Prime Ministers and political parties come and go, but the Empire endures!"

"Quite so."

A minute passed without either of them saying anything, the only sound in the dining room, other than the ticking of the ormolu clock on the mantelpiece, the scrape of Barty's cutlery on his plate as he chased the last of the fried mushrooms around his plate.

"But just the same. Page *seven*?"

"Anyway, apart from nothing of significance about you," Barty said with strained good humour, "what else is in the news today?"

"Oh, you know, the usual," Ulysses muttered, shaking the paper out in front of him as he finally moved on from his brief mention on page seven. "More about Valentine and his attempts to turn back the tide, or rather, in his case, the Smog."

"Right little Canute, isn't he?"

"You could say that." Ulysses said half under his breath, eyes scanning the newsprint in front of him.

"And?"

"Oh, how wonderful. It says here that Petunia Chase is being considered for the recently vacated post of Director of Kew. Bully for her!"

"Anything else?"

"There's something about Oddfellow's return as well."

"Oh yes?" Barty said, soundly properly interested now. "Any mention of your other lady friend? What was her name again? Emily? Amelia?"

"Emilia, with an 'E'."

"Oh yes, that was it," Barty said locking onto this little nugget, seeing how Ulysses was squirming at his interrogation. There weren't many occasions when Barty had the chance to feel superior to his brother, so when one did come along, he liked to make the most of it. "You never did tell me how the two of you got on."

"No, I didn't," Ulysses snapped.

"How long has it been, now?'

"Listen to this!" Ulysses suddenly exclaimed, behaving as if the last two minutes of conversation had never happened. "A mermaid has been stolen from an exhibition, right here in London!"

Realising that Ulysses wasn't going to be drawn further on the subject of him and his old flame Emilia Oddfellow, no matter how much he badgered, Barty gave in and feigned interest in the article Ulysses was reading.

"What? You mean like the figurehead of some ship, or something."

"No, I mean like a half-human, half-fish hybrid. Comb, mirror, siren song, beloved of sailors. I swear on our mother's grave –"

"There's no need for that," Barty protested.

" –it's the genuine article. A sailor's wet dream, I tell you."

"Oh, you mean like a manatee, or sea cow, or whatever they're called."

There was a suggestion of mania about both Ulysses' tone and his expression now. "No. I mean a mermaid!" he said, delighted.

"You can't be serious. You're having me on."

"No honestly."

"It has to be a hoax."

"No, it's in *The Times*."

"But everyone knows that mermaid's don't exist," Barty persisted, even though by the gleam in his brother's eye he already knew he was fighting a losing battle. But he had to persist, for sanity's sake.

"Oh, I wouldn't bet on it." *Not after what I saw, within the rusting chambers of Marianas Base,* he added to himself. "There's a photograph and everything, if you don't believe me."

He roughly folded the broadsheet pages back on themselves and then in half again, proffering the rustling wodge of pages to his brother across the pristine white linen of the tablecloth, exposing the grainy, unbelievable black and white image. Barty took it from him.

"But it's a fake, obviously," he said, taking in the hideous image of what looked like some species of primate melded with the lower half of a large fish – a sturgeon perhaps – with just a hint of doubt entering his voice. Whatever it was made up of, it was a truly repugnant creature.

No matter how much he wanted to hide it, the soupçon of uncertainty was there nonetheless.

"There's no such thing as mermaids," he pronounced again, as if the more times he reiterated that fact, the truer it became.

"You're sure about that are you?" Ulysses challenged, the same manic rictus grin still distorting his features.

Barty looked at the picture again, studying it more closely.

"Look, it's a fake. It's obvious. Look at how the two halves don't match up."

"How do you mean?"

"I mean in terms of scale. The proportions are all wrong. Surely something as skinny as the monkey half would have to have a much more slender lower body – if you believed mermaids really existed, which they don't!"

"Go on."

"And you can practically see where the two halves have been sewn together. It doesn't look so much like a chimpanzee has been bothering a trout, and this was the obscene offspring of the unnatural coupling, as it looks like someone just chopped a monkey and a fish in half, and then stuck the two together. There's probably a tuna-headed chimp masquerading as some kind of fishman at the same exhibition; part of a matching set."

He thrust the paper back into his brother's hands.

"Well, listen to this," Ulysses said, releasing Barty from his scrutinous gaze and applying it to *The Times* again.

"'The exhibit known as the Whitby Mermaid has been stolen from the Cruickshank's Cabinet of Curiosities exhibition, which has taken up residence within the Holbrook Museum for the duration of the London leg of its nationwide tour,'" Ulysses read.

Bartholomew Quicksilver put down his knife and fork to listen more intently.

"'Mr Mycroft Cruickshank told *The Times* that nothing else was taken from the exhibition of the bizarre and the macabre.'" Ulysses went on. "'Police are baffled' – but then, aren't they always? – 'as there appears to be no sign of a break-in. The question also remains as to why the Whitby Mermaid was singled out by the thieves.'"

"You're telling me," Barty interrupted. "Why would anyone want to steal what is so obviously a fake? Where did it come from anyway?"

Continuing to scan the meat of the article, paraphrasing Ulysses said: "Apparently it was caught off the coast of North Yorkshire, near Whitby, by one," – there was a brief hiatus, as he looked for the name that he had seen earlier – "George Craven. Says here it's made him and the freak show's owner, Mycroft Cruickshank, a pretty penny. And the longer the tour continues, the more they'll rake in, but not with their prize exhibit gone."

"Frauds and charlatans," Barty pronounced, imperiously, conveniently forgetting that Ulysses might have said the same thing of him less than six months before.

"Craven claims to have caught the thing whilst out

fishing, and he claims that it was alive when he hauled it in, only it suffocated once it was out of the water, before he could do anything to save it."

"Oh, what a shame. How inconvenient," Barty sneered.

"Says he's given up his old job to travel with the tour and see the sights while the exhibition's in London."

"Bully for him."

"Now, don't be like that, Barty," Ulysses chided. "You wouldn't deny a fellow man, who had been down on his luck, a little good fortune, would you?"

"S'pose not," Barty mumbled ungraciously. "Still looks fake to me, though. Don't tell me you think that thing's the genuine article," he said, stabbing an accusing finger at the picture in the paper.

"Perhaps not."

"Perhaps? There's no 'perhaps' about it! Why I'd bet you anything that somewhere in this farce there's someone with a big fat sail needle, a ball of twine and a bloody big knife," Barty finished, a triumphant look in his eyes.

"If you were a gambling man."

Barty suddenly looked sheepish and cast his eyes down at the tablecloth.

"Which you're not."

"No. No anymore."

"Not anymore indeed."

"But it's still fake."

"But if that's the case, why would anyone want to go to all the trouble of stealing this mermaid, and it alone?"

"That one I can't answer," Barty admitted, stumped. "But you're the one with all the deductive reasoning. I'll let you work that one out, Ully."

"Right you are then!" Ulysses said with gleeful delight and jumped to his feet.

"What?"

"I said, right you are then," Ulysses repeated.

"But what are you doing?"

"I'm taking your advice, Barty. I'm going to find out for myself, as you so rightly pointed out, why someone would bother to steal a fake."

"What, now?"

"There's no time like the present. Are you coming?"

"But it's barely ten o'clock. I'm not seen out these days before noon," Barty said, looking at the clock on the mantelpiece. "So, if you don't mind, I think I'll pass. I don't want to ruin my carefully cultivated reputation."

"Heaven forbid," Ulysses scoffed and pulled the cord hanging between the drapes and the door. A moment later a voice crackled over an intercom speaker half-hidden in an aspidistra pot.

"You rang, sir?" came the carefully cultivated tone of disinterest of gentlemen's menservants the world over.

"I did indeed, Nimrod. We're going out."

"Very good, sir." Nimrod continued in the same unemotional manner. "Will you be needing the car?"

"Yes, why not? I like to travel in style. Fire up the Phantom."

"Might I enquire as to where we are going, sir?"

"The Holbrook Museum, old chap. We have an appointment with one Mr Cruickshank who inexplicably finds his freak show short of one freak."

CHAPTER THREE

A Cabinet of Curiosities

"Sorry, sir. I can't let you in there," the well-meaning yet resolute guard at the door to the museum instructed Ulysses.

"Really?" Ulysses said, exaggeratedly, looking somewhat taken aback.

"'Fraid so. It's a crime scene, see?"

"Yes, I know," Ulysses said, looking the man directly in the eye. "The Whitby Mermaid was stolen from here two nights ago. It was in the paper. That's why I'm here."

"Really, sir?" Now it was the slow-thinking guardsman's turn to look taken aback. He wasn't stupid exactly, just single-minded of purpose and very forward focused in his thinking. He did what he was told.

With one deft movement, Ulysses dipped his hand into an inside pocket of the morning frock coat he was wearing and whipped out a leather card-holder. With an equally assured flick of the wrist he opened it and held it up in the guard's narrow-minded field of vision.

There was a pause as the guard read what was printed on the card inside. Ulysses could see the moment the penny dropped from the way the man's features contorted in, if not confusion, then bewildered understanding.

"Oh. I see, sir. I'm very sorry. If you would like to step this way?"

"Don't mind if I do," Ulysses said breezily and bounded up the last few steps, making for the door to the museum.

As the man's attention moved onto Nimrod on the steps

behind him, Ulysses saw the way in which the guard's former steadfastness was regrouping in his features and pre-empted any further delay with a brusque, "He's with me."

Passing through a gloomy walnut-panelled hallway, motes of disturbed dust spinning lazily in the thin beams of autumn sunlight that managed to penetrate the grimy leaded windows, the dandy and his batman followed the signs to the exhibition and came at last to the hallowed hall of ephemera that was Cruickshank's Cabinet of Curiosities.

They had barely crossed the threshold of the equally drear and dusty room in which the exhibition was temporarily being housed when they were met by an anxiously fidgeting man sporting an startling yellow checked waistcoat under his even more startling crushed green velvet jacket – that made him look like some kind of showman, which, Ulysses considered, was probably precisely what he was. He had an impressive belly – no doubt the product of a strong attraction to ale – and an even more impressive curled handlebar moustache. In fact, this sideshow man appeared to have made a feature of his hair; his moustache was matched by his bushy eyebrows which looked like they were trying to take flight to join the curly, upstanding knot on the top of his head. Between the eyebrows and the moustache, the man's face was a podgy pink mass of broken veins and purple cheeks, a bulbous, gout-swollen nose and a pair of beady black eyes buried amidst all the flesh.

"And who are you?" Ulysses asked, even though there could be no doubt.

"I, sir, am the curator and owner of this museum of marvels, this assembly of astonishments," the man blustered, going red in the face as he did so. "I, sir, am Cruickshank – Mycroft Cruickshank." It looked to Ulysses like the curator's moustache might unravel itself as he seethed away, his complexion steadily turning to beetroot. "And who, sir, are you?"

"Oh, don't you recognise me? You really don't know?"

"Such arrogance!" Cruickshank bridled. "Why the arrogance of you, sir!"

"It's just that I thought you might have recognised me from the papers or the MBBC newscasts."

From a few feet behind him, Ulysses heard Nimrod sigh in polite impatience. Goading pompous fools might be sport for Ulysses but it was a game others soon tired of, including the Quicksilver family's long-suffering butler.

"No, sir, I do not!"

In a trice Ulysses had whipped out his card-holder again. "Ulysses Quicksilver, at your service."

"Oh," was all the exhibition's proprietor could muster as he read the details of Ulysses' ID. And then, recovering himself again: "I see. But your services are not required, sir."

"Look, I'm sorry if we got off on the wrong foot, but I could be of help here."

Cruickshank looked Ulysses up and down, while Ulysses gave the curator a second once-over.

"You know about the debacle surrounding Her Majesty's 160th jubilee celebrations," Ulysses went on.

"Well, yes, of course," Cruickshank had to admit.

"And the loss of the cruise-liner *Neptune* was widely reportedly in the press I believe."

"What? Yes, I did read of it."

"Well, that was me. I was the one who got everyone out of some rather tight spots."

"Oh, I see."

"So, if you wouldn't mind letting us carry on with

our work, I'll make sure we keep out of your way. All right?"

Ulysses took a step forward but Cruickshank moved to block him again.

"It's not that," he said, bushy brows beetling, his face already a much calmer shade of cerise. "It's just that Mr Wraith is already on the case."

"What?" The muscles of Ulysses' face tightening and a bloom of colour now came to *his* cheeks.

"Yes. Mr Wraith is already helping the police solve this mystery."

"Wraith?" Ulysses gasped incredulously. "Gabriel Wraith?"

"The very same, sir. London's foremost consulting detective. We are most fortunate. Perhaps now we'll discover just what's been going on around here." Cruickshank cast his eyes around the panelled room and its many and varied glass display cases.

"When did *he* get here?"

Cruickshank consulted his pocket watch. "Almost an hour ago. It would appear that your services are not required after all."

Ulysses stood there, stunned, not knowing what to say. He glanced back at this manservant who raised his left eyebrow in response; as much of a look of surprise as Nimrod was ever likely to give.

This wasn't getting him anywhere, Ulysses thought, and now that Gabriel Wraith was involved he was even more intrigued. *Time to turn on the old Quicksilver charm.*

"Very well," Ulysses said, relaxing his posture, suddenly aware of how tense he had become at mention of his rival's name. "Fair's fair, I suppose. The early bird, and all that. But it's a personal shame, it really is. A real pity."

"What is?" Cruickshank asked, unable to help

himself, wrong-footed by Ulysses' sudden change of temperament.

"I've heard so much about your little exhibition here that I was going to offer my services for free, simply to be able to say that I had some small part to play with the phenomenon of the season."

"Really?" Cruickshank said, his ears pricking up at the mention of 'services for free', Ulysses supposed. "Well, that's very kind of you, Mr Quicksilver. But, as I said, Mr Wraith is already on the case."

Ulysses detected the barely concealed disappointment in Cruickshank's tone, like that of a man who realises he's just missed out on that most elusive of meals – a free lunch. Ulysses also noted that Cruickshank hadn't bothered to question why, if he was so eager to visit the freak show he had waited until after the theft to bother to come at all.

"I've heard tell that it is the finest collection this side of Dusseldorf."

"And so it should be, sir. It has taken me nearly thirty years to gather this most... unique of collections."

Vanity and self-importance had done their bit. He had the proprietor on side now.

"Well, seeing as how we're here now, you don't mind if we take a look around for ourselves, do you?"

"Be my guest, sir."

"We'll be sure to keep out of Mr Wraith's way."

"Very good, sir."

Cruickshank moved aside, and Ulysses strode into the man's inner sanctum, into his chamber of delights, as it were, Nimrod close behind as usual.

Ulysses took in the entirety of the collection laid out around the room, having to turn his head and crane his neck to take in all its wonders. And there was certainly a very great deal crammed into the room, for the benefit of the viewing public.

It seemed to Ulysses' experienced eye that there wasn't a walnut-panel that was free of some manner of exhibit, if not several. Hung from the walls or filling dusty glass display cases were holy relics recovered from the wreck of a Spanish galleon, their gold-leaf and gesso decorations scoured clean by the relentless attentions of the sea; earthenware pitchers and porcelain from China; an icon of Madonna and Child from Russia, the wood dry and cracked; a necklace of monkey teeth; the broken-off top of a Celtic stone cross; the carved dragon-prow of a Viking longship; a Javanese ritual-dance mask, that of a red-eyed, leering demon; Egyptian galibaias – he had worn such a thing himself whilst on secondment to the land of the pharaohs; a snake-charmer's basket and pipes from Bombay; human skulls, their eye-sockets filled with clay and flints; the baubles and bells of King Henry VIII's fool; the Turkish Emperor's gold seal; a pharaoh's death-mask; scrolls of papyrus; an Aztec codex; an intricately worked astrolabe; a Viking lodestone compass; a Neolithic quern-stone; and a morose limestone gargoyle, pilfered from a church in Antwerp.

Or at least that was what the exhibits all claimed to be, each label carefully filled out in a tight copperplate hand.

Ulysses half expected to see the green-eyed monkey god of Sumatra snuck in there, buried amongst the other items, having mysteriously become part of the exhibition.

And the objects – or object d'art, as Mycroft Cruickshank might have preferred it – were not all man-made either; far from it. There were the polished shells of sea turtles and giant tortoises; the horn and tail of a rhinoceros; the scalp and one tusk of a mammoth – although Ulysses didn't understand what was so special about that when one could still see the real thing roaming the tundra of Siberia, if one was lucky.

A number of the exhibits had been stuffed to preserve them but they were not the finest examples of the taxidermist's art. There was an elephant's head, minus its ivory; a still-born two-headed lamb; a stuffed pangolin; a two-tailed lizard; various cases of pin-stuck butterflies, moths, spiders and scorpions; and then there was a large pickling jar containing the knotted form of an octopus, which reminded him far too vividly of his jaunt to the Pacific only a few months before.

He was disappointed not to see much in the way of dinosaurian artefacts. Thought of the terrible lizards then took him back to London Zoo and the breakout from the Challenger Enclosure nearly six months previously, and his rather too close an encounter with a fully-grown megasaur. What had happened to the brute after he brought it down in Parliament Square, he wondered.

And there were plants too; dried vanilla pods; the rump-shaped seed of the Coco-de-Mer palm; and, supposedly, a mandrake root, but which to Ulysses looked more like a prize-winning obscenely shaped vegetable at a village flower show. He had seen the genuine article, and it looked nothing like a cheekily-shaped parsnip.

But none of the plants on show here were as amazing, or as deadly, as the others he had encountered within the Amaranth House at Kew.

Suspended from the ceiling by means of a complicated system of pulleys and wires was a hollowed-out bark canoe that had once belonged to a lost Amazonian tribe; a gaudily-painted totem pole of the Gitxsan Indians of Canada, painted in what would have once been bright, overpowering primary colours; a slice taken out of a Californian giant redwood; and the hull of a Chinese junk.

"It's as if the spirit of Pitt Rivers is alive and well, and residing here in London," Ulysses announced with something like delight in his voice. "Oh, I've got one of those," he said, pointing at a Balinese fetish mask, "or at least I should say I had one of those, before the fire and all."

It amazed Ulysses how many items there were. It seemed that it was not enough merely to own the tusk of a narwhal; Cruickshank needed to possess at least three of the things, each carefully labelled and catalogued with its provenance, including where and when it was acquired, or killed, in the case of the whale tusks.

It a less enlightened age, when the world was a much larger and more mysterious place, such tusks were passed off as the horns of unicorns, and for a suitably unreal price too. Recalling to mind the photograph of the Whitby Mermaid from the paper, Ulysses was almost disappointed not to find one of the horns screwed into the skull of a stuffed antelope or llama with the proud boast that this was the last unicorn to die on British soil. However, his faith in human nature, specifically man's ability and desire to dupe his fellow man, and man's readiness, in turn, to be duped, was restored when he spotted what was purported to be the shed skin of a basilisk – in truth, a cobra's skin with cockerel's wattles sewn on.

The Germans had a wonderful word for collections such as these; they called them *Wunderkammer* – literally "Cabinet of Wonders." But Cabinet of Curiosities seemed to suit this place better. Most of the objects on display weren't wonders; they were tired, faded, deteriorating scrag-ends of dubious provenance, or downright fakes. There wasn't anything wonderful about them although they did make Ulysses wonder as to the obsessive hoarding nature of the man who had gathered this disparate collection together. Yes, curiosities, not wonders.

"Excuse me, constable," Ulysses said, putting a fraternal hand on the shoulder of a young policeman whose misfortune it had been to be put on this case. "But who's the officer in charge?"

There weren't any robots Peelers on the case. Apparently it wasn't deemed important enough to warrant that sort of interest or protection. No, it was going to be up to the Bobby in the street to solve this one.

Ulysses supposed that it was an unimportant matter, when one considered what went on in a city the size of Londinium Maximum on a daily basis. It was only the curious nature of the object that had been stolen, and the public's insatiable appetite for the bizarre and macabre that had meant it had even made it into the papers.

Catching the confident look in Ulysses' eye, the policeman – who looked like he hadn't even started shaving yet, now Ulysses came to consider it – swallowed nervously before answering. "Inspector Wallace," he said, pointing at an immaculately turned out gentleman standing in the middle of the room, wearing a sharp pin-striped suit with a tailored trench coat over the top.

Not for the first time that morning – the day was still just shy of noon – Ulysses was unable to hide the look of surprise that seized his face, his emotions as readable as an open book.

"Oh, not Inspector Allardyce then? I would have thought this one would be his territory."

"It would normally, sir," the constable agreed, "but Inspector Allardyce is on holiday at present."

"On holiday? Really? I always took him to be the kind

of man who ate, drank and slept the job."

"Not this week, sir." The constable gave a wry smile. "Did you want to speak to Inspector Wallace at all?"

"No, no, don't trouble him." Ulysses was looking beyond the constable and the curiosities now to a darkly-attired man in the far corner of the room. "I'm just here to catch up with an old friend."

The early bird that had caught this particular worm was studying an empty glass display case, the front panel of it hanging open.

"Well, well, well. Gabriel Wraith," Ulysses declared, approaching the cabinet in the corner. "Who'd have thought it?"

The man spun round on his heel, otherwise maintaining his carefully poised, and yet ironing board straight, posture and glowered at the beaming Ulysses.

"Quicksilver."

"Fancy meeting you here."

"Fancy indeed."

Ignoring Ulysses, Wraith turned back to his examination of the display case.

Ignoring the rebuff, Ulysses peered over his shoulder none too subtly to get a view of the case for himself. Resting on the black velvet mount at the base of the cabinet, looking rather forlorn now, was a handwritten card bearing the inscription, 'Whitby Mermaid'.

As Wraith picked at pieces of fluff attached to the velvet with a pair of tweezers, Ulysses also saw now that the consulting detective was wearing crisp white cotton gloves, so as not to contaminate any evidence he might find there.

Wraith snorted irritably at Ulysses' continued and obviously unwanted presence. "Is there something I can help you with?" he asked icily, still refusing to actually face the interloper.

"So, any ideas?"

"I am considering a number of alternative hypotheses at the moment."

"Hmm, a mystery, isn't it?"

"No, not really. Not to someone with a logical mind."

"So you have an answer then?"

"There is always an answer, a logical answer, arrived at following careful consideration of the evidence. It just takes a disciplined mind to uncover it."

"So, you think you'll find the answer?" Ulysses pressed, with all the enthusiasm of an eager puppy, much to Wraith's obvious annoyance.

"I have no doubt that I shall solve this – as you put it – 'mystery', although there is nothing mysterious about it. And I certainly don't need your help." A cold smile suddenly appeared on Wraith's pinched lips. "I understand you had something to do with the fire at Kew," he said, brightly. "You're a walking liability, Quicksilver. First the Crystal Palace, then the loss of that cruise-liner and now Kew Gardens has felt the fell hand of the Quicksilver curse upon it. Why, wasn't your own home gutted by fire not so long ago?"

"That incident suffered from gross exaggeration by the press," Ulysses suddenly found himself at pains to point out.

"Yes, I remember the papers reported your death. Pity."

Hearing hurried footsteps tap-tapping their way across the parquet floor of the room, Ulysses turned to see a yet again red-faced Mycroft Cruickshank steaming his way over to where they were inspecting the cabinet together.

"Ah, Mr Cruickshank. Would you like to give us your considered opinion as to who broke in here and how they got away? Perhaps you could fill in a few gaps for me; clarify a few details," Ulysses began.

Cruickshank glared at him with those piggy black eyes of his from out of the doughy arrangement of his face. From the colour of the curator's face, Ulysses just knew that all this stress couldn't be doing his blood pressure any good.

"I'm sorry, Mr Wraith, is this gentlemen bothering you?"

"Yes he is, Mr Cruickshank."

"Mr Quicksilver, you are here thanks to my gracious goodwill, sir. Please don't abuse that generosity of spirit."

"Of course not. So the break-in was two nights ago now?" Ulysses deftly side-stepped the subject, just as he deftly ushered the curator of this weird and wonderful collection of the macabre and downright bizarre away from where Wraith was working, as if it was he who had interrupted the private detective's investigation of the crime scene.

"What? Yes," Cruickshank replied caught out by Ulysses' abrupt change of conversational direction.

"And you reported it to the police yesterday morning when you discovered that the mermaid was missing, is that right?"

"Er, yes."

Ulysses waited, eyeing Cruickshank expectantly, as if waiting for him to speak. The bewildered proprietor obliging took his cue and began to spill the beans.

"I came in to open up, as it were, as usual and was caught out by the chill draft that was sweeping the room."

"And where was this draft coming from?"

"A window in the one of the – *ahem* – conveniences

had been left open."

"The door hadn't been tampered with?"

"No. It was locked, just as I had left it the night before."

"And who else has a key?"

"Only, Mr Gallowglass, the director of the museum. But the police have already questioned him and his alibi stands up to the closest scrutiny. Besides, he's a trustworthy sort of a fellow."

"And where are these – *ahem* – conveniences?"

"Over there," Cruickshank pointed to a door in the adjacent corner half hidden behind the sarcophagus of a ninth dynasty Egyptian king.

"And is there any other way of reaching them?"

"No, only from this room."

"Well then, if it wasn't Mr Gallowglass, and I have to say, why would a man of his standing be interested in stealing a forgery –"

"I'll have you know I have it on the best authority that it is – *was* – the genuine article!" Cruickshank blazed.

"– and unless it was you, planning some insurance scam –"

"What are you trying to say, sir?"

"– which I sincerely doubt, otherwise you'd have taken something of more obvious value that the mermaid. And talking of fakes," Ulysses said, "where did the Whitby Mermaid come from? And don't say 'Whitby'." Cruickshank looked like he was about to protest again but instead made a face like a goldfish gasping for air. "You don't honestly expect anyone to believe that it was the real deal, do you?"

Cruickshank's manner changed in an instant. He drew Ulysses to one side, an arm around his shoulders and dropped his voice to a conspiratorial hush.

"You're a man of the world, Mr Quicksilver, I can see that, so I won't try to fool you in this regard. If you ask me the thing's a fake. You can even see the stitching if you look closely enough – or at least the scars where the stitches would have been, they're not there now – but old Craven was adamant that when he caught the thing in his nets it was alive, gasping for air on the deck of his little boat as he looked on in disbelief. He swears on the Bible it's the truth, but it hardly seems credible, does it?"

Ulysses gave that thought some consideration for a moment. There were certainly many strange and downright weird things in this world, and he had seen a fair few of them, but mermaids? That just seemed one sea dog's tale too far.

"But nonetheless you saw fit to reveal this abomination, anomaly – call it what you will – to the world."

"Of course. I saw it as my duty, to let the viewing public decide for themselves," Cruickshank said, putting a showman's spin on the subject.

"And you cut Mr Craven in for a share of the proceeds raised from the viewing public?"

"Of course, sir."

"Well, I'm sure that whatever it was you offered him, it was a fair cut, once you take off your, no doubt, not inconsiderable running costs."

"That's right," Cruickshank said, warily. A confidence trickster was always going to be a hard man to play when he was already wise to the tricks played by others.

"Putting that aside for the moment," Ulysses went on, "the fact is that the mermaid was stolen and the only way the felon could have entered was through the open window in the conveniences?"

"But that's impossible. No-one could get in through there; it's hardly bigger than a letterbox!"

"Not impossible, Cruickshank, old boy, only highly improbable."

"What?"

"And once you have ruled out the impossible, what's left, no matter how improbable it might appear, holds the key to the truth!" Ulysses declared triumphantly. "And the cabinet wasn't forced either?"

"No." The cabinet of curiosities' curator was wearing an expression of confusion on his face now.

"Then I would say that the scoundrel we're after is a dab hand with lock picks as well," Ulysses mused, a thoughtful hand supporting his chin. "Good day to you, Mr Cruickshank."

"What? You're going?" Cruickshank exclaimed, as Ulysses strode off, making for the exit, wrong-footed once again. Strangely, he sounded, if not disappointed, then at least annoyed that Ulysses was ready to depart as quickly as he arrived.

"We have all the information we need, haven't we, Nimrod?"

"It would seem so, sir," Nimrod replied in that familiar disinterested tone of his.

"And we wouldn't want to trouble you or Mr Wraith any longer. You don't want us getting under your feet more than is necessary, I'm sure?"

"Well... No?"

"Then good day to you, sir, and I hope Mr Wraith comes up trumps for you, I really do."

And with that, Ulysses left Cruickshank's Cabinet of Curiosities.

As he and Nimrod descended the steps in front of the Holbrook Museum, his ever-faithful manservant asked: "You're not really leaving the matter in the hands of Mr Wraith, are you, sir?"

"You know me better than that, Nimrod," Ulysses replied, unable to hide the look of glee on his face. He was always the same when he was at the beginning of a new adventure. The hunt was all.

"The game is afoot, Nimrod. We have a mystery to solve. And I think it's about time you looked up some of your old acquaintances again."

CHAPTER FOUR

The Whitechapel Irregulars

"Why is it that your 'contacts' always want to meet in such charming places?" Ulysses asked, as he took in the black looming tombs and ivy-clad gravestones of Highgate Cemetery. The skeletal branches of the trees scratched at the night's sky with their talon-like tips, the twigs rattling like dry bones in the chill November wind.

Regardless of the fact that they were still within the bounds of the capital, right at this moment civilisation seemed a long way away. They might as well have been out in the desolate wilds in the middle of nowhere, with only the bodies of the dead for company.

"I understand that they are of the underworld, but do they really need to get so close to the real thing? Does it provide them with some sense of security or something?"

"It goes with the territory, sir, so to speak," Nimrod explained patiently. "No-one else comes to graveyards after dark."

"Indeed. Hardly surprising, is it?"

"The view from the other side, eh, sir?"

"I suppose you could call it that. Although the other side of what?"

Ulysses strained his eyes to peer uneasily between the crypts and iron-speared fences of guarded graves. His edginess didn't arise from a fear of such places, or from being reminded of one's mortality. Ulysses had witnessed the death of others and faced death himself more times than he would care to remember in his years as a dandy

50

adventurer and agent of the throne of Magna Britannia.

No, his unease arose from a desire to get a move on with his latest case. If there was something Ulysses Quicksilver didn't like, it was pointlessly hanging around. What he enjoyed – what he craved – was the thrill of the chase, whether it was pursuing a mystery to its conclusion, battling enemies of the state, life or death struggles or, as it had once been, setting about capturing the heart – or at least the libido – of whichever lovely it was that currently caught his eye.

"You did say nine o'clock, didn't you, Nimrod?"

"I did, sir," Nimrod replied in the same indefatigably patient manner.

"Then where is he?"

And then he felt it, the hairs on the back of his neck rising, his skin goose-pimpling as that ever reliable sixth sense of his kicked in.

"Oh, don' chou worry," came a voice whose words were distorted by a broad cockney drawl, "I'm 'ere. 'Ave bin for the last ten minutes. 'Eard every word you said, din' I?"

Ulysses' head snapped round and his eyes locked on the empty space between a towering unkempt yew and a long forgotten family's house-sized tomb. Only it wasn't empty. There was a figure there, a silhouette darker still against the already oppressive blackness of another Smog-shrouded London night.

But now that Ulysses knew where the man was, he could see subtle signs of movement as Nimrod's contact approached.

"'Evenin', Mr Nimrod," he said, nodding to Ulysses' manservant.

"Good evening, Rat." Nimrod spoke to the shadow no differently to how he would address his master or even Her Majesty Queen Victoria herself. But it sounded strange to hear him pronounce a name such as Rat in the clipped syllables of that well-bred accent of his. "May I introduce my employer, Mr Quicksilver."

The man said nothing but merely regarded Ulysses with the kind of scowl that implied that he rated the dandy barely above something he might find on the bottom of his shoe. Ulysses put this down to the natural distrust of the criminal for any figure of authority or with a higher social status than himself.

Ulysses in turn regarded Nimrod's contact with a look of intense curiosity. He had a scruffy, worn appearance. Everything he wore from the crumpled cloth cap that barely kept an unruly grey thatch in check, to the scuffed hobnail boots on his feet, even if it hadn't started out as a uniform had nevertheless ended up that way.

The man himself appeared to have worn even less well than his clothes, his jutting, angular features marked with the tell-tale scars of smallpox and other scars acquired through misadventure rather than misfortune. He hadn't shaved for a number of days and he didn't appear to have washed either. But he did have most of his own teeth by the look of things.

As to how old he was, it was anyone's guess. The grey hair with its straw-like texture could put him at as old as fifty, but there was a certain youthful sparkle in his eye that could have made him prematurely grey at thirty.

Deciding that someone needed to do something to progress this meeting, Ulysses held out his hand to the wastrel. "Mr Rat. Delighted to meet you."

"It's just Rat," he said, leaving Ulysses' hand well alone.

"Nimrod's told me so much about you," Ulysses went on, feeling that he wasn't getting anywhere very fast with his current tack.

"Has 'e?" Rat replied suspiciously, taking a wary step backwards, glancing between Ulysses and his manservant, his features knotted into a feral grimace. Ulysses could see now why the name Rat suited this ne'er-do-well so well. Nimrod shook his head, never once taking his eyes off the shady character.

"Well, no, he hasn't," Ulysses admitted, "but he has told me that you're the man who has all the answers."

The man known as Rat appeared to relax, although only ever so slightly. He still looked like he could turn tail and run at any moment. "For a price," he said, by way of confirmation, his own appraising gaze fixed firmly on Ulysses again.

"That's understood. Nimrod has made your terms clear to me."

Rat said nothing but continued to subject Ulysses to uncomfortable scrutiny.

"'Ere, I know you," he said suddenly, with devilish glee.

"Well, I should hope so; we have just been introduced."

"Yeah," Rat continued, as if Ulysses hadn't said anything at all. "I've seen your mug on the cast screens."

"Oh, you know me like that, you mean."

"Yeah. I'm right, aren't I?"

"Well, how privileged you are. You seem to have *me* at something of a disadvantage," Ulysses said, tiring of the grass's cocky swaggering manner.

Ulysses had not taken his eyes off the man's face since the two of them had been introduced. He saw Rat's eyes narrow and could almost hear the *k-ching* of the ringing cash register.

"Is there a problem?" Ulysses asked with icy calm, the hairs on the back of his neck bristling, already knowing what the other was about to say.

"Well that changes things, see?"

"In what way?"

"Information is a valuable commodity, isn't it?" Rat spoke the word commodity as if every syllable was a separate word. "Much more valuable than say, gold, jewels or... a bit of the foldin' stuff. And much more valuable to a man of your... standing, Mr Quicksilver, who, at the present time, if I might say so, one might be so bold as to presume is not short of the latter but sadly lacking in the former."

The grass grinned, revealing the yellow pegs of his teeth. This simple action made him look even more like his namesake.

"Rat," Nimrod spoke up suddenly, "we agreed terms at the same time as we arranged this meeting."

"Ah, but Mr Nimrod, you weren't entirely honest with me, were you?"

"I am scrupulously honest," Nimrod growled.

"Well then, let's just say you weren't entirely... forthcoming regarding all the particulars of this 'ere exchange."

"Don't worry, Nimrod," Ulysses said wearily, still not taking his eyes off the opportunist thief as he reached into his coat. "I'll handle this."

Rat's eyes began to sparkle, as if shining with the reflected shine of the money he was hoping to acquire.

"Will this suffice?"

Ulysses' hand came free of his coat in one sudden sharp movement, but it wasn't as sharp as the rapier blade he was now holding under Rat's chin, the sheaf formed by his black wood cane in his other hand.

His body rigid with fear, Rat swallowed, his Adam's apple sliding against the razor-edge of the blade, which gleamed darkly.

"Let's get one thing clear, Mr Rat," Ulysses said, he voice like steel. "No one rips me off!"

Rat said nothing, his bulging eyes darting from Ulysses' own steely gaze to the steel of his sword-cane and back again.

"Do I make myself perfectly clear?"

Rat gulped again and nodded slowly, anxious not to cut himself on the keenly-honed blade.

"Good. I'm glad we've got that sorted out."

Ulysses waited for a moment, holding his fencer's stance, his blade at the grass' throat, before slowly withdrawing the rapier and sheathing it.

"Now, Mr Rat, I am sure that we both have places we would rather be right now so, let's not waste each other's time any longer. I think the expression is, spill the beans. The theft of the Whitby Mermaid – what do you know?"

Rat gulped again and despite the rapier blade being sheathed and safe it still seemed to be hovering there, a metaphorical ghost of itself, just under his chin.

It took him a moment to find his voice. When he did speak, his earlier cocksureness was gone, his voice cracked, his tongue sticking to the roof of his mouth, parched from fear.

"Word is, the Whitechapel Irregulars had something to do with it," he managed at last.

"And who might they be?"

"Gang of thieving street urchins. Conniving little bleeders, if you ask me."

"And where would I find them?"

A momentary look of disbelief knotted the man's face and he opened his mouth as if he was about to make some sarcastic comment.

Ulysses pre-empted any such inappropriateness by

arching an eyebrow at the still quivering man.

"Humour me," was all he needed to say to make his point.

"Make your way to Whitechapel and if you don't find them first they'll be sure to find you, I 'ave no doubt." Rat gave Ulysses a bitter smile. "Failin' that, you could look in the Blind Beggar. That's all I know."

Ulysses relaxed a little. "There. That wasn't so bad, was it?"

Rat said nothing but just glowered at him in return.

"Now then, Mr Rat," Ulysses said happily as, beaming, he reached inside his coat again. Rat tensed. But rather than a blade, this time Ulysses brought out his wallet. "The matter of your fee."

"So, this is Whitechapel?" Ulysses declared, as the cab pulled away, a look of child-like wonder on his face.

"Yes, sir."

Ulysses paused, cane in hand, looking all around him and inhaled deeply, absorbing the aroma of the place as much as the sight of the slums. The teeming hordes making their way through the streets of Whitechapel – hawkers, pedlars, navvies, dockers, gong cleaners, street sweepers, whores and scruffy children by the score – milled around and past him, not giving him a second look.

There were few droids present here; it wasn't the sort of place where (a) people could afford them, or (b) where it was safe to send them; within an hour they could be melted down for scrap, or disassembled and their parts cannibalised to make something else or sold on the black market. Neither was it the sort of place Ulysses wanted to risk his Rolls Royce Mark IV Silver Phantom, hence the need for the cab.

Here, the desperate and the destitute laboured under the almost permanent shadow of the Smog as the factories of the industrialised East End belched their foul clouds of toxicants into the atmosphere. It was said that inhaling the lungfuls of dust present in the air here shortened people's lives considerably.

"Incredible, isn't it? In all my years living in this teeming metropolis and hunting down villains within its winding streets, and I've never set foot in Whitechapel." He turned and looked at his manservant. "I suppose you've been here many times before, Nimrod. In the past, I mean."

"Oh, I know it well, sir. You might say, far too well."

Ulysses took a step forward. He looked up at the street sign nailed to the crumbling brick of a junction above him, letting the tide of struggling humanity wash past him.

"Old Montague Street," he said. "And where's the Blind Beggar?"

"Up this way." Nimrod pointed, indicating the crowded street ahead of them. The way was packed with all manner of people going about their daily business, minding their own, while other more prying eyes looked on.

"Well, no point in hanging around here. If we're going to do this, we'd best get going."

Beggars and others skulked in the many secreting shadows, small bright eyes watching their every move by the light of crackling electric street lamps and a chestnut seller's brazier.

The night was cold, this close to winter – for all the talk that certain meteorologists and protest groups spoke of the new-fangled phenomenon of 'global warming' – and come the morning a crust of ice would cover the effluent streams running down the street. A bag of hot roast chestnuts wouldn't go amiss on a night such as this, Ulysses thought, pulling his scarf tight at his neck. While he was at it, he pulled the cashmere up over his mouth to filter out the worst of the ripe stench of raw sewage and lung-tarring smoke. The noxious stink seemed to characterise Whitechapel rather too well.

This place had been the haunt of prostitutes, thieves and ne'er-do-wells for centuries. When Covent Garden had been cleared, the scum had ended up here, washed east like the rest of the effluent produced by the city.

Ulysses paused again. That old familiar feeling that was both reassuring and at the same time unnerving, had returned; his near-prescient sixth sense scratching away at the edges of his conscious mind.

"Tell me, Nimrod, do you get the feeling that we're being watched?" he said.

"Indubitably, sir."

"Then we have their attention."

"I should say so, sir."

"Excellent. Then let's be having them, as the Peelers would put it."

The two men continued on their way up Old Montague Street, navigating the bustling crowds, Ulysses looking like a fop out to find some diverting entertainment for the evening, with his fixer-manservant at hand to keep an eye on him; just the sort of image they wanted to portray, in fact.

Ulysses had the manner of a hedonistic cad down pat, quite possibly because that was what he himself had once been. The enticements offered by the ladies of night were not totally unknown to him, as the infamous Queen of Hearts herself could vouch.

But that wasn't what he was looking for tonight as he enjoyed the change of scene from the more conservative streets of Mayfair and Bloomsbury. Whitechapel had a look all of its own, its walls plastered with layer upon layer of bill posters – promoting everything from the Chinese magician Lao Shen's show at the Palace Theatre to the new panacea of the modern age, Dr Feelgood's Tonic Stout – until Ulysses could quite believe that it was these layers of paper and glue that were all that was holding some of these crumbling tenements together.

And then, the dull throb of his subconscious became a white hot flare of awareness, just as Ulysses felt what might have been someone simply brushing past his coat tails, but wasn't.

He spun round, fast as a pouncing panther and grabbed the child by the wrist in a grip of iron. The urchin – his clothes rags, his face a smear of soot, the whites of his eyes almost all that was visible beneath the grime, a mop of filthy, lice-ridden hair contained within a cloth cap that was obviously too big for him – squealed like a stuck pig. Meanwhile, a waist-coated monkey, with an ugly, old man's face, jumped up and down on the boy's shoulder shrieking, tugging at the string the boy was still holding fast in his free hand.

Ulysses bent low, eyes blazing and he looked into the boy's terrified pale face. His devilish gleeful grin only made his aspect all the more terrifying as far as the cowering child was concerned.

A triumphant laugh escaped Ulysses' lips. "Got you!" he growled.

CHAPTER FIVE

The House of Monkeys

"So, Sidney, where do you want to begin?"

The boy put down his tankard, containing a double measure of gin, but did not relinquish his grip on the handle.

"Don't send me back to the spike, sir. Please, sir. Not that, sir."

"No one said anything about the workhouse, did they Nimrod?" Ulysses said calmly, regarding the boy's anxious expression with something somewhere between suspicion and almost paternal concern.

His manservant muttered something under his breath that obviously wasn't really intended for his master's ears, and continued to nurse his hand. The monkey had bitten him when he had tried to wrest it from the boy's grasp, Ulysses having apprehended the would-be pickpocket. That had been the last straw as far as Nimrod was concerned, and if Ulysses hadn't stopped him he would have throttled the simian with its own leash. The creature now sat hiding behind the boy's head, peering at the older man with a malevolent, gargoyle scowl whilst picking the occasional louse out of Sidney's hair to chew on.

Ulysses looked to his companion again. "You all right there, old chap?"

"I've suffered worse, sir." That was true, Ulysses thought. "The whiskey's helping." With that Nimrod dipped his bloodied handkerchief into the glass again and dabbed it onto the bite. He hadn't swallowed a drop of the stuff.

"Soon as we're done here, we'll see about getting you a tetanus jab."

"Very good, sir."

Ulysses turned his attention back to the boy, who was taking another noisy slurp of gin. Ulysses didn't have any children of his own – at least none that he knew of – but if there were any of his bastard progeny out there, then he hoped that they were growing up with people who loved them and who could care for them, and not scraping a living from the streets – if it could be called a living – like the poor wretch in front of him.

The boy was small. Under all the dirt and hand-me-down rags he appeared to be about seven or eight years old. He was pale-faced, like so many who lived under the permanent pall of the Smog and thin through obvious malnutrition. The gin probably didn't help, but it was what the boy had wanted.

He was strong, Ulysses would give him that. There'd been a tussle when the dandy had first seized the young dip-thief. The boy had kicked and screamed and tried to get away, as Nimrod tried to stop the monkey from joining in the fracas, but Ulysses had won in the end, bundling the boy away under one arm, the hand of the other covering his mouth. People in the street had watched the confrontation and resulting abduction with nothing more than passing interest and nobody acted to stop Ulysses or Nimrod. It just went to show that such incidents weren't uncommon in the rougher parts of town. The general consensus of opinion seemed to be that it was best just to avert your gaze and mind your own business. The boy had probably wronged the finely-attired gentleman in some way they figured, or owed him for services paid for but not yet rendered. Best to keep out of it.

If Ulysses had stopped to consider it for a moment, he might have pondered on what manner of life could crush a person's spirit so much that any sense of compassion for one's fellow man had been crushed along with it.

"How old are you, Sidney?" Ulysses asked, lowering his voice so that he came across as unthreatening as possible.

"Eleven years old, sir," the child said proudly. Appearances could be deceiving, Ulysses mused. "At least so's I'm told," he added.

"How do you mean?" Ulysses asked.

"That's what they told me at the workhouse where I's was born. Born in the flood of '86, they said, when the Thames burst its banks. Don't send me back there, sir. Don't send me back to the beadles. Please don't."

"Look, calm down. No one's going anywhere at the moment, Sidney."

The boy looked at him with wide, watery brown eyes. They appeared large in comparison to the rest of his head, doeishly cute and appealing, thanks to his stunted growth.

"You're one of the Irregulars, isn't that right?"

"Irregular what, sir? Don't know whatcha mean." The boy's sudden show of bravado told Ulysses everything he needed to know.

"Best gang in the East End, I heard."

The boy eyed him suspiciously, knocking back the last of the rotgut that passed for gin round these parts.

"Another drink?"

"Don't mind if I do, guv'nor! Seein' as 'ow you're payin'."

Once Ulysses had the boy in his grasp and had carried him away from the main thoroughfare of Old Montague Street, he had dropped him in the archwayed entrance to a blind alley. By that point the boy had realised that it was pointless trying to run, at least for the time being, and so had sat and listened as Ulysses had made his claim that he only wanted to ask him a few questions over a drink. The child had certainly had much worse threatened to be done to him, so he had taken the two high-falutin' gents to a drinking den he knew.

There had been little conversation made over the first round but now the gin was starting to loosen the boy's tongue, as Ulysses had hoped. He did not stop to consider the moral implications of getting the boy drunk so that he might disgorge all that Ulysses' needed to know about the urchin street-gang. If he had done, he might as well have given up on ever solving the case of the missing Whitby Mermaid altogether, and he wasn't prepared to do that, not by a long shot.

Ulysses watched his aide's progress at the bar, through the blue fug of tobacco smoke. The barkeep gave Nimrod what could only be called 'a look' but didn't refuse him his drinks. His money was good and money was all that mattered here. This was Victorian England after all and what rich gentlemen got up to with young waifs and strays wasn't anyone's business but their own. There was always the possibility that the man was a philanthropist who would rescue the boy from poverty and take him away to a better life somewhere else. At least that was what the barkeep tried to tell himself as he looked away from their table again.

"So," Ulysses went on, when the refreshed tankard of gin had been placed in front of the boy, "you were telling me about the Whitechapel Irregulars."

"Was I?" the boy asked, innocently, raising the pewter to his lips.

Ulysses' reply was an arching eyebrow, pregnant with

meaning. The monkey glared at him before starting to nuzzle the boy's ear, chattering and chirruping in its shrill simian voice.

And then, seemingly under the influence of the eyebrow, Sidney relented at last. He might have little or no education to speak of, but he wasn't stupid; he knew when he was beaten.

"Like I said, best gang in the East End." Ulysses said.

"Then you 'eard wrong. Best gang in the whole of London more like."

Ulysses smiled in the face of the boy's indefatigable bravado. "Been running with them long?"

"Four years, give or take," Sidney announced proudly, "ever since I hopped spike."

"And how exactly did you get away from there?"

"Got meself taken out with the rest of the shit when the night soil collectors did their round, along with Nobby Clark, didn't I?"

"Very resourceful," was all Ulysses could think to say. He had thought the boy smelt bad before, but now the aroma of unwashed bodies and the street suddenly seemed that much worse.

"Yeah, bin one of thieving Magpie's boys ever since."

Ulysses' ears pricked up at the mention of a name at last – at least at the mention of what was as close to a real name as he felt he was going to get.

"Who's Magpie?"

"That's *Mr* Magpie to you, if you don't mind," the boy said curtly, his former anxiety regarding the workhouse having apparently evaporated.

"So, who is he?"

"You've not heard of the Magpie?" the boy mocked, as if he was as well-known as Queen Victoria herself.

"Humour me," Ulysses continued in the same calm

manner but with an edge of steel to his voice now; the same tone in which he had addressed the informant known as Rat.

"Well that's why he's the master, ain't it! He's so good he don't get caught." Sidney took another swig from the tankard in his hands. "I doubt Scotland Yard even knows 'e exists, but 'e's got fingers in all sorts of pies." He was beginning to noticeably slur his words. "But if they ever found out about the thieving Magpie, if they ever *did* catch 'im, they'd probably be able to solve an 'undred cases in one go. Not that they will ever catch 'im though!" The boy suddenly riled, real venom in his voice.

Whatever hold this Magpie had over the boys in his – to put it loosely – employ, it produced a powerful sense of loyalty among the Whitechapel Irregulars. If the rest of the urchins were like Sidney, Ulysses wouldn't be surprised if they would in fact be loyal to their master – the one who had 'rescued' them from the streets, taken them in, given them a home – even unto death. That thought sent a shiver down his spine. The way Sidney spoke, Ulysses could well believe that the Magpie was like some Messianic figure to his boys.

"'Is boys 'e calls us; 'is bonny darlin's. Princes of the street, that's what 'e calls us. 'Is lovely boys." Sidney's mouth was starting to run away with him.

Sidney suddenly looked anxious, a look that suggested that he had only just realised what Ulysses and Nimrod already knew, that he had said too much.

"But they won't catch 'im, will they? Not the Magpie."

"Who won't?"

"The Peelers, Scotland Yard, them robo-Bobbies in blue," Sidney pressed, the anxiety clear in his voice now. "They won't find out about 'im will they?" The boy started to scan the snug nervously, shooting darting glances into the shadows of booths and unlit corners. "You won't tell them, will you, sir. I'll be brown bread if you do!"

Sidney was nothing more than a scared child again. Who was this man, this Magpie, Ulysses wondered that he could instil a religious fervour in one of his 'lovely boys' one minute and have him fearing for his wretched excuse for a life the next?

"Your Mr Magpie... Do you know if he had anything to do with a certain missing mermaid?"

"I wouldn't know, sir," Sidney said in a small voice, apparently unphased by the mention of an aquatic impossibility. "'E sends us out on all sorts of errands. It's 'ard to keep track sometimes; so many jobs on the go. Like I said, fingers in lots of pies."

The boy was now distractedly rubbing at his ribs, the sparse flesh covering them hidden beneath his ill-fitting attire, a distant look in his watery eyes, as if he were remembering past punishments. But were they ones received at the hands of the beadles or his new messiah?

"But what if the Magpie were to, fly the nest, shall we say? He couldn't hurt you then, could he?" Ulysses stated calmly, letting the implications of what he had said sink in, watching the boy's face intently as he processed what the dandy was suggesting.

The monkey had been watching the exchange with its own intense simian scrutiny. As Sidney considered Ulysses' words, the ape started shrieking and jumping up and down on the boy's shoulder again, attracting the attention of a number of nearby drinkers.

Nimrod glared at the monkey, raising his handkerchief-bound hand, as if he was about to slap the primate from its perch.

The monkey abruptly stopped its screeching and settled down beside the boy's ear and returned to foraging within his messy mop of hair, looking for any choice, wriggling morsels that might be hidden there.

Ulysses watched the creature for a moment as the monkey chattered into the boy's ear. If he hadn't of known better he might have said that it was actually talking to the young scallywag.

"I could take you to 'im," the boy suddenly announced, his whole face lighting up under its coating of grime. "I could lead you to 'is lair. 'E's cocky, 'e is, the Magpie. 'E'd never suspect anyone 'e didn't want snooping around could find 'is way into the rookeries." Sidney boasted, his face aglow.

"You'd do that for us, Sidney?"

"Well, you know 'ow it goes. You scratch my back... Deal?" The boy wiped a filthy hand on his even filthier trouser leg and then, hawking a gobbet of phlegm into the back of his throat spat on it noisily, and held it out to Ulysses.

The finely-turned out dandy looked at the boy's palm with obvious discomfort but after only a moment's pause, he took hold of it in a solid grasp.

"We have a deal."

The boy led them through the labyrinthine side-streets and half hidden, built-over alleyways of Whitechapel's slum rookeries. After countless twists and turns, double blinds, cul-de-sacs and doubling back through cellars and under arch-spans, Ulysses didn't know where he was or how far they had actually travelled. He had lost all sense of direction, the sky and its pall of ever-present choking cloud was no longer visible, hidden as it was beyond a roof of timbers and brick archways.

They came at last to an enclosed octagonal space between the crumbling ruins of a huddle of tenement housing. The structures could have been there since the 18th century Ulysses supposed, looking at them, only they were so rundown now that there were no discerning features by which to date the basic architecture of the place. A forest of bamboo scaffolding had been raised before the facades of the buildings, strung with rope and timber walkways, ladders leading ever upwards towards the canvas awnings that formed a roof over this place.

These were the rookeries; there could be no doubt. The crumbling square smelt of damp, mould, rotting wood and ammonia. A stream gurgled under the planking at their feet, a steady flow of piss and effluent sloshing its way along the boarded-over drain emptying out of the seemingly lifeless slum around them – an indication that there must be some life here, despite initial appearances – on its way to join the Thames or one of the capital's lost waterways, like the Fleet, or the Effra or the Wallbrook. Ulysses might have had an idea as to which if he had had a better notion of where the boy had led them.

The boy stopped beside a dusty tarpaulin, abandoned on the ground and covered in a dusting of broken plaster. He looked back at Ulysses and Nimrod, who looked the most uncomfortable, picking his way through the dust, filth and wreckage. Ulysses knew, however, that he had put up with much worse in his time.

Perched on the boy's shoulder, the monkey scratched its arse and then nibbled at something it found there. Sidney watched the progress of the other two with a look akin to delight on his face.

"At the risk of sounding trite, are we there yet?" Ulysses asked, suddenly conscious of how loud his voice sounded in the muffled near silence of the octagon. You wouldn't have known you were at the heart of the largest metropolis on Earth, not here.

The quiet unnerved him. There was the steady *drip-drip-drip* of a pipe overflowing somewhere, or a tear in an awning letting in overspill from the Upper City way overhead. There was the distant, inescapable rattle and clatter of the Overground system. There was the creak and groan of the awnings as they were pulled by unseen breezes and changes in air pressure. But the presence of any sound to suggest that anything lived here – even pigeons or rats – was absent.

And yet, even here, there was another of those cheerful advertisements for the latest restorative drink – Dr Feelgood's Tonic Stout.

Ulysses suddenly felt very exposed. This was hardly the way to go about creeping up on such a supposedly elusive criminal mastermind.

"We're nearly there now," Sidney said, pointing through a broken doorway, a network of smashed timbers just about visible in the shadows beyond. "We'll need to be quiet from 'ere on in. We're not exactly goin' in the front door, if you know what I mean – it's not even the tradesmen entrance – but 'e's got eyes and ears everywhere."

"I can well believe it," Ulysses said. "Can't be too careful in his line of business, I'm sure." He turned to his manservant, still a few steps behind him. "As they said in the Boy Scouts, be prepared, and all that, eh, Nimrod?" and he took out the pistol he kept holstered under his left arm and checked the chamber. On cue, Nimrod produced his own weapon and readied it.

Sidney acknowledged the presence of the guns with a widening of those puppy dog eyes of his but said nothing. From here on in, silence was key.

"Sir, if you don't mind me saying so, I don't like this," Nimrod whispered at Ulysses' shoulder.

"Don't worry, old chap," Ulysses blustered, instinctive bravado covering up the doubt he felt on his part. "This is our only lead."

"I'm just saying, sir. That's all."

"Duly noted," Ulysses hissed. "Now, can we be about our business?"

They followed their urchin guide through the doorway, their progress slowing considerably as they clambered over the web of broken beams whilst trying to keep their weapons aimed ahead of them, just in case. The underdeveloped boy had no such trouble, scurrying through the spaces between the beams at their feet, his monkey, loosed from its string-leash, bounding ahead, as if scouting a way through the tangle of fallen floorboards and roof supports.

The two men followed as best they could, as quickly and as quietly as possible, which with stealth being of the utmost importance, meant that their progress was not quick at all. And then they were past the hindering obstacles.

As they progressed, a soft orange glow grew in intensity ahead of them, the passageway they were following steadily lightening until the three of them stood huddled at the entrance to a wide open atrium within the rookery. They were on the ground floor, which was covered in rough planks, the space opening up to a height of at least three storeys above them.

Daring to peer further around the edge of the door jamb, Ulysses saw a spider's web of wooden walkways, suspended rope bridges and ladders of one sort or another. From somewhere near his waist Sidney whispered: "It's all right, they're not here."

Ulysses looked again. The web of walkways was slung with glowing hurricane lamps and guttering torches, even the occasional caged halogen light. He could see little in the dark spaces between the hazy spheres of light but still his senses told him that the situation hadn't changed and that the potential threat facing them was no different than when they had started on their journey into the rookery

"Are you sure?" he asked, just the same.

"Sure I'm sure. They'll all be out dipping the pockets of the rich."

"So where will we find the Magpie?"

"'E'll be in 'is counting house," Sidney said, his voice a breathy whisper. "Come on, it's this way."

"Feathering his nest, I suppose," Ulysses said, trying to make light of the situation, but it was a poor attempt to hide how he was really feeling.

The boy started out across the middle of the floor beneath the walkways, scampering ahead as before, only something had changed. Halfway across the void Ulysses realised what it was.

He stopped and Nimrod halted too. A moment later, realising Ulysses' footfalls over the boards behind him had come to a halt, the boy stopped and turned.

"Come on, guv'nor!" he hissed. "Whatcha waitin' for? Bleeding Christmas?"

"Where's your monkey?" Ulysses asked, his voice still quiet but nonetheless commanding for all that.

"What?" the boy asked, his face a picture of pure incomprehension.

"Where's your monkey?"

Ulysses could feel the dull throb of his hypothalamus swelling to a subconscious ache. Something wasn't right.

His head snapped back and he looked up into the glowing constellation of lamps suspended above them. There was movement at the corner of his eye. He followed it and saw another scampering shape elsewhere at the periphery of his vision.

Squinting, he began to see shapes forming amidst the contrasting shadows and sunspots.

And then, there on a walkway ten feet above his head, he saw, quite clearly, a lithe black and yellow shape run along a rope stretched taught across the void, seeming to defy gravity with its inverted aerial run. It wasn't Sidney's missing companion, but another simian altogether.

And then there were more. As if he now knew what he was looking for, Ulysses could hardly miss them. There were rhesus monkeys dangling from ropes and walkways, gnawing nuts and bits of fruit; spider monkeys by the dozen, family groups gathered on shelf-like perches attached to the walls; mandrills scaling vertically suspended ropes. He even thought he could make out the squatting shape and orange fur of an orang-utan on one of the higher levels, half-hidden in shadow behind a balcony.

"Don't bother answering that," Ulysses said coldly, his hind-brain hot with alarm, his grip on the gun in his hand tightening to knuckle white. "Where's the Magpie?"

Preternatural awareness flashed through his brain like a migraine.

"Right here!" came a cackle from the rafters above them. "As is you, Mr Quicksilver, as is you. Right where I wants ya!"

CHAPTER SIX

One for Sorrow

"Welcome to the House of Monkeys, my fine gentlemen."

Ulysses peered up at the rows of balconies above them, shielding his eyes with one hand to try to cut out the glare from the myriad lamps hung from the network of walkways.

His whole body was tensed, ready to spring into action, although Ulysses didn't rate their chances; he and Nimrod were like sitting ducks where they stood out in the open.

"Mr Magpie, I presume," he called up to the galleries, trying to locate their welcomer, his own voice bouncing back to him from the crumbling plaster walls.

"You presume right, Mr Quicksilver," the voice confirmed. "At your service, sah."

"I highly doubt that," Ulysses muttered under his breath.

He was struggling to place the accent. The metropolis of Londinium Maximum was a melting pot of cultures and nationalities, even if outwardly it appeared to be British to the core. But in reality there wasn't a more cosmopolitan city on the planet. Off-planet, that was a different matter, but on Earth the empire of Magna Britannia ruled supreme, governed from the seat of power that was old London town.

Ulysses continued to try to penetrate the dark spaces between the swaying lights. He could see that the apes that obviously gave the place its name were everywhere, larger orders of primate, including whey-faced chimps, slouched on the higher walkways or with their over-long arms wrapped around the supporting pillars of the tiered balconies, while the smaller simians scuttled and bounded between swinging rope ladders and branch-like perches with gay abandon. None of them seemed particularly interested in the presence of the two interlopers.

When Ulysses said nothing else, the master of this den of thieves spoke up again instead.

"So, Mr Quicksilver, what can I do for you?"

"I thought you said you had me right where *you* wanted *me*," Ulysses pointed out, scanning for ways out, should the opportunity arise for them to make their escape.

"So I did, Mr Quicksilver. So I did." The Magpie chuckled.

And there he was. A shadow, a silhouette, no more. The Magpie had positioned himself directly in front of a bright electric light, legs apart, hands on hips, surrounded by a suffused angelic glow. It was a stance that screamed confidence. It said, *you are in my domain. I am king here. Here my word is law. Watch your step.*

The master thief's tone only served to enhance the idea that this was an individual you didn't want to mess with. Not here, not anywhere.

Nonetheless, trying to avoid making any obvious sudden movement, Ulysses slowly angled the muzzle of his gun upwards, aiming it at the silhouette.

"I should watch where you're pointing that thing, if I were you, Mr Quicksilver," Magpie warned, his intent as clear and as lethal as arsenic.

As if on cue, a myriad pairs of simian eyes turned and locked on him from out of the darkness, the flickering light of the oil lamps reflecting redly from their corneas, tiny coals in the semi-darkness. A raucous chattering and screeching swelled from every corner of the space, reverberating from the enclosing walls and setting Ulysses' nerves on edge. He took his eyes off Magpie to glance at where his manservant stood tensed behind him; he looked just as perturbed as Ulysses was feeling. There was also the unmistakeable fleshy thumping of simian fists beating their chests.

Ulysses' hand stopped moving.

Gradually the cacophony subsided, but the inhabitants of the House of Monkeys had made their feelings plain.

"Tell me, Mr Quicksilver. What did you hope to achieve by coming here?"

Ulysses realised he had been given an unprecedented opportunity to find out more, to have his theories about this puzzling case confirmed or denied, one way or the other.

"Very well, then," he began. "Word is that you were involved in the theft of the Whitby Mermaid."

"Well now, you heard right." He wasn't even going to make a show of denying it. The flagrant arrogance of the man! It also only went to show how supremely confident he felt within his own petty kingdom.

"So, how did you do it?" Ulysses went on, remaining outwardly cool, calm and collected, despite feeling riled by the man's arrogance on the inside, his words slow with cold anger.

"He can't even see it," Magpie said, as if he was speaking to someone else. "It's right before his eyes, and he can't even see it."

As if in response to his comment the apes started hooting and chattering again, only this time Ulysses could have sworn they were laughing.

It was just as Ulysses had suspected. The Magpie's mastery of his pets must have been unrivalled in all the empire, outside of the Congo.

Loosely holding the pistol in his hand by only a couple of fingers, Ulysses raised both hands and began a slow clap, each slap of palm on palm reverberating loudly, amplified by the acoustics of the strange monkey house.

"I applaud you, Magpie. An incredible example of man's mastery of the lower forms of life on this planet. The window, the picked lock, it all makes sense to me now."

The silhouette shifted as the villain bowed, luxuriating in the chance to boast of his daring exploits before someone who could appreciate his work, even if he could not condone it.

"But why?"

"Ah," the Magpie mused, obviously delighted to have someone with whom he could share the truth of his cunning, "there it is, the unanswerable question. The one for which any answer, no matter what, can still be interpreted with the same question again; why? Why, why, why?"

Trained monkeys, Ulysses thought. Imagine all the places they could go without ever even arousing any suspicions. He wondered how many other unsolved crimes – or even as yet unnoticed thefts – were the work of Magpie and his monkeys.

"So, why?" Ulysses repeated. "What is a fake, such as the Whitby Mermaid, worth to you?"

"Oh, not to me, Mr Quicksilver, not to me," the Magpie chuckled.

"Then who?"

"Ah, Mr Quicksilver. Now that would be telling, wouldn't it?" Magpie teased.

"But what have you got to lose?" Ulysses pressed. "Who's going to know? Who am I going to tell? Something tells me you're not going to let me walk out of here Scot free."

The Magpie chuckled again. "I do have a reputation to uphold."

"And I have a desperate desire to know. To have got so close to the answer. What can it hurt? What about granting a condemned man's final wish?"

"But what would life be without a little mystery? Where would be the excitement in that?"

That was what all this was about, Ulysses realised, having a little fun. It was all for the thrill; the chase was everything.

"Indeed."

Ulysses aimed his gun, and fired.

The bulb that had been doing such a good job of silhouetting his target exploded and, as the light died, Ulysses caught a glimpse of the Magpie throwing his arms up to protect his head. And then, he was moving.

"Nimrod, duck and cover!"

At his command, his manservant went for the shelter of the doorway by which they had entered the place.

As Ulysses raced for the shadows the only sound he could hear was the mass intake of breath as the House of Monkeys recoiled at his audacity. He raised his gun and fired a second shot towards the network of aerial walkways.

There was a second explosive crack as his shot exploded a lamp, and an angry, animalistic roar as the resulting shower of oil ignited, even as it rained down on the flammable boards and bindings.

"I would appear that you missed, Mr Quicksilver," the voice came from elsewhere now.

"Did I?"

"You are a fool, Mr Quicksilver. A fool. You won't get a second chance."

The Magpie gave a shrill whistle and, with a cacophony of simian shrieks and near-human cries, it started raining monkeys.

The primates dropped from their perches or swung down from the burning boards and bridges above, all gunning for the gunman... even as, after the initial shower of monkeys, fire began to rain down within the House of Monkeys.

The screams of the apes increased ten-fold as burning oil splashed their hairy hides, setting them alight.

Something man-like – and yet too strangely proportioned to be a man – launched itself at Ulysses out of the whirling rabble and landed heavily in the middle of his chest. He was thrown backwards by the baboon that now sat astride him as he landed on top of an apple crate, which turned to matchwood beneath them.

The baboon raised its powerful fists above its head and, snarling, bared yellow predator's fangs. Ulysses bit his own lip as fresh pain shot through his shoulder; an old wound suddenly remembered.

Ulysses heard a gun bark – he knew it wasn't his – and the ape was thrown from him as the bullet punched into it between the eyes.

Ulysses scrambled to his feet, and dusted himself down, testing his flaring shoulder joint. The pain was passing. He assessed that it wasn't going to hamper him.

A gun barked again and another shambling ape fell face down on the boards.

"Nimrod, go!" Ulysses shouted over the shrieks of the terrified animals and hungry roar of the spreading fires. "Get back-up!"

He didn't bother to try to see if his faithful manservant had followed his instructions. They had been in such circumstances too many times, and they both knew the drill. If he were able, Nimrod would be on his way now, re-negotiating the labyrinth of the rookeries to escape their bounds and get help. A cunning criminal mastermind was making his escape and Ulysses wanted him alive – he wasn't done with the Magpie yet!

Moving out from the shelter of the first tier of balconies, Ulysses dared another glance upwards. Somewhere up there, the Magpie was getting away. And there were still questions to be answered, to begin with the one which had been bothering Ulysses ever since he had first read of the theft of the Whitby Mermaid; why anyone would go to so much trouble to steal what was so obviously a fake?

Fire was eating away at the walkway nearest to the oil lamp that Ulysses had exploded with one shot from his pistol, the strands of the ropes holding it up burning through and snapping free under tension, one by one. It would be only a matter of seconds before the whole thing came crashing down, Ulysses guessed. He had to get out of there and fast.

He looked from the burning rope-bridge to the ropes securing it in place, to an iron-cast eyelet punched into the wall high above him which one of the thicker, mooring ropes ran through before descending to a securing bolt in the floor only a few paces away.

Kicking a gambolling monkey aside, Ulysses ran for the rope, holstering his gun as he did so, and grabbed hold with his left hand. With his right he drew his rapier from the sheath of its cane and slashed through the anchoring rope with one strong sweep of the razor-sharp blade.

Its mooring support gone, the bridge went slack and unravelled as the fire did the rest. The walkway dropped, trailing flames, with an animal roar, as it plummeted towards the mass of milling bodies and Ulysses headed skyward.

Ulysses hurtled upwards, pulled through the flames and falling bodies of burning monkeys as the rope ran out through the iron ring in the wall still two floors above him.

Something that was all arms and legs leapt at him as he rocketed upwards, but a sharp thrust of his blade put pay to whatever intentions the ape might have had for him. The rope-bridge crashed to the ground, crushing apes beneath it and sending a rippling blast of air to fan the flames of the other fires that had already taken hold.

And then his ascent came to a sudden stop. Dangling there, twenty feet above the inferno, Ulysses jerked and kicked, attempting to swing closer to the balustrades of a balcony which was tantalizingly out of reach. He had better be quick about it too or the rope would burn through at the bottom and drop him back into the blaze below.

Ever so slowly, it seemed, the rope began to swing. The tips of his toes scraped against the edge of the balcony. Ulysses put both feet against the wall and pushed off again. Like the weight at the end of a pendulum he swung backwards.

The gulf between him and the balcony cruelly widened. When he was at the apex of his swing, with the space between him and safety Ulysses felt the rope sag. It was burning through.

And then he was swinging back again. The rope gave again and he felt himself drop several dangerous inches. Knees bent, feet out flat before him, he connected with the banisters of the balustrade as the rope gave way completely.

Crashing through the timbers, the rope slack in his hands, he rolled across the creaking wooden floor, athletically coming out of the roll and into a fighting stance, rapier blade poised.

There was no sign of anyone who might pass for the villain through the smoke and heat haze. The Magpie had flown.

Picking himself up, and taking a moment to dust himself down, sword-cane in hand, Ulysses set off in hot pursuit, into the dancing shadows.

CHAPTER SEVEN

Flight of the Magpie

Ulysses found himself running through what appeared to be one large room, sub-divided into smaller areas by temporary partitions, stretches of canvas and old blankets nailed to the wooden pillars that supported the floor of the level above.

Behind him he could hear the jabbering screams of the apes, trapped within the blazing conflagration as the fire took hold. Occasionally a smouldering blackened shape would go knuckling by on all fours, leaving behind a trail of smoke and the stink of singed fur.

Ahead of him he could pick out running footsteps, beating a tattoo of panicked flight on the splintering floorboards. And all around him an anxious hubbub of bewilderment and panic swelled to fill the space between.

As he raced on, through the makeshift partitions he saw them – Magpie's lovely boys, the urchin-thieves that made up the Whitechapel Irregulars. He saw grimy face after grimy faces, gap-toothed expressions of curiosity, wide bewildered eyes, the first suggestion of tears of fear in those of the younger members of the gang, children as young as four or five, to look at them, although his experiences with Sidney told him that that didn't mean as much here.

Some had been sleeping, until the growing commotion roused them, bleary eyes blinking from faces half-buried under threadbare blankets and pilfered rag-rugs slung over their hammock-beds. Others appeared to be playing games of chance, some with clay pipes clamped between their teeth, betting for anything that might pass for possessions among the boys – teeth, coloured glass beads, scrag-ends of stale bread, waxy rinds of cheese, cigarette butts. Yet more appeared to have been playing a game that tested the boys' pick-pocketing skills, with a more experienced rogue cast in the role of gentleman-about-town, and acting as their teacher too, as the younger boys tried to relieve him of silk handkerchiefs and a bottle top on the end of a plug-chain, in place of a genuine pocket watch.

Their attire could only be described as haphazard. The boys obviously wore any clothes they could get their hands on, whether they were hand-me-downs from older gang members or stolen from washing lines within the neighbouring streets. There were jackets, dated frock coats, waistcoats, breeches, trews, cloth caps, battered top hats, hobnail boots and wooden clogs. The fashions were worn and dated, patched so many times in some cases that there was practically nothing left of the original item of clothing, and little – if anything – fitted, many of the items being adult's clothing. Amongst the rags was the occasional, much richer item – silk scarves, cravats, gold waistcoat buttons – prizes the boys had won for themselves out on the streets as they ran errands for their master, or simply to pass the time between one meagre meal and the next.

Some of the boys were eating, huddled round small cook-stoves, hunched over mess tins, mismatched pilfered plates and bowls, a thin, grey soup that was unmistakeably gruel, barely covering the bottom of each container.

Most of the children looked startled to see him. One scrawny, whey-faced child stood before the cold iron pot, ladling out portions of the gruel into the wooden bowls and empty food tins that the boys held possessively between thin fingers.

And was it his imagination, or did some of the monkeys look worryingly like boys, whilst some of the boys were beginning to look like apes to him now – all eating the same stuff. What was it doing to them? As he moved in and out of the shadows he tried to convince himself that it was only an optical illusion caused by the changing patterns of light and dark, but nonetheless, to his haggard mind some of the boys were starting to look like monkeys and vice versa.

Ulysses ran on, trying not to look at any of boys' half-human faces – upper lips distended, noses flattened to simian snouts, arms held awkwardly as if they were longer than they should be, shoeless feet wiggling with toes that were too much like fingers for his liking. He had seen all manner of terrible things in his life, and he had been exposed to the dire predicaments of the destitute and the dispossessed before, but it was those hybrid child-ape faces that would haunt his dreams in the dark watches of the nights to come.

Forcing the disturbing expressions from his mind, he focused again on his sole intent – to halt the Magpie's flight.

Still running, Ulysses tossed his sword-cane into his left hand and unholstered his gun again with his right. As he ran on he recounted how many shots he had already fired. The first shot had broken the light behind the Magpie, the second had shattered the oil lamp that started the fire. He had started the night with a full load which meant that he had four bullets left, before he would have to reload.

And then he saw the villain, flying through another crooked doorway before he disappeared into the shadows of a landing. The Magpie was way ahead of him. If he didn't stop him soon, Ulysses would be lucky to even catch one last sight of him before he lost himself in the tangled rat-runs of the rookeries.

He had one chance, and now was the time to act. As the Magpie disappeared into the darkness Ulysses fired.

The crack of the pistol was loud in the compressed space between the gang's living quarters but, despite that, Ulysses was sure that there had been no cry following the shot before he heard, quite clearly, the dull thud, as of a body dropping onto bare boards. Could it be that he had accidentally killed his quarry?

Ignoring the gaggle of children that seemed to be gravitating towards him, alerted by the flight of their master while others moved to escape from the fire behind them, roused by the smoke and heat approaching from the other end of the house, Ulysses vaulted a tumbled tea chest and made for the doorway and the landing beyond.

But now the press of children was greater, fear of the fire spreading faster than the fire itself. Among them were more of the weird not-quite-human-yet-not-quite-simian creatures, but all of them, no matter what they were, were shouting, hooting and screaming in terror.

He had to push them aside; he could not allow anything to hamper his progress now or he might lose this momentary advantage.

His shoe connected with a child and he kicked the boy aside. The heel of his other shoe crunched down on the splayed fingers of a monkey, a shrill animal scream accompanying the soft crunch of breaking bones.

And then he was through the panicking throng and into the shadows of the landing. Here the air was sharp and cold. Above him a rusting skylight swung in the breeze.

Beyond lay access to the rooftops of the rookeries, still in shadow under the pall cast by the Smog and the towering edifices of the Upper City.

Ulysses paused, scanning the darkness. Nimrod should be on his way back to civilisation by now, tracking down the authorities, getting help.

Where could his quarry be, he thought. *Concentrate!* he willed himself.

The skills he had learnt during his brief stay with the monks of Shangri-la, as he recovered at their pagoda-temple, within the jasmine-scented lost valley of the Himalayas, still kept him in good stead. Although not a master like the monks with whom he had stayed as his body healed and his mind was tempered and strengthened, he still had a mastery of his senses that few others possessed.

Shrinking the world around him, straining out the extraneous background noise and the other sensations emitted by the growing conflagration, he held his breath and concentrated on putting the thrumming of his own racing pulse from his mind. He listened instead for the panting breaths of another, the sound of footfalls on wood, or the clatter of feet on the tiles of the rooftops beyond.

Awareness flared in Ulysses' mind. He turned as something at the periphery of his vision detached itself from the darkness, breaking his concentration. A scrawny, spindle-limbed shape launched itself at his face with a savage shrill scream. And then there was movement behind him too.

Ulysses threw up his hands – there was no time to bring sword or gun to bear – grabbing hold of the monkey before it could claw his face. As he grabbed the monkey out of the air he spun on his heel and thrust it towards the man who had tried to come at him from behind, putting all his weight and the momentum of the monkey's leap behind the push.

The monkey gave a strangled cry and tensed momentarily before going limp in Ulysses' hands, a point of metal glistening darkly with the creature's blood, protruding from the middle of its chest.

Then the monkey was pulled savagely from Ulysses' hands as the Magpie shook the dead animal from his blade, and for the first time the dandy got a good look at the robber-king of the Whitechapel Irregulars, the master of the House of Monkeys.

He was both shorter and slighter than Ulysses. A scruffy mess of black hair hid much of his face, but he caught a glimpse, nonetheless of a nose as sharp as a knife. The villain's clothes don't seem to fit him either – just like those of his urchin-sons – a rag-cloak of grey, white, black and blue, making him look like his eponymous magpie! He patently had a taste for the theatrical, as had been evidenced by everything Ulysses had seen of him since entering his lair.

The tiny ape rolled onto the floor and lay limply where it landed, arms, legs and tail all at unnatural angles, blood staining the faded green waistcoat it wore.

Ulysses pressed home his advantage, hoping to wrong-foot the Magpie still further and bring him down. The knife flashed in the near dark. Ulysses yelped in pain as the serrated blade cut into the meat of his wrist. His fingers spasmed open, his gun clattering onto the bare boards at his feet.

Ulysses lurched backwards as the Magpie danced in below his guard with the knife again. He heard the rip and felt the snag as the tip of the blade caught the edge of a buttonhole on his coat and tore through the fabric.

He was dimly aware of the bouncing thuds and bangs of his gun as it continued to tumble down the staircase from the landing, and far out of reach. But for the time being he was more concerned about the dextrous knife-fighting abilities of the rogue in front of him.

As the Magpie bounded forwards again Ulysses took two steps back. The palm of his right hand was wet with blood now but the adrenalin of the moment helped him to put aside the pain in his wrist. Instead, focusing all his energies on the fight, he brought his rapier blade to bear again.

He sensed the Magpie hesitate and knew that he had already turned the tide of battle. Now it was his turn to lunge forward but the Magpie had already made his move. The felon flung himself at the ladder to the skylight and, displaying all the agility of a monkey, scampered up it, heading for the roof.

Ulysses pressed forward again, slashing his sword down onto the ladder, slicing splinters from the wooden rungs. And then his quarry was gone. Without a moment's hesitation Ulysses grabbed the ladder and was up it after the Magpie.

As he pulled himself through the open skylight, the felon's fleeing footfalls carried to him over the roofs of the rookery.

In an instant Ulysses was on his feet. As he took a swaying moment to gain his balance, he took in his surroundings. He was standing on the edge of the roof of the slum building. Only a few feet below him, the slanting lip of the roof dropped into a dark void, many storeys high. Above and to his left, at the apex of the roof, the Magpie was making a run for it, away over the rooftops. He looked like a prancing demon, given a hellish cast, as he was, by the fire and smoke rising up from the centre of the rookery, crackling hungrily in the cold November air. Beyond lay a sparse forest of chimney stacks, aerial masts and cast-iron escape fire escapes. And above it all loomed the might and magnificence of the Upper City, a spider's web of Overground lines twisting and turning between the towering edifices.

There was no time to lose. Sword still in hand, Ulysses scrambled up the sloping tiles towards the crest of the roof. Several times his feet slipped on the smooth shingle and once a tile came free beneath him as he kicked against it. But then he made the apex and, following the Magpie's example, rose cautiously to his feet. Then, arms outstretched, he began to scamper after the rogue again.

But where the Magpie's movements were like those of a dancer, almost balletic, Ulysses' pursuit of the fleeing felon was a clumsy, stumbling run, as he tried to make the next nearest chimney stack before he lost his balance and went sliding away down the steeply sloping roof to the drop beyond.

As he staggered after the Magpie, he found himself calling to mind his close-quarters combat with the reactionary Jago Kane atop the speeding Overground train, only seven months before. Although he was in a perilous position skittering over the rooftops now, at least they weren't rattling and rumbling beneath him.

He glanced up. Incredibly, he appeared to be closing on the Magpie, who seemed to be pausing for breath as he clung to a chimney stack not ten feet from Ulysses.

Ulysses threw himself towards the chimney, but before he slammed into the tottering brick structure, the Magpie was away again. Gasping for breath, heart racing, Ulysses watched as the man sprinted to the end of the roof and launched himself into space.

A second later, the Magpie landed with a crash of

breaking tiles on top of the roof of the next slum tenement. It was only as he let out a pent-up lungful of air that Ulysses realised he'd been holding his breath. And then there was only one thing for it.

He couldn't think about what he was going to do, he simply had to do it. Relinquishing the security of the chimney stack, he sprinted for the gable-end of the building, the void between the slums seeming to widen with every bounding step. And then, with one almighty leap, he threw himself out over the vertiginous void, horrid images of plummeting airships and death-defying leaps from the top of speeding trains returning to haunt him.

The lip of the roof beyond loomed large before him, but then it was directly in his eye-line, and then all he could see before his face were crumbling bricks and mortar. He flung his arms out and up, felt them grab hold of the lip of the roof, braced himself as his body slammed into the wall, knocking the wind from him, and the flesh of the fingertips of his left hand tore as his own body weight pulled them across the rough surface, the skin of the knuckles of his right scraping red raw as he refused to relinquish his hold on his sword, barely managing to cling on. But cling on he did, like a limpet to a rock at low tide.

He hung there for a moment, gasping to get some air back into his empty lungs. But there was no time to delay; right at this moment, the Magpie was making his escape. The muscles of his back and arms straining, the toes of his shoes scuffing as he tried to get a purchase on the wall, Ulysses began to heave himself upwards.

There was the crunch of gravel above him and a face, like that of some leering gargoyle, peered out over the drop. He needn't have worried about his quarry getting away; the Magpie had come to him.

"Well, well, Mr Quicksilver. Not so quick now, are you? It would appear that you need a hand," the thief-lord gloated.

"No, I'm alright thanks," Ulysses managed through gritted teeth.

"Alright then. Here, let me give you a foot."

The felon's boot heel smashed down on Ulysses' sword hand. Bones ground.

With a cry of anguish, Ulysses pulled his hand away and let go of his precious sword at last. Through the agony of his broken fingers, only a second later, he heard the clattering jangle of metal ringing on metal below him. And despite the pain, that instinctive part of his brain that had seen him through so many scrapes before told him what he needed to do.

Before the Magpie could move his foot again, with all the strength he could muster, Ulysses jerked himself up enough with his left arm to release his hold on the parapet and grab hold of the Magpie's ankle instead. With all his weight hanging off the man's leg, he pulled.

With the Magpie already balanced precariously at the edge of the roof, and Ulysses the more heavily built of the two, it did not take much to gain the desired result. The felon lost his footing, falling heavily on his rump on the edge of the wall before the two men fell into the space between the tightly-packed buildings.

Only a matter of a few seconds later – that seemed more like minutes to Ulysses – he and the Magpie crashed down together on the narrow metal walkway of a fire escape bolted to the side of the building, still three storeys above the ground.

Lashing out, the Magpie quickly extricated himself from the tangle of Ulysses limbs, but Ulysses' hadn't been interested in restraining the rogue. In an instant he was on his feet, sword held tightly in his left hand now, the broken fingers of his right clamped tightly under his armpit, still gasping for breath.

The Magpie sprang cat-like to his feet, knife back in his hand, but where the master criminal was agile as a panther, Ulysses had pain and rage on his side.

Bellowing like some injured animal, he charged the Magpie, forcing the man back towards the railings at the end of the walkway, releasing his fury in an unstoppable assault. Their blades rang as the two traded blows but in no time, Ulysses had hacked his way through the best defence the Magpie could offer. With a final lunge he thrust the tip of his rapier blade at the man's eye; although Ulysses still needed the villain alive for interrogation, something small, like being blinded in one eye, seemed like a perfectly valid option, if it meant he could bring the Magpie in for questioning.

Still possessed of all the poise and grace of a puma, The Magpie sidestepped the blow, but Ulysses still felt the briefest resistance in his blade, as if he had made contact.

And then, with one hand on the railing behind him, the Magpie swung himself over the edge and dropped, body held straight as an arrow as he plummeted to the alley below.

Ulysses watched, transfixed by the man's daring, as his quarry escaped him again, landing in a feline crouch amidst the debris and detritus covering the cobbles below.

For a moment Ulysses was rooted to the spot, as he assessed the jump the Magpie had made. But if that felon could make it, then so could he, Ulysses realised. Snapping himself out of his momentary hiatus, the pain in his hand like a distant memory, Ulysses clambered over the railings and then, after a second or two, his pulse pounding in his ears, he took a deep breath, and jumped.

He landed awkwardly among the piles of rotting rubbish, a sack of something soft and mouldering breaking his fall, but he still ended up splayed on his hands and knees on the cold, wet, filthy cobbles.

Even as he picked himself up he knew that he was too late, that the Magpie had flown. He strained his ears, but all he could hear were the sounds of the unsettled city, the ever-present rattle of locomotives above, the crackle and roar of the fire rampaging through the rookeries and the distant wailing sirens of the approaching fire brigade.

What he couldn't hear were the tell-tale footfalls of the fleeing felon.

Ulysses looked around him, at the maze of side-streets, alleyways and dead-ends he now found himself in. This was the Magpie's territory. In the time it would take him to find his way back to a main thoroughfare – any thoroughfare that he could at least read the name of – his quarry would be long gone.

Yet despite the throbbing hurt of his hands and wrist, and all the other injuries he had sustained in his pursuit of the Magpie, a dark smile spread across Ulysses' face, as something clicked inside his head. The thrill of the chase was all, and the chase wasn't over yet.

Extracting his personal communicator from a coat pocket, he began to key in a number.

CHAPTER EIGHT

The Game is Afoot

The cab pulled up outside the Bloomsbury residence with a screech, tyres skidding on the wet leaves clogging the gutter. A door flew open and Ulysses Quicksilver bundled out of the vehicle, quickly followed by his manservant Nimrod.

The street lamps were dim at this late hour – or should it have been classed as early now, Ulysses wondered – and there was no one else around in this part of town, although not so far away the city was as alive and awake as ever.

Ulysses looked up at the imposing facade in front of him. *This is the place*, he thought as he read the name on the brass plate beside the grand columned entrance. And there was a light burning in one of the windows on the first floor.

It had taken him a good half an hour to find his way out of the maze of rookery rat-runs and be reunited with his manservant, who by that point had already managed to procure them a cab to carry them out of Whitechapel. The journey to Bloomsbury had not taken long, but had given Ulysses enough time to order his thoughts and decide on the best course of action to follow next. And that was to not waste time beating about the bush.

He felt for the reassuring presence of the sword-cane currently tucked into the belt of his trousers.

Taking the steps to the front door two at a time, Ulysses went to ring the door bell. He winced in pain, almost crying out, as he tried to close his ruined fingers around the bell-pull and withdrew his hand sharply.

"Let me, sir," Nimrod said stepping past Ulysses.

A bell clattered and jangled noisily somewhere within the dark house.

"Come on!" Ulysses hissed impatiently, his foot tapping on the step as he listened for any sign of someone coming to answer the door. "Ring it again," he ordered. "And if they don't answer this time, we're breaking the door down!"

Nimrod tugged sharply on the bell-pull again. A renewed jangling disturbed the peace of this exclusive address once more.

As the ringing died away, Ulysses heard the *tap-tap-tapping* of leather soles on floor tiles. A few seconds later the front door opened and a scowling face greeted them, peering gargoyle-like from the gloom beyond.

"Do you know what time it is, sir?" the face demanded crossly.

Ulysses made a show of taking out his pocket watch. "As it happens, I do," he said. "Half past one, as you're asking. And that is relevant, why?"

"Mr Wraith is not used to receiving guests in the middle of the night, sir!" the butler said with some vehemence.

Awkwardly, using his left hand, Ulysses extracted the leather cardholder from his jacket pocket and flipped it open. The butler scanned the details so presented.

"Mr Quicksilver," he said, maintaining the same disapproving tone – like a schoolmaster giving a misbehaving pupil a dressing down – "Mr Wraith is not receiving guests at this hour."

Ulysses was taken aback. He was not used to people challenging the authority referred to on his Department ID, not unless he was already wrestling them on top of a train or negotiating with the use of extreme force.

"Oh, I see. That authority not good enough for you, eh? Then try this. Nimrod?"

Ulysses stepped aside, Nimrod forcing his way past the threshold.

"I must protest!" the butler spluttered, his carefully created demeanour of arrogant correctitude crumbling in an instant.

"Must you?" Ulysses said, wearily.

Before the butler knew what was going on, Nimrod's bunched fist connected with his face. He went down, stunned, falling to his knees as he whimpered in shock and pain, his hands pressed to his bloodied nose.

The two men barged past the stunned retainer and into the house.

"Carstairs? Who is it?" came a man's muffled voice from somewhere above.

Saying nothing, Ulysses grabbed his manservant's sleeve and jerked his head upwards, indicating the floor above.

Trying to tread as lightly as he could on the plush carpet covering the grand staircase, Ulysses dashed up it to the first floor, Nimrod following after. Ahead of him, at the end of a darkened landing, stood a set of double doors, light from the room beyond escaping through the cracks where the doors met the frame.

"Carstairs?" came the voice again, warier now and closer, as if its owner stood just on the other side of the doors.

Without hesitation, Ulysses grabbed a brass handle and forced the door open violently, catching the man who had been standing behind it by surprise.

Gabriel Wraith danced back, hastily trying to regain his composure. He stood there in full evening dress, hair slicked down as smoothly as ever with half a tin of pomade.

"Quicksilver!" he yelped in what Ulysses imagined was a more nervously high-pitched tone that he had intended. "What is the meaning of this?"

"With have things to discuss, Wraith," Ulysses announced as he strode into the room, the other man backing into the corner as far as his reading desk, before his unstoppable, glacial advance.

"Things? What do you mean, man, barging in like this?" he demanded, his voice like cold steel now. "What things?"

"The Whitby Mermaid, the Whitechapel Irregulars, the House of Monkeys," Ulysses reeled off the list. "What do you know of th –"

He stopped abruptly, catching sight of the drop of blood, a single crimson droplet oozing from the otherwise almost indistinguishable nick on the consulting detective's otherwise immaculately pale cheek.

"What happened to your face?" Ulysses asked, eyes narrowing as he pointed an accusing, wrongly-angled finger at Wraith.

"I cut myself shaving," he answered icily, subconsciously feeling for the wound. With an arrogant motion he tossed his head back. "You're raving man. I would be grateful if you would depart these premises immediately!"

But even as the words were out of his mouth it was obvious that Gabriel Wraith knew that it was too late, that he had been rumbled. Even as Ulysses went for his blade, pulling the rapier free of its cane-scabbard, Wraith went for his. And then the heavy knife was in his hand again.

"How did you know?" Wraith demanded as he dropped into a fighting stance, more befitting of his criminal alter ego than a respectable Bloomsbury gentleman.

"What, that Gabriel Wraith and the Magpie were one and the same?" Ulysses said. "I didn't know, I only suspected."

"What?" the other man shrieked in angry disbelief.

"But now you've confirmed that fact yourself, the similarities are clear; you're both light on your feet, balletic you might say, face sharp as a blade, mind to match, a propensity for repeating words and phrases. I suppose it would explain your success as a consulting detective as well, if you were the one responsible for the thefts in the first place." Ulysses flashed the icily furious man a devilish grin. "Oh, and you're both arrogant bastards," Ulysses snarled.

"Well then, it would appear we have unfinished business, you and I," Gabriel Wraith declared as he shifted his balance from one foot to the other, preparing himself for the moment when he could duck in under Ulysses' guard and deliver a fatal blow.

"Indeed," Ulysses agreed, hefting the blade in his left hand – not his preferred hand but competent enough, nonetheless. There was the click of a pistol being cocked behind him. "Shame, it appears it's going to have to stay that way, me old fruit. Now drop the knife, or my man here will drop you."

Wraith grimaced and made a sound like an animal snarl. "Idiot!" he hissed.

"What, you or me?"

With a roar born of frustration, rage and despair, Gabriel Wraith sprang at Ulysses, suddenly all semblance of composure gone.

Ulysses raised his own blade just in time to parry the maniac's descending sweep. So angry was the man that, what skill and finesse he might have had was lost as blind rage took over. Ulysses sidestepped and kicked out at the same time, sending his opponent sprawling across the remarkable Turkish carpet that covered the floor of Wraith's consultation chamber.

Before he could recover himself, Nimrod stepped forward, the barrel of the pistol pointed directly at Wraith's face. The rogue's features lost what little colour they still retained as he realised that he had come to the end of the line.

"Go on then – kill me, if that's what you're going to do. Just don't make a damned meal of it."

"Don't be so bloody stupid," Ulysses laughed. "I've not hunted you through Whitechapel and chased you over rooftops simply to kill you now. As you said yourself, Mr Magpie, we have unfinished business you and I."

Wraith looked up into Ulysses' cruelly smiling face and felt his bowels turn to water. He suddenly felt much worse than he had done when he just thought that Ulysses was going to have him killed.

"I hope you have a head for heights," Ulysses hissed as Nimrod delivered a blow to the head with the butt of his pistol.

Slowly a bleary consciousness returned and Gabriel Wraith opened his eyes. He immediately let out a wail of fear as the street appeared four storeys above him, gently swaying from side to side. His head felt thick, engorged with the blood that seemed to be collecting within his skull. The shock of his situation merely helped to bring him round more completely.

Gradually reality reasserted itself and he realised the seriousness of his predicament. He looked up, straining his neck and could see the cord around his ankle just as he became aware of the dull throb there. Beyond that lay only the dark pall of the Smog, under-lit a satanic red by the blinking lights of the city below, the Overground network a dark spider's web against it. The cord ran up and over a bent aerial mast and back to a window on the fourth floor of the house.

"Ah, you're awake. Had a nice sleep, did you?"

Wraith froze. The familiarity of the voice cut through him like a blade of ice and brought with it sudden remembrance of the night-time chase over the rooftops of Whitechapel and Quicksilver's sudden attack within his own home.

Wraith's lip curled into an angry sneer. "Quicksilver, you bastard," he snarled. "What are you doing? What, precisely, do you think you are doing?"

"I'll give you a clue," Quicksilver said, the same cruel smile still locked on his face. "Nimrod?"

At once the line holding him up went slack and suddenly he was falling. The cord whizzed over the mast, accompanied by the sharp smell of scorched rope.

He cried out in fear as the slabs of the pavement and the points of the railings shot rapidly closer.

He was only vaguely aware of Quicksilver shouting for his manservant to halt his descent.

"You said... you weren't... going to... kill me!" the panicking Wraith protested, as he panted for breath. "That's what you said!"

He could see Quicksilver's manservant now, standing at another window on the top floor of the house, the rope held tightly in his great bunched fists.

"I said I hadn't come all this way to kill you *then*," the other clarified, an expression of cruel delight etched onto his clean cut aristocratic features. "But your fate now depends on whether you answer my questions truthfully.

You see, there are things that you know Wraith – or should that be Magpie? – things that I *need* to know."

"And what makes you I'll give you the answers?" Wraith retorted pathetically, making one last ditch attempt at a rebellious front.

"Because I believe you to be a sensible man," Quicksilver said calmly. "Nimrod?"

The cord went loose again and Wraith dropped, another involuntary cry escaping his lips.

It took longer for his fall to be slowed this time and, with a growing sense of dread, Wraith realised that Quicksilver quite possibly was willing to do anything to get the answers he wanted.

As he hung there, swinging from the end of the thin line, upside down, like a fish on a hook, gravity pushing his eyes out of his head, he had a clear view of the spear-tipped railings outside his Bloomsbury residence. Were he to fall he would be lucky if all he ended up with was a fractured skull and a broken neck; at least that way death would be instantaneous. If he was unlucky, he might puncture a kidney, or skewer some other vital internal organ, before bleeding to death in agonising pain, like a stuck pig on the railings.

He felt the cord jerk again, but this time he was being pulled upwards. When he was level with the sadistically-smiling face once more, Quicksilver spoke again. "If you're suspended uncomfortably, then we'll begin."

Wraith nodded slowly; he didn't see that he had any other option.

"You were behind the theft of the Whitby Mermaid, weren't you?" Quicksilver stated calmly.

Wraith paused for a moment. He had determined to be defiant to the end, but the fire had gone from him now. All that stubbornness would save him, other than his pride, was a painful death on the pavement below.

He nodded again. "Yes."

"But why steal a fake? What was it worth to you?"

"A fair amount. It was stolen to order," Wraith stated flatly.

For the first time something other than an absolute conviction in his own arrogant opinion crossed Quicksilver's features. It was the one thing that gave Wraith some small nugget of satisfaction.

"To order?" Quicksilver echoed.

"That's what I said."

"Who for?"

The pedant in Wraith couldn't resist: "I think you mean 'for whom?'"

The cord went slack again. Wraith dropped a floor before the rope pulled taut, tugging sharply on his hip. He almost bit through his tongue with the shock of it.

"Bellerophon," he gasped, blood spraying from his mouth as he spat the name.

"Who is Bellerophon? And don't tell me he's a hero from Greek myth."

"I don't know," Wraith snarled. "It was just a name. There was never any face to face meeting."

"What does Bellerophon want with a fake?" Quicksilver pressed.

"I don't know! I didn't ask!"

"You just took the money."

"As you say," Wraith snarled, "I just took the money."

"So, where is it now? The mermaid."

"There were instructions to send it north, to Whitby."

"Back to Whitby, eh?" Quicksilver pondered. "It keeps coming back to Whitby. But I still don't understand why someone would go to so much trouble to steal what appears to be – what *must* be – a fake." He stepped back from his place by the window and Wraith heard him say to his manservant: "We're not done with this mystery yet, Nimrod. But we're done here."

Disbelieving doubt was soon ousted by cold horror as Wraith awakened to his fate as he watched the one called Nimrod tie off the cord to something inside the room. Quicksilver turned from the window, immediately disappearing into the shadows of the room beyond.

"You can't just leave me here!" Wraith screamed after him, all his fear and anxiety suddenly taking hold.

There was a moment's pause and then his tormentor appeared at the window again.

"Oh, can't I? Goodnight, Mr Wraith." He turned and then was gone, for good this time.

Wraith stared up at the heaving morass of the Smog that hung over the city like a funeral shroud and listened as the distant sounds of police sirens grew louder.

It was the end of the line for the Magpie, and, more importantly, it was the end for Gabriel Wraith as well.

His eyes on the cord cutting into his aching ankle, he reached deep inside a trouser pocket, searching for the pen knife that he always kept there.

This night would see the end of both the master of the House of Monkeys, the Magpie, and Gabriel Wraith, London's finest consulting detective. And all thanks to that smug-faced bastard, Ulysses Quicksilver.

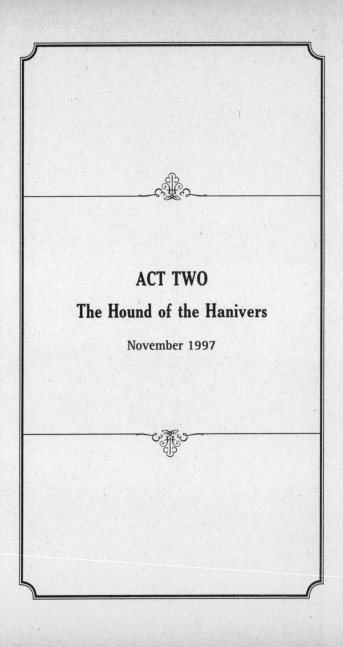

ACT TWO

The Hound of the Hanivers

November 1997

CHAPTER NINE

A Word to the Wise

The journey north took no time at all, or so it seemed, once the train had left St Pancras and the looming edifices of London. Heavily built-up suburban conurbation gave way – along with the ever-present, tangible tobacco-yellow Smog – to pleasant green countryside beyond the furthest limits of Londinium Maximum as they passed through Hertfordshire, Bedfordshire and Northamptonshire. Stations, villages and towns whipped past in an anonymous blur as the speeding locomotive ate up the miles.

The further north they travelled the darker loomed the sky ahead of them as the clear cerulean blue, drawn with streaks of white cotton clouds, steadily gave way to the polluted skies of the North. The towns of the Midlands had been swallowed by the rampant industrialisation that had continued throughout the twentieth century leaving the conurbations as islands of miserable, second-rate civilisation, separated by great expanses of automated factories and industry-polluted wasteland. At this point in the journey, stewards took care to secure all the windows, least the sulphurous fumes of that region proved disagreeable to those travelling on the ten thirty from St Pancras.

What had started out as a relatively fine day in London – and that had become a clear, chill autumnal day in the farmland beyond – now gave way to the permanently overcast misery of Nottinghamshire. The toxic wasteland gave way at last as the train diverted across the windswept moors of Yorkshire, this natural wilderness seeming almost as desolate as the industry-spoiled wasteland through which they had passed on the way.

Having left London only that morning, that same afternoon saw the huffing and puffing locomotive hissing to a halt amidst a rising cloud of steam at Whitby Station, the end of the line, the tracks coming to a stop less than half a mile from the sea.

It being late in the day, the dandy and his manservant set about finding lodgings for the duration of their stay. After making enquiries at the station master's office, they took a horse-drawn cab to the East Crescent and took rooms at a superior lodging house there that had plenty of vacancies, for those few visitors Whitby still received at this time of year; people looking to benefit from the curious properties of the sea air or wishing to follow in the footsteps of Mr Stoker's Dracula.

Determining to begin their search for the mysterious Mr Bellerophon – an assumed name, Ulysses presumed – first thing the following morning, He and Nimrod retired for the night in their suite of rooms on the second floor, Ulysses taking the master bedroom, while Nimrod made for the significantly smaller valet's chamber off the suite's day room-cum-dining room.

"Nimrod, that was a triumph," Ulysses declared, placing his knife and fork together on the grease-smeared plate before him.

"I shall pass your compliments to Mrs Scoresby, sir," Nimrod replied.

"There's nothing like a full English to set oneself up for the day. And I do like black pudding."

"More coffee, sir?"

"Yes, why not, old chap?"

Ulysses lent back in his chair, putting his arms behind his head. His wrist still hurt as did the broken fingers of his right hand which were still bound together to aid their healing.

Nimrod dutifully got up from his seat at the breakfast table opposite his master, draped a freshly-pressed napkin over one arm, lifted the cafetiere from its silver-plated salver, walked round the table to where Ulysses sat stretched out in his dressing gown, and carefully re-filled the dandy's coffee cup.

"Thank you, Nimrod," he said as his manservant placed the cafetiere back on the salver in the middle of the table and returned to his seat. Nimrod nodded in polite acknowledgement.

Ulysses deposited a heaped teaspoon of sugar into the dark steaming fluid and began to stir languidly.

"So, where to start?" he mused, not so much asking Nimrod for his advice as simply giving voice to his own thoughts.

His eyes drifted across to the front page of the local paper that had been laid on the pristine white tablecloth next to his place setting.

"Hey, look at this will you, Nimrod?"

Eyebrows arching, Nimrod looked down his nose, concentrating as he read the inverted headline in front of him.

"'Ghestdale Beast claims Tenth Victim'," he read. "Hmm, it sounds... intriguing, sir."

"I'd say!" Ulysses exclaimed excitedly, scanning the column inches beneath the attention-grabbing banner headline.

"Tabloid scare-mongering?" Nimrod queried as Ulysses reached the bottom of the page and looked up again, a delighted grin on his face.

"It says here that the body of some poor sod was found up on the moors yesterday with his throat and intestines torn out."

"Sounds ghastly," Nimrod said dispassionately.

"Apparently he was found by a sheep farmer who's lost a number of his sheep to wild animal attacks over the last few months."

"Wild animals, sir?"

"That's what it says here."

"But the British Isles have very few natural predators left, certainly nothing big enough to take down a man, surely. I must be some kind of feral dog, or perhaps one of those big cats that keep getting lose from private zoos."

"That's what the editor of this local rag thinks too." Ulysses pointed to the editorial comment at the top of the second page. "At least, local rumour's blaming it on the Barghest, some local legend, a phantom hound said to stalk Ghestdale Moor."

"A phantom hound, sir?"

"According to folklore, those who see the beast don't live to see another day."

"If that's the case, how can anybody have ever reported that that is the case?"

"You can't over-analyse folklore, Nimrod," Ulysses pointed out. "That's what it says here."

"Surely they can't be serious."

"Well, according to this, there have been ten confirmed deaths, supposedly perpetrated by this hobgoblin hound, and just as many people have simply disappeared over the last four months. Most of the bodies were discovered on Ghestdale, the expanse of moorland that lies south-east of Whitby, close to the coast and the notorious Beast Cliff, which is said to be another haunt of the Barghest."

"If you don't mind me saying so, sir, that is nothing but a load of old poppycock."

"But something's responsible for all those deaths."

Nimrod's eyes narrowed as he attempted to assess his employer's true opinion regarding the matter.

"How did the others die?"

"All in a similarly savage manner, from what I can gather from this. Gutted, throats torn out, internal organs missing; some of the bodies were even partially devoured."

"Delightful. It really is a mystery, sir."

"A mystery indeed. And you know how I feel about mysteries."

"Indeed I do, sir," Nimrod said with what Ulysses hoped was feigned weariness.

"But," Ulysses went on, with what sounded like profound disappointment, "we already have one mystery on our hands; that of the identity of the elusive Mr Bellerophon, which is, I have to assume, an assumed name."

"Quite, sir," Nimrod agreed. "So, if I might be so bold as to ask, how do you suggest we move things forward from here?"

Putting the paper to one side, Ulysses devoted all his attention to the older man seated opposite him, immaculate as ever in his simple self-styled butler's uniform.

"You know what, Nimrod? I think it's about time we played the part of tourists to the full and took in the sights of Whitby, starting with some of those delightful looking ale-quaffing establishments down by the docks."

"Very good, sir. Shall I unpack the pistols, or will the bloodstone suffice?"

By the time Ulysses was dressed and ready to face the day – wearing a light tweed suit underneath a long check overcoat, finished off with a crimson cravat held in place with a diamond pin – it was already past ten.

Leaving their lodging house on the Crescent, the dandy and his manservant made their way to the East Terrace and the footpath that led down towards the estuary of the Esk, passing through the whale bone arch – a reminder of Whitby's whaling past – to emerge at the harbour end of the great stone West Pier. From there, the two men skirted the Esk, following the river back upstream through the old fishing town. The air was thick with the smell of fish, wood smoke and the ever-present pollution that drifted down off the moors from the vast brick-built factories with the morning mist.

Through the bobbing forest formed by the masts and rigging of the ships moored in the Lower Harbour, Ulysses could just make out the grey ghost of the Abbey, up there on the windswept crown of East Cliff, through shifting spaces between the smoke billowing from chimneys up and down the town.

Whitby was all of a bustle at this time in the day and even though it wasn't the height of the tourist season, there was still plenty for the local populace to do; the fishing and jet industries were still the life-blood of the old town.

Passing the swing bridge that crossed the silt-brown river as if flowed on its inexorable way to the sea, following the smell of bubbling pitch and the echoing clamour of sawing and hammering, Ulysses led the two of them towards the shipyards of Endeavour Wharf and onto New Quay Road.

They stopped at last outside the white painted facade of

a large, five storey building that sported a sign declaring that this was 'The Angel Hotel'.

"This looks like just the place to start making our enquiries," he said, looking past the stacks of lobster pots to what had all the appearance of being one of Whitby's principal drinking establishments, "don't you think?"

"If you're sure that this is the best way to go about our business here, sir," Nimrod replied with a hint of wariness in his voice.

"Oh, don't be such an old woman," Ulysses chided the older man good-humouredly. "Come on, it'll be fun!"

Five drinking establishments later, and Ulysses Quicksilver and his manservant found themselves in the blue-fugged bar-room of the Black Swan Inn on Baxtergate. It was just like every other. Although it was still only the middle of the day, the taverns in the vicinity of the docks were heaving, the fishermen and many of the stevedores having finished work for the day and made it the few yards to the public houses of Whitby to start spending their wages straight away.

Such was certainly true of the fish-reeking clientele of the Black Swan. For many of them, the working day had finished hours ago, and the men were well into their cups, having been at their seats in the bar since the pub first opened its doors to the desperate drinkers.

Ulysses stepped into the lamp-lit dark of the snug and, blinking against the change in light levels, he casually took in the sprawl of the bar – with its low beams and closeted drinking stalls – which looked just like every other tavern he had entered that morning.

As flamboyantly dressed as he was and as out of place

he would obviously appear no matter how he carried himself, Ulysses saw no point in being anything other than the dandy he truly was, striding across the bar-room with a cocky swagger and an all-embracing smile on his face. Such misplaced confidence made people wrong-footed and that gave him the advantage.

He could feel the eyes of everyone on him and couldn't help but allow himself a private smile. Nimrod followed behind, as ever, apparently above it all, whether he was faced with cocky arrogance or disgruntled hostility.

From the furtive glances he kept giving the two of them, it looked like the barman – his belly swollen from beer, his cheeks jowly, his eyes small back holes amongst the flab – was doing his best to keep a clandestine eye on them. The bar-top looked like it had been made from the warped timbers of a ship's deck, uneven and stained almost black.

Ulysses tapped three times on the wooden counter with his cane and grinned as he saw the man twitch. With a face as overcast and thundery as the dull November day outside, finally admitting defeat, he looked up at his newest customers.

The man eyed Ulysses and Nimrod uncomfortably from under beetling brows. Sweat covered his face like grease. He started wiping the beer glass he held in one hand vigorously with the grubby rag he held in the other.

"Yes?" he asked, grudgingly.

"Good –" Ulysses paused and made a show of taking out his pocket watch and checking the time, before putting it back. "– afternoon, my good man. I wonder if I might take a moment of your time."

"Case you hadn't noticed, this is a pub."

Ulysses looked almost bewildered for a moment and then said: "Ah, yes, of course. I see. Cognac, please.

Nimrod?"

"This, is a *pub*," the barman repeated.

"Oh. Better make it a pint of... What would you recommend?"

"Bitter is what most people drink round these parts."

"Then make it a pint of bitter please, barman."

The sweating barkeep scowled as he filled the glass he had been smearing with the dirty cloth with something the colour and clarity of watered down sewage from an age-worn pump on the bar.

"What'll 'e 'ave?" he asked, jerking his head towards Nimrod who stood impassively, and straight as a lamppost, at Ulysses' shoulder.

"Nimrod?"

"A glass of orange juice will suffice, sir."

"This. Is. A. Pub," the barkeep growled.

Ulysses looked at Nimrod and raised both eyebrows.

"A glass of tap water then."

The barkeep muttered something under his breath that sounded like it was along the lines of "Soft, southern poofs" and looked for another glass for Nimrod's water. It was then that Ulysses struck.

"I don't suppose you would have happened to have heard of a Mr Bellerophon, would you?"

"A who?"

"Bellerophon. Mr Bellerophon. After that chap from Greek myth."

"The what?"

"Greek myth," Ulysses persisted in the face of such over-bearing obstinacy and ignorance. "Bellerophon. Chap who Pegasus, the wing-horsed, and killed the Chi –"

Ulysses stopped abruptly, in mid-sentence, a split second before he felt the heavy hand come to rest on his arm, his whole body tensing, as his genetically-inherited fight or flight response prepared him for whatever might befall him next. He couldn't help noticing the change in the barkeep's expression either; sullen unhelpfulness had transformed into fearful uncertainty.

Ulysses looked down at the ham-sized hand, the fat, calloused fingers, the scar-tissue knotted knuckles, the doubloon-sized signet ring. He followed the large hand to a ragged coat-sleeve, tufts of wiry black hair sprouting from the wrist beneath, up past the well-worn coarse wool and eventually to the man's face.

To Ulysses he looked not unlike a Toby jug in terms of broadness and his stout shape. He was tall, taller than Ulysses, and broad; built like a brick shithouse would have been how he would have been described in the vernacular. His face was brown as a nut from exposure to the wind and weather, and he was ugly, although he smiled broadly through his Neanderthal features. His nose looked like it had been broken several times and was now a flattened pug-snout.

He was wearing a pork pie hat on top of a messy mop of matted grey tresses, and a bright mustard yellow neckerchief was tied in a knot at his neck. Under his coat he wore a tatty waistcoat that must once have been red and must also have once had more than the three brass buttons it sported now.

And the man smelt, although it wasn't of fish, like the Black Swan's other customers. He smelt of animals, musty and with an ever-present aroma of ammonia about him. And when he spoke Ulysses almost gagged at the rank smell of stale tobacco that was exhaled his way.

"I'd be careful what you say in here, sir," the man said in a harsh whisper.

Ulysses stared into the ivory whites of the other's eyes,

his expression suddenly hard as stone. "And why might that be, I wonder?"

The large man smiled broadly through lumpen features that made him look like someone had beaten him about the head with a fence post. "What I mean, sir, is that if I were you, a stranger in town and all, I wouldn't be going about asking such questions so – 'ow shall I put it? – so brazenly. That's all."

"Is that right, Mr...?"

"Rudge, sir. Just call me Rudge," the man smiled, his expression as warm as a sunny autumn day, and released his grip on Ulysses' arm. "There are some – 'ow might I put it? – some dodgy characters about, sir. Untrustworthy types," he glowered at the barkeep as the fat man placed Ulysses' pint unceremoniously on the uneven counter, slopping the brown liquid over the bar top as he did so, "that's all."

Ulysses relaxed slightly, picked up his pint and took a sip. His mouth tensed again; the stuff tasted as bad as it looked. Bitter was obviously an acquired taste, and Ulysses didn't think he had the patience or the desire to acquire it.

"So, Mr Rudge, do you know of a Mr Bellerophon?"

The man grimaced, shoulders hunched, hands up in front of him as if to shush Ulysses' prattling mouth. "I told you, sir, not so bold, if you please."

"Then, I take it you do."

"It's not as simple as that, sir. Things are a little – 'ow shall I put it? – a little delicate in that regard."

"But you can help us, Mr Rudge?"

Rudge took up the pint of bitter that the barkeep had pulled for him, apparently without having to be asked, and took a careless gulp from the glass, rivulets of beer coursing down the sides of his chin and into the stubble at his neck, to eventually be soaked up by the neckerchief. Suddenly the pint glass appeared to be half empty.

"I can help you, Mr...?"

"Quicksilver," Ulysses replied.

"Mr Quicksilver. But not here, sir. Not here."

"Where then?"

Rudge shot the blubbery barkeep a look full of meaning and menace, given extra emphasis by his disenchanting features, and the piggy man found something else to do at the other end of the bar.

"Up on the moors, sir, up beyond the town. Follow the cliff path until you reach a lone standing stone of black granite. From there head west onto the moors. You'll find a tumbledown shepherd's shelter. You can't miss it. It's a few miles walk mind. I'll meet you there in a couple of hours. Something I've got to finish here in Whitby first. Then we can talk."

"Very well. Shall we say, three o'clock?"

"Three o'clock it is, sir."

With that, Rudge downed the rest of his pint with a few economical, if noisy, gulps, put the empty glass back on the counter and, with a tip of his hat to Ulysses, he walked out of the Black Swan.

Ulysses watched the large man as he squeezed his huge frame through the door of the pub and then turned to Nimrod, a wry smile on his face.

"We have a lead, Nimrod. A lead at last."

"Indeed, sir," his manservant replied unenthusiastically, taking a sip from his glass of none-too-clean-looking tap water.

"And we have an afternoon on the moors to look forward to. It's not such an awful day. An afternoon's stroll will be bracing. Maybe we'll be able to clear the stink of fish from our nostrils."

"If you say so, sir." Nimrod replied, still stubbornly unenthusiastic at the prospect.

"I do, old chap, I do." Forgetting himself for a moment, Ulysses took a swig of his own drink and instantly regretted it, grimacing at the bitter aftertaste the ale left in his mouth. What he wouldn't do for a decent glass of Rémy Martin right now.

"The game is afoot, Nimrod. The game is most definitely afoot."

CHAPTER TEN

The Circus of Wonders

The wind came down off the moors in fitful gusts, like the final breaths of a dying asthmatic, rippling the long grass of the cliff top meadow above the town. Ulysses Quicksilver tugged the deerstalker, that he had purchased in the town, down tight over his ears and pulled the tweed cape tighter about his shoulders. If Nimrod felt the cold underneath his funereal black coat, he wasn't showing it.

As the two men strode on their way Ulysses turned to the older man. "What did you make of our friend, Mr Rudge?"

Nimrod took a deep breath of the cold moorland air and, keeping his eyes on the grey horizon, even in the face of the biting breeze, said: "I think you should be careful, sir. I don't think we can trust him."

"Why ever not, Nimrod?" Ulysses asked jovially.

The older man gave him a withering look. "Do I really need to answer that question, sir?"

"I suppose not, old chap," Ulysses laughed.

"But we are obviously going to meet with him anyway."

"Absolutely," Ulysses grinned. "We all need a little risk in our lives to keep us on our toes, to keep us sharp – although possibly not quite as much risk as Barty seems to favour," he added, almost as an aside. "Besides, he's the only lead we've got as far as this Bellerophon fellow is concerned."

"You're certain it's an assumed name, sir?" Nimrod

probed.

"Oh yes – a name like that? And, that aside, I don't think anyone who chooses to deal with a reprobate like Magpie, or Wraith, or whatever he wants to call himself, would risk divulging his true identity to a felon like that, in case the plan went tits up."

The initial climb up from the town and past the skeletal Abbey ruins had left the two of them a little puffed, but they were getting into their stride now.

Having left the Black Swan Inn and its curmudgeonly barkeep, the two men had crossed the river by the swing bridge that spanned the Esk, turned into Church Street and climbed the one hundred and ninety-nine well-worn steps of the Church Stair to the Abbey ruins at the top of the headland, where they stood like some silent sentinel, a stone bastion guarding the town from the predations of sea and sky. They then set off along the packed earth path that led past the grey-black ruins along the cliff path and to the blasted moors beyond.

"Bellerophon," Nimrod said after a moment, as if he had been pondering the name. "The prince of Corinth who slew the dread Chimera with the aid of Pegasus the winged horse."

"Yes, I've been wondering about the significance of that too," Ulysses admitted. "Bellerophon may well be an assumed name, but there may well be a subtle subconscious reasoning behind that particular choice, or even a significant overt one, which we merely aren't party to yet."

"Where there's a hero, there's usually a monster."

"Yes, there's usually a monster," Ulysses agreed, images of the tentacled Kraken, the serum-warped lizard man, and half a dozen other horrors suddenly surfacing from the dark depths of his memory.

The wind blew sour here over the scraggy grass, rank with the smell of petrochemical pollutants, and redolent with the stink of rotting peat bogs and bitter salt sea spray. As they came over the rise at the crest of the hill, St Hild's abbey now nothing more than a charcoal sketch against the sky behind them, they gained their first glimpse of the Circus of Wonders.

The main tent was a mildewed expanse of tarred canvas, stretched taut by thick, green guy-ropes. In places the faded and peeling remnants of brighter colours were just visible against the flapping fabric of the bedraggled Big Top.

That was the first thing Ulysses noticed. The second thing was the police presence.

"'Ello, 'ello, 'ello! What's going on 'ere then?" he asked with enthusiastic interest.

"It would appear to me that the circus folk are helping the police with their enquiries," his manservant replied.

"Come on, Nimrod," Ulysses went in the same vein of boyish delight. "Let's find out for ourselves!"

As they neared the conglomeration of tents and steam-wagons, Ulysses saw huddles of circus folk and policemen gathered between the sanctuary of the main tent and a cordon of police vehicles. The two groups couldn't be more different. There were the uniformed police officers – not an automaton-drone among them, Ulysses noted – notebooks out, licked pencil stubs scratching away, all with unimpressed, or uncomprehending, expressions on their faces. And then there were the circus folk.

To Ulysses it looked like they had stepped out of another time, and one that had never really existed. It was as if a band of medieval mummers had suddenly found themselves living in a Dickens' novel. They were all attired in a similar manner, in that none of them were wearing what could be described as new clothes. Every costume had been carefully created from an amalgam of hand-me-downs.

The circus performers' uniquely individual costumes actually gave them their own uniform, a sense of identity, marking them out as something not quite of this world; something out of kilter with the rest of the empire of Magna Britannia. It provided them with a sense of belonging. And for many of them, their bizarre costumes only served to enhance the other, more unusual, aspects that some of them possessed – the traits that marked them out as members of a freakshow.

Ulysses began to notice these just as he became aware of the signs and billboards littering the grounds around the main tent, all designed and arranged to lure a macabrely-fascinated public inside the 'Circus of Wonders.'

Without really being conscious of where they were going, the two men now found themselves beyond the ramshackle police cordon, treading between knotty tufts of grass, drawn by the lure of the scene.

Glancing at an anxious huddle of performers, who appeared to be trying to keep the police at arm's length, he saw a dwarf, wearing nothing but a leather waistcoat over his muscular, tattooed torso, his bulging biceps bare, a larger lady, her fuller figure squeezed into a lace and taffeta creation, the curled ringlets of her full beard carefully plaited, and a stick thin, pale-skinned man who was wearing nothing but what appeared to be a loin-cloth and ribboned top hat, despite the November chill, his exposed skin a painted canvas of intricate tattoos and body piercings, copious rings drawn through the scrawny, pinched flesh of his shoulders, arms, neck and knees, as well as having bones and feathers thrust through his ears, nose and eyebrows.

Close by them a tall man, with mantis-like limbs and a skeletally gaunt face – his eyes dramatic white orbs within the shadowed pits of their sockets – wearing scuffed top hat and tails, and wholly inappropriate skin-tight, black leggings, and long-toed pixie boots, giving the impression, once again, of a medieval antecedent – was talking animatedly with an unimaginative constable. Everything about his demeanour and the fact that he was the centre of the police's attention, suggested to Ulysses that this was the freakshow's master of ceremonies and *de facto* leader.

A young woman with ridiculously long straw-blond hair – so long, in fact, that it was tied like a belt at her waist to stop it dragging in the dirt – plaited with pink and purple ribbons, beads and even shells, was huddled nervously beside the master of ceremonies. Her dress might have once been the ball gown of a Versailles courtier, but was now a dusty and faded shadow of the glorious centrepiece costume it had once been. The embroidered bodice was loose upon her skinny frame and her slight chest could not hope to fill it. A knitted shawl about her shoulders added to the impression of the impoverished gypsy lifestyle.

A bald, near giant of a man, with the quizzical expression of a three-year old on his prominently-browed face, was led away docilely by the hand into the main tent, by a girl of no more than eleven or twelve, revealing the trio of policemen, deep in conversation, that his hulking frame had obscured from view.

"I don't bloody believe it!" Ulysses exclaimed, a broad grin spreading across his face.

"Ah," Nimrod said as he caught sight of the tuft of orange hair only a moment after his master.

"Ah, indeed, Nimrod! It's only Inspector sodding

Allardyce," Ulysses laughed. "Here, in North Yorkshire!"

Casting his eyes heavenward and letting out a long breathy sigh, Nimrod followed as his master quickened his steps towards the unmistakeable ginger-haired figure of Inspector Allardyce of Scotland Yard, and Ulysses' regular sparring partner.

"Hello, Maurice." The inspector's eyes flashed with furious fire. Allardyce's venomous look came with an accompaniment of spluttering grunts and snorts as the other policemen attempted to suppress their sniggers. "And what brings you here?"

"I don't bloody believe it," the put-upon inspector grumbled. "Quicksilver! What the hell are *you* doing here?"

"Oh, you know, enjoying a little unseasonal sea air. I hear it's very good for one's constitution."

"You're joking, right? Air's as polluted in this godforsaken place as it is back in the Big Smoke. And what do you think you look like in that get up? Get dressed in the dark, did you?"

"And what brings you here?"

Inspector Maurice Allardyce pulled himself up to his full height – all five foot six inches of it – and tugged at the lapels of his grey trench coat. "I'll have you know that I am investigating a series of most foul and savage murders."

"Ah, that's funny, because I'd heard you were on holiday. Although, if that *is* the case, it looks more like a busman's holiday to me."

The policemen exchanged knowing glances at this. Allardyce's face reddened still further.

"Well, yes, I may happen to have been holidaying in the area, visiting the wife's sister."

"But as soon as we heard that Inspector Allardyce of

Scotland Yard was staying here, in Whitby," said an enthusiastic young constable, coming to Allardyce's aid, something like hero-worship sparkling in his eyes, "we knew that we just had to get him on the case."

Allardyce smiled, looking half embarrassed and half delighted with the complement he had just been paid.

"Ah, so it *is* a busman's holiday then."

"You could say that," Allardyce conceded. "Now, Quicksilver, if you wouldn't mind being about your business, then I can be about mine."

Pushing past Ulysses, Allardyce approached the belligerent constable still questioning the increasingly irritated ringmaster.

The near-skeletal MC gave Ulysses the impression that he was an incredibly patient man – having developed his tolerant attitude in the face of society's mistrust and ostracising, coupled with its fascination, nonetheless, for the freaks that inhabited the otherworld of which he was the master – and yet who was now being pushed to his absolute limit.

Allardyce interrupted the constable's ongoing fruitless line of questioning with an abrupt: "Have you finished with this one?" pointing an accusing finger at the ghoulish ringmaster. To his mind, the man had already been tried and convicted, and now he was ready to see sentence passed.

Ulysses sidestepped past the inspector and extended a hand towards the suddenly startled master of the Circus of Wonders. "Ulysses Quicksilver, special investigator of rum goings-on and uncanny occurrences," he said. "And you are?"

Eyeing him like a hawk, the circus-master ignored Ulysses' proffered hand and instead doffed his hat – to expose a few straggly strings of lank grey shoulder-length hair – and took a bow, bending low at the waist.

"They call me Steerpike, and I am indeed master of ceremonies at this Circus of Wonders," he announced, unfolding his body again and returning the hat to his head. "I am also known as the Incredible Eating Man," he said.

With a flourish, he took an Edison bulb from a pocket of his tailcoat, a clockmaker's hammer from another, and then proceeded to break the bulb into a fingerless-mittened hand, and popped one of the larger pieces of glass into his mouth. There followed an uncomfortable crunching sound that set Ulysses' teeth on edge, which was followed by some moments of mastication, that sounded like the man was chewing a mouthful of grit, before Steerpike swallowed noisily and with an exaggerated dip and rise of his head. He opened his mouth wide, sticking out a long pink tongue, to show all assembled that his mouth was now completely empty, ever the showman to the last.

"Very impressive," Ulysses said, offering up a short burst of applause.

"Never mind all that," Inspector Allardyce butted in, his face locked in a grimace that made Ulysses think of a pit-bull chewing a wasp, and demanded of the man, "what have you found out?"

"Still claims 'e and 'is freaks are innocent," the constable sighed with frustration.

"Innocent?" Ulysses said, his ears pricking up at the merest hint of any miscarriage of justice taking place here.

"Oh, here we go," Allardyce complained.

"Innocent of what, exactly?" Ulysses asked, visions of local newspaper headlines cramming his head.

"Murder, of course! I thought you had to be clever

to go to Eton," the inspector added, giving Ulysses a disparaging look.

"But not to be a policeman, eh? Just blinkered," Ulysses countered.

"Look, if you're not off my patch in the next thirty seconds, I'll have you up before the local magistrate for obstructing police business!" Allardyce snarled. "Or perhaps," he said, suddenly smiling darkly, "you know more than you're letting on, and I should take *you* in for questioning."

"Oh you know me, Inspector; nothing to hide here. In fact I would gladly offer myself up for interrogation, if you feel that it would help you bring this particularly nasty case to a satisfactory conclusion," Ulysses offered magnanimously.

"Not bloody likely," Allardyce snarled. "Now bugger off."

"Gladly, Inspector," Ulysses said, doffing his deerstalker to the red-faced policeman. "We wouldn't want to get in the way of justice now, would we, Nimrod?"

"No, sir. Good day, Inspector."

Without another word, Ulysses turned and began to stride away from the enticing Circus of Wonders and Inspector Allardyce's ham-fisted murder investigation.

He glanced back over his shoulder once and caught the eye of the enigmatic Steerpike, and the waif-like girl now hanging off his arm, as the labouring policeman attempted to wheedle anything that might amount to an admission of guilt from the circus folk. Such a thing would wrap up this case nicely and be a feather in the cap of the disgraced copper as he was no doubt still trying to live down the disaster that had been the Jubilee debacle.

Ulysses was certain that the mysterious master of ceremonies and his cronies had plenty of things to hide

– secrets that they didn't want the rest of the world knowing about – but murder? Ulysses wasn't so sure. Why hang around in the wake of ten murders, when they could have packed up and been on their way by dawn the next day, if they were responsible? Travellers like those who made up the Circus of Wonders were good at avoiding unwanted attention by never staying in any one place for too long.

And besides, the paper had recorded that the killings appeared to have been carried out by a wild animal of some kind. Some of the circus performers might be a little wilder than was the norm, but unless the freakshow's star attraction was the Hound of the Baskervilles, Ulysses sincerely doubted that anyone from the circus had anything to do with the mysterious deaths.

"What did you make of that little lot, Nimrod?" he asked when they had left the Circus of Wonders well behind them.

"If you ask me, sir, they're queer coves the lot of them," Nimrod said, his impeccably cultured tones dismissively aloof.

"Hmm, I thought you'd say that," said Ulysses. "Anyway, we'd best not dally here any longer; we have an appointment to keep with our new friend Mr Rudge, do we not?"

From behind a grassy hummock, inquisitive eyes watched the man in the deerstalker and his servant leave the circus behind and continue on their way, along the path that would lead them to the blasted expanse of Ghestdale.

The sentience behind those eyes hoped that the men

knew what they were letting themselves in for. Surely they had heard about the deaths. They had just been talking with the very policemen who were investigating the Barghest killings after all.

Those same eyes had observed the meeting between the man in the deerstalker and the ginger-haired inspector with interest. There was obviously a history between the two of them and a mutual lack of respect.

And yet still the man in the deerstalker and his companion were leaving to continue on alone to Ghestdale, that most damnable godforsaken place.

Keeping low, out of sight of both the policemen and the circus folk, the watcher left the cover of the hummock and, keeping to the shelter of an ancient ditch, set off after the dandy and his valet.

CHAPTER ELEVEN

A Damsel in Distress

Scuds of cloud raced across the leaden face of heaven, the greens, yellows and blues of sub-dermal hematomas bruising the corpse-grey epidermis of the sky.

Everything in this wilderness had been shaped by the elements – the wind most of all – from the few gale-bent trees, looking like dowager-stooped witches, and the storm-scoured slabs of sandstone, denuded of any living thing other than the ever tenacious lichen, to the hardy heather and prickly gorse. Springs bubbled up to gurgle their way between the roots of grassy mounds, reshaping the landscape with geological slowness.

With the rock-gnawing wind pricking the exposed skin of hands and faces, Ulysses took out his pocket watch for the umpteenth time since he and his manservant had begun their trek over the blasted heather and gorse-blanketed moors, between the wind-scoured tors of tumbled boulders and skirted the meandering streams and bogs of Ghestdale.

He *harrumphed* and, flicking the case of his father's watch shut again, returned it to his waistcoat pocket.

Nimrod looked at him, raising one expectant eyebrow.

"Three thirty. He's late."

Eyes straining, Ulysses peered at the horizon, where the grey, overcast sky met the blasted moors, seeking the big man's brick shithouse silhouette. If it hadn't been for his trusty pocket watch he wouldn't have had any idea as to what time it was; it could have been any time between dawn and dusk, the quality of the light hadn't changed once since sun-up.

Ulysses scanned the horizon again, as he had done every thirty minutes or so since they had come upon the tumbledown shepherd's hut. Rudge might only be half an hour late, but Ulysses had been waiting to meet with him again as soon as he and Nimrod had left the Black Swan three hours before.

"It looks like the mysterious Mr Rudge is going to prove himself to be as untrustworthy as you at first suspected, Nimrod," Ulysses said, with a bitter sigh.

"It would appear so, sir," Nimrod agreed. "If it helps to settle your mind at all, I do so hate it when I'm right."

"Thanks, Nimrod, but don't worry, old chap. We'll give him until four, shall we, before heading back?"

"As you wish, sir."

Ulysses felt irritable, a condition brought on not only by Rudge's failure to make their meeting. It was also exacerbated by the biting cold and the gurgling, churning hunger gnawing away at his belly. He realised now that he hadn't eaten anything since putting away the full English Nimrod had served up that morning back at the guest house. The only sustenance he had had since then were a couple of drinks back in Whitby and the revitalising effects of the alcohol had long since worn off.

It was already beginning to get dark, the texture of the sky becoming still more leaden as the sun sank steadily towards the horizon, behind the ever-present pall of cloud. It was as if North Yorkshire had its own inescapable pall, just like London had its ever-present Smog.

For want of anything better to do, considering the circumstances, and as a means of trying to keep the marrow-numbing cold at bay, Ulysses continued picking his way between the hummocks of knotty, yellowing grass and the peaty bog-holes that could so easily ensnare the unwary.

A hundred yards away he could see the start of a defile among the otherwise near-featureless rolling moorlands of Ghestdale; a stream-cut hollow between scrubby bushes, exposed sandstone stacks. The air was redolent with the peaty smell of standing water and no doubt buzzing with moorland midges. Ulysses turned his steps towards the moorland morass, watchful for rabbit holes and half-hidden sink-holes between the tufts of grass and tangle-stemmed bushes of gorse.

There were worse things than rabbit holes on Ghestdale that might endanger the unwary explorer, of course. First there were the peat-steeped pot holes, sucking hollows of saturated peat-mud, perfectly blended into the surrounding landscape thanks to the rafts of sphagnum moss and grasses that anchored their roots in the rich loam, insubstantial as water and yet with all the lethal clinging might of quicksand. Any who stumbled into one of them had better have some means of getting themselves out again or they would be swallowed up within a matter of minutes, drowning in the soupy mud.

And then there were the abandoned mine-workings that riddled the rocks beneath Ghestdale. Whitby and its immediate environs possessed some of the finest deposits of jet in, not only the British Isles, but the whole of the empire of Magna Britannia and, in fact, the world. A black, fossilized wood, jet could be intricately carved and given a superb polish which made for some fabulous pieces of jewellery and other trinkets. The stuff had been mined in the region for centuries and during the mid-nineteenth Whitby supported a very successful jet industry, the interest from the royal family at the time helping it become highly fashionable.

Although the manufacture of jet jewellery and the

like still took place in the town, it was nowhere near the peak it had enjoyed a hundred years before. The mines, however, remained, many of them worked out completely, treacherous tunnels left neglected, pit-props left to rot, galleries becoming water-logged by the run-off that was once pumped out, so that now many tunnels were unsafe, or flooded, or had collapsed under the weight of rock and earth above them.

Ulysses was roused from his distracted musings by the cry of a woman.

"Did you hear that?" he asked, turning to his companion.

"Yes, sir, I did."

"Unless I'm very much mistaken, that sounded like a damsel in distress," Ulysses said, his pace already quickening to a run, forcing Nimrod to lengthen his strides to keep up.

Running as fast as he could, almost entirely heedless now of any potential pitfalls that might catch him out, Ulysses sprinted for the defile hidden between the gorse, from where he was certain the cry had come.

And as he ran, so his mind raced too, as – adrenalin flooding his system – he began to imagine what might await them. The first thought that came into his head was that the woman had been attacked; the next moment his mind was flooded with images of savaged bodies, like those unfortunate wretches that had been found dead here on the moors, carcasses slashed open, gutted by gouging claws, arms and legs bent at unnatural angles, looking like so many discarded ragdolls. Suddenly his comment about there being a damsel in distress seemed in terribly bad taste.

Reaching the top of the defile, he flung himself through a tangled thicket of thorns, tearing the lining of his cape open as he ran, stumbling down over the tumbled stones at his feet. He rounded a spur in the defile, half-expecting to see the body of a young woman lying there, gutted and jointed like a Sunday roast, some monstrous hellhound – all black fur and glowing-coal eyes – standing over its trophy, blood dripping from its cruel jaws; so much so, that he stumbled to an abrupt halt in surprise when that wasn't what confronted him in the hollow at all.

Sitting rather uncomfortably on the damp ground, with her back to him, was indeed a young woman, her taut figure hidden beneath a well-tailored Harris tweed jacket and knickerbockers of the same material, long woollen socks covering the shapely curve of her well-toned calves, with practical walking boots on her feet and her long blonde hair carefully plaited and tied up in a bun beneath her hat. And rather than further cries of pain or terror, Ulysses could hear her berating herself.

"You fool girl," she said, "you've been out on these moors a hundred times and look at you, caught out by a rabbit hole! You can be such an idiot!"

The expectant look of horror on Ulysses' face turning to one of curious delight, he picked his way across the floor of the shallow gorge that he might come to the aid of his damsel in distress.

His highly developed sixth sense flared, shaking him out of his ever-so slightly lecherous reverie, with white hot awareness. He already had his hands up to defend himself as the animal launched itself at him, yapping furiously.

Hearing the noise, the woman's head suddenly snapped round, and for a moment, Ulysses fancied he could see the image of the devil dog reflected in the pupil's of her wide brown eyes, behind the lenses of her round, wire-rimmed glasses, as if she too were half-expecting to see the same thing that his imagination had conjured. And then, with a blink, the imagined monster was gone, as was the brief grimace of terror, to be replaced by a pink-cheeked look of embarrassment.

"Rover!" she barked at the terrier now leaping up and down in front of Ulysses. "Leave the poor gentleman alone. Now, Rover! Heel!"

"Oh, don't mind him," Ulysses said, keeping his hands out low at his waist, just in case, "he's only looking out for his mistress."

"That's very gracious of you, Mr...?"

"Quicksilver, Miss, but call me Ulysses, please."

For a moment something like recognition or curiosity flashed across the young woman's features. Her clear complexion and soft, yet firm skin gave her the natural, understated beauty of an English Rose. Ulysses judged that she couldn't have been older than thirty and was most likely still in her mid-to late twenties.

"But his mistress should be looking out for herself, the silly thing," she said crossly. It took Ulysses a moment to realise that the 'silly thing' she was referring to was herself and not the terrier, which was now prancing around the young woman, watching Ulysses intently and giving off the occasional small growl to remind this interloper who the alpha male was around here.

Ulysses knelt down beside her, meeting her worried, embarrassed look with a kind smile. "Now, what seems to be the problem, Miss...?"

"Haniver. Jennifer Haniver."

"Haniver," Ulysses repeated. There was something strangely familiar about that name. Now, where had he heard it before?

Ulysses offered her his hand and she took it, surprising him with the firmness of her shake.

"Pleased to meet you, Miss Haniver," unable to be anything other than utterly charming, finding himself in the company of another attractive young woman. There was a tired sigh from Nimrod behind him and Ulysses could imagine his manservant's eyebrows raised in disapproval and exasperation.

"It's my ankle," she explained, rubbing at the joint beneath her sock. "I caught my foot in a rabbit hole – silly old fool – and went over on it. Should've been looking where I was going, rather than for paw-prints, shouldn't I?"

"May I?" Ulysses asked, reaching out towards the young woman's ankle.

"No, please do."

He carefully squeezed the flesh beneath the wool.

"Out doing a bit of hunting, were you?" he asked, innocuously.

"You might say that."

"Partridge? Woodcock, was it?"

The young woman paused for a moment before answering, as if trying to assess how this stranger might take her next remark. "The Barghest Beast, actually."

With a sharp intake of breath Miss Haniver flinched, trying to pull her foot away, which only caused her to actually cry out in pain.

"I'm sorry. I'm being as careful as I can."

"Go on," Jennifer said, holding her leg and biting her lip, in an effort not to jerk her leg away again. "I'll try not to move this time – I promise."

Holding the back of her leg in his right hand, Ulysses tentatively felt the flesh around the ankle itself.

"You say you were following animal tracks," Ulysses commented as he stared into the middle distance, concentrating on his examination.

"Er, yes."

"But I thought you said you were out hunting."

"Well they're one and the same thing really."

"You looking for this Barghest beast of yours?"

"Th-That's right," the young woman replied, tensing again under the ministrations of Ulysses probing fingertips.

"I've never heard of a Barghest before." Ulysses said, remembering full well the reference to the ghostly hound in the newspaper article in which he had read of the recent killings. "Do you mind telling me what it is?"

Jennifer Haniver looked down at the boggy ground, her cheeks flushing pink again.

"You'd probably think me even more foolish than you doubtless already do for having fallen down a rabbit hole."

"Well, when you put it like that," Ulysses said with a grin, "what have you got to lose? You couldn't be any more embarrassed than you already are."

She smiled at him, her warm hazel eyes staring directly into his. And, if anything, the flush in her cheeks deepened.

She came across as so lacking in any kind of egotism or narcissism that her way of not making any effort to draw attention to her own attractiveness simply made her appear all the more appealing.

"I suppose not," she admitted, returning Ulysses' smile for the first time since they had met. "The Barghest is a phantom hound said to haunt the area known as Beast Cliff and the moors beyond."

"Ah, a ghost story," Ulysses said. "I've heard such tales of phantom hounds before."

"Of course, practically every county of the British Isles has its own legends of black dogs or hellhounds as they are also called. East Anglia has its Black Shuck, Cornwall the Shony and even the Channel Island of Jersey has its own Black Dog of Death.

"To most, the Barghest is nothing more than a fanciful phantasm, imagined into existence by less enlightened people from times past who didn't know any better, as they tried to explain away natural phenomena they didn't understand." Jennifer Haniver paused, distracted for a moment by the pain from her ankle.

"To most," Ulysses' attention was fully focused on what the young woman had to say now; he wasn't even examining her ankle any more. "But not, I take it, to you."

"Well, no."

"So what do you know that the rest of us don't," Ulysses asked with a wry grin.

"I am a cryptozoologist, Mr Quicksilver. Investigating the mysteries of the natural world – the supposedly impossible, the unsubstantiated and the allegedly extinct – is what I do. I take it you're not a local man yourself."

"No."

"Then what brings you to Yorkshire?"

"A little hunting myself, actually."

Jennifer smiled.

"So what are you hunting for, Ulysses?" she asked, trying the informal for a change.

"Mermaids, as it happens."

"Mermaids? Up here, on the moors?"

"Now who's feeling embarrassed?"

"Then, have you heard of the recent attacks?"

"I only know what I read in the paper this morning."

"Well, to my mind, these attacks have all the hallmarks of a large dog."

"And the Barghest is, supposedly, just that. A big

dog?"

"Exactly, Mr Quicksilver; the biggest." The fading flush returned to her cheeks for a moment. There was something particularly appealing about that. "You don't think me absurd to talk of such things?"

"Not at all," Ulysses admitted. "I have seen too many weird and wonderful things in my life to dismiss anything too readily."

"You don't know what a relief it is to hear you say that," Jennifer gushed.

"Glad to be of service," Ulysses said, his gaze locking with hers again. This time he felt his own cheeks glowing.

"So, doctor, what's your diagnosis?"

"What?" Ulysses shook himself from his pleasant reverie.

"My ankle, Mr Quicksilver. Is it broken?"

"I'm sorry? Your ankle, of course," he said, stumbling over himself, trying to remember what it was that he was supposed to be doing. "Well, I don't think you've broken it, but I would say that it's sprained."

"Silly dithering idiot!" the young woman chided herself again. "Should have been looking where you were going, shouldn't you?"

"Look, I think your hunt for the Barghest is over for the time being, don't you? You're not going to get very far on that ankle by yourself, so is there somewhere that we can help you to. Where are you staying?"

"That's very chivalrous of you," she said, blushing again. "But I feel as though you've done enough for me already."

"But I don't think you're really in a position to refuse us, are you? I mean, it'll be getting dark soon and I'm sure you don't want to be hobbling around out here on your own, with a monster hound on the loose."

"No, of course not. You're quite right," Miss Haniver agreed. "Hunter's Lodge – my father's house; I've lived with him there, since his... retirement."

"What did he do?"

"You might have heard of him; Hannibal Haniver? He was someone, once. A naturalist; a leader in his field."

"Haniver. Hannibal Haniver," Ulysses repeated. "I knew that name sounded familiar. Yes, I've heard of him."

"Well, like I say, he was someone – *once.*"

"Give us a hand will you, Nimrod?" Ulysses said, with one arm already around the young woman's waist.

The terrier still skipping and yapping at their heels, Ulysses and Nimrod helped her stand and then, with one either side, her arms across their shoulders, they set off.

"What sort of signs were you hoping to find?" Ulysses asked, as much as by way of finding something to distract them all – but mostly himself – from the sudden enforced intimacy the three of them suddenly found themselves sharing.

"Spoor, claw-marks, a paw-print if I was lucky."

"Like this one you mean, ma'am?" Nimrod said in his usual underwhelmed monotone, raising an eyebrow at something on the ground – or rather, an impression in the ground.

And there, in front of them, partially hidden by tufts of grass and moss, was the nonetheless still clear indentation of four claw marks and the pads to match.

"That's it!" Jennifer shrieked in delight. "You've found it!"

"By Jove, old chap! Score one to you, eh? But bloody hell!" Ulysses exclaimed as he studied the mark for himself. "Look at the size of it!"

The single, threatening paw-print was more the size

of a horse's hoof than the impression left by a dog, even something as large as a Great Dane. The terrier's feet were dwarfed by it, in comparison.

"It looks like you were right, Jennifer!" he added excitedly.

"Yes, it does rather, doesn't it?" she replied just as excitedly, for the moment the pain in her ankle forgotten. "We should take an impression. I have a mould and some plaster of Paris in my bag. It shouldn't take us more than about –"

"Sir," Nimrod suddenly butted in, eyes turned to the subtly darkening blanket of clouds that covered these desolate moors, "I hate to put a damper on things, but dusk is drawing on and we have just found the very evidence Miss Haniver was looking for to prove that there *is* a ravening beast at large on Ghestdale."

Suddenly realising what he was saying, he looked at the sky again and noted how much greyer and gloomier the moors appeared than when they had first arrived at this spot. Dusk came early this late in the year, frighteningly early.

"Nimrod's right," Ulysses said. "We have to press on. We can come back here again in force, after someone's seen to that ankle of yours. But have no fear, Jennifer, I do believe you've made the discovery of the deca –"

"Ulysses?" the young woman asked, looking anxiously at her knight in shining armour, who was now suddenly doubled up beside her.

"Sir? Are you all right?" Nimrod sounded genuinely concerned, his voice laden with unaccustomed emotion.

A hand pressed to his temple, Ulysses straightened again as the shock of the migraine-flash of awareness began to pass.

"Oh, Nimrod, I do so hate it when you're right."

And then they all heard the deep-throated, guttural growl behind them.

CHAPTER TWELVE

The Barghest

All three of them snapped their heads round at the same time, terror-widened eyes staring through the encroaching gloom at the entrance to the narrow defile by which Ulysses and Nimrod had come to find Jennifer Haniver.

There, standing stock still on four thick legs was a black shape, a blot of darkness against the dimming horizon, a threatening shadow charged with menace and power. It seemed to exude an aura of malevolence that hit the three of them with a wave of nausea-inducing fear.

And Ulysses knew that the beast was watching them just as intently. He almost fancied he could see its eyes glowing red in the darkness, and then he chided himself for allowing such fanciful imaginings to subsume all rational thought. He needed to keep his wits about him: now was the time for action, not for macabre, doom-laden fantasies.

The creature stood rigid, apparently simply watching them. Ulysses knew that they had to run, that if they were to survive the surely inevitable attack that was sure to come, they had to give themselves as much of a head-start as possible.

And there was no doubt that it *was* the Barghest beast. Everything about it exuded malign threat, even at this distance. It looked like it was as big as a pony, although there was something about the shape of its silhouette, and the way the creature held itself, that suggested its essence could not be contained by something as ordinary as a dog's hide.

As Ulysses watched, transfixed by the appalling majesty of the animal standing there, the dog-beast threw back its head and howled.

The sound – one long ululating howl of savage animal delight and hunger – echoed from the walls of the enclosing defile, screwing Ulysses' stomach into a knot, an icy chill rippling through every part of him. He felt his skin contract, the hairs of his arms standing on end, and heard the rapid *dub-dub dub-dub* tattoo of his quickening pulse pounding in his ears, as the old adrenalin-fuelled flight or fight response kicked in.

And then – still unable to take his eyes off the ominous black shadow-shape – Ulysses saw the creature drop its head and look straight at the compromised trio. He saw its stance visibly tighten, thick cords of muscle knotting beneath its velvet-black hide. The Barghest was tensing, ready to spring. And then something in Ulysses snapped.

"Come on!" he hissed at his manservant and the girl, muscles moving again now that he was freed of the paralysis of unbridled fear. "We have to get out of here."

"Yes, sir!" Nimrod acknowledged his master emphatically.

Jennifer, however, now that she was faced with the truth of what had so far only been her academic pursuit of the Barghest beast, could only whimper and mutter to herself, her own anxiety overwhelming her.

Ulysses' gut instinct told him that it was now a case of when, not if, the creature would launch an attack. With the deadliest of intent.

"Come on, Jenny, you can do it, I know you can," Ulysses encouraged her, trying to make his words as calm and reassuring as possible, worried as he himself was that the young woman's own fear might prove more crippling than her injured ankle. "We have to keep moving."

"Nimrod," he said, turning to his manservant, his voice hushed but as hard as iron, "arm yourself, just in case."

He heard the click of Nimrod's pistol chamber being closed again, his ever-reliable manservant close to being a mind-reader himself, having already unholstered his gun and checked its load.

"Already done, sir. Just in case."

"Yes, just in case," Ulysses repeated, as if the animal's attack was anything but inevitable, clinging onto the desperate hope that they could all still get out of this alive.

"We're doomed!" Jennifer hissed. Ulysses could feel her body shaking, pressed against his as it was. "Those who hear the Barghest's howl are doomed to die."

"You know what always made me laugh about folk tales like that?" Ulysses said between puffs and sharp intakes of breath as the three of them attempted to quicken their pace, like competitors in some bizarre four-legged race.

"What?" Jennifer found herself replying.

"If all those who hear its howl always die, then who was it who passed on that little titbit of information?"

And then, the adrenalin-high emotion of the moment catching her completely off-guard, a burst of laughter escaped Jennifer's lips, startling herself so much that she suddenly fell silent again.

"That's more like it," Ulysses gasped, as they continued their stumbling run.

But Ulysses' forced good humour was short lived as he looked back over his shoulder and was unable to stifle his own moan of shock and horror.

"What is it?" Jennifer gasped. "It's gaining on us, isn't it?"

"You could say that," Ulysses had to agree.

Jennifer turned her head.

"Hey," Ulysses snapped, "I think we should concentrate our energies on keeping going, don't you?"

Jennifer gave up on her attempted observation and instead re-doubled her own efforts, pushing hard with her good leg, her hops helping the others carry her over the uneven ground.

Ulysses had only had a split-second's look at the beast, but it had been more than enough. In that split-second the monstrous appearance of the creature had indelibly seared itself onto his retinas. Although it roughly resembled a dog in shape and form – hunched shoulders and slavering muscular jaws screaming its canine ancestry – at the same time it was like no dog he had ever seen.

First of all, the thing's head appeared too large for its body, the thick hump of its broadly-muscled shoulders seeming to have to compensate for the extra weight. Its skin appeared to be pulled too tight against its skull, and this aspect of its appearance wasn't down to the creature being malnourished either. It might have a ravenous hunger – Ulysses could well believe it, seeing the thick strings of saliva dripping from its tusk-like teeth – but if so, it was by design rather than due to the fact that the creature hadn't fed well.

The flesh of the dog's head was drawn back from jaws that seemed too large for even its over-sized skull. It was as if a lion's skull had been forced inside the tight sack of the dog's skin. Jutting fangs, far larger than those of any naturally evolved canine, thrust from glistening gums and partially denuded bone, while the skin at the side of the creature's head was pulled back in creased rolls that seemed close to tearing. Its muzzle was practically debrided bone, giving its snout a bat-like appearance. In fact, the stretched nostrils, jutting, over-sized fangs, red eyes and midnight-black pelt gave the beast a sinister, vampiric quality on top of everything else.

The rest of the beast's body, its heaving ribcage, its lithe, muscular flanks – even its thick, heavy, tail that in the half-light appeared to glisten as might a snake's – spoke of strength, savagery and ferocity. A nightmarish terror-dog; the perfectly designed killing machine.

"Nimrod, leave me to it," Ulysses said, indicating Jennifer with a nod of his head. "I want you to concentrate on emptying your gun into that thing as soon as it's close enough, preferably right between its eyes."

"Very good, sir."

Leaving the young woman solely to his master's attentions, Nimrod turned to face the approaching monster, continuing his half-run backwards, parallel to the other two, pistol out straight in front of him, aimed at the beast.

Just for a moment, Ulysses looked Nimrod's way, just to check that his manservant was all right, and then wished he hadn't. He could not remember the last time he had seen such a look of shock and unadulterated terror on his aide's face. And that unsettled him even more than the appearance of the beast closing on their position.

It unsettled him to the point where, his usual indefatigable positivity suddenly crushed, for the first time he dared to allow the possibility to enter his mind that perhaps the three of them weren't going to get out of this one alive; that he had met his nemesis at last, in the form of unbridled, savage nature, blood red in tooth and claw.

And then they were out of the defile, with nothing but open moorland between them and the twinkling lights of a house, visible on the horizon, a postage stamp of shadow against the rapidly darkening, overcast sky.

The fading twilight played tricks on the eyes, as Ulysses was well aware, but the house still appeared to be a long way away; further than they could ever hope to reach before the terror-dog surely caught up with them.

And then the shooting started.

The first shot was loud and close. The pistol-crack caused Ulysses' body to tense automatically, almost as if he had been shot himself. Jennifer gave a gasp of surprise and hugged herself to him even more tightly as he redoubled his efforts once again.

"If you'll excuse me, Miss Haniver," Ulysses said as he hastily swept Jennifer up in his arms. She in response, put both arms around his neck and clung on tightly. Momentarily her eyes locked onto his, limpid pools of fear meeting his steely gaze.

Biting his lip against the pain, Ulysses ran on, adrenalin spurring him forward. It felt like the fingers of his right hand were being broken all over again, while his irksome old shoulder injury was flaring up under the added duress. But he focused his mind on the house on the horizon, compartmentalising the pain, so that it might be dealt with later – if there was to be a later – the cocktail of chemicals being released into the bloodstream by his own body helping to numb the searing agony in his hand.

More shots followed, seeming to mark his own fleeing footsteps.

Then several things happened in close succession that sent Ulysses' world into a whirl.

The first thing he was aware of was the savage snarling of the dog, so close behind them that, his overwrought imagination working overtime, he felt as if the unnatural animal's hot, fetid breath was gusting on the back of his neck.

He heard two more shots. *Five, six.*

He suddenly realised he had been subconsciously counting how many bullets had been fired. And now Nimrod's pistol was empty and Ulysses doubted that he would have any hope of reloading in time.

And then he heard a cry, followed by a sharp, splintering crack, and Nimrod was suddenly no longer gallivanting backwards beside them. His manservant was down, but all Ulysses could do was keep running. He had no choice.

Ulysses did not need his uncanny sixth sense to warn him when the beast was about to strike, as it finally caught up with them. He could hear its slavering, panting snarls, smell its rank breath and the stinking filth of its blood-matted fur.

As the Barghest pounced, Ulysses dropped. He, and the young woman in his arms, had their landing cushioned by a blanket of heather.

A springing ambush that should have knocked the two of them flat on the ground, the dog-beast crushing Ulysses with its massive bulk as it sank its knife-like talons into his spine, instead sent the beast flying over their heads, to land on the uneven ground beyond.

Ulysses' action had been a hastily calculated risk, and it wasn't going to give them much time but hopefully it would be enough.

Snarling in impotent rage, the animal skidded to a halt, arresting its momentum by unsheathing its claws, gouging muddy ruts in the earth as it turned to face them.

The Barghest bared its horribly distended jaws and barked ferociously, only a few feet from them now.

Ulysses' gun barked twice, silencing the monster. He was right; it had been enough time.

But then another, forbidding guttural growl rumbled

up from deep inside the dog's ribcage and it was clawing the ground again to gain purchase.

"But I hit it!" Ulysses gasped in dismay and disbelief. "I know I was using my left hand, but I hit it; twice, in the head, from only five feet away. That should have floored it."

Too shocked and stunned to do anything other than stare at the resolutely still standing monster he did not think to raise his gun and try again. Recovering itself, the Barghest began to pace towards them, more warily now, perhaps, but nonetheless its savage bloodlust still driving it towards its goal of their bloody demise.

"Ulysses!" the stricken young woman screamed, as she struggled onto her hands and knees in a futile, yet determined, effort to escape her inevitable end, tears of terror streaming down her cheeks. "Ulysses! Move! We have to get away! Shoot it again!"

Her plaintive, desperate, quavering cry was enough to shake Ulysses from his reverie. As the beast closed the gap between them, he took aim and fired. Although not enough to halt the monster in its tracks, it was enough to enrage it. The animal leapt again. This time Ulysses was ready for it.

Tugging at the tied lace at his throat with shaking, pain-numbed fingers, Ulysses pulled the cape free and swung it at the Barghest's muzzle, using it like a matador's cloak. The creature baulked, giving Ulysses enough time to scramble to his feet again.

Slowly, backing away from the beast, watching as it worried at the cape – the cloth becoming more and more tangled around its fangs – breathing deeply, trying to slow his racing heartbeat, Ulysses took careful aim once more. He was beginning to doubt that his gun *could* stop the monster – Nimrod's hadn't, nor had the shots he had loosed into the beast so far – but he had little else he could try. His sword-cane was still there, tucked into his belt, but he hadn't even had a chance to draw.

Ulysses knew the rapidly disintegrating cape would only be a temporary distraction, but with every second that passed, Jennifer was able to get a little further away from the savage creature.

One eye still on the enraged monster, the other on Jennifer as she continued to crawl out of reach of the Barghest, Ulysses began to wonder about what had actually happened to his loyal manservant. Was he dead? Was he alive, but terribly injured? Had he somehow managed to escape his encounter with the brute?

And where was Jennifer's terrier, Ambrose?

Ulysses took his eyes from the hulking devil dog and the damsel for only a moment, shooting desperate glances around him at the darkening moor, eyes straining against the failing light. He saw the faint flicker of movement – the white cuff of a shirt waving in the gathering gloom – as his ears picked up the cry of: "Over here, sir!"

Ulysses looked again, not entirely sure he could trust what he had seen the first time. It looked like half of his manservant was missing. Ulysses couldn't see Nimrod's legs. It looked like he was half buried in the ground, only visible from the waist up. For a split second he wondered if the monster had managed to tear Nimrod in half, but then, if that had been the case, he wouldn't have been in any position to sit up and wave, whilst calling out to his master.

"Quickly, sir. I have an idea."

With one more glance at the Barghest – which was still struggling to free itself from the snare of the cape – Ulysses made a snap decision.

"Nimrod, old chap! I can't tell you how happy I am to

see you're still alive!" Ulysses declared, arriving at his companion's side.

"The feeling is mutual, sir. But with all due respect, the pleasantries can wait. I would be most grateful, however, if you could pull me out of this hole."

"Hole?" Ulysses repeated, bewildered, as he offered his manservant his left hand. Nimrod took it gladly and Ulysses heaved him up. As he did so, he saw the mouldering planks half hidden by the growth of unruly grasses.

"Yes, sir. It would appear that in my efforts to escape imminent death at the claws of the beast, I have inadvertently discovered the boarded up entrance to an old mineshaft."

"Have you now?" Ulysses said, a smile creeping across his face in the darkness.

And then, suddenly, there was a way out of their impossible predicament – a faint glimmer of light, no more than a candle-flicker, in the encroaching darkness.

"Are you thinking what I'm thinking."

"I'm way ahead of you, sir."

"Excellent, then let's make some noise."

The two men began hollering and whooping; anything to get the beast's attention.

"Hey! Over here!" Ulysses shouted, waving his hands in the air.

The dog-monster pulled the last shredded remnant of Ulysses' cape from its muzzle – the flesh there criss-crossed with a myriad bloody scratches – and bared its teeth, issuing another menacing challenge, sounding like an angry wolf. The beast looked at Ulysses directly with blood and fury in its eyes.

And yet despite the obvious rage it held in its black heart, just when Ulysses was certain the beast had taken the bait, it turned away from him and, seeing Jennifer still struggling to get away on her hands and knees, for a moment looked like it might take its fury out on her.

"Bad dog!" Ulysses shouted, took aim and fired. A chunk of meat flew from the bunching shoulders of the beast in a welter of black blood.

With a snarl the Barghest turned.

"There, that's got your attention again!"

And suddenly it was a bounding blur of darkness as it bore down on Ulysses. There was no way the beast was going to stop now, not until it had torn him limb from limb and left his body as something that was indistinguishable from the offal found at the end of the day on an abattoir floor.

When there was almost no more ground between them, Ulysses saw the creature's muscles bunch as it readied itself to leap, and tensed himself. When it leapt, he dropped.

Only this time the hellhound had learnt from the last time it had been caught out that way. In that split second Ulysses pulled the trigger again. The chamber returned empty.

And then the firearm was knocked from his hand as the beast landed on top of him, the heavy swipe of a paw sending the weapon flying while Ulysses was thrown back onto the ground, the full weight of the creature on top of him forcing the wind from his lungs, the nauseous dead-meat stink of the devil dog's rank breath washing over his face in intolerable waves.

But, even as the monster sent him tumbling backwards, short of the pit shaft, Ulysses boldly grabbed great handfuls of its matted fur, nearly hard enough to pull great clumps of it from the creature's hide.

As he rolled onto his back, with the beast on top of

him, those terrible snapping jaws mere inches from his suddenly vulnerable face, he kicked upwards with his feet with all the strength he could muster, even as the breath was violently forced from his lungs.

For a moment something like surprise appeared in the creature's soulless eyes. And then, using its own mass and the momentum of his own fall against it, Ulysses bodily hurled the Barghest over his head. It hit what remained of the boarded-up pit cover and smashed through it as if it were nothing more than plywood.

And then it was gone. All that remained were angry howls and pained yelps, receding into the darkness, accompanied by the occasional scrape of claws, skittering showers of stone and dull thuds.

Ulysses lay where he had fallen, his head hanging over the edge of the pit-shaft, his deerstalker having gone the way of the devil dog – Nimrod on the other side – gasping for breath as he listened to the creature's descent.

And then there was only silence. When at last he felt able to move, broken fingers throbbing with pain, his shoulder feeling nearly as bad, Ulysses cautiously sat up.

"Ulysses!" It was Jennifer, the pale features of her worried face peering at him, ghost-like out of the encroaching dusk. "You're all right. I thought there, for a moment, that..." But she couldn't bring herself to put her imagined horrors into words.

"Yeah, me too," he said, his half-smile turned to a grimace of pain.

"Sir, I would suggest we keep on to Miss Haniver's home, as originally planned. Both of you have injuries that need to be attended to."

"And you, Nimrod?"

Ulysses saw his manservant's usually so rigid aquiline

features soften in the presence of an unaccustomed smile at hearing of his master's concern. "There's nothing wrong with me sir that a good cup of Earl Grey wouldn't put right."

"Glad to hear it, old boy. Glad to hear it."

Suddenly something bounded into Ulysses' lap, yapping furiously.

"I see you're all right then," he said.

"Ambrose!" Jennifer shrieked in delight. "Come here, you naughty boy. Come here at once!"

Nimrod coughed politely. "I'm sure we don't want to be caught out in the open by the beast again, do we, sir?" he pointed out ominously, Ulysses' body tensing again at the unwelcome thought that the monster might have survived its fall and was even now making its way back to the surface to exact its revenge. "Best to keep moving, just in case."

"Just in case." The echo of Nimrod's words sounded hollow, as the anxiety Ulysses had felt himself, in the face of the monster's attack, returned. "Come on then. You help Miss Haniver and I'll –" He winced again in pain. "I'll do my best to keep up."

It was so dark now, dusk leading inexorably into night, that the three survivors were nothing more than black paper cut-outs against the horizon-wide blanket of clouds.

He had caught up with them at the same time as the beast. It had been pure luck that the prevailing wind had meant that the creature picked up the scent of the dandy before it had sniffed him out, otherwise he wouldn't have been alive now.

He had wanted to do more to help, dearly wished that there was something he could have done, but he was impotent. He was unarmed and he did not have the obvious physical skills that the other – who had previously been wearing the deerstalker – had. But there had been a moment then, when the monster looked like it was going to turn on the lady, the one he had admired from afar for so many months now, that he had been about to fling himself between the beauty and the beast, ready to sacrifice himself so that she might live. But, thanks to the actions of the other, in the end it hadn't come to that.

At that thought he offered up a prayer to his Lord. Surely it wasn't a sin to sacrifice one's own life for that of another, even if it did mean taking on what was effectively a suicide mission.

But then, of course, it hadn't come to that.

And so he followed them as they continued on their way towards the sanctuary of the house on the crest of the rise, always keeping a respectful distance so that he wouldn't be seen or heard. It wouldn't pay to be seen by them after all. No, not at all.

Making his way onwards, picking his way carefully between hidden sink holes and peaty morasses, he followed them, into the embrace of the forgiving darkness.

CHAPTER THIRTEEN

The Naturalist

The sturdy front door to the lodge house opened with a groan of protesting hinges and a pale grey, skeletal face appeared out of the semi-darkness of the candle-lit hallway beyond. The old man was completely bald but had apparently tried to make up for his extreme hair loss by growing a bushy white beard on his chin instead.

"Who is it?" the crotchety face demanded. "What do you wan– Oh my god, Jenny!" he suddenly exclaimed, coming to horrified life as his eyes moved from Ulysses' haggard face and that of his weary manservant to the young woman they were supporting between them.

He hurried out, his walking stick clattering to the black and white diamond check tiles of the hall as he crossed the threshold.

"What happened?" he demanded of her, taking her faces in his hands, his own visage as white as a sheet. "It's already dark. What have you been doing?"

"I was searching for the beast, Father."

"But out on these moors, with that monster on the loose?"

"That's exactly why, Daddy. That's precisely why I had to go out."

"Sunset came and I began worrying about where you had got to." His tone was chiding, precisely that of a parent punishing a child purely as a result of their own feelings of fear, panic and love.

"I sprained my ankle," Jennifer admitted.

"Where's the dog?" the old man suddenly asked, his

over-wrought mind flitting from one thought to the next. "Where's Ambrose?"

At the merest mention of its name, the terrier darted between Ulysses' legs, past the old man and into the warmth of the house.

Ulysses cleared his throat loudly; they needed to get Jennifer inside so that they might examine her ankle more closely. And besides, he felt like he could do with a sit down and a glass of cognac. "Excuse me, sir," he began, "but might we –"

"What are you doing just standing there?" the old man suddenly snapped. "Bring her inside. We need to take a look at that ankle."

With an exasperated *harrumph*, Ulysses helped Jennifer over the doorstep and into the antler-festooned hallway beyond. He noticed that Nimrod wiped his feet on the stiff brush doormat before entering; ever mindful of his place within the social hierarchy.

"Bring her through to the drawing room," the old man instructed, leading them inside the house, one hand on the wall to steady himself. "Make her comfortable. Get her foot up. I'll get some ice from the pantry."

"Your stick, sir," Nimrod said, proffering the handle towards the old man. He took it, barely giving Nimrod a second look.

"Now come on. Chop chop!" he ordered, stopping at the entrance to a corridor.

"Welcome to Hunter's Lodge, gentlemen," Jennifer offered somewhat belatedly, as they entered the warm embrace of the house.

Ulysses followed the old man's pointed directions, passing a dining room to his left, then on through the hall, with the staircase leading to the first floor on the right and a door marked 'LIBRARY' to the left, and finally, through the last door on the left. This lead into the drawing room itself, while the old man disappeared along a corridor opposite the dining room his stick *tap-tap*-tapping on the tiles as he went on his way.

On entering the drawing room, Ulysses helped Jennifer onto a sofa facing a roaring fire – a number of logs blazing away within the grate, filling the room with heat and flickering orange light – and made her comfortable. He plumped up a pair of cushions for her to lie against whilst he used another to help him prop up her swollen ankle.

There were two other chairs in the room. The one closest to the fire had a table next to it on which lay a pile of dusty-looking books. The tome on the top of the pile looked to be about botany. Discarded on the rug in front of the chair was a tartan-patterned woollen blanket.

"Your father feels the cold," Ulysses said, as he helped Jennifer remove her walking boots.

"Yes. He's not a well man, hasn't been for a long time."

"I'm sorry to hear that."

He unrolled the long, knee-length sock – revealing the supple, well-toned calf beneath – and Jennifer winced as he pulled it over the bruised and swollen joint. "Yup, it's definitely sprained," he said. "Sorry. Plenty of rest – that's what you need. So, what's the matter with him? Your father, I mean."

"It's not what's the matter," Jennifer tried to explain, "so much as what happened to him."

"Oh?"

Jennifer looked like she was about to say something more but at that moment the old man returned, a bucket of ice and a tea towel in his free hand.

"Here, get that on there. Wrap it up nice and tight

too, mind," the girl's father instructed, pointing at his daughter's ankle with his stick.

"Yes, sir," Ulysses replied, unable to negate the sarcastic sneer that entered his voice. He never had responded well to authority, especially when it resulted in someone treating him like an idiot.

Ulysses took the bucket and immediately grimaced in pain as his damaged fingers took the weight. He let go again quickly, the tin bucket dropping to the floor with a clang.

"Can you see to Miss Haniver's leg?" he winced, addressing his manservant. "It's just that I appear to be somewhat incapacitated."

"Of course, sir. You should take a seat yourself. You look like you could do with a rest."

Ulysses regarded his manservant with unashamed admiration. He had been through just as much as the rest of them as they had fled from the predations of the Ghestdale beast and yet here he was, taking the strain and helping out, carrying on as he would with his usual duties, as if nothing were amiss.

Nimrod was, Ulysses decided, really something else. And he had always been the same, such as when Hercules Quicksilver, Ulysses' father, had been alive.

Not needing to be told twice to take the weight off his feet, Ulysses gratefully collapsed into a chair by the fire. His deerstalker and cape were gone, lost to the moors and the Barghest, but at least that was all that had been taken. Things could have been so much worse..

"So, Jennifer tells me you're a naturalist," Ulysses said, by way of making light conversation.

Hannibal Haniver, his face a wizened mask, but one that still spoke of former glory, looked myopically at Ulysses and then, without saying anything, turned his face to the fire, losing himself in the hypnotic, inconstant flames.

"I've heard your name mentioned before, certainly," Ulysses went on, in an effort to break the uncomfortable silence. He sensed Jennifer tense where she lay on the sofa, now with a cup of hot, sweet tea in her hands, the drink being intended to take away the chill of the moors and the shock that both the accident and the beast had wrought.

Ulysses swirled the cognac in the glass in his hands – a very fine Courvoisier – and then downed the last of it, enjoying the sinus clearing blast of alcoholic vapour as its essence filled his mouth.

"I might have been someone," Haniver replied eventually, with a weary sigh, "once."

"And you still are someone," Jennifer chided him, speaking up in his defence. Ulysses was reminded, however, of the fact that it had not been so long ago that Jennifer had said precisely the same thing of her father. "It's just that my father doesn't enjoy as good health as he once did," she went on.

"She is such a comfort to me, you have no idea," Haniver said. "She is not only my eyes and ears in the world beyond this house. She is so kind and gentle – just like her mother. So beautiful." The old man's eyes hazed over, as if he was looking at something that only he could see, gazing back across the years to a time when he was a younger, stronger man and his wife was still alive.

"Is that her?" Ulysses asked, pointing at a portrait hung above the fireplace.

"That's her," the old man replied wistfully. "So beautiful.

I never knew what she saw in an old man like me."

Ulysses studied the painting thoughtfully for a moment. The likeness that Jennifer and her mother shared was clear.

"Yes, I know what you're thinking, and you are right," Haniver suddenly blurted out irascibly. "What is a fool like him doing with a beautiful, young daughter? Well, the truth is, I met Jenny's mother when I was already well on in years, but she made me feel young again. And she gave me some of the happiest years of my life, even though it wasn't to last."

"She died in childbirth," Jennifer said matter-of-factly, gazing into her tea.

"Oh, I'm sorry," Ulysses faltered, feeling that he should say something in acknowledgement of such a personal revelation.

"It's all right, I don't mind talking about it," Jennifer stated. "There are no feelings of guilt there. I do not have any issues to deal with in that regard. You see, I never knew her."

"But you are so like her," her father repeated and Jennifer smiled weakly. The old man turned from the flickering flames in the grate and his memories to Ulysses. "Jennifer is all I have now. I have no career or reputation to speak of, after all. No, she really is all I've got."

"There you go again," Jennifer muttered wearily. "If you would just let me explain..."

"Hush now, Jenny. Quicksilver and his man don't need to learn of all the ins and outs of my shame."

"Your shame? Oh, you're too proud!" Jennifer scolded. "I think they do, Father, because it shouldn't be your shame. We have proof now. You can go back to the Royal Society, as one utterly vindicated!"

"What?" The old man's eyes were suddenly alive with

something other than the dancing firelight as he turned to look at his daughter.

"We found it, father!" Jennifer said excitedly, her former fear now replaced by an excited euphoria.

"You found it? The beast itself, not just a sign?" The old man sounded just as excited as his daughter now, and clapped his hands together in delight, his heavily-lined face lighting up with unadulterated glee.

"It was more like it found us," Ulysses added coolly.

"Yes, Daddy, we found it!"

"Oh, my poor Jenny," the old man extolled, looking like he was about to well up. "My poor child. It must have been terrifying for you. You could have been killed! I should never have let you go out on the moor alone."

"I wasn't alone; Ambrose was with me. And besides, I'm not a *child*, Daddy."

"You are!" the old man countered, his rheumy eyes wet with tears. "You're *my* child."

He took out a handkerchief, blew his nose into it, and then looked to his daughter expectantly again, the smile returning to his face.

"But how wonderful for you as well! What was it like?"

"As big as a Shetland pony, covered in a thick, black hide. Half-Rottweiler, half-wolf, half-lion, all nightmare," she gushed excitedly as she described the beast that had tried to kill them all.

"Breath like an unwashed abattoir, claws like kitchen knives," Ulysses put in, remembering the injuries he himself had suffered, "all the wit and charm of a Scotsman."

"So it's *not* just another feral dog, beaten and abused and now living wild on the moors?" Hannibal asked, although, from his tone, it sounded as though he didn't really need to be convinced that Jennifer was telling the truth.

"Oh no, not at all. It's definitely our killer."

"I don't know about you, but I feel like I could eat a horse," Ulysses suddenly threw in, interrupting the conversation. "I've not eaten anything since... since breakfast, in fact!"

Hannibal Haniver broke off from his discussion with his daughter and gave Ulysses a look that revealed exactly how he felt about the dandy and his rude interruptions, regardless of whether he had saved his precious child's life or not.

"I wouldn't mind something to eat myself," Jennifer chipped in, looking at the grandmother clock in the corner of the room. "It's past six o'clock, and I forgot to have that sandwich I made for myself I was so absorbed in my search for the beast."

"Very well, then. But I want to continue this discussion over supper."

"It's only cold cuts, I'm afraid," Hannibal Haniver said as they all took their places at the table in the lodge's dining room. Ulysses helped Jennifer to a place at the table, Nimrod pulling out Haniver's chair for him.

As master of the house, Hannibal Haniver had taken his place at the head of the table while Jennifer sat to his right, where she was able to put her injured leg up on the chair next to her. Ulysses sat opposite. Nimrod had not set a place for himself; Ulysses assumed he would eat by himself in the kitchen after they had finished their meal.

There were another six potential seats at the table, the place opposite Haniver at the foot of the table close to the heavy maroon drapes hiding a set of French windows, firmly shut and locked now against the wind and weather until the spring returned.

The chamber was decorated much like the rest of the house, all oak panelling and dark heavy drapes to keep out the coming winter chill, over-filled with heavy pieces of furniture, making the room appear even darker and more cramped than it really was.

"I would have asked Jennifer to prepare something for us," good manners dictating that the host apologise for any failings in his ability to cater for his dinner guest, "but, under the circumstances... Anyway, it looks like your batman has managed to rustle something up," he went on, surveying the epicurean feast that awaited them.

There were slices of ham, tongue and corned beef, all laid out immaculately on china platters, a bowl of picked onions, a cheese still in its rind and a radish salad.

"Only cold cuts eh, Haniver? Then I'd like to see what Christmas dinner's like at Hunter's Lodge."

"Your man," Hannibal said under his breath, towards Ulysses, "is he, quite, well, you know."

"Oh, absolutely," Ulysses said with a smile at the disparaging expression the older man offered him in response.

Nimrod, wearing a frilly pink pinny over his waistcoat, having dispensed with his coat and butler's tails, placed a jar of piccalilli on a mat in front of Haniver.

"Suits you, old man," Ulysses said, nodding at his valet. "Pink."

Nimrod didn't bat an eyelid. "Thank you, sir. I like to think that it brings out the blue of my eyes," he said, as poker-faced as ever.

"So, Haniver, who usually keeps house for you?"

"A woman from Stainsacre, a village on the edge of the moor, a Mrs Pritchard. I would have got her to concoct us something – cook us one of her venison pies or prepare a pan of her legendary Scotch broth – but her son came to collect her in that infernal jalopy of his," he said as an aside to Jennifer, "before dusk. You know what people are like since the killings began and the Press started their scare-mongering. No-one wants to find themselves caught out on the moors after dark."

"Well you can add before dark as well now, in light of our little run in with your phantom hound."

"Oh, it's no phantom, Quicksilver, I can assure you of that," the naturalist said vehemently.

"I know. I can vouch for that fact myself," Ulysses pointed out, riled by the old man's defensive attack. "I only meant that the legend of the Barghest has been perpetuated for centuries and what I saw on the moors today looked nothing like the product of any natural birth."

"What are you saying, sir?" the curmudgeonly Haniver challenged. Before Ulysses had a chance to explain himself, the old man turned to the girl again. "Is that right, Jennifer?"

"Well, Daddy, it was getting dark and we were hardly in the best position to see, but the creature was certainly unlike any dog that I have ever seen before, or any wolf for that matter."

"How do you mean? In what way was it different?"

Jennifer put down her knife and fork and thought for a moment. "In that its various body parts didn't seem to fit together properly, quite as they should, in that... I know this is going to sound ridiculous, but in that it appeared cobbled together. In that it was greater than the sum of its parts."

"Precisely!" Ulysses crowed triumphantly.

"What are you getting at, Mr Quicksilver?"

"Jennifer's just told you! It was greater than the sum of its parts."

"I'm sorry, I don't follow you."

"But, that aside, what I want to know is where did it come from? And why now?"

"What are you saying, Ulysses?"

All eyes were on Ulysses now.

"When did the first death occur?"

"The first Barghest killing, you mean?" Haniver asked.

"Yes," Ulysses nodded.

"Back in September," Jennifer said, "a rambler, not far from here in fact, up on Fencher's Tor, at the edge of the Umbridge estate."

"Not Umbridge as in Josiah Umbridge, famous industrialist who's dropped out of the public eye due to poor health?"

"That's right." The old man was a picture of bewilderment.

"And yet the legend of the Barghest has been around for centuries, hasn't it?"

"There have been reported sightings from as far back as the twelfth century," Haniver proffered the information from his obviously encyclopaedic knowledge of the legend.

"But these deaths are the first that can be properly tied to the beast in, what, a hundred years?"

"There was a report from the seventeenth century that a farm worker witnessed the Barghest carry off a woman accused of witchcraft after it was said she had poisoned her husband."

"But the first substantiated report of a death to occur in this century happened two months or so ago?"

"What are you getting at, Mr Quicksilver?"

"What was it you said just now, Jennifer, about the beast?"

"I think I said that it looked like it had been cobbled together."

"Precisely!" Ulysses put down his knife and fork and, resting his elbows on the starched white tablecloth, gently cupped his injured right hand in his left. "What do you know of the Whitby Mermaid?"

Hannibal Haniver grunted in annoyance. "Is there any danger of you actually giving us a simple answer to a simple question? First we're talking about the Black Dog of Beast Cliff and now you've thrown mermaids into the equation."

"If I might beg your indulgence for a moment? The Whitby Mermaid – have you heard of it?"

"But of course, this isn't the arse end of beyond, you know. I do read *The Times*. And of course it was reported in the local paper – huge furore. I would have liked to have looked into that one more closely myself, but that scoundrel Cruikshank saw to it that the thing was whisked away to London before myself, or Jennifer – or anyone else for that matter – could take a closer look. And now the damn thing's been stolen, hasn't it?" A spark of excitement appeared in the old man's eyes again. "Have you seen it, Quicksilver?"

"Only a photograph. Not in the flesh, as it were. I would have liked to though. For a start it might have made my current investigation a little more straightforward. But I've seen enough to know it's a fake."

"Your investigation?" Jennifer asked.

"Yes, Quicksilver, you haven't told us what brings you to Ghestdale," Haniver said, almost accusingly.

"And you haven't told me why a leader in his field,

like yourself, is living as a recluse at the edge of these godforsaken moors."

"The impudent cheek. I'll have you know that this is God's own county!"

"My apologies," Ulysses said hastily, making an instant retraction.

"I find that this is the perfect environment in which to pursue my studies."

"Would that be your studies in natural history or cryptozoology?"

"Mr Quicksilver! I will not be made a mockery of in my own home!" the old man fumed, slamming a fist down on the table. "I am going to have to ask you to leave!"

"Daddy," Jennifer said, stepping in. "I do not believe that Ulysses is trying to mock you."

"No, not at all, sir," Ulysses backed her up, trying to sound as sincere as possible. "Considering how events have escalated recently, I really would appreciate your input in this matter. As you will know from reading *The Times*, the Whitby mermaid was stolen, but what you probably don't know is that it was stolen to order, and sent back to Whitby."

"Do you know *who* it was sent to?" The old man was intrigued now.

"Only that it was stolen on the orders of one Mr Bellerophon."

"Bellerophon? I've never heard of anyone by that name living in these parts."

"No, and I wouldn't have expected you to."

"But back to the mermaid; it was obviously a fake," Haniver said. "You could just about see the stitch marks in the photograph."

"But who's to say that it wasn't stitched together while it was still alive." Ulysses smiled wryly.

"Are you saying that it was a vivisect?" Haniver blustered in wondrous disbelief.

"Are you serious, Ulysses?" Jennifer asked, sounding just as astonished.

"Like the Barghest hound."

For a moment everyone around the table was silent; only the chink of silverware on the finest bones china disturbed the eerily tense atmosphere, as Ulysses dissected a slice of ham on his plate.

"You speak of such things as if you have encountered them before," Haniver pointed out. "Have you seen something like this before, Quicksilver?"

"Yes, actually I have."

The stunned silence returned.

With a deafening crash of breaking glass, the French windows exploded into the room as something huge and terrible hurtled through them, tearing the heavy drapes from their curtain pole to trail the thick velvet hangings.

Shards of broken glass whickered through the air like a crystalline hailstorm as the beast landed in the centre of the table, its varnished surface splintering under its weight.

Jennifer screamed.

The beast roared.

And Ulysses Quicksilver stared death in the face.

CHAPTER FOURTEEN

Red in Tooth and Claw

The beast's roar silenced the screaming Jennifer. Struggling to know what else to do she pushed herself back into her chair, as if somehow that would save her from the slavering jaws and razor talons of the monster.

For a moment the Barghest simply sat there, not looking at any of them. Its nose in the air, the grossly malformed hound sniffed sharply several times while all those present in the room could do was watch in stunned horror.

The monster must have found a way out of the jet mine, Ulysses thought, climbing back above ground before hunting them to the house.

In the brightly-lit dining room, with the beast mere inches from his face again, Ulysses saw the monster clearly for the first time as it squatted there in the centre of the table, panting heavily. The room filled with the stink of its steaming body, its filth-matted hide, a stomach-turning blend of wet dog and spoiled meat.

In that same instant, Ulysses' over-wrought mind took in every hideous detail. The creature's short black pelt glistened wetly in the suffused candle-light, the bristles of its fur standing on end. Ulysses fancied he could see every one of its killingly-powerful muscles as they slid and bunched beneath the scabrous skin of its hide.

Up close he could also make out every one of the injuries it had already sustained. There were grazes and lacerations acquired, no doubt, when it fell into the mine shaft. In fact, the creature's right eye had been practically gouged out, no doubt by some outcropping rock. Cuts flecked its shoulders, forelimbs and flanks. Some still had diamond-sharp splinters of glass embedded within them. The beast's blood mixed with the mud its paws had smeared over the tablecloth.

And then there were the gunshot wounds. Ulysses could see the hole he had managed to blast in its shoulder, and one ear was now a ragged mess thanks to where another shot had pulverised half of it. Both he and Nimrod had actually hit the thing then – he had been beginning to wonder if they really had, seeing it there in front of him now – but none of their shots had been killing shots. The beast's resilience and stamina must be incredible, practically any of the other shots would have been enough to floor a lesser animal.

It was bold too, in a way that other dogs weren't. Not even a wolf would have thrown itself through a set of French windows to get at its prey. It must have followed their scent to the house and then, attracted to the noise they had made during dinner, it knew where to attack. But now Ulysses was almost certain that the Barghest was looking for one person in particular. And then he saw the dull metal box sunk into the flesh at the base of its skull, and that was enough to shock him into action: he had seen such a thing before.

He lunged for the carving knife beside the ham, even as the dog turned.

"Get out of here!" he yelled as he slashed at the dog's debrided snout, cutting through the string of flesh that separated its nostrils. Thank goodness the Hanivers' housekeeper liked to keep the knives sharp.

A combination of his natural instinct for survival and a greatly developed subconscious prescience, sent Ulysses leaping from his chair. Spinning round, he grabbed the chair in time to use it to shield himself from the Barghest's attack when it came a split second later.

The creature struck out with a massive paw, claws tearing through the upholstered chair as though it were matchwood. Ulysses' shield was gone, utterly destroyed, having only bought him one second more. Backed up against a heavy sideboard, with two-hundred and fifty pounds of killer dog bearing down on him, looking like it was ready to drive him through the wall, Ulysses tightened his grip on the carving knife. If only he had kept his sword-cane with him, rather than leaving it in the drawing room along with his jacket.

And then Nimrod was at the door, as Hannibal Haniver and his daughter both made for the way out, Jennifer sobbing in pain and fear as she was forced to put weight on her wrecked ankle. Still in his pink pinny and shirt sleeves, Nimrod assumed a marksman's stance, a fresh load in his pistol. The shot came sharp and loud, like a thunderclap in the close confines of the dining-room. It hit the creature's grasping forelimb and punched clean through flesh and bone. The Barghest gave up a surprisingly shrill yelp of pain.

Ulysses suddenly felt very cold, but it wasn't just down to the fact that the creature's destructive entrance had brought the cold night in after it.

The creature snarled and lunged at Nimrod from its perch on the table, muscles shifting as it lashed out at the butler. The swipe knocked the gun from Nimrod's hands, forcing him back towards the door, as Jennifer and her father ducked through it behind him.

Ulysses' manservant had probably just saved his life for the umpteenth time, but in doing so had now brought the monster's ire upon himself. If he didn't do something quickly he had no doubt that Nimrod was going to die.

Ulysses felt impotent against the beast. He had no gun, no sword and no chance of overcoming the beast for as long as he remained trapped in the dining room. He was up against an enemy that could not be placated, that could not be reasoned with and that would not stop, or so it seemed – no matter what they threw at it – until either it or they were dead, and right now, Ulysses didn't fancy their chances much.

But in the height of adrenalin-fuelled desperation, instinct took over.

Ulysses grabbed chair. Raising it in front of him, as might a lion tamer, with a roar of his own, putting all his weight behind the thrust he pushed forwards.

The chair connected with the side of the monster's over-sized head, clubbing it violently sideways. For a moment the beast was caught off balance and looked like it might slip off the edge of the table. Then it recovered and lunged again, making a swipe for the chair. But Ulysses was already moving for the door, after the retreating Nimrod, letting go of the chair as the monster's jaws shattered it.

Nimrod was safely out of the room and Ulysses was now moving to the open doorway himself.

He felt the flash of prescience even as Nimrod gave a shouted "Sir!" Both told him that there wasn't a hope of him making the door before the beast clawed him to the floor.

He stepped swiftly sideways. The fireplace was next to him, the poker that he himself had used to stoke it before dinner, still protruding from amid the white-hot coals. Ulysses' right hand closed around the hot metal, a welter of scalding pain flared across his palm to join with the breath-catching agony of his broken fingers. At this rate they were never going to heal!

Adrenalin and an instinct for self-preservation helping

him to put the pain aside, Ulysses swung the smoking tip of the poker in an arc, smacking the snapping Barghest across the end of its muzzle. The creature gave a piercing scream like a gin-trapped wolf and recoiled, the stink of scorched fur causing Ulysses to do the same, his nose wrinkled in disgust.

And that was enough for him to cover the last few feet left between him and the dining room door, throw himself through, and slam it behind him. He heard the latch bolt catch in the lock plate.

Three ashen faces and sets of anxious eyes stared into his.

With a crash the door shook in its frame as the beast slammed into it from the other side, panels splintering under the force of the impact.

"Move!" Ulysses shouted.

"Where to?" Hannibal Haniver spluttered.

"The kitchen!" Jennifer shouted, already beginning to move herself.

The old man said something but his words were drowned out by the savage barking of the dog behind them and the cruel sound of splintering wood as the Barghest demolished the dining-room door.

With Jennifer leading the way, the four of them stumbled, limped and ran for the kitchen passageway. The creature lunged through the shredded door panels, snagging the tail-end of Ulysses' waistcoat with a sickle-blade claw. Jaws snapping, it came no closer, its great bulk wedged between the ruptured boards.

Tearing free of its grasping paw, Ulysses herded the rest of them into the passageway. He knew that they had only been granted a moment's grace; in no time at all the Barghest would be upon them.

"Come on!" he urged. "We can't stop!"

Old man Haniver was gasping for breath as he managed something close to a run along the narrow tiled passageway. Ulysses wondered how Haniver's ill-health manifested itself. How was the old man's heart, say? He didn't want him dropping dead of a heart attack before he'd had a chance to bring the devil-dog to heel.

Then the animal was through; Ulysses heard the wooden tearing of the door as it came apart, and then the scrabbling of clawed feet on smooth tiles that paved the way to the kitchen.

Re-doubling his own efforts, he spurred them all onwards.

Ulysses was dimly aware of passing a darkened adjoining passageway to the right that ended at a descending staircase, and then he was entering the lamp-lit brightness of an immaculately-kept kitchen.

As he turned to close the door behind him he was faced by the appalling aspect of the brutally deformed Barghest as it bounded down the passageway towards him, its flanks scraping against the walls either side of the corridor as it closed the gap between them.

Ulysses slammed the kitchen door shut and, keeping his hands pressed against the wood, braced his body against it. The Barghest slammed into the door and Ulysses was pushed backwards several inches as the wood around the lock splintered.

Looking down he saw the tips of the predator's tusk-like teeth appear through the gap as the dog pushed against the door. Ulysses kicked out viciously, catching the dog squarely on the nose. There was a yelp of pain which transformed into a snarl of snapping rage. The dog pulled back, Ulysses assumed in readiness to ram the door again.

Desperate eyes scanned the kitchen for some means

of barricading the door, and fell upon the tall wooden dresser to his left.

"Quick, Nimrod, the dresser." But his quick-thinking manservant already had his shoulder against the other end of the heavy piece of kitchen furniture, as the dog's second charge met with the sundered door.

With an agonisingly-shrill screech, like fingernails scraping across a blackboard, the dresser shifted, crockery shaken loose from its shelves crashing down onto the terracotta tiles of the kitchen floor, as Nimrod put all his weight behind it. The sliding dresser hit the beast squarely on the muzzle as it tried to push itself further through the widening gap. There was a meaty tearing sound, another protest of pain, and the muzzle was pulled back again, the solid piece of furniture sliding into place across the door, barricading them all inside.

Ulysses took in the strained, uncertain expressions of the others. But there was more to be read in their faces and the way they held themselves than just the heightened emotions they were feeling at present. He could see that Jennifer was in pain, the extra strain she was putting on her ankle obviously taking its toll and giving her a sickening pallor. If Jennifer looked like she was suffering, the old man looked much worse.

Even Nimrod was no longer his usual self, his eyes sunken within dark rings of shadow.

"Now what?" Jennifer asked, her voice almost a shout as the dog crashed against the kitchen door again, sending more of the teetering crockery on the dresser crashing to the floor.

His thoughts awhirl, Ulysses took a moment to consider their options.

"You don't know, do you?" the old man blustered, his words punctuated by great wheezing gasps.

Ignoring Hannibal Haniver, Ulysses focused all of his attention on Jennifer, who was propping herself up against the cold, porcelain basin of the kitchen sink.

"Is there another way out of here? Another door leading outside?"

"No," she replied, her voice betraying that she was on the verge of hysteria.

"We're trapped in here, aren't we?" the old man challenged. Part of Ulysses' brain understood that Hannibal Haniver's anger was born of fear and incomprehension, faced with such a dire predicament, but it didn't make him any easier to put up with.

There was another crash from behind the rocking dresser.

"Think, Jennifer," he pressed, "is there any other way out?"

"There's the scullery window, but that's probably too small." And then enlightenment dawned across her face, and the effect was like the sun appearing from behind the clouds on a rainy day. "But there are the back stairs!"

"That'll do," Ulysses said with relief, a nervous grin taking shape upon his own haggard features. "How do I get to them?"

"Through there," Jennifer pointed to a door on the other side of the kitchen.

"Right, that dresser's not going to hold forever, but just for now I want you to wait here," he commanded. "I'll be as quick as I can."

"What do you plan to do, sir?"

"Plan?" Ulysses laughed. "You know me, Nimrod! Since when did I ever have a plan?"

Then he saw the crestfallen expression on the face of Hannibal Haniver and saw the glimmer of hope fade from Jennifer's eyes and her face sagged in abject despair.

"I'm kidding! I'm kidding," he said, desperately wishing he could retract his last flippant statement. "I'm going to create a distraction."

He turned to Nimrod, meeting the butler's piercing sapphire stare. "As soon as you can get these two somewhere safe." He looked back at Jennifer. "We passed the stairs to a cellar on the way to the kitchen."

"Then what, sir?"

"Well then I'd appreciate it if you could see to giving me a hand with this wayward hound of ours."

"Very good, sir."

Ulysses turned and made for the door.

"Good luck, Ulysses," Jennifer said, the look in her eyes a confused mixture of anxiety, affection and even adoration.

"Yes, good luck, Quicksilver," Hannibal Haniver added.

Once through the door Ulysses entered a servant's passageway, finding the twisting back stairs directly in front of him.

He could still hear the shuddering crashes of the relentless beast throwing itself at the barricaded kitchen door as he made his way up to the first floor of the house. At the top of the stairs a short landing led to a narrow door which, in turn, led into an empty bedroom. Through that he entered a carpeted, oak-panelled passageway that ran past another bedroom, down a couple of steps and finally turned right onto the main landing, at the top of the central staircase of Hunter's Lodge. From here he could hear the scrabbling of the monster's claws tearing up the tiles of the scullery passageway as it tried to gain purchase, so that it might push its way through the kitchen door at last.

And as he had made his way through the house he

had desperately tried to formulate some sort of a plan. If he could get back down the main stairs while the dog was still distracted, he could retrieve his sword-cane from where he had left it in the drawing-room and then at least he would have a fighting chance against the beast. Perhaps he could hamstring the thing before plunging his blade into the base of its skull.

He didn't think the beast's heightened sense of smell would detect that he had left the kitchen and was now upstairs, not after the mess he had made of its nose. Probably the only thing the creature could smell now was its own blood.

His heart in his mouth, he took his first step down the staircase. The stair cried out like a creaking coffin lid as he put his weight onto his leading foot, and he froze. Surely the monster would have heard that.

Then he heard the cacophonous crash of the dresser finally toppling over, every last piece of crockery still stored inside smashing to smithereens upon the hard floor of the kitchen. Ulysses realised that if he didn't do something fast, Nimrod and the others would all soon be dead.

"Here doggy-doggy!" he bellowed at the top of his voice.

In the silence that followed, all he could hear was the solemn ticking of the grandfather clock in the hallway below, and the dub-dub dub-dub of his pulse, right at the centre of his head.

And then he heard the savage, wolfish snarling of the Barghest, the scrape of talons clawing up the floorboards of the hall below and his blood turned to ice in his veins.

For a moment he found himself frozen to the spot, two million years of evolution unable to erase the memory that for much of that time man had been the prey and not the hunter.

What have I done? he wondered. The monster was coming for him and he had nothing to defend himself with. He had hoped to have had enough time to descend the staircase, at least retrieve his sword-cane from the drawing room before he had to face the beast again.

Another instinct taking over now, he went for his gun. But it was only when his aching fingers found nothing there in the holster under his arm that he remembered how he had lost it during his first run-in with the beast-dog.

And then it was there, at the bottom of the stairs, ruined muzzle sniffing the air, those massively mishapen jaws now missing more than just a couple of fangs. A moment later it caught sight of Ulysses, the darkly burning pin-pricks of its eyes narrowing with cold animal hatred.

His petrified muscles miraculously unfreezing, Ulysses didn't hang around to find out what the monster would do next. Turning, he threw himself through the door nearest to him, finding himself inside a bedroom – quite possibly Hannibal Haniver's by the look of things. He slammed the door shut behind him, knowing that it would only slow the beast for a second.

Eyes scanning the room for anything that he could turn into a weapon, Ulysses took note of a large, heavy-looking lamp on a bedside table, and even the table itself.

And all the time, at the back of his mind, bubbling away beneath his surface thoughts, he found himself wondering whether Jennifer was all right, and whether Nimrod was leading the girl and her curmudgeonly father to safety in the cellars beneath the house.

"I don't believe it!" the old man fumed as he took in the state of his kitchen, the terracotta tiles buried beneath a porcelain-white snowfall of broken china shards. "This is my home. My *home*!"

"Quickly, sir!" Nimrod hissed. "We have to go now!"

"Daddy, come on!" Jennifer urged, her voice strained with emotion, her eyes red from crying.

Picking his way over the carpet of broken pottery, taking care not to crunch any of it beneath the soles of his shoes – keen not to do anything to attract the monster's attention again – Nimrod led the naturalist and his daughter out of the kitchen, into the passageway beyond, and down to the cellars.

"I mean I've been hunting the thing my whole life and now that pompous idiot has brought it *here*, it's destroying my home! God damn it, its ruining everything!" old man Haniver went on, incensed.

"Hush, father!" Jennifer whimpered, from fear of the monster coming after them again, rather than from the pain of her ankle.

A loud crash reverberated through the house from the floor above: the monster must be hunting his master now, Nimrod considered, which would hopefully give him enough time to discharge his duties towards the old man and his daughter.

Leading the way, Nimrod helped Miss Haniver down the steps to the cellar. At the foot of the stairs she scrabbled with the key that had been left in the lock and opened the door.

"Mind that last step, sir," he said, turning to help the girl's father and then said nothing more as he realised the old man was no longer with them.

"Mr Haniver, sir!" Nimrod called back up the stairs as loudly as he dared.

"Daddy?" Miss Haniver called out, willing her worst fears to be confounded. "Daddy!"

"Miss Haniver," Nimrod said, his voice stern, his tone commanding, "lock yourself in the cellar and wait for me there. I will not be long."

Jennifer said nothing, the tears running freely now down her cheeks and splashing onto the dusty flags at her feet as she slumped awkwardly against the cold bricks of the wall.

What does the old man think he's doing? Nimrod fretted, his long legs taking the cellar steps two at a time, he chased back up them after the old man.

Ulysses burst out of the bathroom and back onto the landing. He could hear the monster's claws scrabbling against the enamelled sides of the bathtub, punctuated by a guttural growling as it tried to extricate itself from the shower curtain.

And then he was at the top of the stairs, staring down the twin barrels of a rifle, held in the hands of a shaking Hannibal Haniver. Ulysses had to grab the roundel at the end of the banister to stop himself careering into the old man and, as a result, lost his footing, his legs sliding out from under him, slipping on the carpeted stair. Falling heavily, he bumped down the first turn of the stairs on his arse towards the gun-toting naturalist.

Feeling a rising sense of panic, Ulysses heard the crash of the bathroom door flying open, the angry shout of the old man and the throaty bellow of the beast.

Lying almost on his back, Ulysses saw the monstrous shape of the Barghest as it leapt over him. He heard the retort of the rifle firing and, ears ringing, closed his eyes against the shower of dust and plaster that fell from the ceiling where the shotgun shells had struck.

The Barghest struck the old man with such force that he bounced off the wall and smashed through the banisters, plunging to the hallway below.

Ulysses got to his feet, stumbling down the stairs in horror as he saw how the old man had landed, limp as a discarded doll, the hunched black form of the devil dog now astride the wretched man.

"Get off him! Leave him alone!" Ulysses screamed at the beast, descending the stairs at a run. Its huge, misshapen head jerked from side to side as it burrowed into the old man's meagre flesh.

Pulling a broken baluster from the ruined staircase, Ulysses hurled it at the animal.

"Bad dog!"

The splintered spar struck the monster's flank, finding an open wound there, and remained lodged in the creature's flesh. It was enough to turn the monster's attention back onto Ulysses.

Leaving the red ruin of the old man, the Barghest paced its way to the foot of the stairs and began to climb, Hannibal Haniver's blood spraying from its gore-drenched muzzle as it barked and snapped at the dandy hastily retreating back up the stairs.

And then, when it felt like there was nowhere left to run, Ulysses heard the shout, "Sir!" and glanced back down to the hallway in time to see Nimrod throw something up to him.

The bloodstone-tipped cane spun through the air and over the banisters. Ulysses reached out an arm and plucked it from the air. Grabbing the black wood shaft of the cane with his left hand, he pulled the rapier blade free of its scabbard as the monster leapt.

In the unnatural stillness that followed Ulysses heard an audible pop and blinked against the wet spray that spurted into his face. He felt the blade meet resistance but it held firm. The dead weight of the monster fell on top of him, outstretched claws raking the wood-panelling behind him, tearing great slivers of veneer from the wall.

Ulysses found himself sitting on the stairs, back pressed up against the wall, gasping for air, all two-hundred and fifty pounds of muscle and evil intent crushing his body below the waist.

And there the monster remained, the stink of its foulness strong in Ulysses' nostrils. It died not with a roar or a whimper but with a last gust of bloody breath and with Ulysses' blade sunk up to the hilt in its one remaining eye.

An awareness of his surroundings returned, as if someone had turned up the volume on a radio set and he heard Jennifer's great gulping sobs of shock and grief on seeing the savaged corpse of her father and Nimrod, unable to hide the emotion from his voice himself now, say: "Sir, are you all right?"

And then he felt tears of relief, hot and uncontrollable, welling up in his eyes and running down his cheeks, and when he could speak again he said simply: "Get me out from under here, would you? I'm a little stuck."

CHAPTER FIFTEEN

A Death in the Family

"I mean look at it, Nimrod," the dandy said, prodding at the flopping jaw of the dead beast, stretched out on the dining table, with the same silvered serving tongs his manservant had used to serve supper only an hour before. "Have you ever seen anything like it?"

"No, sir. Not since our sojourn at the Marianas Base."

"Precisely what I was thinking," Ulysses said, knocking back the rest of the brandy he held in his other hand, unable to take his eyes from the monstrosity in front of them.

It had taken no small effort to get the cooling carcass of the beast back into the dining room and up onto the table. First they had had to shift the thing from where it had collapsed on top of Ulysses. Between himself and Nimrod they had finally managed to roll the monster off Ulysses' legs and through the broken banisters, letting it fall, loose-limbed, onto the floor of the hallway below.

The thud of meat and muscle hitting the floor had startled the weeping girl, kneeling beside her father's lifeless body, his blood-soaked head in her lap, her freely-running tears splashing onto his gore-reddened face. From the expression on the old man's face, if it hadn't been for the torn out larynx and the opened ribcage, Ulysses could have almost believed that he was just sleeping.

Easing himself up from where he had lain squashed under the bulk of the beast, Ulysses descended the stairs to stand at Jennifer's side. Saying nothing he put a comforting hand on her shoulder. Welcoming contact with another human being, she grasped his hand tightly in hers and he was able to help her to her feet.

Guiding her away from the gutted carcass of her father he half-carried her up the stairs, despite feeling exhausted himself, and escorted her to her room. There were more gasps of horror when she saw first-hand the destruction the monster had wrought to her father's chambers in pursuit of Ulysses.

Leaving her sobbing quietly in her bed, the covers pulled up over her still clothed form, he returned to where he had left Nimrod to clear up the mess downstairs.

The ever-reliable Nimrod had already moved Hannibal Haniver's body to the scullery passageway, but not before wrapping it in one of the destroyed dining-room drapes, as much as to hold it together as to not cause any further distress to the dead man's already distraught daughter.

It took both of them to move the body of the dog-beast into the dining-room and onto the table, so that Ulysses might have a closer look at it, in the hope of finding some clues as to the beast's origins. Someone had been trying to kill one of them – but whether the intended victim had been himself or Jenny, or even the old man, he wasn't sure – and he needed to know, in case the killer tried again. Perhaps the beast's handler – and he was sure that it had a handler – had wanted all of them dead.

As Ulysses poured himself the first of several glasses of cognac, and prepared to make his cursory examination of the Barghest's corpse, Nimrod set about mopping the old man's blood from the floor and walls of the hall.

Ulysses refilled his glass sloppily from the bottle on the sideboard next to him and took another swig.

"Sure I can't get you one?" Ulysses asked, proffering the glass to his manservant.

"No thank you, sir. Not while I'm on duty."

Something of Nimrod's indefatigable demeanour had returned, despite the fact that for the last half an hour he had been clearing corpses and mopping up blood. It was just business as usual as far as his butler was concerned.

"On duty? You're never *off* duty," Ulysses said.

He found the alcohol helped; it was relaxing him after his frantic fight with the Barghest, and the fumes of the cognac swirling in the glass provided the added benefit of going some way to mask the excremental stench of the beast itself.

"So, this is a vivisect too," Nimrod said, "like the missing mermaid?"

"I think so," Ulysses replied, wiping splashes of brandy from his chin with the back of his hand. His broken fingers were just a dull ache now; for the time being residual adrenalin in his system and alcohol were having a pain-numbing effect. "I mean there's no way this thing's natural. So far I haven't found any obvious signs of suturing, where one body part has been grafted onto another, but then we have no idea how long ago it was that this thing left the operating table."

"And I suppose the body's rather badly damaged," Nimrod pointed out, looking down his nose at the thing on the table.

"There is that," Ulysses agreed. "But you only have to look at the thing to see that it wasn't born so much as made."

Those are never a dog's jaws. They're not even those of a wolf. They look like they should belong to something the size of a big cat, a tiger or a lion. Its skin doesn't even fit over the skeletal structure beneath. And then there are the claws."

"And the creature's musculature," Nimrod added as he ran an appraising eye over the dead brute. "It definitely looks like its been added to, particularly around the shoulders."

"To support the extra weight that's been added to its skull," Ulysses conjectured. "It would have helped the beast climb out of that mineshaft we dropped it into no doubt."

"And would go some way to explaining how it seemed to shrug off the damage caused by our shots." Nimrod mused.

"Yes, that and an enlarged medulla oblongata, no doubt. I bet if we cut it open we'd find its bones are thicker than they should be, perhaps even reinforced with metal rods.'"

Ulysses stared into the ruined eyes of the creature, one practically gouged out, the other popped by the tip of his own rapier blade. His gaze moved from the creature's ugly bifurcated face to the top of its thickened skull to the hunched, muscle-bound shoulders, slashed and grazed, and with pieces missing from the flesh there.

He gave the small metal box sunk into the thick flesh at the base of the creature's skull a tap with the serving tongs. "What do you make of that, Nimrod? Look familiar, does it?"

Before Nimrod could offer a reply, Ulysses turned to face the ruined doorway of the dining room, the unmistakeable sensation of someone watching him causing the hairs on the back of his neck to stand on end.

Jennifer Haniver stood there, leaning against the ruptured wood, her grime-smeared face streaked with tears, her blouse red with her father's blood, the eyes of both Ulysses and his manservant heavy upon her.

"Jenny," Ulysses said, somewhat surprised to see the wretched girl again so soon. "You should be resting."

"No," she said firmly, in a voice that brooked no

discussion. "I want to know what killed him – what killed my father. I need to... understand why he died." There were no tears, no wailing, no hysterical recriminations or shrieks of protest, just a resolute determination to discover some answers.

Ulysses saw the implacable look in her eyes as she kept them locked firmly on the creature in front of her. "So be it," he said, equally determined, equally resolute.

"What is it?" she demanded. "The Barghest, I mean. What is it really?"

"It's man-made, the work of a skilled vivisectionist," Ulysses explained.

"Where did it come from?" was her next straightforward question. "Who was responsible for its ungodly creation," she hissed, her voice replete with quiet rage.

"You mean, what leads do we have as to who set this thing on us?"

"I think you mean on *me*, Ulysses," Jennifer corrected him coldly.

"We can't be certain which of us the dog was after, but I'm convinced that it was set on us, to hunt one of us down and get us out of the way."

"But I was the one who was out on the moors searching for it and knowing what sort of reputation my father has..." – she broke off, catching herself – "my father *had*, I wouldn't be surprised if people in certain quarters would have known that too. He never made a secret of his quest to uncover the truth, even though it forced his retirement to this godforsaken place!"

"Well, let's just say that I had been making enquiries of my own, regarding the missing mermaid, that were probably just as poorly received in those same quarters."

"Then what of the Barghest's other victims, sir? The ones whose deaths were reported in the local press?"

Nimrod asked, challenging Ulysses' hypothesis, as only one completely loyal to his master could. "Were they all hunted down as part of some nefarious master-plan?"

Ulysses was quiet for a moment, another swig of the honey-coloured alcohol helping lubricate the grinding gears relentlessly turning his thoughts over inside his head.

"I wouldn't be surprised that if Allardyce and his cronies had half a mind to look beyond the obvious they would find something connecting them all. Remind me to look into it when we get back to the guest house will you, old boy?"

"As you wish, sir."

Ulysses looked from his manservant to the dog's carcass and then back again at Nimrod. "You think I'm looking for Machiavellian machinations where there are none?"

"Not at all, sir, I was merely playing devil's advocate. Is it not possible that all of the beast's victims have merely been the terribly unlucky?"

"Maybe so, in the case of the others, but not tonight. I don't believe the beast would have gone to all the trouble off tracking us here simply for revenge. An animal that had already survived a beating like the one we dealt out would have gone back to its lair whimpering, with its tail between its legs, not tracked us for miles across Ghestdale to then leap through a plate glass window to teach us a lesson!

"No, the Barghest was merely a puppet; there's someone pulling the strings, someone behind the scenes," he said, his eyes returning to the metal box clamped to the back of its neck.

"Besides there was someone who knew where we would be this afternoon as well, Nimrod, someone other than Inspector Maurice Allardyce of Scotland Yard and the

North Yorkshire constabulary."

"I was just thinking the same thing myself, sir."

"Who? Who knew?" Jennifer said.

"A man called Rudge. We ran into him whilst pursuing our investigations down in the town. In fact, now I come to think of it, he made his entrance as I was asking a barkeep if he knew the name Bellerophon."

"Rudge?" Jennifer said, surprise raising her voice an octave.

"You know him?"

"Tall as he is broad? Built like a brick... well, you know how that saying goes."

"You *do* know him then!"

"Oh yes, I know him. I suppose you could describe him as a nasty piece of work, a cruel man. No time or regard for his animals, let alone his fellow man."

Nimrod gave Ulysses a look heavy with meaning.

"Really? He was really turning on the charm then when he spoke to us then."

Ulysses put his the brandy balloon to his lips but then paused.

"We come to Whitby looking for Mr Bellerophon but run into Rudge instead. Rudge arranges to meet us on the moors but rather than Rudge, the Barghest turns up..." With a swift jerk of his head, he knocked back the remainder of the brandy.

"So where would we find this Rudge?"

"He's gamekeeper to the Umbridge Estate."

"That name again," Ulysses pondered. "Then we have the lead we need. Come the morning we shall pay a visit to the reclusive Josiah Umbridge."

Putting the empty glass down on the table beside the dead dog-beast Ulysses turned to Jennifer, put both his hands on her shoulders and gazed into her grief-stricken face.

"But for now, let's get some rest. We're all in need of a good night's sleep."

Morning came, it seemed, all too soon, the watery grey light of a dreary dawn oozing across the moors along with the stagnant mists that rose from the peat bogs and waterlogged hollows. Hunter's Lodge having once been precisely that, it had not been a problem finding accommodation for both Ulysses and his manservant, so that each of them was able to have his own room.

Before the three of them had retired for what remained of the night, Jennifer had told both of her gentlemen house guests to feel free to help themselves to anything from her father's wardrobe, to replace that which had been either soiled or ruined during their battles with the Barghest. But she wouldn't enter the old man's room herself. It was all too soon, his death too recent, her loss still too raw. It would take her some time to come to terms with the old man's death, if she could at all.

On rising, Ulysses washed at the basin in the guest room. Peering at himself through bleary, half-closed eyes, he took in all the little nicks and scratches he had sustained battling the beast. There was even a bruise blossoming, like a blue-black carnation, on his cheek under his left eye, but he couldn't actually remember how he had come to sustain such an injury.

He decided that he would look a whole lot better if he shaved and so, finding soap and a brush, set to work, careful not to give himself any further injuries. One last dousing with chill water removed the last of the lather from his face and helped to bring him fully to his senses.

Sleep had come easily to him – exhaustion and alcohol both playing their part – but his slumber had been punctuated by dark dreams of savage dogs and desperate flights across the moors. The moors had given way to the sea and he had found himself at the edge of a cliff, white spume crashing on the black rocks below, like the distended open jaws of a predator. He heard the grunting panting of the black dog bearing down on him and yet he had been unable to take his eyes off the churning, corpse-grey surge of the sea. For there, visible between the rise and fall of the dark waves was a beautiful woman, her naked torso draped with the seaweed that tangled her hair, her pert breasts glistening milky-white against the black waters. He looked from her nakedness to her face and saw Jennifer Haniver staring back at him with anxious eyes, calling to him, her words subsumed beneath the crash of the breakers and the rattling suck of the sea as it retreated, preparing for its next assault on the jagged rocks. And then he could hear her and she was laughing. He watched as Jennifer's skin shrivelled and her hair receded until he was staring into the eyeless face of a mummified monkey. And then, with a flick of its fishy tail, the mermaid was gone.

Ulysses blinked sharply, chasing the last fading images of his disturbing dream from his waking mind. He dressed, Nimrod having already chosen him an appropriate outfit – and one in his size, no less – from the old man's wardrobe. He still felt slightly muzzy-headed, and as he dressed he had to sit down on the bed to put on his spotlessly clean shoes. But that wasn't down to a lack of sleep, but the result of an excess of medicinal cognac the night before.

Attired in a green-check suit and starched white shirt, the whole arrangement set off with a bold paisley-patterned bow-tie, Ulysses descended the stairs to be greeted by Nimrod who had a steaming cafetiere in one hand and a white napkin draped over his other arm.

The ever resourceful manservant appeared to be wearing the same set of clothes in which he had fought off the beast on the moors, cleared away corpses and cleaned up after them. And yet there didn't appear to be a mark on them. With perhaps the exception of a clean shirt from Hannibal Haniver's wardrobe, he must have been up most of the night doing the laundry.

"Good morning, sir. I take it you slept well," he enquired politely.

"As much as might be expected, under the circumstances." Ulysses looked around him in dazed confusion and then realised what it was that had surprised him. Nimrod had already cleared away the detritus from their final showdown with the beast the night before.

"You will find breakfast served in the drawing room this morning, sir."

"Ah yes, breakfast," Ulysses said, eyeing the coffee pot in Nimrod's hand. "A capital idea!"

Ulysses turned at the bottom of the stairs and made his way across the hall to the drawing room. Jennifer was already there and her appearance took Ulysses aback somewhat. He had been preparing himself to have to deal with a puffy-eyed, grief-stricken girl constantly dabbing at her tears with the scrunched up ball of a damp handkerchief and not the resolute young woman stood before him instead.

She looked better than he had ever seen her since they had first met on the moors the previous afternoon. For then she had just sprained her ankle and was suffering from the cold shock brought on by the trauma of the injury.

But now she appeared fresh-faced and with a rosy glow he had not seen before. She had washed and dried her hair, tying it up in a practical bun, and she was wearing an open-necked shirt and a new pair of Harris tweed knickerbockers. He could see from the way the knee-length sock on her right foot bulged that she must have strapped up her ankle well – it certainly didn't appear to be troubling her unduly – and had managed to put on another pair of walking shoes.

Ulysses found himself struck dumb by her simple, natural beauty – his English Rose had blossomed – and so it was Jennifer who initiated their first exchange of the day.

"Good morning, Ulysses. Is something the matter?"

"What? No. No, nothing." He realised he had stopped dead in the doorway of the drawing room on catching sight of Jennifer. Crossing the room, he sat down in an armchair next to the windows through which wan sunlight was streaming. "You're looking well," he said cautiously. "Are you feeling –"

"Yes, quite well, thank you."

"There's nothing quite like the smell of grilling bacon, is there?" he said, by way of making light conversation, anxious not to say anything that might upset Jennifer's seemingly cheerful mood, which he was sure must be balanced on a knife edge.

Nimrod returned and placed a plate laden with bacon, scrambled eggs and black pudding in front of Ulysses. Not only had he managed to rustle up a filling breakfast amidst the devastation of the kitchen, he had even found enough intact plates to serve it on.

"Looks wonderful, old boy," he beamed, inhaling deeply, savouring the succulent aromas of the hot food.

"Thank you, sir."

Having made himself scarce the night before when the much bigger dog had invaded his home, the smell of bacon and other such delights had drawn Ambrose the terrier out from his hiding place under the sofa. The dog squatted down beside Ulysses, hopeful eyes watching every forkful of food with expectant relish, but he wasn't even going to get a look in.

The dandy tucked in straight away, but, as far as he was concerned, the pot of coffee that Nimrod had produced was by far his greatest achievement.

"I'm sure you must ravenous after all your exertions last night," Jennifer said, placing her own knife and fork delicately together on her empty plate.

"What? Oh, yes," he admitted, still somewhat unsettled by her oh-so positive tone.

"Well, come on then, eat up. We're all going to need our strength for what lies ahead of us today, aren't we?"

There was something disconcerting about the way she was speaking so freely, a dark, disquieting edge to her strikingly cheerful tone. As far as she was concerned, there would be time enough to grieve later. For now, determination and a resolution to find her father's true killer was paramount.

"Um, yes," Ulysses managed through a mouthful of black pudding. "I'm looking forward to meeting Mr Umbridge."

Less than half an hour later, with breakfast finished and everyone suitably attired for a clear, cold day on Ghestdale, the trio, made up of the cryptozoologist, the dandy and his manservant, set off west, following the stony track that led across the moors in the direction of the Umbridge estate, Miss Haniver taking the gentleman detective's arm for support.

It had been cold out the night before, but certain that the beast would not be troubling him, he had made a bed of heather and bracken for himself in the lea of a rocky outcrop that sheltered him from the warmth-stealing winds that seemed to constantly scour the moors.

He had risen at first light, as the fragile light of the sun struggled to penetrate the cloying November mists and made his way back to the lodge. From his hiding place behind a dry-stone wall he saw a tattered curtain flapping in the breeze, tugged through the shattered remains of the French windows and wet with dew.

When he had reached the house after the others, the night before, all had seemed well. He too had thought the beast dead, or at least trapped within the warren of mine-workings underground. It was only as he was making his way home, scampering back towards the distant lights of the town, that he heard the blood-curdling howls and the woman's screams.

He had returned to the lodge at a run, but by the time he got there it was all over. It took some minutes for him to realise what had happened. It had been then that he had resolved to wait close by until morning, just in case she needed his help again.

It wasn't until the party were a good two hundred yards along the track – Miss Haniver making confident progress despite her injured ankle – that he left his hiding place and, careful as ever not to be seen, set off after them.

Heavy hobnail boots kicked away the wreckage of the devastated French windows, crunched over broken glass and entered the dining room. There on the table, lying under a blood-soaked tablecloth, was the dog. Yanking the cloth free of the animal's body the man turned his face away; the combination of blood, shit and putrefaction was too revolting to stomach even for him.

Hearing the sound of more heavy footsteps in the hall beyond, the man looked up to see his companion standing there, behind the splintered remains of the dining room door.

"Did ya find 'em?" the first asked gruffly, not bothering to remove the stub of the cigar he was smoking from between his teeth as he spoke.

"Only the old man," the second replied, "wrapped up in a curtain in the scullery."

"Bloody 'ell!" The man kicked at the remains of a shredded upholstered chair.

"The boss isn't going to be happy," the second offered unhelpfully.

"No, 'e's bloody not," the first scowled. He looked down at the corpse stretched out on the table next to him. "Come on, we'd better get on and shift this. We don't want anyone else coming round here and finding the bloody thing, do we? Come one, give me an 'and will ya?"

None too willingly his partner joined him at the end of the tables and took hold of one of the creature's back legs.

"And what do we do when we've moved the bugger?" the second asked.

The first took the cigar from between his teeth and smiled, the few yellow pegs of what teeth he had left looking like a row of discoloured headstones planted within the blood red cemetery of his gums. "What do we do then? Why, then we burn the place," he said, with obvious delight. "To the ground."

CHAPTER SIXTEEN

The Industrialist

Ulysses stood at the top of the flight of broad white stone steps, Jenny waiting nervously beside him, both of them looking up at the awesome facade of the mansion.

Umbridge house had been constructed in the Neo-Classical style. To either side of them stood great columns of white stone which in turn supported a grand pediment which was itself decorated with carved figures from Greek and Roman myth. The whole place looked more like a temple of antiquity, than someone's home.

Considering the imposing edifice in front of him, for a moment Ulysses felt butterflies of nervousness take flight within his stomach.

'Well, here goes nothing,' he said giving the bell-pull a tug.

A moment later a distant bell tolled ominously somewhere away within the vast complex of the building.

They had been able to approach the mansion unhindered, having not seen another human soul since arriving at the main gates half a mile away, down the gravel drive that snaked up to the main house through an acre of sparse woodland. For someone so keen on his privacy, Ulysses would have expected Josiah Umbridge to have had someone on the gate to monitor the approach of strangers.

For not only was Umbridge a recluse, he was also one of the richest, most successful men in the empire and, hence, the world. Umbridge's factories had proliferated across the North York moors, polluting the surrounding environment, in the process making him a very rich man. It was Umbridge Industries that provided other factory-owners with the factory structures themselves and internal machinery they needed to produce the automobiles, automata, steam engines, printing presses, traffic control systems, dirigibles, kinema cameras and scores of other mechanical mechanisms that kept every major city from Edinburgh to Calcutta running.

And of course Ulysses now knew that Josiah Umbridge had had his own part to play in Project Leviathan. He might be an ill man, as was reported in the papers, but ironically, if it hadn't been for his deteriorating state of health he would like as not have been a dead man by now.

Ulysses was roused from the recollection of his last fateful sea voyage by footsteps coming from beyond the closed double doors. There was the rattle of bolts being loosened, a handle being turned and then one of the doors opened a crack. An ancient face peered out at them through the gap, the sagging jowls, the bags of skin under the eyes and scraggy wattles of the butler's neck wobbling loosely as he looked from Ulysses to his female companion and back again.

"Yes?" the butler asked, managing to sound both imperious and irritated at the same time.

"Good morning," Ulysses said brightly. "We're here to see Mr Umbridge."

The butler looked down his nose first at Ulysses and then, even more disdainfully, at Jennifer.

"Mr Umbridge is not receiving visitors."

"He'll see us," Ulysses said confidently, his jaunty tone shot through with steel. Reaching into a jacket pocket he extracted his leather card-holder with his left hand and then almost dropped it as he attempted to flick it open. The butler could not help but be unimpressed by Ulysses' clumsiness.

The butler took a moment or two to read the information presented there on the ID – a moment or two longer than was really necessary, Ulysses thought – all the while looking as though he was being expected to survey the contents of a gutter press publication.

"This way please, sir. Madam," the Umbridge Estate's ancient retainer said, stepping aside and ushering them into the cavernous, echoing entrance hall beyond. Everything was cold and white and palatial, like some eccentric aristocrat's mausoleum, an edifice built to honour the memory of a dead man.

The butler was a good head shorter than Ulysses' own manservant – and even Jennifer was a good few inches taller, and able to see the top of his balding pate – but he still managed to look down at the two of them.

As soon as Ulysses and Jennifer were over the threshold, the butler assiduously closed the door again, shutting out the morning light, returning the white-stoned hall to its previous state of grey shadow, and then, as the two visitors waited for him to show them to his master, simply held out a white-gloved hand.

"I'm sorry," Ulysses said, confused. "Aren't you going to take us to see Mr Umbridge?"

"Your ID, sir," the butler said unsmilingly, "if you would be so kind."

"Oh, I see." Ulysses hesitated for a moment before handing it over.

"Wait here," he said, and then, turning on his spatted heel, strode slowly away into the depths of the house, leaving the two of them alone in the sepulchral atrium.

In the shelter of a sparse stand of beech, Nimrod paused in front of a high stone wall. It extended away from him on both sides. He had approached it from the right, where, one hundred yards away, it turned a sharp corner and headed off northwards across the moors.

Nimrod had parted company with his master and the young Miss Haniver as they made their way along the rough dirt road that skirted the edge of Ghestdale as it tracked its way towards the Umbridge estate. The estate, with its Neo-Classical style mansion set at the north-east corner, came into view when they were still two or three miles away, the house itself framed by formal gardens. The high wall which was blocking Nimrod's own approach to the house, appeared to encompass the entire estate.

It was at this point that Nimrod split from the other two, taking a divergent path which headed back across the undulating acres of bracken and heather towards the rear of the estate. While his master and the naturalist's daughter sought an audience with the industrialist himself, Nimrod's remit had been to try to locate the gamekeeper Rudge – assuming he wasn't ensconced within some Whitby drinking house, or out on the moors – without attracting undue attention to himself. But Master Ulysses had a feeling that the thug wouldn't be too far away, and Nimrod tended to agree. And of course, even if he didn't find the man himself, who knew what other clues or dark secrets he might uncover? Under the circumstances, a little, clandestine exploration could pay dividends.

Nimrod wasn't blessed with the near prescient powers that his master seemed to have acquired during his sojourn with the monks of Shangri-La, but he still had the sudden and uneasy feeling that someone was watching him, right now.

One hand on the butt of the fully loaded pistol in its underarm holster, Nimrod turned, half-expecting to see the burly gamekeeper, pork pie hat pulled down hard on top of his head, bearing down on him, ham-sized fists bunched, ready to give him a pummelling.

For a split second he thought he saw movement, as if somebody had just ducked down out of sight, but then there was nothing. One tussock of coarse, sun-bleached grass looking just like another.

Who was it? Who was out there? Was it the gamekeeper, returning to the estate after unleashing the monstrous hound on the Hanivers?

And then the uneasy feeling was gone.

He turned back to the wall. After making a quick assessment of the arrangement of the stones, Nimrod started to climb, his black leather gloves helping him secure a confident grip. As soon as he could see over the top – the stones there arranged so that their jagged points might cause anyone trying to scale the wall no small discomfort – he scanned the grounds beyond, his gloves protecting his palms and fingertips.

He could see Umbridge house at the top of the hill, a good mile from his current position. Beneath the house and its clinically symmetrical formal gardens, carefully tended lawns stretched down to a babbling stream, the lush green sward a stark contrast to the sombre, almost spectral palette, of Ghestdale itself. The stream itself had clearly been re-engineered to produce a series of pleasantly descending and carefully sculpted cascades that eventually emptied into a lake at the bottom of the valley. Around the man-made mere, a carefully-managed strip of woodland was nestled, protected from the moor-scouring winds by the steeply-rising slopes and the estate wall itself.

Seeing no one within the fastidiously-kept gardens, Nimrod scrambled over the parapet and dropped down on the other side, landing lightly on his feet among the drifts of autumnal leaves that had collected there. Keeping to the shadows on this side of the wall, Nimrod moved as quickly and as quietly as he could towards the leafless wood. For if the gamekeeper had a hovel anywhere within the estate, it would be there.

After what seemed like an eternity, the butler returned. He made no apology for keeping them waiting but simply said: "Follow me."

"I told you he'd see us," Ulysses said in a forced whisper, offering Jennifer his arm again.

"But what are you actually going to say to him?" Jennifer whispered back.

"Don't worry, I do this sort of thing all the time."

"Really?" She looked at him with genuine astonishment.

"Really. And usually I just make something up on the spot."

"You're not serious?"

"No," Ulysses said with a forced grin, "of course I'm not. Not really. Do you think I'd walk in here to confront the man we suspect of masterminding the theft of the Whitby mermaid and the Barghest killings without having some sort of a plan?"

Ulysses wondered if all the white lies he told would catch up with him one day.

The butler led them from funereal white entrance hall into a wood-panelled corridor – clinical and dustless – through another room another hallway, just like those before, and so on. Many of the rooms they passed seemed more like museum pieces, as if the stately home was open for public viewings, the rooms and their contents trapped in time, like galleries in a museum of antiquities. The place certainly didn't feel lived in. It was almost as if the fading Umbridge had actually died long ago.

That was until the diminutive manservant led them into a fire-lit study at the back of the house, and the warmest room in the place they had so far experienced.

The study was small compared with the palatial, columned chambers they had passed – sterile ballrooms, libraries, dining chambers and galleries, all unoccupied – but it was still easily as big as the largest room in Ulysses' own Mayfair residence. Much of one wall was taken up by a huge stone-carved fireplace, the fire that had been set within it blazing away, keeping out the wintry chill that seemed to pervade the rest of the house. Two massive leather armchairs, upholstered in a deep red, had been arranged so as to face the fire.

"Mr Quicksilver and Miss Haniver, sir," the butler announced to someone sitting in the chair with its back to the door, and so still out of sight.

"Show them in," came a reedy, age-cracked voice.

The unsmiling manservant signalled for Ulysses and Jennifer to approach.

As they rounded the side of the unnecessarily large chair, the voice said: "That will be all, Molesworth," and waved the butler away with a skeletally-thin hand, veins visible beneath the parchment-like skin.

Where Hannibal Haniver had appeared aged and withered by ill-health, the older Josiah Umbridge appeared even more so. He looked like little more than a skeleton. There was almost no flesh on his bones, beneath the waxy, liver-spotted skin and his out-dated black suit hung off his sparse frame as if he were no more than a glorified coat-hanger. As well as liver spots, his pallid skin was covered with crusted black pressure sores. From the waist down he was buried beneath a bundle of blankets so that his feet and legs couldn't be seen at all. There was barely a hair left on his head, other than for the occasional, intermittently sprouting strand of grey, which only served to give his head a truly skull-like appearance.

The dying man – and he certainly smelt like he was dying, the air around him already heavy with the smell of death and decay – regarded the two of them from the abyssal pits of his sunken eye-sockets and his thin lips parted in a deaths-head grimace.

"Miss Haniver; what a pleasure it is to meet you at last."

"Mr Umbridge." Jennifer hesitated, having not expected to be the one to have to speak. "Thank you for agreeing to see us at such short notice, um, without an appointment," she said, as if feeling under pressure to give some sort of explanation as to their presence there within his home. "I hope that we are not keeping you from anything important."

"Well, I could hardly refuse now, could I?" Umbridge replied, turning his deathly gaze on Ulysses. "Not when you come bearing such auspicious authority." Still without having actually addressed his other guest directly, Umbridge turned his gaze and his smile back onto Jennifer. "You're dear old Hannibal's daughter, aren't you?"

"Yes."

The atmosphere within the study suddenly became thick with expectation.

"And how is your father?" he asked softly, regarding

her closely from beneath beetling eyebrows. "I trust he is well."

"Actually, he's dead."

Ulysses watched Jennifer closely. She made the announcement without any hint of emotion. *She must still be in a state of shock,* he thought.

In the awkward silence that followed Jennifer's revelation, Ulysses became uncomfortably aware of the inescapable ticking of a clock on the mantelpiece above the fire. Its steady clockwork heartbeat seemed to draw attention to his own mortality, the way it moved on from one second to the next, unceasingly, with never a single one to be reclaimed, to be lived again.

"As am I," Umbridge said at last, his words doing nothing to alleviate the atmosphere of tension and despair.

Ulysses looked at him askance, one cynical eyebrow raised. "Really, Mr Umbridge. Then I must congratulate you on your most excellent impression of a living being."

"I am as good as dead!" the old man suddenly snapped, turning on Ulysses like a tiger cornered by hunters, knowing that its time has come, but determined to fight to the last. "I have a death sentence hanging over me. It's cancer, you know? Whole damn body's riddled with it. There is no cure, hence I am a dead man."

He stared at Ulysses, his caustic gaze intended to strip away the younger man's resolve, but Ulysses Quicksilver was made of sterner stuff than that and simply stared right back.

"I know what you're thinking," Umbridge snarled.

"Oh? And what's that?" Ulysses challenged, calling the old man's bluff.

"You think I deserve everything that's coming to me. You think I'm an old man who's lived beyond his time anyway, getting rich at the expense of the poor downtrodden working classes. I know what people like you are like – like that damned Darwinian Dawn – eco-terrorist sympathisers. You despise me."

"Do any of *us* look like we have much in common with the working classes?" Ulysses pointed out. "And I don't mind telling you, there is little love lost between myself and the Darwinian Dawn."

"But I can see it in your eyes, just the same," Umbridge persisted. It seemed that Ulysses' one chance remark had awoken the lion in the old man's heart. "You claim to care about the empire, about the legacy we are leaving future generations, as custodians of this planet. You think that industry has ruined this green and pleasant land. Well I'll tell you; without those dark satanic mills, your world would not exist. That is the reality we live in, and there is no going back."

Ulysses opened his mouth to speak, but then, for once, thought better of it. At this rate, the old man would have them thrown out before they managed to find out anything.

When he was certain that he had silenced Ulysses with his tirade, Umbridge turned his attention back to the young woman again. "You must excuse me, my dear," he said, his tongue darting out from his mouth to moisten the dry, peeling skin of his lips, "what is it that I can do for you?"

Jenny hesitated, looking to Ulysses for support.

"Go on," he said, encouraging her to speak with a nod of his head.

"Well, it's like this. Last night..."

Jenny broke off abruptly. Taking a deep breath, to calm herself, she started again. "Last night my father was killed, while yesterday afternoon Mr Quicksilver, his manservant, and myself were attacked whilst out on the moors."

"I am very sorry to hear that, my dear. Truly I am. Very sorry to hear of your loss, my dear, very sorry," the old man suddenly looking crestfallen. "Your father was a great man. If there is anything I can do to help at what must be a very difficult time..." he said, his corpse-smile returning, "please do not hesitate to ask, and I will do all I can to assist you. All I can."

"We have reason to believe that your man Rudge might have had something to do with the attacks," Ulysses put in forcefully.

"What, the gamekeeper?"

"I don't know of any other."

"I'm sorry, but do I know you, Mr Quicksilver? Have we met before?"

"No, but I met your man Sylvester last year, on the first and last voyage of the *Neptune*."

"Ah, yes. A most unfortunate business."

"You go in for understatement, do you, Mr Umbridge?"

"I see no point in being melodramatic about these things."

"But do you know why the world's most sophisticated submersible cruise-liner ended up at the bottom of the Pacific Ocean?"

"Perhaps you could enlighten me on another occasion. I'm sure you understand, Mr Quicksilver," – the man's breath was a rattling wheeze in his chest – "that my time is precious; more so now than ever. It takes no little amount of time and effort to keep a ship like Umbridge Industries on course, and I am not blessed with much of either."

"You met my father once though, didn't you?"

"Really? Quicksilver, Quicksilver," the old man mused, as if trawling the fathomless depths of his memory for any recollection that might help make sense of things.

"His name was Hercules. Hercules Quicksilver."

"I must apologise," Umbridge said, the same fixed smile on his face but now full of sinister intent. "I am an old man. My body's riddled with cancer. I'm afraid that my memory is not what it once was."

"But I bet you remember the name Project Leviathan."

"I'm sorry, Mr Quicksilver, but I thought you came here to talk to me about yesterday's dreadful occurrences."

"Indeed."

"And you believe someone in my employ had something to do with this poor young woman's father?"

"I would appreciate the opportunity to discuss the matter with him."

"And on what do you base such a ludicrous supposition?"

"On the fact that I was supposed to meet him at the edge of Ghestdale yesterday, only he didn't turn up and instead I had a run in with the Barghest beast!"

"The Barghest? Will you listen to yourself, man? You sound as bad as those melodramatic gossip-pedlars at the paper. Phantom dogs roaming Ghestdale, taking the lives of all and sundry? You'll be telling me that the Whitby Mermaid was the real deal and not a poorly-conceived fake next."

"Mr Umbridge, I saw the creature with my own eyes, I watched as it tore my father's... my father..." And then, unable to hold back the tears any longer, Jennifer dissolving into a fit of silent sobbing. Ulysses put a comforting arm around her shoulders and pulled her close.

"I am sorry, my dear, really I am, and I don't doubt the

veracity of your words for a moment," Umbridge said, leaning forward in his chair, as if this gave his words an added sense of sincerity. "This is indeed a most distressing matter. I don't believe that Mr Rudge is on estate land at present, but I am very concerned by what you have told me. Leave the matter with me and I promise that I *will* look into it."

The old man slumped back into the chair and closed his eyes, a long rattling breath escaping from his cancerous lungs. For a moment Ulysses wondered if he had actually passed away, there and then, right in front of them. Then his rheumy eyes flicked open and the darting tongue reappeared from between the pale drawn lips.

"Now, if you will excuse me, I am very tired. It's the cancer, you know? A little bit more of me dies every day. So, if you will excuse me, our meeting has quite taken it out of me. I would ask that you leave now." He looked at Jennifer again, with hooded, half-closed eyes. "And have no fear, I *shall* give this matter my utmost attention."

He closed his eyes.

Sensing another presence in the room, Ulysses looked up. Molesworth was standing there, regarding them with that familiar disdainful frown. "This way," the butler said abruptly, ushering them out of the study.

As Molesworth was about to follow after them, Umbridge's eyes flicked open once more, like a corpse waking from its eternal rest, and a wave of his long fingers halted the butler in his tracks. Molesworth looked at his master.

"Sir?"

"They know too much," Umbridge said darkly, his voice a sinister, serpentine hiss. "Get Rudge up here. Miss Haniver and Mr Quicksilver are going to be staying after all."

CHAPTER SEVENTEEN

The Freak

Nimrod looked at his watch for the umpteenth time and then back at where the sky was purpling like a bruise on the horizon. The persistent cloud cover had not let up all day, keeping everything beneath its foggy clutches in a state of permanent cloying dampness.

There was no point lying to himself; he was becoming concerned. Dusk was falling and after four hours neither Master Ulysses nor the young Miss Haniver had returned to the rendezvous point. And he had been waiting at the south-east corner of the estate, back on the Ghestdale side of the wall, since three o'clock that afternoon.

It was perfectly possible that Josiah Umbridge had been the perfect host and had invited the gentleman and his lady friend to stay for supper, but knowing that they had arranged to meet over an hour ago at the latest, Nimrod was now convinced that something untoward had happened to them. He had already tried calling his master using his own personal communicator, and there had been no response.

His own search of the estate grounds had born fruit, up to a point. He had found the gamekeeper's cottage at last – a stone-built refuge, that was not much more than a single-roomed hovel, various ill-kept vicious steel traps hung from nails on the wall, a clutch of dead vermin strung up on a line between two trees outside – not far from a rusted gate that led onto sheep grazing land on the far side of the walled grounds.

But he had not found the gamekeeper himself. A cursory

search of the roughly-furnished cottage had turned up nothing that linked Rudge, the Umbridge estate, or even Josiah Umbridge himself, to the Barghest or the late Hannibal Haniver in anyway. The one thing he had noted in particular was the cudgel hung up in pride of place on the plain whitewashed wall above the cold grate of the fire.

Nimrod was starting to wonder what Master Ulysses and Miss Haniver had uncovered. Whatever it was, it was preventing them from making the rendezvous as planned.

He had promised Ulysses' father that he would look out for his eldest son, no matter what. It was a vow that he took very seriously – even more so after Ulysses' return after an absence of eighteen months, in April that year, having been declared dead after his hot-air balloon went down over the Himalayas – one that he had sworn to uphold with his very life, if necessary. After all, it came, in part, as his repayment of a debt that he could never repay to the late Hercules Quicksilver for having saved his own life, in more ways than one, all those years ago.

For a moment he considered contacting Inspector Allardyce and the local police – he even got as far as taking out his emergency personal communicator – but had then dropped the brass, teak and enamel device back into his pocket. Until he had a better idea of what sort of trouble Master Ulysses had got himself into, Nimrod didn't want to do anything that might make what was already doubtless a dangerous situation even worse. After all, so far they knew that a crazed vivisectionist was involved, a brute of a man who wasn't averse to dishing out a good beating and, possibly, a powerful industrialist.

No, the police would only turn up in a whirlwind of flashing blue lights and wailing sirens, barrelling in there in their clumsy size elevens, and God alone knew what a man who revelled in cutting up living things, a desperate thug, or a man whose position of power and affluence made him believe that he could do anything he wanted, might do.

Leaving the police to their investigations into the Ghestdale killings – even though he already knew who, or rather so far, *what* was responsible – remembering the old adage that if you want something done properly, you'd best do it yourself, Nimrod set off west, following the wall where it demarcated the perimeter of the Umbridge estate.

This time, to avoid drawing attention to himself, Nimrod took the longer, and yet less exposed route, around the outside of the estate wall until he reached the rusted gate, close to where Rudge's hideaway lay.

The decorative ironwork of the gate made it an easy thing to climb, and dropping down on the other side Nimrod re-entered the estate wood. Still unseen, he made his furtive way back to the gamekeeper's cottage through the rapidly encroaching gloom.

Creeping through stands of elm and ash he saw the hovel as now nothing more than a shadowy construction growing out of the murk of the darkening woods. There were no lights shining from the windows and so it seemed likely that there was no one at home.

Placing his feet with care, and moving at a cautious pace – so as not to trip over an exposed tree root or catch his foot in the mouth of an animal burrow – remaining as vigilant as possible in the encroaching dark, Nimrod made his way to the door.

Earlier that afternoon, when he had first explored the estate, he had kept half an eye open for any signs that the Barghest had been there – oversized paw prints, the animal's spoor, claw marks in the trunks of trees – but he had found nothing. But then he hadn't approached the gamekeeper's domain from this direction before: he wondered what he was missing now in the dark, unable to even make out the ground beneath his feet.

Cautiously, one hand on the pistol underneath his arm, Nimrod eased open the door. The hinges complained loudly in the twilight stillness, the protesting metal seeming to scream into the November night. But, when no one shouted in surprise or leapt at him from the darkness, Nimrod stepped inside, closing the door carefully behind him.

Inside, the cottage was just as he had left it before, only now it was in utter darkness. Nimrod knew that if he was going to find anything else here he was going to need to light a lamp, despite the risk that it would alert anyone nearby to his presence within. However, that one slight risk was nothing compared to the terrible fate that could befall his master the more time he wasted here, blundering about in the dark.

He could see a hurricane lamp on a window sill, silhouetted against the window behind it: that would do. With the lamp lit, its warm amber glow suffusing the cottage, playing a game of cat and mouse with the shadows at the corners of the single room, Nimrod took another, closer look around.

Last time he had only really been looking for the gamekeeper, or any sign of a connection to the Barghest beast. Now he was looking for anything, *anything* that might give him a clue as to what might have happened to his master. And it wasn't as if he could just walk in through the front door of Umbridge House. That was how Master Ulysses had made his move and, chances were, that was what had got him into trouble. No, he had the certain growing suspicion that he had missed something the last time he had been here and that he was missing it all over again.

Standing in the middle of the room, he held the lamp high and looked all around him, peering into every darkened corner, at every piece of furniture.

There was a simple sink and a stove next to the small hearth built into the chimney breast. In one corner stood the gamekeeper's rough, unmade bed, a chamber pot underneath. In the opposite corner was a rocking chair with a knitted blanket thrown over one arm.

There were other seemingly incongruous homely touches – the rag rug on the floor, a picture of an old mop-capped woman, that might have been the man's mother, over the range, an anonymous brass trinket of some kind – but on the whole it looked like precisely what it was, the simple home of a middle-aged man with few, if any, attachments in the world, a man with simple needs, the torture of defenceless creatures being one of them.

Nimrod turned around to look at the other side of the room and felt something shift beneath him, heard the subtle creak of wood giving under his weight.

He stopped and looked down at the rug on which he was standing. Shifting his weight from one foot to the other he heard the creak again. Stepping off the rug, he took hold of a corner and lifted it up. Pulling the rug away completely, there, revealed in the middle of the flagstoned floor of the hut, was a trapdoor.

Nimrod's pulse began to quicken. He took hold of the iron ring recessed into it at one end and pulled it open. A waft of cold, earthy air hit him full in the face. He could see a set of worn stone steps leading down into the dank darkness below.

Laying the open trapdoor carefully down on the discarded rug, so as not to alert anyone who might be down there already, Nimrod crouched down, lowering the hurricane lamp into the hole.

Six feet or so down, the steps met with the floor of a rough-hewn tunnel, cut from the rock and earth that lay beneath the foundations of the cottage. Here and there he could see where tree-roots penetrated the underground passageway. He breathed deeply and caught the aroma of peaty soil and mould.

Who knew how far down the tunnel went or where it led, other than that, to begin with at least, it appeared to lead in the direction of the house? The steps certainly didn't lead down to a cellar – after all, why would such a small dwelling even have one – and it seemed as likely that the tunnel would connect it to the house, as anywhere.

There was nothing else for it. If Nimrod was to find out where the tunnel led for sure, he was going to have to follow it.

Lantern held high to illuminate his way, eyes peering into the darkness at the limit of the lantern's sphere of radiance, ears listening for any indication that he might not be alone down there, Nimrod descended the steps and set off along the tunnel. Taking care to place his feet lightly on the dirt floor, he had to crouch to keep from grazing his scalp on the low ceiling of the passageway.

The tunnel proceeded in a straight line for some forty yards until it reached another set of steps. These had been cut from the bedrock itself, rather than being laid stones, like the first flight, and were slick with water. Steadying himself against the sides of the rock-cut passageway, Nimrod descended still further, the uneven, steps twisting this way and that down through a chimney in the rock, a natural formation in part creating by the erosive action of water seeping through from the moors above and into the fissure-riven sandstone on which Ghestdale rested.

Reaching the bottom of this haphazard flight, Nimrod found himself on one side of a wide gallery, the roof of which ascended out of reach of the lantern's circle of light, and knew exactly where he was. He could make out the marks left by digging tools on the rocks around him quite clearly. The air was moist down here and Nimrod found himself pulling his coat tighter about him against the bone-numbing chill that permeated the tunnels.

He was inside the hollowed-out innards of an abandoned mine, any deposits of jet it might once have had having been stripped out long ago, possibly as far back as the end of the nineteenth century. It had since become absorbed into the Umbridge estate, providing a network of secret tunnels that connected the gamekeeper's cottage to the main house, Nimrod expected, and who knew where else? Nimrod surmised that there were half a dozen hidden entrance points up on the moors and possibly as far away as the coast and Beast Cliff itself that led into and out of the Umbridge estate.

One of them could even have been the shaft into which Master Ulysses had first bundled the Barghest. And if the beast had originated from somewhere within the estate, it may well have already been familiar with the tunnels, using its enhanced sense of smell to sniff its way out again, and back onto their trail.

The Barghest may well have known its way around these tunnels, but that did not change the fact that Nimrod did not. And so, although he might know in principle where he was, he didn't know where he needed to go next. And so the question remained: which way should he go now?

Hearing the skitter of stone on stone he held his breath. In the eerie stillness he listened for the sound again. And then, there is was; the sandpaper scrape of grit on stone. It had come from his right.

Nimrod set off. There was no point dousing his light – without it he would be utterly lost. Instead he reached for his holstered pistol.

He could hear the footfalls ahead of him quite clearly now, their pace quickening, any pretence at stealth rejected in favour of flight. His quarry was on the run.

Picking up the pace, Nimrod hurried on through the worked-out mine. The tunnel twisted and turned, the ceiling of bedrock undulating above him, so that from time to time he found himself having to duck again to avoid knocking himself out on the downward pointing rocks.

For a moment he saw the bobbing will-o'-the-wisp flicker of another light source ahead of him. But then it was gone. He came to a halt. The running footsteps were gone too.

Slowly, ever so warily, Nimrod continued his advance, trying to tread as lightly as he could on the sandy floor of the tunnel, avoiding the noisy ripple and splash of stepping into puddles. Gun in hand, he kept going, trying to judge at what location the second light had disappeared.

Ten yards. Nine yards.

He kept going at the same steady pace, pistol tight in his hand, muzzle pointing forwards.

Five yards. Four.

His steps slowed, footfalls near silent in the smothering darkness, the only other sounds disturbing the oppressive stillness, the *drip-drip-drip* of water elsewhere within the mine, the sound carried as hollow echoes by the eerie acoustics of the place, and –

Two. One.

– nervous, panting breaths.

Nimrod spun round, shining his light into the natural cleft within the rock face in front of him, taking aim with his pistol.

Something hideous and misshapen – a lumpen body, uncoordinated limbs, a face that was only human thanks to it having the requisite features – surfaced from the thickly-cast shadows like a phantasm walking through a wall.

Its equally misshapen mouth agape, fists like cudgels raised before it, pin-pricks of eyes amidst the mass of deformities that was its face glittering in the light of the hurricane lamp, strangled vocal cords giving voice to a terrible wailing howl, the horror threw itself at Nimrod.

CHAPTER EIGHTEEN

An Appointment with Doktor Seziermesser

Ulysses half-opened his eyes and then shut them again tightly, against the brilliant fury of the lights in front of his face. Aware of the glare now, he tried again, still blinking against the harsh glare. He could feel the raw heat of the bulbs against the skin of his face, hot as sunburn.

He tried to raise a hand to shield his face from the incandescent glare. It was only then that he realised his arms had been restrained at the wrists. And now he was also aware that he was lying prostrate on his back. That certain knowledge didn't help how he was feeling right that moment, not when he considered what had almost happened to him the last time he had come to lying on his back and restrained.

He tried his legs but these too had been strapped down, restrained by what felt like a leather strap around his ankles. Somebody didn't want him going anywhere in a hurry.

He turned his head as he tugged against the restraint binding his left arm. The old injury his shoulder had suffered nearly two years ago now – as his hot air balloon plummeted groundwards amid the snow-capped peaks of the Himalayas, the basket locked in a spiralling, deathly embrace with the Black Mamba's gondola – grumbled in protest.

He understood now: he had been strapped to some kind of operating table. His arms had been restrained so that they were at right angles to his torso. They were held tightly at the wrists by buckled leather straps and Ulysses could also feel a tightness just below the ball and socket joints of both his shoulders. And he was shirtless.

In frustration Ulysses pulled and kicked and attempted to arch his back, but all to no avail. There was another belt strap around his middle.

He still felt muzzy-headed, his recollections of what had happened to him prior to ending up in this most undignified and uncomfortable of predicaments a jumble of sepia-blurred images, like out of focus photographs. Focusing all his mental energies on recollection, Ulysses tried to piece together what had happened. If he could re-order his dream-like recollections perhaps he then might remember who it was that had done this to him and why? And if he could understand his enemy's motivations, then he might yet talk his way out of this predicament.

He remembered the meeting with the industrialist. He remembered being escorted to the front door by the dour-faced butler. Then he remembered the first itch of prescience at the back of his skull, a moment before the butler opened the door and a hulking silhouette appeared there, quickly resolving into the outline of the elusive Mr Rudge.

Ulysses was already going for his sword-cane and pushing Jennifer aside as the brute came at them, cosh raised. And there had been someone else with him, a snivelling weasel of a man. Ulysses remembered thinking that two against one weren't such bad odds but then his tingling sixth sense screamed a warning and he turned to see that it wasn't two against one at all, but three. As the butler came at him with the chloroform-soaked handkerchief, Rudge barrelled in too.

Distracted, suddenly forced to defend himself on two fronts, with Jennifer's screams filling his ears, he took on none of his attackers particularly effectively. His broken fingers didn't help. Rudge's cosh descended, black stars going supernova inside Ulysses' brain, and then the butler's doping cloth finished what the thug's beating had started.

Cold panic gripped his heart and squeezed, as Ulysses' mind turned to thoughts of Jennifer. What had happened to the girl?

Violently twisting his head from one side to the other, Ulysses struggled to see if she was anywhere nearby. He tried calling her name but his tongue felt thick and heavy inside his mouth, and all that came out was an incomprehensible splutter.

'Ah, I see you are awake.'

Ulysses turned his head in the same direction that the voice had come from. It took his addled mind a moment to realise that the words he had heard had been spoken with a clipped German accent.

An indistinct shape moved between him and the punishing lights. His eyes taking a moment to adjust to the sudden change in light levels, Ulysses peered at the features now sharpening into focus from the man-shaped shadow before him.

There was something unsettlingly familiar about the man's appearance, as he regarded Ulysses from behind curiously protruding, telescopic spectacles, a haughty expression on his time-worn face. It felt to Ulysses as if he must have once run into the man's son, or the man himself, only when he was younger. He was wearing what must have once been a white lab coat, but was now a faded grey, interspersed with patches of rusty brown.

And he could see other things now behind the man, beyond the glare of the lights – walls of crumbling red brick, metal work surfaces, a range of wheeled stands and gurneys bearing all manner of surgical instruments and devices.

The cold knot of nausea took hold of his guts and twisted. He tried to speak again, but panic and his sluggish tongue conspired to ensure that nothing comprehensible came out.

"I shouldn't try to speak," the other suggested. "I would just relax if I were you. It's better that way." The man wasn't looking at Ulysses as he spoke but was busying himself with laying out the tools of his trade, ready to set to work.

Ulysses swallowed, grimacing at the taste of stale saliva and old blood in his mouth.

He tried to speak again. "Where's Jenny?" he managed.

"Jenny? Who is this Jenny?"

"She was with me," he struggled, slurring his words with the effort of speech.

"Ah, I understand now," the German said, as he continued to prepare for whatever was to come next. "All in good time, Herr Quicksilver. All in good time."

Ulysses craned his head forward in an attempt to see what the man was doing. For a moment, in the reflecting glare of the lights, he saw quite clearly the serrated blade of a bone-saw.

Ulysses felt sick. With a sudden shout of frustration he kicked and bucked, a part of him knowing that it wouldn't make any difference, but the fighter in him knowing that he had to do something, that he couldn't just lie there and wait for this strangely bespectacled other to decide his fate for him.

"Now, now, Herr Quicksilver. Struggling will only make it worse."

With one last muscle-tearing convulsion of effort,

Ulysses relented and fell back on the table. His skin was cold against the bare metal, as the sweat of his exertions began to evaporate.

"Who are you?" Ulysses hissed through gritted teeth.

The man turned to face him again and this time Ulysses realised that his spectacles had been fitted with decreasing sizes of magnifying lenses, that could be flicked down in front of the main lens as and when required. They gave the impression that his eyes were too big to fit within the orbits of his skull.

"I am sorry, Herr Quicksilver, how rude of me. Where are my manners? You must forgive me. I was so caught up in my preparations... But, that is not important. I am Doktor Seziermesser and I will be your surgeon for the duration of this procedure."

Ulysses' mind raced. *Procedure? What procedure?*

"You!" he gasped. "You're Mr Bellerophon."

"I am sorry, but you are mistaken, Herr Quicksilver. No, I assure you, I am Doktor Seziermesser." Ulysses could hear the 'k' in doktor quite clearly.

Seziermesser. Seziermesser. Where had he heard that name before?

"I thought you had already met my employer."

"What?"

"I am afraid that it was because of me that he had to create the alternative persona of Herr Bellerophon. The mermaid's escape was the result of carelessness on my part. But do not worry, I have been suitably punished."

He held up his left hand – or at least the stump of where his left hand had been. In its place a prosthetic metal claw had been strapped to the knot of pink scar tissue that covered the nub of his wrist. The claw itself looked like it had been cobbled together from whatever had been lying around the lab that day.

"I am a surgeon, a master craftsman," Seziermesser continued, gazing at the stump and the artificial claw, a glazed expression on his face. "In fact, I like to think of myself as a sculptor, but one that works in flesh. My hands are my tools. That was why it was only right that I should lose one in payment for my recklessness. But have no fear, I have become quite adept at using this replacement."

The surgeon's voice belied no sense of malice or sarcasm. Instead he appeared suitably chastened, and seemed to bear his master no resentment for what had been done to him.

"It was only right that Herr Umbridge have his man show me the error of my ways. I was becoming distracted from the great work, my life's greatest accomplishment. Indeed, the greatest accomplishment in the history of vivisection!

"And perhaps, if I do a good job on you, when the great work is finished, perhaps Herr Umbridge will deign to let me replace it with something more... appropriate."

Ulysses watched as the man's eyes fell on his own hand, but was only half aware of the fact that it was his right hand which he was regarding with such lascivious intent. There was nothing else for it, nothing else he could do, and although he had tried the self-same thing already, he couldn't let this madman take him apart like a Sunday roast, and so struggled against his bonds again.

"Here, this should help you relax."

Ulysses felt the stab of a needle being thrust into his arm and gasped involuntarily. He was dimly aware of a curious sensation of cold spreading along his arm as the injection was delivered directly into his bloodstream.

The surgeon returned to laying out his scalpels, clamps and bone-saws. Ulysses felt the effect of the drug almost immediately, a strangely welcome warmth taking hold of his aching muscles and easing him back down onto the table, taking him to the very edge of unconsciousness.

But still that name haunted him. *Seziermesser* – where *had* he heard it before?

Heard it, or read it?

"Very good. I think we are ready to begin," the surgeon said, turning back to the operating table and Ulysses' prone form.

"Such a fine specimen," he said, starting to run the fingers of his right hand over the flesh of his arms and torso. His dancing fingertips felt like spiders scuttling over his exposed body. Inside Ulysses raged and riled in frustration but on the outside there was nothing he could do now to resist Seziermesser's probing touch.

Seziermesser. Seziermesser.

And then the memory surfaced from the depths of his subconscious like some great Biblical leviathan. Dark, forgotten domes, tanks of something like rancid primordial soup, indistinct shapes suspended in the slime – arms and legs, webs of skin between their digits, gills where necks should be – faded parchment labels and a name, written in a spidery copperplate; *Seziermesser.*

"Marianas," Ulysses hissed.

"Ah, yes. I understand now. I was still a young man then, a protégé of the late Doktor Waldman, a leader in my field; a trail-blazer, you might say. Just defected from the Frankenstein Corps – with your father's help, as it happens – with wonderful new opportunities ahead of me. And then it all went wrong, but not as a result of *my* work, I can assure you!"

"But that is all in the past. What we are concerned with today is the future, Herr Quicksilver; the future of the human race. So, let us begin."

Ulysses tried to say something else, but his thoughts were becoming clouded. It was as if he were sinking into himself, his mind wandering in a world of its own, as if mind and body were no longer quite one.

A piercing scream cut through the fastidious quiet of the operating theatre, rebounding from the broken brick walls.

"Ah, such sweet music," Seziermesser said distractedly, as if savouring the agonised sound of a body in torment, and then, flicking another lens down in front of his glasses, returned to his work.

Dreamily Ulysses turned his head in another attempt to see what the doktor was doing. Eyes struggling to focus, he saw the crimson tip of the scalpel blade and then watched as it entered the meat of his arm again, as the surgeon made a neat incision right around his arm, just below the ball and socket joint of his shoulder, the man apparently unperturbed by the screaming that now filled the dank chamber.

And in the split second before he lost consciousness, lost in a world of shock and pain, Ulysses realised that the screams were his own.

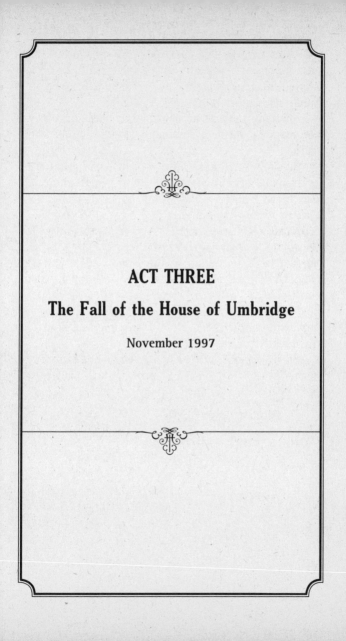

ACT THREE

The Fall of the House of Umbridge

November 1997

CHAPTER NINETEEN

The Menagerie

"There. There it is again," the creature slurred, angling its chin upwards and putting its head on one side, as if that, in some way, helped it to hear more clearly. But there certainly wasn't anything wrong with its hearing – despite everything else that appeared to be physically wrong with it – for Nimrod could hear the sound now too, a gaggle of mewling voices, yammering cries and woeful wails.

Nimrod found it hard to think of the creature as a man: it was the deformities that did it. He looked at the poor wretch again as they moved through the semi-darkness together. Nimrod was no medical man, but it occurred to him that the creature was nothing more than a collection of tumours, his wretched body hung with a conglomeration of abnormal growths. Most noticeable, of course, were those that disfigured his face, giving it a grotesquely asymmetrical structure. The right side of his visage was swollen with sub-dermal growths, that made his ear protrude far from the side of his skull and pulled his mouth into a perpetually open maw.

But the left side of his face hadn't been saved by whatever disfiguring condition it was that he was undoubtedly suffering from. His forehead above his left eye jutted a good two inches from his brow. Hair covered only some parts of his head, the rest bare areas of warty grey scalp. In fact, in the suffused light of the lantern, all of the creature's skin appeared to have the same rough texture and grey tone.

And his disfigurement wasn't just restricted to his head. Even through the rumpled suit of coarse grey cloth, Nimrod could see the lumps and bumps that afflicted the rest of his body. Again, the right hand side appeared to suffer from this condition the most. Certainly the creature's right paw was a twisted, swollen thing with fingers entwined into a club-like fist.

His semblance was more monster than man. It was little wonder that Nimrod had almost killed him on first sight, although he had soon discovered that it was not, in fact, the first time they had met. The wretch had been following he and his master ever since their run in with Inspector Allardyce of Scotland Yard.

Nimrod had not stopped to ask the deformed young man, but he would not have been surprised to learn that his condition was incredibly painful. The strain on his neck alone, in having to support the over-sized head, must have put a great strain on his whole body.

But for all that, he moved agilely and without drawing undue attention to himself, even though he was wearing a battered pair of mismatched boots. And then he stopped, head tilted to one side again.

"Creature, what is it?"

"I heard a scream."

"A man or a woman?" Nimrod pressed. He hadn't heard anything other than the distant background noise of plaintive cries and slack-jawed moans. Certainly nothing as clear and chilling as the cry of a traumatised soul.

"A man. And I would prefer it if you called me Jacob."

"I'm sorry?"

"I would prefer that you not call me creature. My father saw fit to give me a name and I would rather you addressed me by that name."

Knowing that the thing had a name only served

to trouble Nimrod's mind further; that something so inhuman should have such a human name.

"Very well, Jacob," Nimrod said uncomfortably. Something approximating a smile formed on the creature's blistered lips. "The scream: from which direction did it come?"

"The way we are heading."

Nimrod's heart went cold.

"Then let us press on."

As they wended their way onward through the dark Nimrod considered what a sudden reversal of fate he had witnessed. One minute the monstrous freak had seemed intent on smashing out his brains on the rock wall behind him, and then, in the next instant, Nimrod had found himself faced with a cowering wretch, as monstrous and as malformed as anything he would have expected to see stuffed and mounted in a glass display case as part of Cruickshanks' Cabinet of Curiosities.

"Don't shoot! Don't shoot!" the thing had wailed. Nimrod had been almost as surprised by the fact that the creature could speak as he had been by its appearance.

With his gun levelled at the creature, he had carried out his interrogation.

"What are you doing here?"

"I am here to save her."

"Who? Who are you here to save?"

"Miss Jennifer."

"You mean Miss Haniver."

"Yes."

"But how do you know she is here?"

"I followed her – I followed you all – from the lodge."

"You saw what happened there?"

"I have worked it out."

"You worked it out?"

"I was not there."

"You didn't witness the attack?"

"No."

"The beast had nothing to do with you?"

"Nothing, I swear on the Holy Cross – on my mother's grave – I had nothing to do with it!"

"Then how did you know to come to the house?"

"I... I followed *you* there."

"You followed me?"

"You and your master."

"How long had you been trailing us?"

"Since... since you left the town. Since the circus."

"Why?"

"You... intrigued me. And I thought you might be heading into danger."

"Danger?"

"On the moors, what with the Barghest killings and all. You were obviously strangers to these parts. I was concerned that you might fall foul of the beast yourselves."

"Well we did, didn't we? But you already know that. So why didn't you step in to help us then? Why didn't you intervene when Miss Haniver's life was in danger then?"

"I... was scared. It is to my great shame. It is why I have come here now, to make amends. Miss Jennifer is still in danger."

"She's not the only one."

The second revelation, as far as Nimrod was concerned, had been how gentle and well-spoken the creature was. But good manners and a pleasant speaking manner did not an innocent man make. So Nimrod kept his gun on the young man, just in case. He had no reason to believe that this Jacob was truly on his side at all. He had not had the chance to back up his bold words with actions yet, and until that time came, Nimrod judged that it was better to keep him at arm's length, and right where he could see him, with a gun trained on his back at all times.

And, in this manner, they had proceeded together further into the abandoned mine, following the snaking network of tunnels that led them ever onwards under the Umbridge estate.

"Look. Up there," the creature – this Jacob – said, suddenly stopping as he emerged from another low-roofed section of tunnel.

Nimrod quickly followed, and looked. There was a light ahead of them, an electric light.

Jacob turned his misshapen face towards Nimrod. "We're almost there."

There was a skittering of legs upon the uneven rocky floor at his feet and Nimrod nearly jumped as he felt something squeeze past him, its pliable body rubbing against his legs.

He lowered the lantern and looked at the floor. Beetles scuttled away from the light, long-bodied centipedes snapping at one another with nutcracker mandibles, fighting to claim a fissure in the rock for protection. Only they weren't beetles, Nimrod realised, or centipedes, they were both and yet neither, at the same time grotesque man-made creations that were all legs, chitin and mandibles.

He swept his lantern over the undulating mass at his feet. He saw things with the bodies of crabs, propelled across the floor with writhing starfish limbs. He saw something with the body of a snake scuttle past on half a dozen lobster legs. There were many-legged things, things with the bristling limbs of spiders, with the amorphous, oozing bodies of slugs, while something scampered across the wall, nearly brushing Nimrod's ear, before disappearing into the shadows again, that left him with the enduring, unpleasant image of a rat engulfed by an octopus.

"Abominations," the creature that called itself Jacob declared. "Blasphemies against both God and Nature!"

"Vivisects," Nimrod muttered.

"I beg your pardon, sir?"

"I rather feel that these are the work of another Creator entirely."

Placing his feet carefully, so as not to tread on any of the creatures if he could at all help it – not because he cared about the fate of the vivisects but simply because he found the idea of squashed slug-bodies beneath his feet abhorrent – Nimrod took the lead now, the light from his lamp helping to clear a path through the seething mass of bodies in front of them.

And then they were on the other side of the glistening black cavern, Nimrod and his unexpected companion. Ahead, the mined out cave gradually gave way to an obviously man-made tunnel, this one faced with stone. Its damp, moss-covered walls suggested great age to Nimrod. He wondered how long ago the passageway had been created, how old the foundations of the Umbridge House really were.

Had this tunnel been in regular use during the smugglers' heyday of the eighteenth century? He thought it likely. Who knew what had been brought into the country without the revenue men being party to it. Whiskey, tobacco, slaves? Or perhaps this tunnel had been used for more altruistic purposes, as an escape route, to get persecuted men to safety, following the network of caves beyond perhaps as far as the sea.

"We are beneath the house, I think," Jacob said, studying the tunnel with his head still on one side.

"I think you're right," Nimrod agreed. "Keep your wits

about you. We don't want to be discovered now."

The way ahead was lit by dully pulsing caged bulbs, positioned at regular intervals as far as the eye could see. Nimrod placed the hurricane lantern on the floor, at the mouth of the cave, causing a momentary commotion among the encroaching abominations, which slithered back across the rocky floor behind them into the oily darkness. He then set off again with renewed vigour, quickening his pace, now that the surface on which he ran was packed earth rather than moisture-slick, uneven stone. Jacob loped after him.

The passageway gave way to more stone steps, which this time took Nimrod and his companion back up into the bedrock, on which the Umbridge estate stood, he assumed towards the cellars of the house. The further they climbed, the more recent the building work appeared to be.

Reaching the top of the flight Nimrod came to a halt. Jacob stopped below him and looked up quizzically, his head tipped to the right. "What is it?" he asked.

Nimrod silenced the freak with a "Shhh!", a finger on his lips and a wave of his hand. Ahead of him was a network of rooms and corridors, vaulted cellars and storerooms that led off from one central sanded passageway. He could see the brickwork of other walls and further doorways through the archways opening off both sides of this passageway. He did not need Jacob's heightened sense of hearing now to make out the pitiful moaning voices, the dragging of feet – or other body parts – on the sandy floor. And the smell – the smell was indescribable.

Nimrod's grip on the gun in his hand tightened, one gloved finger tensed against the trigger. With his free hand he signalled for Jacob to follow him.

Placing his feet carefully again – this time to avoid grinding the grains of sand beneath his heels as much as he was able – Nimrod led the way through the cellar-dungeon.

He had only gone five yards when he came upon the first of the dungeon's prisoners. He surprised the thing, lying there in the near darkness, and cursed inwardly as it let out a yelp of surprise. Nimrod pointed his gun at the thing's face, his finger tightening on the trigger.

It had been human once – at least part of it had – that much he could tell from its face. But it could hardly be described as human now. It looked more like a human face had somehow become attached to a seal's body. The thing still had one arm – although the elbow seemed to bend the wrong way – but on the other side of its body it had a flipper. Its hide glistened wetly.

On seeing Nimrod the inhuman thing tried to pull itself out of the way, dragging its great body along by its one crooked arm.

Hearing a hiss of aggression from his right, Nimrod spun round, gun raised.

The seal-thing's cry of alarm had attracted more inhuman things. A figure emerged from the shadows contained within an archway. A head shorter than Nimrod, it walked on two legs, like a man, but its features were something wholly other. The roughness of the skin and the jaundiced yellow of its eyes reminded Nimrod of the lizard-creature he and Master Ulysses had run into in the sewers beneath Southwark, while the thin red sliver of a forked tongue darted in and out of its toothless mouth.

Where the seal-thing was naked, this creature wore a basic sackcloth shirt and trews, like someone incarcerated in the poorhouse.

And there were still more abominations crowding in on

them; things that were half-men and half sea-creature, the head of one – entirely hairless, its porcelain pale skin shot through with blue veins – swelled and then deflated again with its own pulsating rhythm, where there should have been a mouth nothing but the fronds of a sea anemone.

One squatted like a toad, its mouth forced open by a set of anglerfish jaws that were far too big for it. Another was only human from the trunk down; its arms were writhing octopoidal tentacles while the beaked head of some large fish sat directly on top of its shoulders. They were like something out of a Hieronymus Bosch painting he had once lifted from an art gallery, the denizens of some macabre garden of unearthly delights.

Nimrod tried to count how many of them there were, moving towards he and Jacob from out of the dank shadows. He reached twenty before another movement to his left distracted him from the task. Certainly there were more than he had bullets for. Perhaps he would only need to kill a few of them before the others gave up the fight.

Another peered around the corner of an archway, and for a moment Nimrod felt relief that there was another normal human being down there with them. The young woman looked at him with puppyish curiosity and then moved into the light cast by the flickering fizzing bulbs. Nimrod took an involuntary step backwards as he realised that the entire left-hand side of her body – the side that had been hidden behind the arch – was in no way human at all.

Half of her head was that of some overgrown insect, a lone mandible clacking uselessly from within the woman's distended mouth. Her torso writhed with unidentifiable pseudopods and she supported the weight of her albino body on a pair of crustacean limbs, as long as a man's arm and with one too many joints.

He bumped into something soft and pliable and spun on his heel again. The slug-like body, the size of a child with the face to match shifting and sliding across the inconstant, rippling flesh of the gastropod mollusc flinched, recoiling into its own mucusy mass.

Nimrod gagged. He was not one to have his stomach turned so easily, but what he and the freak had found down here, dwelling in near darkness under the Umbridge estate was something of another magnitude of appalling horror altogether.

Who would do such a thing? And how, against all the odds, had it been achieved?

As he was so ready to decry, Nimrod was not a medical man, but he knew enough about physiology to understand that any attempt to marry human flesh with that of another species should have resulted in failure and, like as not, death, as a result of tissue rejection.

In his moment of shocked hesitation, the things moved in closer again. He swallowed hard. It was time to take decisive action.

"Take care, Jacob," Nimrod said clearly, so that the other things present might hear him just as well. "They may be hostile."

Nimrod swept his pistol round in an arc in front of him. Instinctively, it seemed, the creatures moved back, as if they were fully aware of the danger the weapon presented. They must have seen such a thing before.

Nimrod set his eyes on the door he could see now at the end of the passageway; solid steel, with a small barred grille at face height.

He took a confident step forward and the gathered pack backed away before him. He poked his gun at a slavering, dog-faced creature and the horde moved away further still. Nimrod took another step forward into the space left by the retreating abominations. He glanced back over his shoulder and saw Jacob still close behind him, the pack moving in to block the way back behind them.

Apart from the occasional discomforting mewling whimper, snake-like hiss or epileptic tapping of chitinous claws, none of the cellar's inhabitants moved to attack them, or to halt their progress. It seemed as though the half-human things were letting Nimrod and his companion pass, almost as if they were keen for them to make it to the door and leave. It was almost as if the creatures were showing them the way out.

As he passed the abominations he looked at them more closely. The things looked back at him with pleading watery eyes. And there was fear there too. He became aware of inflamed knots of scar tissue, where one unnatural body part was joined to another.

There were other marks too, that were not the result of some abominable surgery; burns, grazes, contusions. And there was something about the condition of their skin, the way it clung so closely to whatever passed for a skeleton in each individual case – if they even had such a thing – sunken eyes and bony joints that suggested malnutrition in many cases.

The longer he observed them the more certain he became. These were wretched specimens indeed, but what made their already abominable condition even worse was that they were scared and abused, both mentally and physically. They had been half-starved and beaten into submission. Nimrod was almost amazed that hunger hadn't driven them to fall upon each other. Perhaps they were more human than he had at first realised.

But who could do such a thing to creatures that must once have been human, no matter how unlikely that seemed now.

The rough, broken-nosed face of one individual came to mind immediately: Rudge, the gamekeeper.

The last of the surgical subjects hauled its massive bulk out of the way – a creature with the pallid, hairless physique of a great ape topped off with the head of a child, a languid expression in its eyes, and strings of saliva dangling from its stroke-twisted mouth – and then there was the door in front of them.

Nimrod tried the handle.

"I might have known it," he said gravely, finding himself talking in a whisper, feeling suddenly self-conscious in the expectant stillness that hung over the pack. "It's locked."

"Then where do we go from here?" Jacob asked. The half-human, half-animal things – like the inmates of some macabre and grotesque menagerie – watched them with expectant eyes, as if hoping against hope that Nimrod and his companion would find a way to open the door. "Miss Jennifer needs us."

"As, I suspect, does Master Ulysses," Nimrod said, boldly putting away his gun and taking something else from one of his coat pockets. "But do not worry, I have yet to encounter a lock that I could not pick."

Having chosen a pick from the set on the hoop of metal he had taken from his pocket, Nimrod set to work. Pushing the shaped metal rod into the keyhole, he twisted and turned it, staring blankly ahead of him as he did so, tongue sticking out of the corner of his mouth, visualising in his mind's eye what he could determine from his probing.

He gave one last twist, and a sharp metal click echoed through the stillness of the cellar.

Nimrod remained exactly where he was. Had his release

of the lock sounded as loud in the passageway beyond? Was there someone approaching their position even now, armed and dangerous and ready to deal with them once and for all?

He waited; one second, two seconds, five, ten...

Slowly, Nimrod tried the handle again. This time the door opened a crack.

Not one of the creatures moved: Nimrod had half expected them to make a break for freedom, but they remained where they were, all eyes on him and Jacob as first one, and then the other, passed through the open door and into the corridor beyond.

Nimrod looked back at the gathered pack, as if giving them one last chance to escape, waiting for them to make their move. But no move came. It was as if by some silent consensus the creatures had decided that they had played their part, that they had done enough.

The fear was there in their eyes again, clearer than ever, as if they knew what it was that lay beyond the door and could not bear to confront it again.

Nimrod closed the door, but left it unlocked. He scanned the corridor ahead, lit again by strings of caged electric lights, and wondered what it was that the inhabitants of the bizarre menagerie knew, that he did not.

"What do we do now?" Jacob asked, looking at Nimrod with imploring, anxious eyes from beneath the lumpen growths of his face.

Nimrod put away the lock picks and took out his pistol.

"Now we face our fears," he said.

CHAPTER TWENTY

Last Supper

The snap and crunch of the crab cracker breaking open the cooked crustacean's claw cut sharply through the stillness of the vast dining room. The only sound other than the crunch and clatter of specialised cutlery was the crack and pop of the fire blazing within the vast fireplace.

The polished mahogany table that ran the length of the formal dining chamber was easily large enough to seat thirty, but only two places had been laid this evening. At the head of the table, sat in a wheeled wicker bath chair, was Josiah Umbridge, terminally-ill industrialist, host and kidnapper. Opposite him, at the far end of the table, was Jennifer Haniver, cryptozoologist, orphan and now reluctant dinner guest.

Umbridge scooped fibres of white meat from the crab claw with a fork and stuffed them into his mouth. He ate ravenously, like a condemned man relishing his last meal.

Hands gripping the arms of her chair tightly, Jenny stared down at her plate, having no desire to look her incarcerator in the face.

"It'll get cold," Umbridge pointed out, gesticulating with his fork. "Aren't you hungry?"

"Funnily enough, no," Jenny spat, continuing to stare at the plate in front of her.

There was half a crab, some lobster in there too, and the coils of an octopus's tentacles, some squid and chunks of eel, by the looks of things, but not one of the dead sea creatures that had been served up for the meal was wholly intact. It had all been presented with care and, Jenny had to admit that it smelt delicious, but none of it had been presented in the conventional manner. And besides, no matter how much the aroma of the fish might cause her to salivate, she wouldn't be able to stomach a single mouthful, considering how this little supper for two had come about.

"What is it?" she said, disgust in her voice. "It looks like leftovers."

"I suppose it is, after a manner of speaking. But it is also the finest food that a man could ever hope to feast upon. The fruits of the sea. Surely you would not deny a dying man the chance to be a little extravagant and spoil himself when it came to his last supper."

Jenny looked up, startled. "Your *last* supper?" What did the old man know that she didn't? Was he planning to kill himself, end his agony now?

"That's right, my dear. And so I am sure that you would not deny me only the finest company also for such a meal."

Despite herself, Jenny felt her cheeks redden at the old man's compliment. Perhaps she had judged him too harshly. But that didn't change the fact that she and Ulysses had effectively been abducted against their will. Ulysses himself had received a vicious beating at the hands of the vile gamekeeper Rudge, and she had been taken away by another, a snivelling weasel of a man who looked like his ancestry included a whole host of other vermin as well. Her steely resolve returned in an instant.

She looked at the butler standing patiently beside the door at the other end of the room. He looked back at her, his face an impassive mask of disinterest, and yet which also told her precisely what would happen if she tried anything.

For a moment she thought about taking her knife and making a run for Umbridge, holding him hostage until she was able to get out of there, perhaps even rescue Ulysses too. She considered the possibility for a moment and then dismissed the idea. There was no way she would be able to get away with it. The butler would have Umbridge's heavies there in an instant and then who knew what might happen to her. She had no idea how long the old man's tolerance of her might last, how deep his feelings for her ran; she doubted deep enough to stop him killing her. No, he had something else in mind, she was sure of it, something far more important than the imagined romance with a girl more than a third of his own age.

"Perhaps you would like some wine?" her host and abductor suggested, as he champed away at a mouthful of rubbery octopus flesh. "Molesworth, wine for our guest."

Jenny gazed at Umbridge in disbelief. How could he be so relaxed, carrying on as if she were a willing participant in this fiasco?

"I know," Umbridge laughed, catching her eye. "Chardonnay is not to your liking; you would prefer the claret. Well, hang convention! This is a special occasion. Have what you want."

"What I want?" Jenny seethed, no longer able to contain her frustration and despair in the face of the man's unwarranted good humour. "What I want? What I want is to not be forced to remain in this house a moment longer against my will. What I want is to know what you have done with Mr Quicksilver. What I want is to know why my father had to die!"

"That was a most unfortunate... accident." Umbridge stated flatly.

"An unfortunate accident?" Jenny screamed at him down the length of the table. "He was torn apart by some monstrous dog that, we believe, was under the control of your man Rudge!"

"Please, my dear," Umbridge said, picking up his wine glass and taking a sip. "You are disturbing the ambience. I am trying to enjoy my last meal as a human being."

"Oh, I'm sorry!" Jenny shrieked. "Perhaps you would prefer it if I ate up my food like a good little girl?"

Picking up her plate she hurled it towards the fireplace, the fine bone china smashing to smithereens against the cast iron grate. Crab meat and squid sizzled and popped on the white-hot logs.

For a moment her eyes alighted upon the hideous shrivelled thing that had been mounted in a glass display case on the mantelpiece above the fire. Something not quite fish and yet not quite mammal.

"You really should drink something," Umbridge said, carefully placing his cutlery on the table, his hands bunching to fists, knuckles whitening, his voice suddenly steel.

"Well, here's to you!" Raising her glass to the seething old man at the other end of the table, standing she shot him a grim smile through the tears now streaming down her cheeks and made her toast. "Up yours!" she said and tossed the wineglass into the fire after the plate.

"That was foolish," he said icily, taking another swig of wine from his own glass. "I am told that it will help make the experience that much easier to bear."

"What? What experience?"

He regarded her with an intense, gimlet gaze, all signs of good humour gone from his face.

"The world is changing, my dear, and I, for one, do not intend to be left behind."

"Left behind? But you're dying, you said so yourself," Jenny sobbed, confused and upset, trying to make sense of the madness unfolding around her and into which she felt like she was falling, deeper and deeper.

"This body is dying," he stated matter-of-factly, "but I do not intend to die with it."

"What are you talking about?" she screamed.

"I am going to ascend this pathetic mortal frame of mine. I have spent too long building my company, lived through too much to lose it all now... to cancer! The inheritors of Darwin's legacy will have to create a new classification for me, for I shall be the first of a new species. I shall become *homo superior*. The textbooks will have to be re-written in my honour."

"What?" she gasped, cruel realisation slowly dawning on her.

"You were right, Miss Haniver," Umbridge said, his voice calm again. "The creature that killed your father was just one step on the way to achieving perfection and the accomplishment of my dream – every man's dream – the desire for immortality. I do not intend to die today or tomorrow, or whenever fate and the cancer consuming my body choose." A dark smile crept across his face. "I do not intend to die at all."

Jenny collapsed back into her chair as she realised that she was at the mercy of a madman, the sheer level of insanity on display too much to cope with.

"Our planet is sick," Umbridge went on. "This country, the empire, the whole world, is sickening, is changing. Every day it becomes ever more polluted and no matter what Prime Minister Valentine and his toadies might say, we are long past the point of no return. No, this is what our world has become, and we should embrace that change, as failed custodians of planet Earth.

"I shall be the first of this wondrous new species. But if I am to be father to a new race, I shall need a consort," Jenny stared at him in horror, mouth open in a silent scream, body frozen rigid with terror, "which is where you come in. A much preferable choice than the scullery maid I had marked down for that purpose, I must say, my dear, to your credit. You know, you really should drink something."

"You're mad," Jenny spluttered, finding her voice again, and, with it, the ability to move. She began to lift herself out of the chair, keeping her eyes on Umbridge's right-hand man all the time.

There was nothing else for it now. She grabbed the knife with her right hand. She had to get out of there now. She had to try, no matter what they might do to her, no matter how hard she had to fight. Anything, even death, had to be better than the horrific fate Umbridge had in mind for her.

Umbridge nodded to someone over Jenny's shoulder. She glanced back to see Rudge and his weasely accomplice closing on her position, having entered by some disguised doorway at the back of the room.

Jenny was still half out of her chair when the two rogues made a grab for her.

She spun round, lashing out with the knife in her hand as she did so. For a moment she felt resistance as the serrated edge made contact with something and then froze in shocked surprise as she saw blood beading across the burly gamekeeper's cheek and the bridge of his nose. He put a hand to his face and then looked at the blood now painting his fingertips.

"Bitch!" Rudge snapped and struck out with the flat of his ham-sized hand, slapping her hard across the face.

Stunned, Jenny lost coordination, making it all the

more easy for the two ruffians to restrain her and drag her from the room.

The heels of her walking boots kicked against the polished floorboards as she tried to do something – anything – in the hope of breaking free and somehow, against all the odds, getting away. The pain in her ankle was as nothing compared to her fear of what Umbridge had in store for her.

"You're insane!" she screamed as she was hauled from the room. "Insane!"

The young woman's cries echoing back to him along the sepulchral halls and passageways of the great house, Josiah Umbridge continued his meal – alone.

How will food taste after I have ascended? he wondered, as he tucked into a platter of roast pheasant, honey-roast parsnips, rosti potatoes and shallots. Indeed, how would he experience any of his senses through his new body?

Would he still only be able to see in the conventional optical spectrum? Would he touch, taste and hear in the same way, smell in the same way? Surely not; not when his new body offered him so many more ways in which to experience the world around him. One thing was for certain, it would be far superior to the cancer-riddled, corpse-in-waiting he inhabited at present. As far as Umbridge was concerned, his longed-for transformation could not come quickly enough.

After the pheasant there came a magnificent dessert of crème Brule and chocolate chestnut truffles, and after that the cheese platter, the crackers and grapes as well.

Just as he was savouring his last mouthful, a telephone rang in an adjacent room.

"If you'll excuse me, sir," Molesworth mumbled before departing the dining room to take the call on his master's behalf. He returned only a few minutes later.

The butler approached the table and coughed politely.

"Yes, Molesworth?"

"Doktor Seziermesser is ready for you now, sir."

"Excellent," Umbridge said, dabbing at the corners of his mouth with his napkin before laying it beside his empty plate. "Excellent! The time has come, Molesworth. The time has come at last!"

"Yes, sir."

Umbridge let out an almost girlish giggle. "Tonight I say farewell to this feeble flesh, this mortal coil. Tonight I become immortal. Tonight I shall ascend to godhood!"

"Yes, sir," Molesworth said impassively and wheeled the wizened old man, hunched in his bath chair, from the room.

CHAPTER TWENTY-ONE

The Doktor Will See You Now

Cautiously, pistol cinched close to his waist, Nimrod peered around the cracked plaster corner of another bend in the passageway. "This is more like it," he said to himself.

The corridor ahead of him was the most modern-seeming and clearly the most regularly used of any they had come across so far. The lights were brighter here, gently humming fluorescent tubes placed at regular intervals so that nothing was left in darkness. The floor, rather than being made of compacted earth, or sand-dusted brick, was tiled. Tiles also covered the lower half of the walls, while above that they were painted a dull hospital blue.

Not that there was much blue to be seen. The place still didn't look like it had been cleaned recently, a thin veneer of grease and grime covering everything. One beneficent consequence of this was that Nimrod could clearly see the footprints of those who had passed along here most recently as smeary marks on the sticky floor tiles.

Three doors led off from the clinical corridor to the left, another to the right, and at the end of the brightly-lit passageway, a flight of steps led up to, what Nimrod imagined must be, the ground floor of the house.

Jacob waiting patiently behind Nimrod, happy for the more experienced man to lead the way into whatever danger might await them here.

Nimrod listened. He could hear unsettling sounds, a muffled sobbing from behind one of the doors, the rattling purr and rumble of an engine somewhere and, clearly audible above them all, the insidious dentist-drill whirr of an electrical cutting tool being put to use.

Nimrod took a step forward – feeling suddenly very exposed under the neon glare of the lights – feeling the adhesive resistance of whatever it was that covered the tiled floor with its sticky residue. He decided not to spend too long dwelling on what it might be; it had a greasy sheen and when he moved the smell of rancid fat rose from the floor.

He paused at the first door on his left. Over the other noises coming to him down the passageway he could hear a plaintive moaning.

He tried to handle. It wasn't locked.

He opened the door a crack. Dirty yellow light spilled out. The moaning voice became louder. Pistol at the ready, Nimrod pushed the door open fully.

The sight that met his eyes shocked him far more than anything he had so far witnessed within this den of vivisection and madness.

Master Ulysses lay huddled on the sparse straw mattress of a pallet bed. He was rocking from side to side, his eyes tight shut, hair plastered to his head with sweat, his abused body wet with it.

From the waist up he was naked – his jacket and blood-stained shirt had been laid carefully over a wooden stool. The dark blooms of bruises were visible over his ribs, his chest, his back. His face was pale, his eyes grey-ringed hollows, the bandages bound around the stump of his left arm crimson with blood.

Without pausing to check whether the coast was clear, Nimrod ran to his master's side, and fell on his knees beside the shabby cot. Encircling him with both his arms, Nimrod hugged him close, rocking backwards and forwards in time with the deliriously moaning man, tears streaming down his face.

"It's alright, sir. I'm here now. It's alright," he whispered softly, into Ulysses' ear. "It's alright. They can't hurt you anymore. I wouldn't let them hurt you anymore."

He manoeuvred his right hand and examined the stump of his master's arm by touch alone. He could feel the nub of clean-cut bone beneath the folds of skin that had been roughly-stitched together over the severed humerus.

Ulysses flinched at Nimrod's touch, his constant moaning becoming more pained, but still his eyes remained closed.

"It's alright now," Nimrod repeated, stroking the delirious man's sweat-slick hair out of his face, his own freely-flowing tears splashing onto Ulysses' eyelids. "It's going to be alright."

Hearing the scraping drag of clubfeet on the tiled floor of the cell, Nimrod looked up and for a moment appeared almost surprised to see the lumpen-headed Jacob standing there.

The lips of the freak's sagging mouth moved, as if he was about to speak, and then he seemed to think better of it. He had no words for what had happened here.

Nimrod stared at the other plaintively, with an expression of desperation, as if pleading with the malformed young man to help, to do something – anything. And then his features took on a terrifying aspect, tightening into a look of unadulterated hatred, the eyes hardening to diamond, cold and piercing, the tears blinked away in a moment.

"Someone is going to pay for this," he hissed with barely restrained fury. "Someone will pay!"

Jacob took a nervous step backwards in the face of Nimrod's rage.

Carefully laying his master back onto the sweat-drenched mattress and pulling a discarded grey blanket from the foot of the bed over his shivering form, Nimrod sprang to his feet.

"Watch him," he instructed Jacob, in a voice that brooked no debate, and strode from the room.

Pistol in hand, Nimrod proceeded along the empty passageway and stopped outside the second door. Putting his ear to the unsmoothed wooden planks, he listened.

The sound of sobbing came from beyond. Nimrod had little doubt who it was making them, although as to her current condition, that was another matter altogether.

And there was something else. Mingled with the stale disinfectant and unwashed bodies smell wafting through the corridor, another aroma seemed to ooze from under the door, the ammonia and dung smell of terrified animals.

He tried the handle. The door was unlocked, like the last.

Eschewing stealth for urgency now, he stepped boldly into the room. In was much like the last, except that a matted mess of rotten straw and faeces covered the floor here. It looked like it had been used as a holding pen for animals – before they were subjected to the incomprehensible whims of an over-eager surgeon. Another door in the far corner of the room connected the stinking cell to the room beyond, from which came the unmistakeable rattling whirr and squeal of mechanical cutting blades.

It was as he had expected; Miss Haniver sat sprawled against the wall on the other side of the dimly-lit cell, hands pulled up above her head, bound together with cord at the wrists which had then been tied again to a rusted iron ring hammered into the wall. The young woman's ankles had been bound as well, the cord cutting into the puffy flesh of her sprained right ankle in particular. And she had been gagged, but that didn't stop her sobs and couldn't hold back her tears of terror.

At first she pulled back, seeing Nimrod silhouetted there within the doorway, the brighter light of the passageway behind him, turning him into a shadow whose body language spoke of deadly intent. But then, as he entered the room, terror was replaced by a surge of relief and her sobs of resigned despair became gasping sobs of delight.

Unsheathing a pocketknife, Nimrod cut through the cords binding her wrists and her ankles. He helped her to her feet and then, putting a finger to his lips, he helped her pull the gag free.

The two of them stood there for a moment in the stinking cell, listening to the sound of the powered cutting blade, the young woman attempting to read Nimrod's intentions from his steely expression. Placing the knife into her shaking hands, he guided her back towards the door, from there into the corridor, and then to the cell where he had left his master. Before opening the second cell door, he fixed her with his sapphire stare and put a finger to his lips. Only then did he direct her through it.

Ignoring the involuntary sobbing gasp he heard, Nimrod re-entered the holding pen and approached the door in the far corner. With a dying whine, he heard the mechanical cutter come to a stop.

Pressing himself against the damp brickwork beside the door, he tested the handle. It turned with a click.

He froze. Had whoever was on the other side heard it too?

He waited, his breath shallow, his heart beating a tattoo of adrenalin-heightened anticipation against his ribcage.

He heard voices, and they were coming his way. Pistol at the ready once more, he prepared to meet whoever was approaching. Rubbing his eyes with the back of a sleeve he pulled at the handle and opened the door just a fraction, trying to get a glimpse of who, or what, awaited him on the other side.

From what Nimrod could see, it looked like the room beyond was decorated in the same way as the neon-lit corridor outside – all white tiles and blue paint – but here they were stained with the rust-red traces of dried blood.

The sour smell of disinfectant, the strong iron reek of blood, and something else – something strangely familiar, like aniseed mixed in with the rancid meat smell of the laboratory – permeated the place.

"Take him back to the cell," he heard someone say in a clipped German accent. "The anaesthetic will start to wear off soon." Nimrod didn't recognise the voice.

"Right you are, doc," he heard another man say. This voice he knew; it belonged to Rudge the gamekeeper. He had tracked him down at last.

"And if I were you, I'd make sure I wasn't in the same room as Mr Umbridge when he comes round," the German went on. "It might take him a little time to... adjust."

"Don't worry, I wasn't planning on being," Rudge replied, his voice receding.

Someone walked right past the door – grubby, once-white lab-coat, shock of untidy grey hair, long vulcanised rubber gloves, and strangely-lensed spectacles – their sudden appearance startling Nimrod.

He pressed himself flat against the wall, holding his breath. For a moment he considered simply bursting into the room and taking on the peculiar scientist. But whatever thoughts of vengeance he might now harbour in his heart – and he was not a man to let a trespass go unpunished – acting on them would have to wait.

What was of prime importance now was finding a way of putting right the wrong that had been done to Ulysses Quicksilver.

He was going to have to choose his moment carefully. Someone had amputated Master Ulysses' arm with surgical precision and Nimrod planned to make that same someone undo the damage he had caused, ideally reversing the procedure, if he could. If not, then the faithful retainer's wrath would know no bounds.

There was the sound of movement, like something large – something very large – moving sluggishly around inside the room. There was a sudden crash as a tray of metal tools was sent cascading onto the tiled floor.

"Please be careful, Mr Rudge," the German's voice came again.

"I can't 'elp it, like. Its legs are 'alf asleep as well. How much of the knock-out juice did you give it?"

"Do I tell you how to do your job, Mr Rudge?"

Nimrod did not hear the gamekeeper's answer as the sluggish thing he was trying to shift bashed into a cabinet. But he heard the doctor's response.

"Then kindly do not tell me how to do mine. The rest of the subject should be anaesthetised enough that it can be guided but remains docile until Mr Umbridge can exert his will and take control of the body."

There was another crash.

"But I would not take too long about it. Anaesthesia is not an exact science in a case such as this."

"I thought you said you knew what you were doing," Rudge's complaining voice came again.

Nimrod heard the other reply with a *harrumph* of annoyance.

"Don't worry, doc. I know how to handle this thing."

The doctor sighed. "I know you do, and I do wish you

would refrain from tormenting it so. I would prefer not to have to perform another skin graft."

"I thought you weren't going to tell me how to do my job."

"But you have Mr Umbridge in your tender care now. You would do well to remember that, Mr Rudge."

The gamekeeper muttered something in return that was subsumed by more grating scrapes as whatever it was that Rudge was trying to manoeuvre dragged a steel gurney after it.

"I shall just check on our other guest," Nimrod heard the surgeon say as Rudge, and whatever it was he had with him, left the operating theatre, the German's voice getting louder as he approached the door to the holding cell.

The unkempt surgeon opened the door without a second thought and entered the pen. Before he had even clocked that his guest was gone, Nimrod grabbed him, twisting one arm up behind the man's back. With his other hand he seized doctor around the neck, putting pressure on his windpipe, so that the surgeon couldn't cry out and yet, at the same time, could see the gun in his hand.

"And who might you be?" Nimrod hissed into his hostage's ear.

Nimrod continued to squeeze the man's throat, pressing the muzzle of his pistol into the soft flesh under his jaw.

"And, before I let you answer, just remember that I can carry out a little operation of my own in a split second – a craniotomy, if you like. I can transplant your brain from inside your skull to the wall behind us with one simple incision. So, your name."

"Seziermesser," the German croaked as Nimrod eased the pressure on his windpipe slightly. At the same time he increased the pressure on the arm he had forced behind the man's back.

"Well done, Doktor Seziermesser. Very good. Now I take it that you are the one who removed Mr Quicksilver's arm, are you not?"

The surgeon did not answer immediately, as if weighing up the merits of trying to pass the blame onto someone else, but then obviously thought better of it. He nodded.

"Excellent. Excellent."

The pressure on Seziermesser's arm increased, almost to the point where his wrist was ready to snap. The surgeon's cry of pain was stifled by Nimrod's arm tightening around his neck again.

"Why?" Nimrod hissed sharply in his ear.

"For... For the great work," the doktor replied, as if that was all the explanation that was needed.

"But that was a mistake, wasn't it?"

Nimrod felt the man's Adam's apple bob as he swallowed hard.

"And now you have the opportunity to correct your little mistake, because you're going to put it back."

Nimrod eased the tightness of his hold on the surgeon's arm. After all, he didn't want to break his arm when Seziermesser needed his hands to operate on Master Ulysses again.

The doktor craned his head round, trying to look Nimrod in the eye. "But I can't."

"What?" Nimrod snarled, his anger bubbling to boiling point. "Why not?"

"Because it has become part of the great work. I no longer have it."

"Then you are of no further use to me."

Nimrod pushed the doktor away from him violently, hooking one foot around the man's ankles and pulling his feet out from under him. The surgeon went sprawling in the muck and mouldering straw that covered the cell floor.

Gripping his pistol firmly in two hands, Nimrod took aim and began to squeeze the trigger.

"Wait!" the other screeched, turning desperate lens-magnified eyes on his would-be executioner, holding up his hands as if in surrender. It was then that, for the first time, Nimrod saw that the surgeon's own left hand was missing, a two-pronged metal claw poking out of the sleeve of his filthy coat.

"Why?" Nimrod said coldly. "You no longer have the arm, ergo you cannot make amends for your crime, hence you are of no further use to me. You have seen my face, you know I'm here. I cannot allow you to live."

"No, I-I said I don't have *his* arm," the doktor stammered, desperate for his plea to be heard before Nimrod shot him. "But I do have another. Please, just don't shoot me!"

Nimrod slowly lowered the gun. The surgeon continued to regard him with wide, anxious eyes.

"Another arm?"

Tentatively, never once taking his eyes off Nimrod, the man struggled to his feet, pushing at the stones of the floor with his crude claw.

"It's this way," he said, indicating the door to the operating theatre. "Come this way."

CHAPTER TWENTY-TWO

A Fate Worse Than Death

He woke to the sound of distant roaring. It was a terrible, savage sound, a sound like fury, a sound like bloodlust, a sound like nothing he had ever heard before – the bellow of a bull, the roar of a lion and the scream of a man all rolled into one. It spoke of rage, frustration, horror and madness. Such a sound could surely only be made by a creature from his nightmares, not by any actual living thing.

Perhaps, Ulysses Quicksilver considered, he was delirious or trapped in some waking nightmare.

He blinked his eyes and saw three figures standing there looking down at him, outlined by grimy yellow light. There, to his right, was Jennifer, holding his hand tightly, and that knowledge and her touch were enough to make him want to smile.

He raised his head. Pain rolled around his skull, as if a heavy metal ball was trapped in there, forcing him to lie back and making him close his eyes. But before he did so, he saw that there was someone else standing by the door, beyond the three, someone who looked like his head should be too heavy for his neck to support.

He lay still for a moment before opening his eyes again, and found Jennifer's tear-stained face once more. As he gazed into the young woman's glistening eyes he couldn't quite shake the feeling that there was something he had forgotten, something that he really should try to remember. It was like a memory-shaped hole inside his head, a fading thought like a dream that, on waking, refuses to be forgotten, wanting to be remembered.

But as he struggled to recall what it was that he really should have remembered, a dull ache grew within his mind, as if the effort of recollection was too much, an ache that began to permeate every part of his body, from his arms to his legs.

His arms... It was something about his arms...

Ulysses moved his gaze from his dear, sweet Jenny to the tall, lean figure, standing at the foot of the cot he was lying on. There stood Nimrod, looking like some grim-faced guardian angel, as stern as Ulysses had ever seen him look. He had his arms folded in front of him, his gun in his right hand, cocked and ready.

And then suddenly he was seeing Nimrod in his mind's eye, tears streaming down his face – which was most unlike the old, emotional cold fish that he was – and he heard his manservant's voice in his ear again, as if from far away: *"It's alright now. It's going to be alright."*

He turned from Nimrod to the figure to his left, the one who was monitoring a drip that had been set up next to his bed.

And then the memories came flooding back, in a torrent of unmitigated horror and excruciating agony.

"No!" Ulysses screamed, suddenly finding his voice, drawing himself up at the head of the bed, anything to get away from the maniac surgeon.

"He is awake," Doktor Seziermesser said with unbelievable calm.

"It's alright, Ulysses," he could hear Jenny saying, but his mind refused to believe that it could be, not with that scalpel-wielding madman there in the room.

"No! Get him out of here!" he bawled. His desperate eyes fixed on Jennifer, his imploring gaze transfixing her own. "You don't know what he did to me!"

"But it's alright now, Ulysses."

This had to be a dream; some sick nightmare. Jennifer didn't know what she was saying! It couldn't be real, because the reality of the situation was too terrible to bear.

Recalling what the unbearable truth was now, remembered pain lancing his body, Ulysses pulled his hand from her desperate grasp and felt for the stump of his left arm. But before his fingers reached the bony nub he felt them come into contact with a covering of coarse hair.

Surprise seizing hold of him again, he looked at what his hand had found.

Black fur covered leathery grey skin, stretched taut over a pronounced and unusual musculature.

The agitated Ulysses traced the shape of the arm from the overly-long fingers and the grey leather palm of the hand to where stitching formed the boundary where his own shoulder ended and the primate's arm began.

"What have you done?" he shrieked at the vivisectionist.

"What had to be done," Nimrod said frankly.

Ulysses' turned back to his most trusted companion.

"Nimrod," he gasped, "he's given me a monkey's arm!"

"It is that of a chimpanzee, actually," Seziermesser corrected him, "not a monkey."

Ulysses' appalled stare returned to the surgeon.

"You did this to me!" he screamed, rising from what he now realised was the operating table, as shock turned to anger and anger swiftly blackened to hatred.

Jenny clutched her hands together in anxiety, as if waiting for someone else to make the move to stop him. Nimrod didn't move a muscle but watched the furious

Ulysses advance on the maleficent Seziermesser, a grim smile playing about his lips.

Seziermesser took a shuffling step backwards, looking from Ulysses to Jennifer and Nimrod and back again, as if somehow hoping against all hope that one of them might intervene.

"*You did this to me!*" Ulysses screamed directly into Seziermesser's face, spittle flying from his lips. He seized the doktor by the lapels of his filthy lab-coat, with both his one human hand and the chimp substitute. The drip-stand rattled as the tube in his arm pulled taut. Releasing the doktor for a moment, Ulysses yanked the tube from his simian arm, a yellowish liquid dribbling onto the floor of the operating theatre. His nose curled as his nostrils were assailed by the acrid stink of aniseed and spoiled beef.

He grabbed hold of the doktor again and slammed him into a counter, sending a tray of tools flying.

"Where is my arm? *Where is my arm?*"

And just when everyone in the room thought that Ulysses was going to crack the vivisectionist's skull open, to everyone's surprise, including his own, he released his hold on the surgeon. Seziermesser dropped onto the metal counter with a crash, glass bottles tinkling together in reply.

Ulysses turned away in disgust, his whole body suddenly sagging as if the trauma of what had happened to him was at last starting to sink in.

Despite that fact that he had been either unconscious or delirious for God knows how many hours, his unerring sixth sense still played its part, awareness blooming hotly in his hindbrain. He turned in time to see Seziermesser, scalpel gripped tightly in his right hand, pushing himself off from the counter, using his blunt steel claw to give himself extra leverage.

Acting virtually on instinct alone, Ulysses lashed out. The bunched fingers of the simian hand struck the man, connecting with the side of his head before the surgeon could land his own poorly-judged attack.

The blow lifted Seziermesser off his feet and sent him crashing into the operating table, the drip-stand clattering to the floor beneath him. He lay sprawled where he fell, the scalpel slipping from slack fingers, a dazed groan of pain escaping his lips. His magnifying spectacles skittered across the floor to come to rest several feet away.

And then Ulysses was leaning over him again, pulling the dazed Seziermesser up by the lapels of his coat, until he was practically nose to nose with the surgeon.

"How did you do it, eh, doktor?" Ulysses growled. "How did you do this?" He glanced sharply at the ape arm clutching a handful of the surgeon's lab-coat. "*How did you do it?*"

Blinking myopically, Seziermesser craned his head backwards. Ulysses followed his gaze as the surgeon tried to see what was on top of the counter behind him. Ulysses peered at the collection of bottles, flasks and other vessels, eyes darting from one container to the next, desperately trying to see what must be right there, staring him in the face.

And then, there it was; an unassuming flask, with no label or other distinguishing marks whatsoever, other than for the yellow-green liquid that half-filled it.

Dropping the wretched physician again, Ulysses stepped over him and grabbed the container. He sniffed at the neck of the flask. The heady scent of fennel and spoiled steak rose from the liquid within. Ulysses' quizzical frown became a gargoyle grimace of utter hatred.

"We have the Alchemist to thank for that," Seziermesser said mysteriously.

Ignoring him, stepping back over the prone surgeon, not even giving him a second glance, Ulysses walked over to Nimrod.

"Get him out of my sight," he snarled.

"Yes, sir. With pleasure, sir."

Hauling Seziermesser to his feet by the scruff of his neck, without another word Nimrod dragged the unnervingly quiet surgeon from the room.

Nimrod led the slouching surgeon along the tiled corridor and into the dungeon-like cellars beyond. They stopped at last in front of a large steel door with a barred grille set into it at head height.

"What are you going to do to me?" the doktor asked at last, as if resigned to the fact that there was no hope for him now.

"Oh, it's not what *I'm* going to do to you."

A cold shiver coursing down his spine and into his stomach, Seziermesser turned and saw the other's dark, shark-like smile, revealed as they passed through the dirty cylinders of sodium light cast by the crackling nicotine-brown bulbs. Fear of the uncertain fate that awaited him consumed him completely now.

His despair deepened when he looked back at the door and a chill realisation seeped into his brain, as cold as glacial melt-water. He had not been here himself for some time – care of the test subjects had always been one of Rudge's responsibilities – but Seziermesser recognised it now, faced with the ominous, rust-streaked door again.

In the quiet of the corridor, Seziermesser listened. He could hear slavering sounds, pitiful mewling cries and a noise like an old woman weeping. And there were other, more sinister – more threatening – sounds too, animalistic grunts and guttural growls.

"No, please no," he begged, knowing in his heart that it wouldn't make any difference anyway, that they had passed the point of no return.

Nimrod raised a sarcastic eyebrow at the doktor, checked the load in his gun and then promptly shot the man through the left kneecap.

Seziermesser cried out in shock and pain, and fell to the floor. Nimrod roughly hauled him to his feet and opened the door. The sounds became louder and a pungent, vile odour assailed their nostrils – an acrid mix of rank, unwashed bodies, like fish guts and faeces. Shapes moved in the gloom beyond.

"Goodbye, doktor," Nimrod said calmly, before throwing him through the opening and slamming the door shut after him.

Nimrod returned a few minutes later, alone, by which time Ulysses had put on his borrowed shirt and jacket again, and introductions, of a sort, had been made.

The dandy looked almost like his old self again, other than for the fact that his shirt was stained with blood, his face was the colour and texture of a candle, and the incongruous grey chimp's hand protruding from the end of one sleeve.

"Nimrod," he said. "Give me your gloves."

Nimrod obediently took them off and handed them to his master. Without saying anything, Ulysses pulled them on, struggling a little to get the left glove on over his differently-proportioned ape hand.

And all the while the bestial howls and bellowing

continued.

"What is that?" Ulysses asked finally having managed to put on both of the black leather gloves.

"I can't be certain, sir, but –" Nimrod began, before Jennifer interrupted him.

"I know what it is," she said. "It's Umbridge."

"It's what?"

"Before I ended up down here, before all this," she said, taking in the cell, and, by extension, all that had befallen them in the dungeons beneath Umbridge House, with a wave of her arm, "he shared his plans with me."

"So what you're telling me is that the sick old man we met earlier, the old bastard dying of cancer, has since become... *that*?" Ulysses challenged as another bellow rattled the light fittings of the room.

The reticent Jacob said nothing, listening intently to the exchange taking place between the dandy, his servant and Jennifer.

"But that's insane!"

"I know it is!" Jennifer answered shrilly. "I know it's insane, but he told me that he was going to ascend... be the first of a new species, that the doktor was building him a brand new body, and that I was to be his bride." She broke up in another fit of sobbing.

The poor girl had been pushed to the limit, Ulysses considered, thinking about someone else for the first time since he had come round from his traumatised delirious half-sleep. But then he too had been pushed to the edge and then right over it. As far as he was concerned, somebody still had to pay for what had been done to him.

"Then our work is not yet done here," he stated coldly. "I think it's time we put the poor bastard out of his misery, don't you?"

He took in the faces of those around him: the darkly smiling Nimrod; the puffy-eyed Jennifer; the anxious freak.

"But before we do, there is one last thing I have to do here."

Choosing a bottle from among those lined up on the metal counter labelled 'Ethanol' he pulled out the glass stopper – his nose wrinkling as the whiff of industrial alcohol hit him hard in the face – and then started sloshing its contents liberally around the room; over the operating table, over the tiled and stainless steel surfaces. He threw the empty bottle onto the floor, apparently uncaring of the fact that he might alert other servants of the insane industrialist to what he was doing.

"Nimrod, a light."

Without hesitation, his manservant reached into another well-resourced coat pocket and took out something square and silver, that gleamed dully in the bright lights of the operating theatre. Ulysses took the lighter and flicked it open, spinning the flint-wheel as he did so.

Without a second thought, He tossed the lighter into the middle of the room. The alcohol ignited with a satisfying *whoomph*, orange and blue flames rising right across the room, licking up the walls and embracing everything within its fiery clutches.

"That's better," Ulysses said, a cruel smile on his face, and turned to exit the operating theatre.

Out in the corridor, Jacob turned to Nimrod. "What did you do with the doktor?" he asked.

At that moment, a high-pitched scream echoed through the cellar-dungeons beneath the house, briefly even drowning out the bellows of the beast that lurked, unseen, elsewhere.

"As the saying goes," Nimrod said sagely, "ask me no

questions and I'll tell you no lies."

Leaving the door open behind him, Ulysses followed the others as they hurried towards the steps at the end of the tarnished corridor. At least someone seemed to know where they were going, and it was Jenny who was leading the way, closely followed by Nimrod and the stray he appeared to have picked up along the way.

Giving the vivisectionist's burning lair one last lingering look, satisfied that nothing would ever be tortured and diced up there again, he stumbled after the others.

He could hear a voice now, coming from behind the lone door to the right, the last one that led off from the corridor, before the cellar steps. He would have known that traitorous voice anywhere. "Get away, yer bastard!" it barked, before adding. "I mean, sir. Keep back! Or you'll be gettin' another taste of the lash."

Ulysses quickened his steps.

When he was only a few feet away from the start of the staircase, the door opened, and Rudge stepped through.

"What the bloody 'ell's goin' on out 'ere?" he asked of no-one in particular. Then he saw Ulysses, his startled gaze moving quickly from the dandy's unsmiling face, to his left arm, his look of surprise becoming all the more pronounced.

As the two of them stood, frozen to the spot, staring at each other in bewildered surprise, something massive began to squeeze itself through the open doorway behind Rudge.

A huge hand, its skin grey leather, thick with black hair, grabbed the doorframe. Huge fingers dug into the mouldering wall on one side of the door, while on the other, a chitinous talon appeared – just as large as the hand – plaster cracking and crumbling beneath its indelicate touch as the claw sank into the brickwork beneath. And then another grasping forelimb appeared, and another, and lastly a startlingly human hand – compared to all the others – and one that Ulysses recognised.

Muscles bunching, crustacean claws levered the appalling bulk of the creature half through the door. The thing straightened, attempting to draw itself upright and its hulking shoulders, at least six feet across, scraped the ceiling of the passageway.

Atop the massive, multiple-armed torso – which appeared to be not one thing but created from parts of many different specimens – between the muscled mass of its unbalanced shoulders, Ulysses saw the face of Josiah Umbridge staring down at him.

The old man's eyes latched onto Ulysses, looking down at where he stood, isolated from his companions, his own appalled expression a mixture of revulsion, contempt and disbelief. Seeing who it was, cowering there before its grotesque majesty, the eyes narrowed as they continued to bore into Ulysses own horror-widened gaze.

And then the abomination spoke, its voice a booming guttural growl, that wasn't quite a bullish roar and yet wasn't entirely human either.

"*Quiiick-siiil-verrr,*" it rasped.

CHAPTER TWENTY-THREE

The Chimera

Ulysses stared at the monstrous thing as it continued to heave its malformed mass out of the door, the flickering firelight behind him and the neon strip lights above illuminating it all the more clearly now.

It was clear to Ulysses that the old man's head had been transplanted onto a hideous, man-made body, created by the insane vivisectionist Seziermesser. And what a piece of work it was – the great work that the surgeon had spoken of – a true chimera, stitched together from pieces of a plethora of other creatures. The torso in particular was criss-crossed with livid pink and purple scarring, demonstrating quite clearly where one body part had been connected to another, as the vivisectionist had pieced it together like some monstrous flesh-puzzle.

It looked like the torso had been created around that of a large silverback gorilla, that had also provided the chimera with one of its left arms, but much had been added to both the ape's skeletal structure, as well as its musculature, judging by the curious contours of its patchy hide. Externally it looked like there might even be some bull or bear in there, while smooth grey seal skin had been used to fill some of the gaps where the monster's skin had split under pressure from the shifting musculature beneath.

There had obviously been a need to add additional muscle groups to support the vivisect's unbalanced and wholly unnatural physique. The creature's right shoulder was noticeably larger than the left, and in places heaving red wet muscles could be seen moving through further rents in the chimera's patchwork hide. But then the thing needed all that muscle to provide support and movement for three upper arms – if they could be called arms – on the right-hand side of its body.

Uppermost there was a long crustacean-like claw that must have been made from more than one creature, judging by its length and the unnatural number of joints it possessed. Close to the body was what appeared to be the hairy orange-furred arm of an orang-utan. Between these two was an arm that was more human in appearance, except that this one had two elbows and the vivid scarring where one bicep had been sewn onto the second elbow was clearly visible.

It was this one appendage that Ulysses recognised. Slowly a spark of anger reignited the ire deep inside him. Well he should recognise it. Admittedly, it appeared to have been inverted and now possessed a hideous purple hue, but nonetheless, it was still his arm!

A deep rage taking hold, Ulysses took in the rest of the abomination. It only had two limbs protruding from the left side of its upper body. The dominant limb was that of the gorilla, having been severed from the torso only to be stitched back on again but now with a slick-skinned protrusion beneath it, that didn't seem to have any bone structure at all, but writhed and twisted like a cephalopod's tentacle, although it ended in a huge, crushing crab's claw.

Even the old man's swaying head was not as it should be. While he had been putting the finishing touches to his last masterpiece, the mad doktor had added a little something here. The mouth was no longer able to shut properly as it looked like Seziermesser had managed to cram the teeth of another predatory killer in there, the skin around the hinging joint of the jawbone appearing stretched and more elastic.

Having used its arms to pull itself through the restricted opening of the doorway, the creature reared up before the incredulous dandy, its head nearly scraping the ceiling a good four feet above Ulysses' head. And it still wasn't fully out of the door.

The thing cantered forwards on a host of legs that could only have belonged to a giant spider crab – one of the monstrous twenty foot specimens that trawlers occasionally dragged up from rocky holes at the bottom of the North sea. The eight shell-encased limbs knocked hollowly on the tiled floor of the corridor.

And now Ulysses could see the monster in all its terrible glory. From the waist down its mammalian characteristics gave way to the mid-section of a crocodile – no doubt one of those century old monsters that could still be found lurking in the fetid jungle rivers at the heart of the Dark Continent – with its rough grey-green scale-armour and softer white underbelly. It was to this part that the giant spider crab legs had been attached. Reptilian flesh in turn gave way to the thick, fleshy grey tail of a shark, made up of almost nothing but the dagger-like rudder of the caudal fin.

Ulysses backed away from the monstrosity blocking their path to freedom.

"So, you wanted to become a new species, did you?" Ulysses asked the beast quietly, looking into the old man's unblinking eyes. "Well, as they say, you should be careful what you wish for, or you might just get it."

Unable to tear his gaze from Umbridge's tiny head, swaying hypnotically like a cobra between the brutish, adapted shoulders, he slowly became aware of another sound over the laboured snorting of the chimera, and the crackle and pop of the fire spreading behind him. It was a filthy, repugnant sound, like a boarish snorting. It was the sound of Rudge laughing.

There was no doubt about it: with the fire licking at the doorframe of the laboratory behind him, feeling its incandescent heat on his back, and with Rudge and the Umbridge-chimera in front of him, Ulysses was trapped.

Rudge's howls of laughter increased in volume as the Umbridge-chimera towered over him, the old man's distorted features peering at Ulysses with malign intent. Lips rolled back, exposing a double row of teeth, everything from canine fangs to the serrated triangular tips of shark's teeth. A thick, grey tongue slipped between them and the chimera hissed at Ulysses.

As he stared into the bloodshot eyes of the insane industrialist, transfixed by the old man's unblinking gaze – he was dimly aware that the thing's jaws were stretching open, far wider than was humanly possible. But then what had once been Josiah Umbridge wasn't truly human anymore. Their eyes still locked together, the old man's head glided closer on its twisting neck, as if Umbridge somehow intended to bite off his head.

The Umbridge-chimera opened its mouth and a reptilian bark emerged as smoke began to fill the passageway. Ulysses coughed and instinctively put a hand to his mouth as he suddenly came to his senses.

There was the cracking pop and shatter of glass breaking as the fire inside the laboratory grew in intensity. The chimera barked again, its head darting from side to side in distress.

It's afraid of the fire, Ulysses realised. And then he saw the burn marks – the scorched patches of fur, the shiny pink scar tissue on its flanks. Ulysses could only guess at their origins, but to look at the cruelly laughing

Rudge, it wasn't hard to imagine that the gamekeeper had caused those injuries, long before Josiah Umbridge's head had been transplanted onto the vivisect body. The abuse had probably taken place over a period of some months, judging by the way some of the burns had healed; a means of keeping the growing abomination under control.

God alone knew what kind of primitive brain had been used to keep the vivisect's autonomic processes working until it was ready to receive the old man's head. Perhaps that rudimentary collection of ganglia had never been removed, left in to aid the old man in controlling all the disparate body parts. And what the chimerical body remembered, from the time before it had become the Umbridge-chimera, was that fire was to be feared.

And the primal fear of fire was now coupled with the old man's desperate desire to survive.

Ulysses wished he had his sword-cane with him as he watched the monster and its handler's every move, in case they unwittingly provided him with an opportunity to escape.

Then he saw it, tucked into the gamekeeper's trousers. He had obviously decided to keep that particular trinket for himself.

"Not so fast," Rudge growled, seeing where Ulysses' gaze had fallen, and put a possessive calloused hand over the end of it. "It's mine now."

Behind Rudge the chimera reared up on its spider-crab legs and let out a shriek. Flames were licking the ceiling now, the smoke thickening, accompanied by the acrid stink of boiling chemicals. It wouldn't be long before all of them were overcome by the smoke.

The creature was becoming more and more agitated. It skittered backwards and forwards, its great armoured limbs fidgeting restlessly beneath it. Its thick shark's tail lashed in alarm, sending Rudge suddenly stumbling towards Ulysses.

As Ulysses readied himself to make a grab for the exposed sword-cane at the big man's belt, Rudge turned sharply on the beast and, without a second thought, smacked it across the torso with the heavy cosh in his hands.

"Watch it, yer big bastard!" he shouted at the vivisect and the huge monstrosity retreated before the gamekeeper's blows, as its body-memory was reminded who the master was here.

Smoke billowed along the corridor, carried forward by the currents created in the air as the cold cellar was heated by the fire.

Ulysses edged forwards, closer to the gamekeeper and his monstrous charge, closer to his one hope of getting out of there.

And then he saw a change come over the Umbridge-chimera's expression. Where at first there had been only fear of Rudge's beatings, now there was full-blown desperate panic. The old man's eyes glared down at Rudge as he rained blow after blow onto the vivisect's massive body. The blows themselves didn't particularly hurt the beast, but they reminded it of pain the cruel man had inflicted in the past.

"Get back! Get back!" the gamekeeper shouted, trying to force the chimera back into the chamber from which it had come. "Come on! Move!"

And then its rheumy human eyes narrowed with a vicious intent all of its own. Rudge was the one thing stopping it from escaping from the hungry flames.

When the attack came, it came fast. The chimera lashed out with its crustacean claw and double-jointed arm at the same time, seizing hold of the huge man and lifting him off the ground. Before Rudge really understood what was going on, the tentacle, squid-like, whipped forwards, the huge crab's claw closing around the gamekeeper's kicking legs.

Rudge cried out. His yelp of pain became an agonised scream as the three limbs began to pull in different directions, the horrible high-pitched shriek filling the corridor for a moment before Rudge was suddenly and savagely silenced as the chimera tore him in half.

Loops of steaming intestine splashed to the floor as the gamekeeper gave one last gargling death rattle and a spray of hot, red blood bathed the walls, the floor, the chimera and Ulysses in a ruddy shower.

There was never going to be a better chance than this, Ulysses decided, as he made a break for it. The Umbridge-chimera distracted, ducking past its wildly limbs, as it continued to dismember the gamekeeper's corpse, Ulysses pushed past the creature's scrabbling crab's legs.

And then he was through, only cool air and the cellar steps ahead of him.

At the top of the stairs Ulysses caught up with Nimrod and the others.

"It's this way," Jenny said breathlessly, as she led the party back through the palatial stately home at a run, heading for the entrance hall and a way out of the house.

Entering the dimly lit atrium, Ulysses became aware of several things all at once. The front door was already open and voices raised in argument echoed from the marble columns.

Umbridge's butler was there, valiantly trying to prevent a helmeted policeman from entering the premises. The dulcet tones of another irate officer reached Ulysses' ears, and for the first time in his life he felt pleased to hear Inspector Maurice Allardyce's voice raised in anger.

"Get out of the bloody way!" he heard Allardyce shout as two burly constables barged their way past the startled butler and into the house.

And then Ulysses heard the sound he had been dreading, booming from the passageway behind them.

"And who might you be, sir?" one of the constables asked as he was suddenly confronted by a wild-eyed Ulysses, trailing the smell of smoke with him into the atrium, accompanied by an agitated-looking older man in a long black cloak, a desperate, bedraggled young woman, and what could only be described as a sideshow freak.

"Never mind that!" Ulysses snapped as he pushed past the policeman. "You have to get out of here!"

"Now hang on a minute, sir," the constable said, putting out his arms as if to stop Ulysses' flight from the house. "We've had a report about this place –"

"Quicksilver!" Inspector Allardyce exclaimed as he too pushed his way into the entrance hall. "You look terrible. What have you got yourself mixed up in this time?"

"Allardyce, we all have to get out of here now!"

"What? But we've only just got here!"

"Are your men armed?" Ulysses said, half over his shoulder, as he continued to make for the door, Nimrod and the others close behind him.

"No."

"Then get them out of here now. You have to withdraw!"

"Now look here, Quicksilver! You can't just charge in

here and start ordering me around like this, I'll have you know."

"Allardyce!" Ulysses roared in frustration. And then his face fell, as he caught sight of what had entered the hallway after them. "Just run," he said, his voice suddenly horribly quiet.

"What?" The confused inspector turned from the ashen-faced Ulysses to see what it was that had caused what little colour there was to drain from his waxy cheeks. "You're shitting me," he gasped.

The first to fall foul of the chimera was the policeman who had tried to stop Ulysses. The monster picked the constable up with one claw and then merely tossed him aside. He collided with the top of a column and then dropped fifteen feet to the floor, landing face first on the cold marble tiles without making a sound, other than the sickening crunch of his skull breaking.

Ulysses paused at the doorway and stared at the monster in appalled horror. The wretched butler Molesworth stood beside him staring aghast at the creature that now bore only the vaguest similarity to his master Josiah Umbridge.

Screeching, the vivisect reached for another wretched policeman who was already scrabbling to get away, feet slipping on the highly-polished floor. The Umbridge-chimera lunged forwards, bringing the man down with the point of one crustacean leg. The man screamed as the great weight of the monster pressed down on that one clawed crab's leg, puncturing the flesh of his thigh, and pinning him to the ground.

The chimera regarded the policeman curiously for a moment. Absently-mindedly tossing the gamekeeper's lower body aside – which it had still been holding in the vice-like grip of its monstrous claw – the creature closed its pincer around the constable's head and, with one neat twist, removed it from his shoulders.

"Quick! Get out!" Ulysses screamed as he hurried his friends through the door, hoping that Jenny would not look back and witness any of the carnage consuming the atrium behind them.

Unable to tear his own gaze away, he looked from the twitching corpse of the decapitated policeman to the white-faced Allardyce staring transfixed at the vivisect-beast and the remains of the gamekeeper. Beside the oozing remains was Ulysses' cane.

Scrambling back into the hall, he pulled the black wood cane free, feeling its reassuring weight as he held it in his hand again, and then turned for the door, dragging the dumbfounded Allardyce after him.

Shoving the bewildered inspector ahead of him, Ulysses paused in front of the frozen Molesworth, paralysed now that he was faced with the reality of what his master had become.

Ulysses drew back his left hand and hit the butler full in the face, his new simian arm delivering a powerful punch. Molesworth's head hit an alabaster pedestal behind him and he crumpled to the floor, out cold.

"That's for the knockout drops," Ulysses declared with indignant self-righteousness, and then dashed through the door, after the dazed Allardyce.

Once outside in the biting cold of the November night, he paused again, this time to slam the double doors shut behind him; anything to slow the creature down, even if would only be for a second.

With the beast and its enraged bellows trapped inside the house for the time being, Ulysses caught up with Allardyce as the inspector was making for the gleaming black police car pulled up on the gravel drive.

"This your car?" Ulysses asked.

"Y-Yes," the inspector stammered.

"Everyone, get in!" Ulysses commanded, pulling open a door. "Keys?"

"In the ignition."

"Good. I'll drive. Now, get in!"

CHAPTER TWENTY-FOUR

Fight or Flight

Ulysses pushed the accelerator pedal to the floor, and the car took off, throwing up a spray of gravel behind it. Almost as an afterthought he found the right switch on the dashboard and flicked on the headlights. Two powerful white beams cut through the dark, illuminating the driveway ahead and reaching as far as the boundary wall of the estate.

For a few moments, the only sounds inside the car – other than the rising and falling tone of the engine – were the gasping pants of its occupants as they all tried to recover their breath and make sense of what had happened to them back at the house.

Ulysses tore up the driveway, accelerating into the gentle curve of the gravel road as it pulled round parallel with the Neo-Classical facade of the stately home.

"What *was* that?" Allardyce demanded, turning in his seat to face Ulysses. Ulysses' eyes remained firmly on the drive ahead, a manic gleam ablaze there.

"By *that* I take it you mean the monster that just tore apart your friends from the North Yorks constabulary."

"Of course that's what I bloody mean!" Allardyce shrieked.

"Didn't you recognise him? That was the renowned industrialist billionaire recluse Josiah Umbridge. Although it looks like he's not such a recluse any more, doesn't it?"

Allardyce gawped at the dandy, hunched over the steering wheel, a haunted expression on his face as he peered beyond the windscreen of the car. Details flashed into existence out of the darkness as the beams of the police car's headlights briefly illuminated trees and topiary before the night swallowed them up again.

"Nimrod, any sign?" Ulysses asked his manservant, who had bundled into the back of the car with Jenny and the freak.

Nimrod peered out of the window next to him, trying to discern anything through the darkness. Behind them the great house was aglow, the fire having spread.

"I see it, sir!" he suddenly shouted. "Approaching from the right!"

Holding the steering wheel straight, Ulysses dared a glance. The chimera was moving towards them at speed across the carefully tended lawns, galloping through the water of an ornamental pool in its rush to catch up with them.

The landscape designer who had laid out the estate and the approach to it along the drive had planned it so that visitors might enjoy unprecedented views of the whole of the carefully constructed Neo-Classical facade of the house as they entered the grounds.

However, the curve of the drive, provided the thing, of which Josiah Umbridge had become a part, with a shortcut by which to intercept the escaping police car and its passengers.

Teeth gritted, knuckles white around the steering wheel – his left arm aching right down to the bone – Ulysses watched as the chimera hove into view, galloping over the last rise of turf to reach the road.

The only way out was the private estate road that cut across Ghestdale, but to make it they were first going to have to pass through the stone-pillared gates and, right now, that meant confronting the chimera head-on.

Ulysses pushed his right foot down as hard as he could, as if trying to ram the pedal beneath through the floor.

"Look out!" Allardyce yelled, and pulled hard on the steering wheel, as the creature skidded onto the road, its hideousness revealed again by the wildly swinging headlights.

"Get off!" Ulysses shouted, fighting to get the car under control as it bounced off the gravel drive, its tyres gouging ruts in the perfectly-manicured lawn.

The car swung back onto the road with a squeal of tyres.

There was a resounding crash and the car lurched sideways. Jennifer screamed and the freak that she had named Jacob moaned in terror as well.

"Bloody hell!" was all the inspector could think to say.

Allardyce looked out of the driver's window. He saw the dark mass of the chimera moving alongside the car, maintaining a galloping to keep pace with the speeding vehicle. And then he cried out in unintelligible dread as the chimera's old man's face appeared, craning forwards over the top of the car on its elongated neck.

There was another crash and the police car's passengers were shaken out of their seats, Jennifer falling into Jacob's lap.

"What's he trying to do?" Jenny wailed.

"My guess would be that Umbridge is attempting to ram us off the road." Ulysses glanced back over his shoulder at Jenny. "To get to you. You were to be his bride, after all."

Jennifer face in reaction to this statement said it all.

"But don't worry, that's not going to happen. I'm going to get you out of here. We're all getting out of here!"

And then the stone pillars of the estate entrance stood ahead of them. Desperately willing the car towards them as it powered up the drive, Ulysses aimed right for the middle of the open gateway.

With another resounding crash, the chimera collided with the car again, denting the driver's door and crazing the window, such was the force of its attack. The wheels on the nearside left the ground and the car scraped against a gate post as it hurtled through, this second collision righting the vehicle again.

Ulysses was sure he heard a squeal of pain and thought he saw the Umbridge-chimera run headlong into the opposite pillar, out of the corner of his eye.

With the road across the moors clear ahead of them, Ulysses risked looking in the car's rear-view mirror. He could see the house, flames dancing high into the sky, the brilliant orange blaze lighting up the estate like a beacon. Visible against the burning house was the malformed shadow of the vivisect-beast. Ulysses thought he saw the creature shaking its head – as if the old man was trying to recover his senses – and then the monster was on the move again, dogged in its pursuit of them. But they had the advantage; on a straight run, Ulysses sincerely doubted that the beast would be able to keep up with the car.

"So, what now?" Allardyce asked, turning back to Ulysses.

"Now?" Ulysses said, as if this was genuinely the first time he had considered where they should go from here. "Now, we head in to town for reinforcements and then head back up here to run down the beast and put an end to it!"

"Reinforcements?" Allardyce screeched. "Where do you think we are? This isn't London, you know. There are no automata-Peeler grunts here."

"Call ahead!" Ulysses demanded, thinking on his feet.

"Tell your friends at the Whitby constabulary that you need them up here now, with everything they've got!"

"I don't bloody believe this," Allardyce muttered under his breath as he took out his police-issue personal communicator.

"What don't you bloody believe?" Ulysses challenged, his dander up.

"Any of this. Is your life always like this?" Allardyce demanded. "Is it always this mad?"

"Not all of the time," Ulysses muttered, taking his right hand off the wheel to massage the place where the ape's arm had been attached to his body. "What were you and your men doing at Umbridge House anyway?"

"We had an anonymous tip-off that something was up."

"I took the liberty of calling for back-up, sir, when I became fully aware of the seriousness of our situation," Nimrod explained.

"So it was you?" the policeman railed.

"Yes, inspector."

"I don't believe it! *You* called me for back-up?"

"I know. I couldn't believe it either, as I was making the call, sir."

The car's occupants fell silent.

Ulysses returned to massaging his arm. It still pained him, but then he had undergone major surgery only a few hours ago.

How had Seziermesser done it? he wondered. How long had he taken to perfect his technique and test the properties of his secret formula? And where had he got the animals from? He and Umbridge must have been planning this for months, if not longer; two madmen sharing the same twisted vision but with entirely different motives.

Ulysses had to admire the vivisectionist on one level,

to have accomplished such a feat of creation. But for the most part it appalled him. If it hadn't been for the good doktor, then Ulysses would still have his arm. But then, if it hadn't been for the surgeon's skill with a needle and nerve-splicer he wouldn't have been in any fit state to fight back against the crazed beast that old man Umbridge had become.

And it must have been quite some cocktail of drugs that Seziermesser had plied him with, (a) to overcome his body's natural defences to stop it rejecting the chimp's arm, (b) for him not to be doubled up in agony, gibbering like a moron on the laboratory floor, and (c) for him to have come round so quickly, without feeling any extreme ill-effects. He wondered how long he had until their effects wore off.

Or was it something else that was keeping him going? Had the doktor in fact attached additional adrenal glands to his body while he was poking around inside him, reattaching his shoulder? Was that what was keeping his body stimulated to the point of euphoria?

His mind starting to wander, as he tried to make sense of all that had happened to him in the last twelve hours or so, Ulysses did not see the dip in the rutted moorland road. The car flew into it, its bumper impacting into the road surface on the other side, before bouncing out again. For a split second Ulysses lost control of the vehicle and, breaking, spun it on the loose dirt surface of the track, sending it off the road.

Shouts of panic and surprise filled the police car as it slid to a halt facing the wrong way amidst a knot of gorsy tussocks. The engine died.

"What the hell are you playing at, Quicksilver?" Allardyce shouted.

Slowly Ulysses released his white-knuckled grip on the

steering wheel.

"Look, get this ruddy thing started, you bloody idiot!"

"Are you alright, sir?" Nimrod asked from the backseat. "Would you like me to drive?"

In a daze Ulysses reached for the ignition key and turned it.

"Yeah, that's it. Get your man to drive. Or here's a better idea. Swap seats and I'll drive."

The engine rattled into life again.

"I'm alright," Ulysses said, coming out of his stupor.

"No, let me drive!" the agitated inspector demanded.

"I'm alright! I – *Hnnn!*" Ulysses winced and threw up a hand to his temple.

"Look, Quicksilver, you're obviously in no fit state... Bloody hell! You've got to be frigging joking!"

The look in the inspector's eyes demanded that Ulysses follow it, although his screaming sixth sense had already told him all he needed to know.

Leaping over the tussocks and trenches, the uneven ground not hindering its progress in any way, the chimera galloped towards them out of the night.

Slamming his foot to the floor, his heart racing, Ulysses willed the car to start moving as the monster bore down on them. The car's wheels spun, churning the damp moorland to mud, and then incredibly they found purchase again. The automobile shot forwards, throwing the passengers around inside the car as it bounced over the rough heath and back onto the rutted track.

But the beast had caught up with them again now. As Ulysses pulled hard on the wheel, spinning the car to the left and onto the moorland road, the chimera made contact. The police car lurched as its rear end briefly left the road. There was a second crash as the monster reared and brought almost its full weight down on the back of the car. The rear window shattered, showering Nimrod, Jenny and Jacob with glass fragments as the monster's crab-claw smashed its way inside.

Tyres gripping the road again, the police car shot forwards, leaving the lethal pincer snapping at thin air.

Giving voice to a booming bellow of frustration the chimera powered after them. The small part of the increasingly feral creature – the primitive part of Umbridge's brain that lusted after Jenny Haniver – was determined not to let her get away, not when she was practically within its clutches.

It hurled its elastic octopus limb at the car again. This time the pincer snapped shut around the rear nearside-wheel of the car. There was another part of the old Umbridge intelligence at work here, the part that demonstrated the old man's cunning that had helped to make him one of the richest men in the Empire.

Those inside the police car heard the loud bang of the tyre bursting as the crushing claw punctured it and proceeded to tear its rubbery remains from the wheel.

Ulysses felt the effects immediately as the car jolted and bounced on the road. He had to fight the steering wheel as it pulled to the left, and the vehicle veered dangerously close to the edge of the road.

Again the car slewed sideways, as the vivisect hit it side on.

"Hold on!" Ulysses shouted, although whether he was addressing himself or his passengers wasn't clear.

He pulled the car sharply to the right and then left again, as the road swerved sharply to avoid an outcropping of rock. He was dimly aware of the monster charging past and thought he heard the clatter of its armoured limbs as it scrabbled over the rocky summit of the obstacle.

And then it was down the other side and the road was

leading the police car back into the path of the persistent beast.

Understanding the limits of his new body better now, or rather the lack of them, the vivisect threw its full weight at the left-hand side of the car.

Wrong-footed, Ulysses overcompensated as the road took them over the crest of a sloping stretch of moorland, the rugged landscape dropping away to Ulysses' right in a sudden incline. The car's right-hand wheels left the road, skidding through the mud and wet grass at its edge.

The inhuman creature's grotesquely human head appeared beside the wailing Allardyce as the beast put all its weight behind its enormous right shoulder. The window beside Allardyce cracked and the metal pillar between the door and the body of the car buckled inwards.

Ulysses' view of the world rolled sideways, as the car left the road. The world began to spin before his eyes and he threw up his hands to shield his face as the windscreen shattered.

Tiny shards of glass filled the air around the five of them as they rolled with the car, the vehicle tumbling down the slope of the hill. The roof dented, window glass popped and shattered, the beams of the headlights spun wildly, illuminating inverted trees, then scrubby moorland, then nothing as the impenetrable darkness passed overhead and then back to moorland again.

With a dull *crump*, the car rolled to a stop against a sandstone boulder.

Ulysses opened his eyes and blinked. He was in darkness, lying on his side, with the befuddled moans of his companions close by.

"Is... Is everyone alright?" he said, desperately trying to shake the clouds of concussion from his mind.

He tried to look round but a sharp pain in his neck

stopped him from trying any more. He slouched even further over to the right as the door beside him was wrenched open.

"This way, sir," he heard Nimrod say from beside him and felt himself being hauled from the battered vehicle. Finding his feet he stumbled after Nimrod as his manservant led him further into the shelter of the rocky outcroppings beside which the car had come to rest.

He was aware of Allardyce running ahead of them and, looking back, saw the freak Jacob assisting Jennifer as she stumbled after them.

His wits felt addled, as if he was having some kind of out of body experience. Was this the effects of the doktor's drug therapy wearing off or a result of the crash, he wondered as his mind began to stray again.

He almost blacked out as preternatural awareness threatened to overwhelm his traumatised mind. A second later he heard the screeching, primeval cry of the triumphant chimera as it bore down on them, having stopped briefly at the crash site to inspected the wreckage of the car for bodies.

His vision swimming into focus again, Ulysses saw the rocky defile ahead of them as Nimrod half-dragged him towards a tight crevice between the sandstone walls. The exposed cleft ran a good ten yards into the feature which towered above them to a height of twenty feet or more. Once they were in there, there would be no way the creature would be able to prise them out again. Then it would simply be a matter of waiting for Allardyce's back-up to reach them.

The scream cut through Ulysses like Seziermesser's scalpel, finally bringing him fully to his senses. There could be no mistaking that cry; it was Jennifer. He pulled free of Nimrod, his feet slipping on the mud and stones, already scrambling back out of the defile towards Jenny.

Jacob lay sprawled on the ground, moaning in pain. And there was Jenny, suspended in mid-air, her feet high off the ground, her body held tight in the clutches of the monster's claw. Her cry was cut short as the chimera squeezed her in its pincer grip, leaving her gasping for air as she struggled.

"Jennifer! Jenny!" he screamed in impotent rage as the Umbridge-chimera, having got what it wanted, turned and began to ascend the slope again, turning back to the road.

And then she was gone, swallowed by the darkness as the creature carried her way into the bitter night.

CHAPTER TWENTY-FIVE

The Abbey

Jennifer Haniver opened her eyes. The world swung past her in dull greys and purples in the pre-dawn twilight. She felt dizzy, her senses reeling from the galloping motion of the beast. She closed her eyes again.

Her chest felt tight. She tried to breathe, but when her lungs were only half-full, she felt the crushing pressure of the claw across her midriff again and let her breath out in a gasp.

Her head felt thick. She half-opened her eyes and craned her whiplash-sore neck, trying to focus on one point on the swaying horizon. Somewhere, far off, she thought she saw stars, until she realised that the yellow-orange pinpricks were lights coming on in the wakening town below the cliff tops.

She blinked, forcing wakefulness upon herself. And as awareness came to her, so did a plethora of other sensations. There was the salt-smell of the wind blowing in off the sea; the cold, damp touch of the wind on her face; the breath of the breeze rippling the long grass of the moors; the colours of pre-dawn painting the landscape in a wash of purple blues and greys; the looming shadows of a building ahead of her; the stomach-turning mammalian musk and fish-stink of the creature filling her nose; the grunt and snort of the thing, as it galloped on, loud in her ears.

They appeared to be heading towards a dark structure on the horizon, shot through with arch-holes of sky, two pinnacles and a pointed triangular pediment, thrusting up towards heaven. Even from the curious angle from which Jennifer was viewing it, it looked familiar.

With a tremendous splashing, the vivisect galloped through the boggy waters of a reed-edged pool. The water splashed up into her face, drenching her hair. And then they were through, the beast clearing the shallow bank on the other side and entering the shadowy sanctuary of the ruined Abbey.

"Come on!" Ulysses urged, maintaining his stumbling run through the wind-blown grass.

They had been in pursuit of the beast for the last hour, ever since it had run the police car off the road and made its escape with Jenny in its clutches. The thought that any harm might come to her cut Ulysses to the quick. He had not known her for long, but in the short, dramatic time they had spent together he had come to feel hugely responsible for her, as if, with her father's death, her welfare had become his concern.

So, ignoring the cuts and bruises he had sustained in the car crash Ulysses kept up his dogged pursuit of the Umbridge-chimera and Jenny Haniver.

"And where are we heading, exactly?" Inspector Allardyce puffed.

Ulysses glanced at the ground. It was not hard to follow the chimera's path, the flattened grass, the stab marks in the mud from its arthropod legs, the occasional gouged area of turf. He looked from the ground and the trail across the heath towards the crest of the cliff, beneath which lay the fishing port of Whitby.

"There!" he panted, pointing.

"It's heading towards the town?" Allardyce exclaimed.

"Not the town, you idiot. *There*."

Ulysses pointed again, towards the remnants of walls and buttresses that was all that was left of the Benedictine monastery of St Peter and St Hilda.

"That old ruin? But what good's that?"

Ulysses paused, considering his answer carefully for a moment.

"Perhaps the creature is seeking sanctuary." Nimrod suggested, coming alongside his master.

"Or absolution."

All turned. It was the freak that had spoken.

"Who knows what the bugger wants. But if that's where it's hiding out, then we have it," Allardyce said with conviction. He was a man who liked to deal in hard facts – not metaphysical musings on man's state of original sin.

Ulysses could see the lights of torch-beams piercing the early morning gloom now as well. The Yorkshire constabulary had arrived.

"Our back-up's here."

The policemen were approaching the ruins from the other side of the East Cliff, a line of ten men.

"It's not going to be enough," Jacob said in a worried tone.

Ulysses looked at him, although it made his skin crawl to do so. But nonetheless, the boy's eyes were human, windows to a troubled soul.

And perhaps the boy was right, Ulysses thought, as he set his eyes on the ruins ahead of them. They had all witnessed what the chimera had done to the policemen back at the house, without even batting an eyelid. Then there had been the resilience it had demonstrated in running a police car off the road. Ulysses doubted that anything the Whitby police could throw at it would do the beast much harm. For a start, they probably weren't even armed.

"You could be right," Ulysses said as he jogged on. He turned back to the boy, only to see him haring away over the grass, back the way they had come.

"I don't bloody believe it!" Allardyce swore. "The coward! I should have him arrested for dereliction of duty!"

"Leave him," Ulysses said coldly. "We don't have the time."

"And to think I thought he had a soft spot for the girl," Nimrod mused behind Ulysses. "After all that he's been through already, I would not have expected this."

Umbridge's pursuers – now numbering only three – helped each other scale the boundary wall of the Abbey's grounds.

The trail left by the beast, more clearly visible as the sky lightened in expectation of the coming dawn, led directly into the abbey's ancient fishpond and then cleared the bank on the other side.

Skirting the pond, lungs aching now – every breath like fire in his throat – Ulysses led Nimrod and the inspector over the undulating mounds of the grassy field in which the ruins stood.

There was no point trying to be subtle now. Time was of the essence and, besides, there wasn't anywhere to hide. Until they reached the sanctuary of the Abbey itself, they remained totally exposed. And besides, Ulysses pondered, God alone knew what other senses Umbridge had acquired since becoming a part of the chimera. It wouldn't surprise him to learn that the thing had heightened hearing, or that it could see by the heat-trace left by their bodies in the infra-red spectrum.

Ahead of them and a little to the left stood the black

oblong of Cholmley House. To the right stood the silhouette of the Abbey. The policemen, more than just sweeping spots of light in the darkness now, were moving towards them on an intercept course between the two structures, having caught sight of the inspector from Scotland Yard and his dishevelled companions.

And then they were standing in the shadows of the once-great Abbey, all dark pillars and empty archways. As Allardyce got his second wind and strode off to make contact with the approaching policemen, Ulysses hung back, keeping one eye firmly on the ruined edifice rising up beside him.

The chimera was here; he was sure of it. Such conviction came from the nagging voice of his subconscious, like an itch at the back of his brain.

He stared up at the ruins – his chest heaving as he lungs dragged air into his body – desperately trying to penetrate the shadow of the Abbey, hoping to see anything – anything at all – that might reveal to him where the creature was lurking.

A little way away from Ulysses and Nimrod now, Allardyce and the policemen were entering the nave of the Abbey through a gaping rift in a ruined wall.

Ulysses followed, Nimrod at his heel, like some faithful hound.

"How many of you are armed?" he heard Allardyce hiss in annoyance.

Ulysses couldn't make out the policeman's reply but he heard the inspector's heartfelt, angry response.

"I don't bloody believe it! And you came on foot?"

"Yes, sir," a bleary-voiced sergeant replied. "Up St Mary's steps."

"You're more out of breath than I am," Ulysses heard Allardyce chide the officer, "and I feel like I've just run halfway across Yorkshire, *and* having just walked away from a car crash, I'll have you know!"

Part of him, annoyed at their lack of professionalism, he supposed, wanted to tell them to be quiet. But there seemed little point. He was sure Umbridge – or whatever passed for Umbridge now – was already well aware of their arrival.

They were standing amidst the grass-covered mounds of rubble that had once been the Choir of the church. In front of them stood what remained of the north transept, one of the more intact parts of the ruin.

"What are we looking for, sir?" a constable asked, looking up at the jagged spurs of broken walls above them.

"You'll know when you see it," Allardyce said, his eyes on the surrounding walls.

Awareness crackled through Ulysses like a bolt of electricity and he ducked, shooting darting glances upwards at the looming columns.

A split second later, there was movement in the darkness, a scraping sound – as of hardened carapace grating against stone – and the whip-crack of a snapping pincer. The curious constable knew what they were looking for now, as the chimera's claw closed around his neck and shoulders and the vivisect pulled him violently off his feet.

All eyes followed the policeman's struggling form as he was dragged into the air, feet kicking uselessly. As horrified eyes caught sight of the vivisect-chimera the constable's struggles became nerveless spasms and a shower of hot, viscous rain fell on those assembled below.

The chimera was peering down at them from its perch, halfway up one of the thick pillars that rose like petrified tree trunks from the earth.

Gasps of horror and revulsion added to the sense of panic, but the bloody shower was as nothing compared to what came thudding down around the party next. The constable's head thudded to the ground only a few feet away from Ulysses, his dismembered torso and legs landing in two entirely different places altogether, but the dandy couldn't have cared less. He had only one thing on his mind and nothing was going to distract him from that over-arching purpose now.

Ulysses peered into the darkness as excited voices began shouting around him, taking a chance to scan the walls nearby. There was the glint of light on a trailing tress of wet hair, and he saw what he was looking for. He had found Jennifer.

She was lying within the crook of an archway above the Choir. The monster must have put her there for safe keeping. Ulysses was certain she was still alive, but also unconscious – thankfully, for her sake!

A shot rang out, the echo of its retort as loud as the crack of doom itself, within the confines of the church.

A bellow of pain or rage – Ulysses wasn't sure which – shook the crumbling structure to its foundations and the crab-claw came sweeping down out of the darkness.

Ulysses followed the sound of the gun shot to its source: Allardyce had been the one to fire on the chimera. His shot had obviously had little impact – if the inspector had hit the thing at all – but now he had made himself the creature's prime target.

Ulysses was already running towards the inspector before his conscious mind had realised that he had decided to move. The rapier-blade slid from the sheath of the black wood cane with a zinging hum of reverberating metal.

He and the chimera landed their blows at the same time. Allardyce was sent flying as the heavy pincer smacked into him, and Ulysses' trusty blade made contact with boneless flesh.

With all his weight behind it, the tempered blade sliced cleanly through the cephalopod limb. The full weight of the unnaturally large claw landed on top of Allardyce, knocking the wind from his lungs, the pincer twitching as lifeless muscles relaxed.

Howling in agony, black inky fluid dripping from the severed limb, the chimera scuttled backwards further up the pillar and out of harm's way. Ulysses could just make out the old man's face snarling and spitting at him from the darkness.

Umbridge was definitely becoming more feral, the bestial body-memory of the vivisect corrupting what was left of his barely human mind.

Another figure was moving among the ruins now, but this one appeared to be scampering up the corner of the north transept, as if it were a monkey climbing a tree. It was a young woman, he could see that much, and the silhouette bore the suggestion of damask and lacy skirts. And she wasn't the only one; there were other figures like her, all bizarrely dressed, scaling the walls of the north transept as if it was the sort of thing they did every day.

Ulysses could see that they were carrying something between them, something that was almost invisible against the twilight sky, but something which each of them had a hand upon as they hauled it up after them. He took in the rest of the transept above him and saw more figures doing the same on two outer sides of the transept. Some had already reached the top now, running along the walls, drawing the net over the apex of the ruin, so that soon the only side not covered was that which opened onto the main body of the church. But give them long enough, Ulysses thought, and they would probably have that covered too.

Where had they got the net from, he wondered, and then realised that it was probably the same net they used to ensure the safety of the high-wire and trapeze artists in the Big Top.

A few moments more and the acrobats of the Circus of Wonders would have the beast trapped within the ruins. What Ulysses needed to do now was keep the chimera there long enough for the circus folk to bring their plan to fruition.

"What's the matter, Umbridge?" Ulysses shouted at the inhuman monster. "Are you scared? Is this all that the world can expect from *homo superior*? What's the matter, did I hurt you?"

His words resounded around the cold dead vault of the Abbey, as did the monster's bellowed response.

"*Quuiiick-siiill-veerrr!*" it snarled, the name of its nemesis becoming a howl of bloodthirsty intent. The creature began to descend the pillar.

"I must be mad," Ulysses said to himself, seeing the monstrosity bearing down on him, its four remaining arms open wide, ready to seize him in its deadly, crushing embrace.

"Yes, I am mad!" he decided, shouting the fact to the world, as he felt the adrenalin quicken the blood in his veins, his pulse thrumming in his ears, nerves tingling, muscles tightening. "In fact I'm utterly furious!' he raged at the beast. 'Because that's my arm you've got there!"

With a roar the creature leapt the last ten feet, aiming to crush Ulysses beneath its spider-crab legs. But Ulysses was too quick for it. Spinning out of the creature's way, his blade scored a cut across its crocodilian midriff. It was not enough to debilitate the vivisect, but it was enough to keep its attention as the circus folk swarmed overhead, pulling their net to the limit of the chancel.

Turning again to deliver a two-handed strike at one of the crustacean limbs, Ulysses saw two of the scrambling figures take a run up and, the edge of the net in their hands, take a leap of faith that reminded him of his own death-defying leap from the top of the Bakerloo Line train as it sped on its way over Trafalgar Square. They fell gracefully through the air in an arcing curve, the cords of the net making a whizzing sound as they were pulled sharply over the broken mortar and weathered stones at the top of the tower.

Momentarily distracted by the acrobats bold act of circus fearlessness, Ulysses only just brought his blade to bear in time as the vivisect stamped down with one stabbing claw-foot and swung at him with its scything talon at the same time. He parried the swipe whilst dodging the claw, but that put him on the wrong foot and left him vulnerable to the sudden tail-lash that came his way.

Ulysses was sent flying into the rough stones of the transept wall, adding another graze to his already cut face. For someone who was so proud of his good looks, he wasn't looking so good anymore. But the injury was nothing more than a superficial abrasion of the cheek and so, with his wits still about him, Ulysses double-bluffed the creature, running straight for it as it cantered towards him, so that it mistimed its next strike as the dandy threw himself under its crocodilian underbelly.

Rolling over on the turf he leapt to his feet again and let out a gasp of surprise as he almost ran slap-bang into the elephantine freak.

"You!" was all he could manage. But it was all he

needed to say.

Jacob stared back at him with open, apologetic eyes.

"You brought back-up!" Ulysses suddenly laughed. The boy was no coward after all, and here he was again, ready to do his part.

The Umbridge-chimera turned, the old man's head swaying on its grotesquely elongated neck, frantically searching for its prey. And then its savage gaze – any semblance of humanity gone from those feral eyes now – found them both and a guttural screech issued from somewhere deep inside its Seziermesser-made chest.

"Help! Somebody?" came a distraught wail from above them. "I'm up here!" Ulysses did not dare take his eyes off the beast again, not for a moment. But then he didn't need to; he knew who the voice belonged to and where the desperate pleas were coming from. It was none other than his poor, traumatised Jenny.

"Jacob," Ulysses said, addressing the deformed young man by his name for the first time since they had met. He spoke with a clarity of mind and purpose, as the chimera took a rhythmic, many-legged step towards them; there wasn't time for any misunderstandings or mistakes. "Get Jenny down and get her out of here!"

The boy didn't need telling twice. "Yes, sir!"

And then he was gone from Ulysses' side as the acrobats landed behind him and closed the net on both the vivisect and the desperate dandy.

CHAPTER TWENTY-SIX

Gods & Monsters

"This way!" Jacob called over the furious berserker screams of the cornered beast. Taking the young woman's hand in his – her long, delicate fingers swamped by his fat, misshapen paw – he made for the cleft in the chancel wall, pulling Jenny after him.

Leaving the desecrated sanctuary of the Abbey, the still standing north wall of the nave to their left, Jenny and the wretched young man stumbled over the undulating turf, past unearthed Saxon tombstones, past the arch of the west door and through the visitor's turnstile, making for the crenulated nave and tower of another church – the parish church of St Mary's.

Their feet pounding over cobbles now, they could both hear the bellows of the beast reverberating from the broken columns of the ruin behind them, the raised voices of the circus folk as they relayed instructions backwards and forwards between themselves, the disorganised shouts of the policemen and the visiting inspector.

Then they were through another gate, pounding down a flagstone path that ran between serried ranks of stone crosses and headstones, the solid walls of the church of St Mary's and the sanctuary they offered directly in front of them.

And now a new and terrible sound reached their ears, a shrill half-human scream of rage, pain and will-shattering insanity, that turned the blood in Jenny's veins to ice-water.

Then a part of her realised what the sound signified.

The Umbridge-chimera had discovered that its mate-to-be had been stolen away, and it was angry; angry like they had never seen it before.

Shots were fired. People cried out and there was an ominous tearing sound, as of ropes being ripped apart.

"It's coming!" she spluttered, allowing Jacob to pull her towards the church door.

Jacob fumbled clumsily at the latch until the door creaked open and they tumbled down the cold stone steps into the church.

"What is the meaning of this?" a grim voice demanded. Jenny looked up, wincing as her eyes adjusted to the dusty, candle-pierced gloom of the church. The instantly recognisable smell of musty hymnals, burnt beeswax and cold stone hit her full in the face, mixed, in this place, with the stale aroma of the fishy faithful.

"I demand to know the meaning of this intrusion."

A figure wearing the severe black cassock of a priest was watching them from the steps leading up to the sanctuary, a dully gleaming metal cross hanging around his neck, smoking taper in hand. He was an austere man, standing as straight as one of the pillars supporting the church roof. The wisps of grey hair that tufted the sides of his head only served to make him appear even more sinister. He looked down his nose at the two bloodied and filthy creatures that had fallen through the church door, regarding them through severe wire-framed spectacles.

On seeing the priest, the exhausted Jacob assumed a fawning stance, the boy casting his eyes down at the stone flags as he approached the vicar, as might a sinful petitioner seeking absolution.

"I am sorry, Father, but we have come seeking the sanctuary of God's holy church. For we are in danger – terrible danger."

The austere priest descended the steps from the sanctuary, the slow, deliberate manner of his approach only enhancing the menacing atmosphere, and making Jenny feel more unwelcome by the second. The vicar was scowling, the corner of his top lip flexed upward in a sneer.

Too exhausted to do anything else, Jenny lay where she had fallen, taking in her surroundings with weary, aching eyes, the cold stones leeching what little warmth was left in her body.

The smell of the place might be familiar to Jenny, but the interior layout of the church was not. Everything about it suggested that the original building had since been modified and refurnished by generations of parishioners, giving this particular place of worship a remarkable and entirely idiosyncratic appearance.

The interior was a hotchpotch of styles and eras. As well as box pews there was an incredible pulpit that ascended through three distinct levels. Behind the pulpit, and astride the chancel arch, a large gallery ran around the walls, supported by twisted columns. There was even what appeared to be a charcoal stove in the middle of the church, its flue rising to the ceiling.

And through the chancel arch could be found the candle-lit sanctuary – that seemed more like a side chapel in its size and design. The painted panes of a stained glass window were already colouring the sanctuary floor with muted tones as the firmament beyond began to lighten in anticipation of the coming dawn.

"Where have you been?" the priest demanded of Jacob, coming to a halt in front of him.

Jacob was practically on his knees now.

"Father, I will explain everything later, but first, lock the door, I beseech you."

Jenny saw the heavy ring of keys at the priest's belt, that jangled together as he moved.

"Have you been out all night?" The priest's tone was cold, like a strict parent chastising a miscreant child. But that was the way of priests the world over, Jenny thought.

Father: it was a term of respect, an honorific. But as Jenny looked from the freak to the priest there was something darkly similar about the two of them.

"Father," Jacob pleading, his voice sounding as though he was close to tears, "please lock the door. There is something after us, an abomination straight from the darkest pits of hell."

"You do not need to lecture me on abominations," the man said making no attempt to hide the spite belying his words.

"Please father. Lock the door. Before it's too late."

Jacob's blubbering plea had barely left his lips when, with a crash that shook the building like an earthquake, the door flew open.

For a moment it almost looked like Josiah Umbridge had regained his natural, human form, as his face peered around the edge of the door, as if he had come to the church seeking absolution. Umbridge stopped, sniffing the air sharply, and then slowly his head turned and his unblinking gaze fell on Jenny. Blood ran from a head-wound obscuring the vision of one bloodshot eye and as Jenny watched in horror, too tired to do anything else, a cruel smile curled the old man's mouth. As his lips parted, the points of arrow-tip teeth became visible.

"*Jeenn-eeee!*" the creature exhaled.

And then all she could hear was the thudding of her heart within her chest; all she could see was the old man's hideous face as it extended into the church on the end of that horrific, vertebrae-ridged neck.

But somehow she found the means to move again, pushing herself backwards on her bottom, using her hands and heels to put herself out of the reach of the monstrosity.

"Miss Jennifer! Run!"

She felt Jacob's hand grab hold of hers, felt him pulling her further out of harm's way. Without being fully aware of what she was doing, the animal instinct to survive seizing hold, she scrambled to her feet and stumbled after her malformed saviour.

Accompanied by the wet crack of wood, and the scraping clatter of crustacean claws, the Umbridge-chimera pulled itself through the door and into the church.

The Reverend Nathaniel Creed stared at the abomination in abject horror. What unholy visitation had his monster of a son summoned from the depths of hell? What new atrocity was this that had been sent to test him?

They had as king over them the angel of the Abyss, whose name in Hebrew is Abaddon.

Was this the living embodiment of God's judgement that came to claim the souls of those who had sinned in his eyes? Had the day of doom come at last, and with it an end to his own hell-on-earth existence?

How long, Sovereign Lord, holy and true until you judge the inhabitants of the earth and avenge our blood?

A cacophony of splintering pews, tumbling candelabra and scraped stone filled the church, the acoustics of the nave amplifying the hellish roars and bellows of the dread beast bearing down on him as the usurper of his life and his whore fled through the vestry door. The creature cast shattered pews before it, crushing them to matchwood beneath its impossibly large body.

And I saw a beast coming out of the sea. He had ten horns and seven heads, and on each head a blasphemous name. The beast I saw resembled a leopard, but had feet like those of a bear and a mouth like that of a lion.

And then the blasphemy was swaying there before him, a huge shark-like tail lashing the air angrily behind it.

The creature peered down at Creed from its lofty position and the tormented priest responded in the only way he knew how.

"Begone, Satan!" the Reverend Creed roared, with all the conviction of his best fire and brimstone preaching voice.

For a moment the abomination paused, cocking its head to one side as it regarded the priest, an almost quizzical look in its inhuman eyes. A breathless snorting noise escaping its flaring nostrils as its patchwork-flesh chest heaved. The stink that came off the beast – of blood and rot and death – could only be described as hellish.

The thing raised its multitude of limbs – one scythe-like claw held high above its head, some vile secretion oozing from the stump of another abominable limb – and the Reverend Creed knew that his time had come.

As the talon descended, Creed took a stumbling step backwards, the natural instinct for survival hard to deny. The tip of the claw caught the cloth of his cassock as he went down hard on his back, the lighted taper falling from his hands, the cast-iron candlestick beside him crashing to the floor, spilling hot wax across the stone flags and trailing fire.

The monster loomed over him, its hideous form a dark stain against the backdrop of the white-emulsion ceiling above, an evil shadow blocking out God's light. The musty, oily stink of its heaving flanks was hot in his nose and made him want to gag.

A human head supported on an elongated, snake-like neck descended, jaws dislocating as the mouth of hell itself yawned open.

Nathaniel Creed closed his eyes; his longed for end had come. The Lord God had seen fit to send his angel of death to take him from this world. And if he were to reside in hell for all eternity, then so be it; it could not be any worse than the living hell he had put himself through these last seventeen years.

Seventeen years since the boy's mother – the street girl whose path had first crossed his when she was barely past her eighteenth year, the same age the wretched boy was now – had turned up at his door again, the TB already too far gone for him to do anything for her other than hear her last confession, give her the last rites, and acknowledge the boy as his own, the result of his one transgression of the flesh.

He was dimly aware of a dull *whommph* and then he felt the fires of hell against his back.

Sudden scorching pain made Creed open his eyes. He found himself staring right into the gullet of the beast. But then, suddenly, the jaws snapped shut, mere inches from the end of his nose, and the blasphemy's old man's face recoiled. Creed could see the fires of hell reflected in the eyes of the demon now, and something else too. If he had not known better he would have named it terror. But what did an angel of the Abyss have to fear from a sinner like him?

Intense burning pain suddenly consumed him, and with it, the priest's addled senses returned. Screaming in pain and panic, Creed leapt to his feet, but he was already too late. His cassock was alight.

Screeching in fear – yes, it was fear that he had seen in the old man's eyes – the monster retreated, all eight legs taking a step backwards as it shrank from the preacher.

Creed took an agonised, shuffling step forwards, arms outstretched towards the beast. "'The Lord your God is a jealous god!'" he screamed, as fire clawed its way up his body with flickering fingers, the hair on his head curling and blackening before the advance of the flames. "'*The Lord revengeth, and is furious; the Lord will take vengeance on his adversaries, and he reserveth wrath for his enemies!'*"

Creed's shambling steps became more urgent as the fire spread. Eyelids burned, melting flesh sealing them shut, his tongue cooking in his mouth, his voice nothing but incoherent screams now, and he half-ran and half-fell towards the beast, seeking its awful embrace.

And fire consumed his soul.

Free of the remnants of the net at last Ulysses pounded down the path to the church no more than a minute behind the beast.

He reached the sundered door to be greeted by a chorus of unholy screams, bestial roars, and the snarl of hungry flames, the church's stained glass lit up in a brilliant rainbow of flickering light from inside. Ulysses grabbed the splintered door jamb to arrest his flight and stop himself falling headfirst over the threshold, rapier blade still in hand, adrenalin and Seziermesser's cocktail of miracle-drugs numbing his broken fingers.

His own subconscious warning scream had Ulysses throwing himself aside, so that he saved himself from being trampled underfoot by the fleeing monster. Trailing the charcoal-stink of the church's burning furnishings behind it, back in the chill embrace of another dull November morning, the Umbridge-chimera raised its face to the sky, the gyrating head performing a peculiar cobra-dance of its own, and sniffed the air. Then with a triumphant howl it set off at a gallop, back across the churchyard.

Ulysses hauled himself to his feet. He felt exhausted. He didn't know how much longer he could maintain the chase. But then if he didn't, who would? And besides, he could not – *would* not – let the beast to escape him again.

Turning away from the fire-lit interior of the church, Ulysses stumbled back along the path. But rather than return to the Abbey and the mob of policemen and circus folk awaiting it there, the chimera turned left past the east end of the church, heading out across the stone-planted field of St Mary's cemetery.

Ulysses rounded the end of the building after it and ran on, his lungs feeling like they were on fire, the monster galloping over the weathered tombstones and monuments that littered the graveyard.

And there, even further ahead, Ulysses could make out the running figures of Jennifer and the freak as they followed the cliff-top path towards the eastern extremity of the cemetery and its perimeter wall.

The creature was closing on them.

The intensity of the moment helping him to focus his mind on tapping the last reserves of energy his body possessed, Ulysses bounded along the well-trodden grass path between the gravestones, towards the crumbling cliff path.

The chimera was only a few lolloping strides from its quarry, its pounding footfalls sending shudders through the turf at Ulysses' feet. For Jacob and Jennifer it was only a matter of another ten yards to the cemetery wall. Soon there would be nowhere else for them to run, nowhere left to hide.

As the chimera bore down on them Jacob turned in a display of astonishing bravery, and with nothing but his bare hands, prepared to make a good account of himself in the face of the vivisect's attack.

The move obviously surprised the tiny part of the old man's mind that remained his own and the creature stumbled to a halt, in a confused flurry of lurching legs. As the creature reared up before them, preparing to make its mantis-like strike at last, Jacob took a bold step forwards, looked directly into the old man's leering face and let out a pained roar of anger, frustration and desperation.

For a moment, the bewildered beast withdrew its head. Then slowly its face came level with the boy's again. The chimera opened its gaping mouth and roared in animal fury, meeting the young man's challenge.

And Ulysses' blade fell.

The monster's roar of fury became a howl of pain as the razor-edged rapier sliced through one arthropod leg.

The howl became a scream as Ulysses pushed against the blade to prise the leg apart. With a horrible sucking sound and a popping crack, the lower part of the crab limb came away from the thigh-like merus. The shorn limb fell uselessly to the ground, trailing stringy white meat from the horny-joint, a watery grey fluid dribbling into the grass at Ulysses' feet.

The chimera wheeled round. Ulysses had its attention again. He took a wary step backwards.

He had faced the impossible hybrid three times now, and on every occasion so far the outcome had been inconclusive. However, they shared a mutual understanding now that this time neither would desist until one, or both of them, was dead.

Its old man's face contorting into a bellow, the chimera charged at Ulysses, hampered by the fact that it had lost one of its eight legs. This incapacitation gave Ulysses all the time he needed to prepare his next move.

The monster rushed in, gorilla-fist drawn back ready to take a swipe at the dandy while the long, disembowelling claw unfolded, ready to tear the man open from sternum to groin.

At the last possible moment, Ulysses launched himself at the beast, sprinting from a standing start to charge in under attack-raised arms. He slammed into the solid wall of muscle that was the vivisect's broad crocodilian midriff, forcing the tip of his sword-cane through the leathery epidermis and into the coils of viscera behind. Umbridge screamed again.

Only Doktor Seziermesser had known what manner of internal organs actually lay buried inside the fleshy shell of the monster's body. For all Ulysses knew his blade might have punctured a kidney, a lung, a stomach, the monster's heart – and who was to say that it only had the one? – or maybe he had even managed to sever a major artery.

Bullets might not have had much of an impact against the unnatural creature but good old-fashioned, tempered British steel – that was quite another matter!

Ulysses kept his hold on the pommel of the blade firm as the monster writhed and kicked, pushing him backwards, but the beast was unable to dislodge him despite its frenzied efforts. But then Ulysses felt strong hands grasp his shoulders, blunt fingers digging into his flesh, worrying at his old shoulder wound and threatening to tear the stitches where the ape's arm had been attached to his other shoulder.

Now it was Ulysses' turn to cry out, moaning through gritted teeth as he desperately tried to keep a hold of his sword. He might have managed to escape the reach of the chimera's larger limbs, but he had still been within reach of its smaller secondary arms.

And then his fingers slipped from the blood-slicked bloodstone-tip of his sword-cane and he suddenly found himself unable to defend himself against the monster's onslaught.

Ulysses had thought that nothing could top the horrors he had witnessed and experienced first-hand, the personal abuses he had suffered. But as his eyes snapped open, excruciating pain lancing through his aching body as the monster tugged at his left arm, he realised how wrong he had been.

For there, right in front of his eyes, the amalgamated flesh of the chimera was starting to bubble and blister. Ulysses watched as the patches of exposed skin began to sizzle and pop, as if its flesh had been subjected to a chemical attack – or as if something was moving beneath the skin. And then, as he peered closer, unable to tear his eyes away, despite the agonies he was suffering, he saw that there *was* something there beneath the shiny, translucent skin, a tiny something inside each and every blister.

Ulysses cried out again as the stitches securing the chimpanzee's arm to his shoulder began to tear and his eyes swivelled round to see for himself what was happening. What he saw filled him first with horror, then revulsion until that feeling too changed to become furious resolve. Seeing his own left arm worrying at the surgery that had been carried out as a result of its amputation gave him the strength and the determination to fight back.

Using the chimera's hold on him to support himself, Ulysses tucked his legs up to his chest and planted both feet firmly against the monster's reptilian abdomen. Tensing his thighs, he pushed with all the strength he had left. His body skewed to the left as the monster maintained its hold on his ape arm, the pain in his shoulder easing immediately, his right arm pulling free of the chimera's own blood-wet hand.

At once he reached for the beast again, swinging precariously from the stubborn grip of his own left hand. The shattered fingers of his right hand clutched at the old man's face and, making a paralytic claw of his maimed digits, he dug in.

The chimera gave voice to another scream – pain and fury indistinguishable now – and Ulysses felt something, soft and pliable as jelly, pop under pressure. With a sharp, spasmodic jerk, the abomination hurled Ulysses away.

For a moment Ulysses sailed through the cold air, both his left arm and shoulder feeling like they were on fire. He landed hard on his back, sliding over the dew-wet grass. He came to a halt – eyes shut tight against whatever terrible disaster might befall him next – and lay there for a moment, listening to the screams of the girl, the shouts of the boy and the incessant roaring of the beast. The salt sea breeze ruffled his hair and stung his face with cold.

Utterly exhausted, as he was, part of him felt like just lying there and doing nothing, waiting for the inevitable end to come, for the beast to take him. But he had hurt the creature now; he had it on the back foot. The advantage was his.

Ulysses tried to push himself up into a seated position and would have gone off the cliff backwards and into the sea, had it not been for the precarious fence that leaned out over the drop. He had come to a stop right on the very edge of the crumbling precipice, and when he had tried to put his hand down under the wire, to find some purchase, he had put all his weight on thin air.

He sluggishly staggered to his feet once more as the chimera bore down on him. With the creature filling his entire field of vision, Ulysses saw the blistering flesh again, great red wheals forming in other places now.

For a moment, he almost believed that the monster's charging run was going to take it off the edge of the cliff, the abomination unable to slow itself in time before hurling both Ulysses and itself over the precipice and into the sea.

Barely on his feet, he bowled himself clear of the great talon-scythe.

As the monster dug all of its remaining arthropod limbs into the soft turf before the fence, Ulysses suddenly found himself caught in the cage it had made of its claws. He was trapped.

He looked up at the pallid underbelly of the beast. There, sticking out of its reptilian flesh, was the glinting pommel of his sword. Reaching up, he grabbed the bloodstone hilt and pulled. The blade came free with an obscenely wet sucking gasp.

Pulling himself upright within the embrace of the abomination, the swelling blisters mere inches from his face now – the embryonic forms of something horribly familiar squirming within the iridescent mother-of-pearl fluid of their birthing sacs – Ulysses brought the blade up cleanly and parried the panicked thrusting of the creature's own chitin blade.

As the monster's talon slid free of his sword, Ulysses twisted his wrist sharply to deliver a downward cutting stroke of his own. His old left arm flopped onto the windswept grass at the cliff's edge.

"Let's see how you like it!" Ulysses said, a look of grim satisfaction on his face.

The dreadful raging screams of the beast suddenly ceased, replaced by a single, breathless cry. The Umbridge-chimera reeled backwards as gouts of thick black blood pumped from the severed brachial artery at the distended limb's second joint. The creature struck the fence, two of its claw-tipped limbs thrusting through the metal mesh, while others pushed against the wire netting on the near side.

Ulysses stepped in again, bringing his blade back up in a sweeping arc. The tip of the bloodied weapon made contact again, denying the old man any memorable last words, even if Umbridge had been able to articulate them. Ulysses' final blow had half cut through the fibrous muscles of the snaking neck, shearing through the creature's oesophagus and windpipe.

The severed stem writhing like a salted slug, the old man's head flopped impossibly to the right. For a moment the thing's staring eyes locked onto his and, in that one look Ulysses thought he saw something that might have passed for a trace of humanity within the dead-eyed fish stare he found there.

And then the creature's body began to fall, toppling almost languidly off the edge of the windswept cliff. First went the heavy shark's tail, the cancroid legs tearing the tangled fence from its roots under the great weight of the body, then the mish-mash of a torso, its flesh bubbling like boiling mud, then the trailing primate and crustacean limbs, and lastly the snake-like neck and the half-human head, gasping for air like a landed fish.

Ulysses staggered to the edge of the cliff, dropping to

his hands and knees at the spot where the monster had fallen. He felt almost ready to go off the edge after it.

Beneath him the monster somersaulted through the air, blood spilling from a multitude of wounds to stomach, limb-stumps, face and neck.

The splash of the abomination entering the sea was lost amidst the white-water torrent of the breakers crashing against the black rocks. And then the abomination was claimed by the hungry waves, the dark surge drawing the vivisect's twitching body down into the freezing, stygian depths.

The roiling waves released the rocks again, pulling back from the rugged coastline, but the creature's carcass was gone. And with the creature gone, Ulysses' body gave in at last.

He collapsed onto the cold, wet grass at the edge of the cliff – the North Sea wind pulling at his clothes and pain-wracked body, stinging his face with cold – and let blissful unconsciousness claim him.

EPILOGUE

Plenty More Fish in the Sea

"So, this is goodbye," Jennifer said, smiling despite the tears welling up at the corners of her eyes. Steam gushed around them as the train prepared to depart.

Standing there, face to face on the platform, Ulysses gently took her hands in his. He caressed her fingers with the soft black leather of his gloves, although inside he was wincing as his right hand throbbed with pain. Plenty of rest, the doctor who had treated him after his wild night on the moors had said.

But Ulysses felt like he had rested enough. He had slept for the whole of the following day, after his battle with the Umbridge-chimera, and had not woken again until well past nine on the morning after that. He had stirred to find Jennifer waiting anxiously at his bedside. He soon discovered that she too was staying at Mrs Scoresby's guesthouse now, as apparently Hunter's Lodge had also suffered the ravages of fire. "Well, they do say these things come in threes," Ulysses had remarked to Nimrod later, in private.

For a moment he had not known where he was or what the girl was doing there. As he came to wakefulness, the events of the previous forty-eight hours had seemed like nothing more than some hideous nightmare. But any such wishful thinking, on Ulysses' part had been banished by the reality of the pain he felt when he tried to move. Every muscle in his body felt either stiff or as if it had been damaged in some way. When eventually he pulled back the sheet, persisting in his struggle to rise, he found his body was a patchwork of bandages and plasters, that covered a myriad cuts and bruises. Nimrod had done a good job of taking care of him – as always.

But there had been one thing that his skilled manservant could do nothing about, not now, and that was his replacement left arm. The limb that he had reclaimed from the vivisect had been packed in ice and kept in the guesthouse's cold cellar – unbeknownst to Mrs Scoresby – but Ulysses feared that the flesh would have begun to necrotise before they could get it to a surgeon with the skill to graft it back onto his body. No, it looked like the chimpanzee's arm was there to stay.

And despite having been prescribed three days of bed rest by the local doctor, if not a whole week, Ulysses had insisted in not only getting out of bed, but of also getting dressed – although it took him rather longer than usual – and going about his business as if nothing untoward had happened at all. The rest of that day had been spent sifting through the smouldering embers of Jennifer's home and trying to make sense of all that had happened over the past few days, while Inspector Allardyce led the local police in an investigation of the burnt-out ruins of Umbridge House.

It crossed Ulysses' mind that the inspector didn't seem overly bothered that his visit to his wife's family had turned into a busman's holiday.

Rest was what the doctor had ordered for Ulysses, but in his own expert medical opinion there would be time to rest later. The curious case of the Whitby Mermaid was not yet closed.

"Yes. Goodbye, for now," Ulysses said softly. "There are matters regarding this case that I need to tie up back in London."

"So, you're going after the one who supplied Doktor

Seziermesser with his flesh-melding potion? This Alchemist?"

"Indeed I am."

"There's more to this than you're telling me, isn't there?"

Ulysses stared into Jennifer's eyes remembering the distinctive aniseed and rancid meat smell of the serum, as well as the nifty box of tricks they had found embedded in the flesh at the base of the Barghest's skull. He had encountered both before, when they had been used in conjunction by certain elements attempting to bring about the end of the British Empire.

"What will you do now?" he asked.

Jennifer sighed. If that was how it had to be, then so be it. "I'm going back to the Umbridge estate."

"After all that happened there?" Ulysses said, somewhat taken aback.

"The police have cleared the house, rounded up those who were in on Umbridge's scheme, those that he didn't kill in the end or that weren't burnt to a crisp by the fire," she added. "But when they came to the cellars they found them empty, apart from what was left of the good doktor, apparently."

Jennifer broke off and cast her gaze from the waiting train, the platform and the station buildings, to the headland on the other side of the Esk valley and the borders of the blasted moorland beyond.

"They're still out there," she said. "Seziermesser's experiments; his other victims. They've probably gone to ground in the caves and mines. Some might have made it to the coast. Others, who knows. But they need to be tracked down and found, so that they can be helped. And I have the expertise... to help."

Ulysses smiled. "Good for you." The girl was more resilient that he had given her credit for. It just went to prove the old adage of that which doesn't kill you only makes you stronger. "If anyone can make sure that those poor wretches get the help they need, it's you," he said warmly.

"Besides," she went on, blushing, "I feel that it will go some way towards vindicating my father's work."

"He'd be proud of you, to hear you say that. Good for you."

Ulysses lent forward and kissed Jennifer softly on the lips. She pulled away, her blush deepening, but did not remove her hands from his.

A sharp whistle cut through the background hubbub of the station, informing those gathered on the platform that the twelve forty-one to London was ready to depart. It was time for last fond farewells to be shared, for passengers to board and for well-wishers to allow them to do so.

Ulysses and Jennifer remained where they were.

"Sir, I hate to intrude," Nimrod interrupted as politely as he could, "but it's time to go. The train is ready to depart."

"One minute, eh, Nimrod old chap?"

"Very good, sir," Nimrod replied with just the slightest hint of annoyance in his voice.

"Jennifer... Jenny," Ulysses began. "There's something I need to say to you, something that I don't think I've said to you once in all this."

"Yes?" she said expectantly, her face drawing close to his again.

"And that's thank you."

"I'm sorry?"

"Thank you for everything you've done. You have been, quite simply, incredible. And if there's anything I can ever do for you, whatever it is –"

"There is one thing," she said, before he could finish – the flush of colour still there in her cheeks but her eyes now staring confidently into his – and with one hand on the back of his neck pulling him close, her warm lips parted to meet his unprotesting mouth.

With the train underway, and the memory of their last lingering kiss still warm on his lips, Ulysses Quicksilver distractedly picked up that morning's copy of *The Times*. The headline read:

AILING INDUSTRIALIST DIES IN HOUSE FIRE

"We made the front page," he said, smiling grimly at Nimrod. It had taken a while for the news to filter down to London, but Umbridge Industries was one of the cornerstones on which the modern British Empire of Magna Britannia was built, so his passing had made headline news – even if all of the facts surrounding the case had not.

The morning after the incident, the local paper had gone with news of another fire, the one that had gutted St Mary's Church and resulted in the death of the Reverend Nathaniel Creed. The fire at Umbridge House and the death therein of the cancer-stricken industrialist Josiah Umbridge had only made page seven.

The boy watched the train are is rattled its way along the track, hugging the banks of the Esk as it first headed south before turning west and starting on its way across the moors. He heard the distant *clickety-clack* of its wheels on the rails and the *peep-peep* of its steam-whistle, softened almost into melody by the distance and the muffling wind sweeping across the headland above the town.

"So, are you coming or what?" a skeletally gaunt man wearing scuffed top hat and tails, and tight black leggings, called from the cavalcade of steam-wagons and horse-drawn carts.

"I'm coming!" Jacob called back as he hefted his own meagre pack onto his shoulder. He hadn't had much that he could call his own to begin with, and thanks to the fire and his father's death, he had even less. The fire and brimstone priest might not have loved him, but he had still cared for him after a manner of speaking for the last seventeen years, and Jacob would miss him, even if the recalcitrant sinner had given him a name that summed up how he felt about the impact he had had on his life, a name that translated from the Hebrew as 'usurper'.

And now that his father was gone, it was time for Jacob Creed to make his own way in the world, and not as a boy but as a man, as part of new family, one that accepted him as he was.

"I'm coming!" he called again.

Throwing the blackened shell of the church one last mournful glance, Jacob trotted after the departing wagon-train as the Circus of Wonders went on its way.

Dawn was still two hours off as George Craven started hauling in his nets after another night's fishing. He had slipped back into the old routine as easily as he had slipped into his old galoshes and sou'wester, as easily as Mrs Craven had taken on the mantle of nagging fish wife again – although now she had something else entirely to complain about.

His life of luxury had not lasted for long, as ephemeral as the fame Mycroft Cruickshank had promised him. What had been headline news a month ago was today's fish and chip papers. And George should know; he had been tucking into a portion of deep-fried haddock only the day before when he had come across the words 'Mermaid Stolen' half-obscured by grease at the bottom of the packet.

He was still considering how quickly fame could turn to notoriety and, in turn, to derision when the glistening, writhing mass of his catch began to spill into the bottom of his boat, the *Mabel*, and it took him a moment to realise that something wasn't quite as it should be.

Amidst the wriggling mass of writhing tentacles, flapping fins and scuttling crustaceans there seemed to be some commotion. There was something in there with the catch, something that was voracious and evil-minded, something that was attacking the sea's bounty that lay suffocating in the bottom of the boat; several somethings in fact.

George Craven peered closer, trying to get a proper look at what it was that was molesting the fish, by the swaying inconstant light of the hurricane lantern secured to the mast.

They were hideous, impossible things, like some unholy cross between a crab, a fish and... and something like the mermaid – something almost human. In fact, in comparison, they made the mermaid seem like a perfectly plausible natural hybrid. But there was nothing natural about these things.

Boldly, George reached down with a thick gloved hand and plucked one of the creatures from the writhing mass of bodies sloshing around his feet. It was bright red in colour and only six or seven inches long from head to tail. Parts of it looked like they were covered in shell, but the shell itself was still soft and pliable, as if the thing were newly hatched. As George peered at it in disbelieving wonder it hissed and twisted in the grip of his thumb and forefinger, snapping at him with one over-sized pincer-claw.

For a moment he considered taking the specimen back to shore alive. He still had Cruikshank's details. Perhaps this could be the start of something big.

"Now hang on there, George," he announced to the sea and the wind. He peered at the impossible amalgam again, with its asymmetrical physiology, seemingly part mammal, part fish and part crab, and saw nothing but trouble. "They'd never believe you!" he said with a sigh.

And with that he tossed it overboard, back into the cold surge of the sea. Snatching the others from among the morning's catch, one by one, he sent them over the side after the first. The squirming creatures plopped into the water, quickly sinking from view into the black depths of the North Sea.

"How'd you do this morning, George?" the fisherman said aloud, playing all the parts in some imagined conversation he might have later that morning, back at the docks.

"Not bad, not bad."

"No mermaids today?"

"No, not today."

"A good catch then?"

"Yeah, a good catch. But you should've seen the one that got away."

THE END

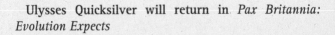

Ulysses Quicksilver will return in *Pax Britannia: Evolution Expects*

Jonathan Green lives and works in West London. He is well known for his contributions to the *Fighting Fantasy* range of adventure gamebooks, as well as his novels set within Games Workshop's worlds of *Warhammer* and *Warhammer 40,000*. He has written fiction for such diverse properties as *Sonic the Hedgehog* and *Doctor Who*, and non-fiction books including the titles *Match Wits with the Kids* and *What is Myrrh Anyway?* The co-creator of the world of Pax Britannia, *Human Nature* is his third novel for Abaddon Books and the fourth in the series. To find out more about the world of Pax Britannia, set your Babbage engine's ether-relay to www.paxbritanniablog.blogspot.com

Now read the exclusive short story
"Christmas Past"...

PAX BRITANNIA

CHRISTMAS PAST

JONATHAN GREEN

Abaddon
Books

WWW.ABADDONBOOKS.COM

~ December 1997 ~

I – WHOM THE GODS WOULD DESTROY

The atmosphere within the doctor's study was one of quiet, studious application, the only sounds the crackling of the fire in the grate, the scratching of the pen across the sheet of headed notepaper he had placed on his blotter, and the deathly ticking of the clock as it marked the man's last moments on this earth.

The pre-printed heading on the top of the crisp sheet of vellum notepaper read:

Dr Lockwood Lacey, Doctor of Psychiatry

Beneath it the doctor had written the date – 1st December 1997 – and then, in a meticulous hand, had proceeded to set down his written confession.

It was snug within the study: the curtains had been drawn against the encroaching night outside and the doctor had ensured that he had locked the door before he set about his night's business.

He put down his pen and, having re-read the last paragraph of the letter, took up the bundle of crumpled papers again. Shuffling through them one by one he read each again in turn. It did not take him long. Each was a letter, written on significantly poorer quality paper, torn from a child's jotter. Each was written in bright crayon colours, in the same childish hand, was decorated with simplistic illustrations, and each began in just the same way:

Dear Farthr Krissmus

There were thirty-seven of them in total.

With a sigh the doctor put them back on the desk, shuffling the papers together into a neat pile as he did so. Taking off his glasses he rubbed at his eyes. He felt tired, exhausted in fact. He hadn't slept for days; but he would have his rest soon enough.

Replacing his glasses, he re-read the last paragraph of his own letter. Taking up his pen once more he signed his name with a flourish, and then carefully replaced the lid. He folded the sheet of notepaper and slipped it into the envelope that he had addressed before commencing his act of confession and, licking the gummed strip, sealed it. Having tidied the other papers on his desk, the doctor laid the envelope carefully on top of the small pile in his out tray, his eyes alighting on the name of the addressee once more: The Reverend L. G. Havelock.

Calmly, the doctor rose from his chair, took off his shoes and padded across the carpeted floor of the study, the black dog that no-one else could see but which he knew was there – that was always there – trotting at his side. He stopped before the chair, which he had already had the forethought to place under the light fitting in the middle of the room.

Climbing onto the chair he slipped the noose over his head – the noose that he had also seen fit to prepare before he commenced on the rest of his endeavour, while his mind was still clear, his resolve firm. Kicking the chair away from under him, the doctor hanged himself.

A choking gargling sound disturbed the peace of the room, the spasming body sending jerking shadows dancing about the study in the flickering firelight.

And the black dog wagged its tail in approval.

II – THE DEAD OF JERICHO

Night fell as the Sunday faithful attended evensong, and with it, the first snows of winter drifted down upon the dreaming spires of Oxford. Feathery flakes descended right across the city from the blanket of clouds above.

The snow fell on the streets of Jericho, and the red-brick homes of the employees of the Oxford University Press, as much as it fell on the domiciles of dons and scholars, swirls of white confetti spiralling down between the terraces to form fractal icing sugar patterns on the roofs and roads and pavements.

But such beauty went unappreciated by Noah Hackett who, in his rotgut-induced alcoholic stupor was, for the time being, only concerned with finding a place to sleep. The snow only made things worse. Tonight it would be both cold *and* wet.

The prospect of sleeping rough on the streets of Oxford, amidst all the wealth and splendour of the complacent colleges, even among the less than salubrious warren of streets of Jericho, was never a pleasant one. But the knowledge that the cold and damp would leech what little warmth the last bottle of cheap gin had left in his bones, only made it seem all the more unappealing.

But he knew Jericho well – it was a favoured haunt of his, the memories of better days dragging him back to the area time after time, and there were always the boathouses and lock-ups down by the canal that were worth trying before hunkering down to wait out the night, the snow and the inevitable hangover.

He turned onto Canal Street, hoping to find an appropriately unlocked coach house in which to shelter. It was then that he heard the jingling sound for the first time, although in the drunken haze through which he lived much of his life these days he barely registered it.

The sound provoked in him nothing more than mild amusement, and into his mind, blown like the whirling inconstant snow, came memories of childhood Christmases, twee carol-rhymes rising from his subconscious like the bubbles in a glass of champagne. Not that he got to drink champagne these days.

There was nothing worth celebrating nowadays; it was enough for him that he managed to beg enough pennies from the guilty worthies of the city to furnish himself with another bottle of cheap gin and a bull scrotum pie, if he was lucky.

The tramp stumbled on along Canal Street, pulling the layers of scavenged shirts, cardigans, waistcoats and his heavy coat closer about him. He tugged his woollen cap down tight over his ears and for once was glad of his lice-ridden beard, which helped keep his face warm under its week's accumulation of grime.

Jingle-jingle.

There it was again, the tinkling of Christmas bells.

Noah trudged on through the slushy first fall.

Jingle-jingle.

And again.

This time the tramp turned. He peered through the snow and the night, and his own ever-present alcoholic fog, and glimpsed movement in a patch of shadow beyond the pool of light of the nearest guttering streetlamp. Something crimson swirled in the light escaping from a first floor window of one of the houses.

Jingle-jingle.

And then it was gone.

Confused by what he had seen and heard, but more irritated at still having nowhere to sleep, the tramp continued on his stumbling way, grumbling to himself through his beard.

Reaching the entrance to one of the alleyways that ran down to the Oxford Canal, Noah ducked into it, fervently hoping to give whoever it was that was following him the slip. He had had enough of the police harassing him and of the do-gooders from the Temperance Society sticking their interfering noses into his private business.

Untended weeds clogged the alleyway, poking out from underneath the ill-fitting doors of lock-ups and boathouses. Surely there had to be somewhere suitable round here?

Rattling the doors of the padlocked outhouses, Noah was only dimly aware of the footsteps approaching him. The renewed jingling, however, was enough to alert him to the presence of the stranger behind him.

He shuffled close to the red-brick structure to his right. He had learnt long ago that it was sometimes best just to blend into the background and not draw attention to oneself, especially when you were creeping round behind people's houses. Accusations of theft and trespass sat all too easily on the shoulders of a vagrant, as far as the authorities were concerned.

The thumping footfalls came nearer.

Jingle-jingle.

Noah froze, his weak heart suddenly racing with fretful apprehension. But still he turned round, to see who was following him.

A huge shadow stepped out of the night and into the middle of the alleyway in front of him and stopped abruptly. Noah's gasp of alarm surprised even himself. Cowering before the figure, he peered up into the hood of the crimson cloak that was pulled up over the stranger's head.

He half-expected to see a jolly, rosy-cheeked face with a bushy white beard. The bifurcated brutish face he saw there instead turned his guts to ice-water colder than the snow, and caused him to blurt out another blubbing cry of dismayed disbelief.

"You?" he gasped, recognition coming to him, despite the mind-fogging effects of the gin.

There was a sudden flurry of movement that sent eddying snowflakes spinning into the air, the reflected flash of the streetlamp on finely-honed steel and Noah gasped again as the air was forced from his body by a crippling punch to the stomach.

The figure pulled back. Noah's gaze was drawn to the fist with which the savage blow had been delivered. Four claw-like appendages glistened wetly, speckles of holly-red dripping onto the ground amidst the smattering of snow.

Noah instinctively put a hand to his belly. It came away painted red. In a state of shock the tramp found himself thinking how hot his lifeblood was, when he himself felt so cold.

With a feral wail of its own the red-cloaked figure moved in again with the gutting blades, and the jingling of Christmas bells accompanied the chorus of savage howls and agonised screams that suddenly filled the winter's night.

And all the time the snow fell.

III – THE BODY IN THE LIBRARY

"Not another one," Chief Inspector Thaw muttered grumpily.

"I'm afraid so, sir," his loyal sidekick Detective Sergeant Whately replied, holding the door for his superior to enter the archive ahead of him.

There, between the rows and rows of shelves lay the crumpled body of the Chief Librarian. From his posture and the rigour-set expression on his face, the Chief Inspector could have believed that Everett Willoughby was only sleeping, if it hadn't been for the blood-sodden mass of papers and irreplaceable archive documents on which he was lying.

The air of the archive was redolent with the smell of old books, mildew and the bitter-iron aroma of blood, and there was lots of it.

"Dear God," Thaw uttered in dismay.

"Ah, you're here at last, Chief Inspector," a young woman wearing blood-stained white coveralls said, rising from where she had been crouched beside the corpse.

"And good morning to you too, Doctor Lavish," Thaw replied, absentmindedly combing a hand through the swirls of white-grey hair on his head, in the presence of the attractive younger woman. "You're looking radiant as ever, if I might be permitted to say so?"

"Well compared to our friend the Chief Librarian here, I suppose I am," she smirked, looking down at the dead man's puffy, fish-white face. His eyes were sunken within blotchy purpling hollows.

"Is it our killer?" Thaw asked, returning to the matter in hand.

"That's for you to find out, isn't it Chief Inspector?"

Doctor Lavish said, a twinkle in her eyes.

"Well, yes. Of course, but —"

"But if you mean, is it the same M.O., then yes. Knifed in the stomach with what looks like a fistful of kitchen knives. He was stabbed multiple times. Position and pattern of the wounds suggest that the victim was struck repeatedly with an instrument made up of several long blades."

"You're sure, doctor?"

"Either that, or our killer took the time to meticulously measure the space between each stab wound before administering the next."

The Chief Inspector expressed his irritation by breathing out loudly through his nose. "Point taken."

He turned to his Detective Sergeant. "First it was Higgins, wealthy banker, out for a walk with his dog along Brewer Street, two nights ago. And now this poor bugger."

"Yes, sir," Whately confirmed.

"Two men, two murders, two nights. But what was it that connected the victims? Why were they the targets that our killer chose?"

There was the creak and bang of a door opening and closing, accompanied by the *tap-tap-tap* of footsteps on the polished archive floor.

"And what have we here?" came a cheery voice from behind the Chief Inspector. Thaw turned and came face-to-face with a smartly-dressed man, in his mid-to-late thirties judging by the streaks of grey present at the temples of his thick head of hair. He was handsome, with a well-defined jaw-line, and tall, and the Chief Inspector could see that beneath his long coat and tweed suit he had the physique of an athlete. Behind him, at his shoulder, stood an older man, dressed in the traditional attire of a butler. He was tall like his master and broad across the shoulders, his grey hair swept back from a clearly-defined widow's peak

"Who the bloody hell are you?" Chief Inspector Thaw demanded.

The interloper fixed the policeman with sparkling brown eyes and grinned. "Ulysses Quicksilver, at your service," he said, holding out a black-gloved hand. "You might have heard of me."

"Might I?" the Chief Inspector returned. "Should I have heard of him, Whately?"

"Oh yes, sir," the Detective Sergeant blurted excitedly. "Mr Quicksilver saved her Majesty's life, sir, during the Wormwood Debacle. Don't you remember?"

The Chief Inspector muttered something as undoubtedly unflattering as it was unintelligible.

"It's a pleasure to meet you, sir," the Detective Sergeant said, with all the enthusiasm of an over-excited puppy, taking the proffered handshake where his superior had not.

"Thank you...?"

"Whately. Detective Sergeant Whately."

"Sergeant Whately. A pleasure!"

"Who let you in here anyway?" Thaw snapped.

"Does that matter? I'm here now, and I'm here to help."

"What brings you to Oxford, Mr Quicksilver?" Whately asked, patently awestruck finding himself in the presence of a genuine Hero of the Empire.

"Looking up an old friend," Quicksilver replied. "Or at least I will be when we're done here. Saw all the commotion in the street as we were driving over to Boriel."

"Well, you'll be pleased to hear that we are all done here," the Chief Inspector declared. "Isn't that right, doctor?"

"Yes, Chief Inspector. It's over to you now."

"So thank you for the offer of your help, but we won't need to keep you from renewing your old acquaintance after all."

"What happened to the poor fellow?" Quicksilver pressed, craning to peer past the Chief Inspector at the body lying between the stacks. "Stabbed was he?"

"Yes," Whately replied helpfully, "several times. Just like the other one."

"The other one?"

"Whately!" the irascible Thaw growled.

"Sorry, sir." The Detective Sergeant turned an embarrassed shade of beetroot.

"So, Mr Quicksilver, as we like to say in the Force, there really is nothing to see here. We have everything under control."

"Oh, I'm sure you do, Inspector."

"That's *Chief* Inspector."

"Oh, I *do* beg your pardon, *Chief* Inspector. We wouldn't want to be getting in your way now would we, Nimrod?"

"Indeed not, sir," the dandy's manservant replied in a tone that matched the severity of his expression of aloof disdain as he regarded the two policemen with a stony, sapphire gaze.

"But if you would like my help at all, I'll be in Oxford for the rest of the day, so don't hesitate to get in touch."

He pulled a leather wallet from a jacket pocket and from that extracted a printed calling card, passing it to the still-grinning Sergeant.

"Thank you for your time, *Chief* Inspector. Merry Christmas."

And with that he turned, and left the library.

"Nimrod, I do believe we have tarried here long enough," Ulysses Quicksilver announced as he and his manservant left the crime scene that the Bodleian Library had become. "I rather feel we've kept old Monty waiting far too long already."

"Very good, sir," Nimrod replied matter-of-factly. "Would you like to take the car, sir?"

The two of them ducked under the police line at the arched entrance to the Bodleian Square and turned left, making for where Nimrod had parked the Mark IV Silver Phantom at the entrance to Catte Street.

"Let's leave the car," Ulysses said, buttoning his coat against the cold. "A walk in this bracing air will help clear the remains of last night's excesses from my head, I hope."

"Very good, sir."

A young woman, wearing a woollen beret and full-length coat against the cold, emerged from the throng of curious onlookers collected outside the Bodleian and hurried to intercept them.

"Mr Quicksilver?" she called.

"Who wants to know?" was Ulysses' sharp rebuttal.

"Lucy Gudrun, *Oxford Echo*. What is that brings you to Oxford on Christmas Eve, when only last night you were seen gallivanting at Lord and Lady Rothschild's Christmas Ball?" The young woman suddenly seemed very confident as to Ulysses' identity.

"Personal business."

"And would that same personal business include the investigation of the Christmas Killings?"

Ulysses' carefully-composed grimace of passive indifference slipped and he turned to look at the girl directly. "Killings plural, you say?"

He was caught by her obvious attractiveness, which she seemed at pains to cover up. But even without the application of any obvious make-up, her cheeks still had an appealing rosy glow and her rosebud lips were none the less appealing.

"Everett Willoughby's death is the second in as many days that match the same M.O. within the city."

"How do you know...?" Ulysses broke off. He wasn't that naive. His comment had been a knee jerk reaction. He knew how the press worked. They always 'had their sources'.

"I have my sources," the young woman said with a mixture of smugness and pride.

"I knew you were going to say that," Ulysses said raising a wry eyebrow. She was young and eager, barely into her twenties, if he was any judge, and he was. "Look, Miss Gudrun, I have tarried too long already and have places I need to be, as I'm sure do you. Now if you'll excuse me."

"Just one comment for the *Oxford Echo*?" the plucky reporter pressed, tireless in her efforts.

Ulysses stopped. "Alright, here's a comment for you. *No comment!*" With that he turned on his heel and strode on his way.

"Can I have a comment from you, sir?" the young woman asked, thrusting the hand-held recorder under Nimrod's nose before he even had a chance to follow his master. The young woman almost wilted under his withering sapphire stare.

"Good day, Miss Gudrun," he intoned sonorously, but the look in his eyes said so much more, and none of it pleasant.

She watched them leave.

Lucy Gudrun knew a good story when she stumbled

on one, like a chalk-outlined body on the floor of the Bodleian library, but she also knew when she was pushing her luck and when to admit defeat. Besides, she might have lost this particular battle, but she hadn't lost the war. Not yet.

She turned back to the Great Gate that led from Catte Street into the School's quadrangle and from there into the Bodleian itself. She was just in time to see the curmudgeonly Chief Inspector Thaw and his sidekick Sergeant Whately emerge from beneath the stone gateway and cross the police line.

Ensuring that her hand-held recorder was still running, she trotted towards the pair of policemen. "Chief Inspector!" she shouted. "A word for the *Oxford Echo*?"

IV – THE DAMOCLES CLUB

He knew that something was wrong before the porter even opened the door to the old man's rooms. It was the smell. The iron-rich tang of blood at the back of his throat again, the rancid ammonia smell of voided bowels, the unpleasant and wholly unmistakeable smell of death.

"Bloody 'ell!" the porter swore, his hand slipping from the doorknob as he stood there dumbfounded, the door swinging open to reveal the scene of devastation and death beyond.

"Monty!" Ulysses Quicksilver gasped, pushing past the porter – his bowler hat held tight in his shaking hands now – and into the room.

It had obviously been a mess to begin with. A proliferation of books and manuscripts, along with empty tea cups, half-eaten plates of food, and the skull of an Australopithecus, were scattered over desks and bookcases. The half-expected scholarly clutter of an absent-minded professor even littered the tops of glass-fronted cabinets containing stuffed animals and Neolithic tools, cracked leather chairs, and the Persian rugs on the floor as well. The attack on Professor Montgomery Summerson, had obviously left the study in an even greater state of chaos and confusion.

Ulysses stood there, amidst the disorder and disarray, staring down at the cold carcass of his old tutor. Honeyed sunlight pierced the leadlights of the room's windows, revealing the full horror of the scene in intense, sun-washed colours, predominantly red.

Summerson had called him at home only the evening before, but Ulysses had been out on the town, enjoying the company of tipsy and compliant young socialites at the Rothschild's Christmas Ball, held at his Lordship' Gunnersbury Park estate, west of the capital. Ulysses had missed the call then and hadn't even been aware of it until Nimrod woke him that morning, having checked the calls logged to the house the night before.

"I should have come sooner," he said, his voice barely more than a whisper of regret.

"You were out, sir," Nimrod replied. "You weren't to know that Professor Summerson would call. After all, you have not heard from him in some time."

"I know, but if hadn't been out gallivanting about the place, like the self-indulgent idiot I was in my youth, I wouldn't have missed his call."

"You've had a lot on your mind, sir."

Ulysses swore under his breath. "He was onto something, Nimrod," he said, nudging a pile of papers at his foot. "He wanted my help and because I wasn't there for him he's dead."

Ulysses looked at the body again. It was a mess. He didn't need to be a coroner to pronounce the cause of death. He had been knifed like Willoughby the librarian. His face had been carved up by four slashing knife strokes, while his shirt had been turned wholly red by his own blood.

Ulysses knelt down beside the body. Summerson had died in agony, his body curled into an agonised question mark, as if in death every part of him had wanted to know why he had to die in this manner. As far as Ulysses could tell, he had bled to death, having been stabbed so many times that the blood-sodden fabric of his clothes now lay in tatters over the mangled meat of his chest.

There was blood on his face, on his chest, his arms, blood had pooled on the floor around him, soaking fallen papers, the threadbare Persian rug on which he lay, contorted in his death-agonies, it covered his hands... Only it didn't. Ulysses paused and looked more closely.

The dead man only had blood on the rigoured claw of his right hand, and no signs of any wounds there. The hand was stretched out from the professor's body, his fingers partially obscured by a bloodied document that must have fallen across him as he lay dying on the floor of his study.

Suddenly aware of the rapid beating of his heart, caged within his chest, carefully Ulysses moved the papers aside. His breath caught in his throat. There, formed of bloody finger-strokes, was one semi-congealed word: Damocles.

Monty Summerson had sent Ulysses a final message, written in his own blood.

"I-I'd better call the-the police," the porter stammered, backing out of the room, leaving the door open behind him.

"Just give us half an hour," Ulysses said, without looking at the man, but flashing him the contents of his leather card-holder again just in case he needed reminding who's authority they were working under.

For a moment neither Ulysses nor Nimrod moved. Neither of them said anything, the only sound that broke the stillness of the study the insistent ticking of the clock on the mantelpiece on the other side of the room.

As Ulysses continued to take in every detail of the murder scene, a shadow fell across him from the doorway to the study behind him.

He heard a startled gasp and turned.

In a moment the young woman had composed herself again. "Perhaps you would like to make a comment now, Mr Quicksilver," Lucy Gudrun suggested, recording device pointing towards him.

"Anything that has the name Damocles on it. Anything that might give us any kind of a clue. Anything at all." Ulysses said, frustrated at his own failure to so far discover what it was that his former tutor had been trying to tell him through his last, dying act.

Heedless to what Chief Inspector Thaw might have to say about them disturbing a crime scene, Nimrod set about bringing some semblance of order back to the professor's study – although he made sure that he left the body just as it was – so that Ulysses' search for clues might be made all the easier, while the reporter began going through the papers on the dead man's desk.

Ulysses had taken the attitude that her arrival at Boriel College, having obviously followed them from the Bodleian, had been opportune. She obviously already had a handle on what was going on, and she had seen too much of the scene of Summerson's murder already to be fobbed off, and so he had decided to treat her presence as an asset rather than a hindrance. He had put her to work, promising her the scoop of her career as he set about solving the Christmas Killings. She was tough too, not seeming to mind that the professor's body was still there in the room.

And yet, here they were, with the half hour's grace granted them by the porter almost up, half-expecting the police to turn up at any moment, and still without any answers.

"Here, take a look at this!" Lucy suddenly piped up. Ulysses joined her at the professor's desk. She was poring over a pile of newspapers, among them copies of the *Oxford Echo*. Ulysses peered over her shoulder to see what it was that had caused her outburst.

She had a copy of *The Times* in front of her, folded so

as to expose the obituaries page. Circled in red pen was the obituary of Dr Lockwood Lacey, doctor of psychiatry. Ulysses scanned the piece.

"Fifty-seven years old... worked at the Saint Ophelia Sanatorium for the Mentally Infirm," he read. "Very interesting, but what does this have to do with Damocles, or the other killings, for that matter?"

"Well, your professor friend circled it for a reason and then there's this." She moved the paper to reveal another, with another article circled, this time reporting the murder of one Aloysius Higgins, a banker. "This one just made yesterday's *Echo*."

"When's the obituary from?"

"The eighth of December. It says Lacey died on the first of December."

"And when did Higgins die?"

"The night of the twenty-second."

"So how does this one fit in?" Ulysses asked, lifting another folded newspaper from a pile of books on a chair beside him and placing it on the desk. In this case, Summerson appeared to have circled a few lines at the bottom of an inside page of the local paper, that reported the killing of a tramp well-known in the Jericho area, who went by the name of Noah.

"That's news to me," Lucy admitted. "When did that happen?"

"On..." Ulysses paused, searching for a date at the top of the page. "On the twenty-first. Sunday night."

"And then the Chief Librarian was killed last night, which was the twenty-third," Lucy pondered, gazing thoughtfully into the middle distance.

"Along with Summerson. So, what could possibly connect the Professor of Social Anthropology, the Chief Librarian of the Bodleian, a successful banker, and a homeless tramp?"

"You think something does connect them then?"

"Well, apart from the manner of their deaths? It seems likely, doesn't it to you?"

"Well yes, but a couple of academics, a banker and a tramp?"

"And let's not forget the suicidal doctor of psychiatry." Ulysses' face twisted into a knot of concentration. "Physician, heal thyself," he said quietly to himself.

"Excuse me, sir," Nimrod said interrupting his master's musings, "but I think this might be of interest." He was holding up a framed photograph. The glass was cracked right across the middle, no doubt having been damaged at the same time that Summerson was attacked.

Ulysses crossed the room in a series of excited, leaping strides. "Good show, old chap!"

The photograph showed seven young men, undoubtedly undergraduates, by their dress and apparent age. The picture had been taken within the Boriel College quad. Although the pose was formal, their attitude was anything but. All of them were wearing expressions of smug arrogance or feigned aloof indifference.

"Obnoxious arrogant bastards, convinced of their own superiority over the rest of the human race the lot of them," Ulysses muttered under his breath.

"I couldn't possibly comment, sir," was Nimrod's tactful reply, his gaze lingering on Ulysses.

The sepia-tint photograph was mounted within a card frame, at the bottom of which had been written, in an exaggerated Gothic hand:

The Damocles Club, Michaelmas Term, 1960.

Underneath that were recorded the names of the

individuals in the picture.

"Well, there are a few familiar names here," he stated with glee. Her reporter's sense of curiosity piqued, Lucy rose from her place behind the desk and joined the two men in their inspection of the image. "There's Higgins, the banker, second from the left, and L. Lacey next to him, the suicidal doctor. Two along from him again is poor old Monty, of all people, and next to him, second from the right, is Willoughby."

"You think this is the connection then?" Lucy asked.

"Well, considering that we have the word 'Damocles' written over there on the floor in Monty's blood, and three of the men from this photograph have been murdered within as many days, I can hardly see how it can be anything other," Ulysses declared.

"It's four, actually," Lucy said.

"I beg your pardon?"

"Four men from that list have been found dead since Monday morning."

"Really?"

"If you include old Noah. N. Hackett?"

"Of course!" Ulysses exclaimed, flashing the girl a delighted smile. "The tramp! Oh how the mighty have fallen."

He turned back to the photograph.

"So, one dead by his own hand. Four dead by the hand of another in the last three nights. That just leaves two names on this list, neither of which mean anything to me. But we have to find them, that is most imperative."

"You think they are in danger, sir?" Nimrod asked.

"Indeed I do. One of them could even be our killer. Either way, we have to find them as quickly as possible. Which is where you come in, Miss Gudrun."

"It is?" the young woman met Ulysses intense gaze.

"Indeed it is! I want you to use the immense resources of that local rag you work for to find out who S. Fitzmaurice and V. Ashton-Griffiths are and where they might be found. I have a feeling that it will be somewhere not a million miles from here."

"Very well, but what's in it for me?"

Ulysses' look of childish excitement darkened to become one of bitter disdain. Reporters the world over; they were all the same.

"Do this, for me," he said, "and I'll give you the exclusive of your career. I'll hand you Oxford's Christmas Killer on a platter."

V – SLAY BELLS

"Mr Fitzmaurice?" Ulysses tried, as he entered the fusty darkness of the glasshouse. "Saintjohn Fitzmaurice?" he called a little louder. Eyes straining to see anything through the failing twilight, his manservant cautiously followed him into the building.

The place seemed to be entirely deserted – there wasn't a light on anywhere – but that didn't put pay to the uncomfortable feeling Ulysses' had, like a persistent itch on the inside of his skull, that something wasn't right. There was danger here.

It had been several hours since they had made their hasty exit from the Professor's study, leaving as Chief Inspector Thaw and his attendant officers were making their way into Boriel College by the Longwall Street entrance.

As the reporter returned to the *Oxford Echo's* newsroom and its difference engine database, Ulysses and Nimrod retired to the backroom of the Turf Tavern, Ulysses muttering something about the hair of the dog that had bitten him the night before.

In time, Lucy's scouring of her Babbage engine's reader screen had come up trumps and she had contacted Ulysses, furnishing him with the current whereabouts of Saintjohn Fitzmaurice, formerly of the Damocles Club, now Director of Oxford's Botanic Gardens.

"Mr Fitzmaurice!" Ulysses called again into the gathering gloom between the potted plants, louder this time.

Still no reply.

They had tried the man's home already, only to be told by his housekeeper that he had left earlier that evening in a state of high dudgeon, having taken a handwritten missive at the door, saying something about having to go back to the Gardens.

Ulysses edged forwards slowly. The insistent subconscious scratching on the inside of his skull grew in intensity. Was Fitzmaurice waiting for them, just around the corner, garden fork in hand, ready to do them in? Or had the killer struck already, and the Director was, right now, lying dead, half buried in a compost heap somewhere?

And then Ulysses heard the incongruous sound for the first time, the jingling of bells.

"Come on, Nimrod!" he hissed. "This way!"

And then the two of them were running through the glasshouse. Ahead of them the insistent jingle-jingle of the bells continued, leading them on.

Ulysses reached a glazed divide and pushed through the unlatched door swinging on its hinges, almost tripping over the body lying in the darkness between the trestles of the potting shed.

Ulysses guessed that the figure curled in an expanding pool of his own blood, that glistened black in the darkness, was Saintjohn Fitzmaurice, but there wasn't time to stop and check.

The body groaned weakly.

"Nimrod, stay with him," Ulysses instructed his manservant, hopping over the fatally wounded man and charging on his way in pursuit of the bells.

There was a cacophonous crash of breaking glass and splintering glazing struts from the far end of the glasshouse. Ulysses ran on.

He emerged from the end of the glasshouse through the wreck of another glazed door that it looked like his quarry had run straight through without bothering to open, into the oily darkness of the formal gardens.

He ran on, between carefully-manicured black lawns, along gravel paths, always chasing the steady jingle of the Christmas bells. Sleigh bells.

Shrubs and the dark skeletal shapes of trees loomed ahead of him. There was a change in the rhythm of the jingling, as if, Ulysses imagined, the killer had taken a running jump at the walled boundary of the Gardens. A moment later he heard the thud of someone landing heavily in the street on the other side.

He reached the wall himself only a matter of moments later. Using his unnaturally muscled left arm in particular to help with his ascent, Ulysses pulled himself to the top of the wall that marked the western boundary of the Botanic Gardens.

He peered down into the poorly-lit lane beyond. He couldn't see anybody, either running up or down the road, and, he now realised after his own desperate scramble up the wall, he couldn't hear anything in the way of pounding footfalls or jingling sleigh bells either.

A hissed expletive escaped Ulysses' gritted teeth. They had been so close. If only they had got there sooner, he might have had the Christmas Killer in his clutches right at that very moment. Instead he was no closer to catching the murderer of his old friend and tutor, and all those other men. In fact his failure to act in time had led to another man's death. Not for the first time that day, Ulysses berated himself for not answering his tutor's plea sooner.

It was at that moment that his personal communicator buzzed inside his pocket. Straddling the top of the wall, Ulysses took out the device and pressed the enamelled answer key.

"Yes?" he snapped sharply into the mouthpiece.

"It's Lucy," the woman's voice at the other end of the line said. "Did you get to Fitzmaurice in time?"

"No. We were too late. The killer got here first and now he's got away. I lost him!" he snarled, the rancour evident in his voice.

"Well I think I know where you might find him," Lucy said.

"Really?"

"I've identified the last man in the photograph. Get yourself back to Boriel, it's the Master. It's Virgil Ashton-Griffiths! Either he's the killer or he's the next victim!"

VI – THE GHOST OF CHRISTMAS PAST

"So, tell me about the Damocles Club, Master," Ulysses said, regarding the gargoyle-faced man opposite from over steepled, black-gloved fingers, "and, more specifically, why somebody would want every last member dead."

Ulysses Quicksilver was impressed. The Master had maintained the same stony facade ever since they had invaded his private sanctuary.

The porter – still shaken by his discovery of Montgomery Summerson's eviscerated body – had reluctantly led Ulysses, Nimrod and Lucy through the college buildings to the Master's apartments, as if he half expected to stumble upon another corpse. It had been with some obvious relief that he had opened the door, hearing the Master's voice command them to "Come!" Ulysses' 'by Appointment to Her Majesty' ID had done the rest.

Ulysses and Virgil Ashton-Griffiths met each other's unblinking eyes, each regarding the other by the ruddy glow of the fire crackling in the hearth. For a moment, all that could be heard within the Master's study was the insistent ticking of a clock and the snap and crackle of the fire smouldering in the grate.

And then the older man's expression of steely resolution slowly began to crumble, the hard lines of his hawkish face becoming sagging lines heavy with worry.

"We were undergraduates at the time, here at Boriel College," the Master said quietly. "We were young, we were arrogant –"

"I could see that for myself," Ulysses threw in.

"And we were bored. The idle rich, if you like," Ashton-Griffiths went on.

"So, apart from looking down on everyone else and

your Daddies having more money than you had things to fill your days with, what did you do that would make someone wish you all dead?"

"From what I remember of your own background, Mr Quicksilver, you were not left exactly destitute by your parents when they died." The Master's previous steel had started to return in the face of Ulysses' brusque manner.

"But my name isn't the one that's at the bottom of a list of dead men," Ulysses pointed out darkly.

The Master sighed. "To be honest, it will be a relief to be able to tell someone about it after all these years."

"How many years, precisely?"

"Thirty-seven."

"So, around the time the photograph was taken, when the Damocles Club was at its height."

The Master reached for his cup of tea and took a sip before continuing.

"It was the product of the recklessness of youth, I suppose, a group of like-minded individuals, cast free of boarding school and our mothers' apron strings for the first time, with enough money and status to do pretty much as we pleased. Such youthful exuberance manifested itself at first in terms of ridiculous drinking games at various pubs around the town, but they didn't really appeal to our thrill-seeking natures. It was adrenalin that motivated us, the need to face impossible odds and triumph.

"We began to partake in various gambling pursuits, but when money is no object, when you are not really risking anything in a real sense, it takes away the element of risk and saps the excitement from it. So we started gambling with things that were more precious to us than money. We took up some of the rather more extreme sports, rock-climbing, white-water rafting and the like."

"But we've all done that sort of thing haven't we?"

Ulysses said, recalling the time in his own life when he had frittered his life away in idle pursuits. He had held the Paris-Dakar rally record for eight years running, for a start. And it could be argued that his life now was even more dangerous, and satisfying as a result. Well, most of the time, he thought, rubbing at the shoulder joint of his left arm.

"We fashioned ourselves into the Damocles Club, named after the infamous sword, of course," the Master went on, as if he hadn't heard a word Ulysses had said. "But, unlike Damocles, we liked that feeling of imminent danger, that everything about our position of privilege could be over-turned in an instant."

He paused, returning the teacup and its saucer to the table.

"And then we met Marley."

"Go on."

"Lacey brought him along, I think he had a bit of thing for him to be honest. Lockwood always did go for those rugger types, the old poof. But Marley wasn't one of us. He didn't fit in. He didn't come from the right background."

"What do you mean?" Lucy asked.

"His father was a churchman. They didn't have money." Ashton-Griffiths gave her a disparaging look. Something of the arrogant youth was still there, just beneath the veneer of social responsibility. "Anyway, it was Higgins who suggested the initiation. Hackett provided the gun. His family were of the huntin', shootin' and fishin' variety."

"So you shot him?" Lucy asked, shocked.

"Don't be ridiculous, my dear," Ulysses rebutted her. "I'm guessing that after a bout of heavy drinking the idea of the initiation was raised with this Marley – a game of

Russian roulette was it, Master?"

The older man nodded. He suddenly appeared to have aged ten years, the inconstant shadows cast by the fire giving him a haunted appearance.

"And Marley lost."

"I didn't know Higgins had actually loaded the damn thing! Marley's death shocked us all out of our youthful arrogance and taught us to value what we had more carefully. The Damocles Club was disbanded. We all went our separate ways."

"And yet, almost all of you ended up back in Oxford thirty-seven years later," Ulysses pointed out. "I wonder why that was. A sense of guilt? Unable to completely leave the past behind? Having discovered that you couldn't run from yourselves you all decided to confront your past in some pathetic, subconscious way?"

"So, what do we do now?" The Master raised his head and looked at Ulysses, his eyes glistening in the flickering firelight. "Are you going to have me arrested?"

"Arrested?" Ulysses laughed humourlessly. "But you're not the murderer, are you?"

"But..." Lucy suddenly put in, looking bewildered. "But he's the only one left on the list."

"Yes, but Nimrod and I came straight here, having just chased the killer out of the Botanic Gardens. The Master here is some years older than me and, if you don't mind me saying so Master, he's carrying a few more pounds and he wasn't even out of breath when we arrived. If he had been the killer I wouldn't have expected him to be waiting in his rooms when we arrived and, if by some miracle he was, I would certainly have expected him to be out of breath!"

"But I've just confessed our crime to you," the Master pressed. "I need to pay for the part I played, for being an accessory after the fact."

"If I didn't know any better, I would have to say that I thought you wanted to be arrested, to be put into protective custody and save your own sorry skin."

For a moment the Master was speechless.

"So who's the Christmas Killer?" Lucy asked, completely confused.

"That is, what I suspect, we will all discover before this night is through," Ulysses said, brimful of the sort of arrogant confidence that would have seen him fit quite well with the rest of the Damocles Club where the wretched Marley had not.

"So, what are we going to do now?"

"Now?" Ulysses said, a dark smile forming on his lips. "Now we wait."

VII – SANTA CLAWS IS COMING TO TOWN

The clock in the Master's study was just striking the tenth bell of eleven when Father Christmas paid a call. He broke down the door on the second attempt, but by that time Ulysses' prescient sixth sense had already alerted him to the assailant's approach.

Lucy screamed as the doorjamb splintered and a hulking figure burst into the room. He was shrouded by a deep red cloak and hood, trimmed with white fur, and as he lurched into the study steel claws gleamed in the dying ember-glow emanating from the grate.

With a startled grunt the hulk hesitated, surprised to discover that the Master had company. But his hesitation lasted only a moment. Dogged in his determination, and apparently unconcerned as to the presence of potential witnesses to the crime he was about to commit, the ogre lunged for the Master with a savage roar.

But Ulysses and Nimrod were ready.

The brute was almost as broad as he was tall, built from slabs of muscle, as Ulysses soon learnt to his cost, the man-mountain hurling him across the room by one swipe of his arm, sending the sleigh bells ringing again.

The killer turned his attention back onto the Master who had backed away as far as he could behind his desk, until he was stopped from going any further by a wall of bookshelves.

"Sir!" Nimrod shouted over the furious bellows of the brute, casting an anxious glance Ulysses' way.

"Don't worry about me!" he shouted back, picking himself out of the remains of the side table on which he had landed. "Take him down!"

Nimrod's pistol was in his hands in an instant. Ulysses

looked from the muzzle of the gun to the ogre, batting Lucy aside, claws extended, as he tried to reach the mewling Master. Apart from the fact that there was a mad killer on the loose in the room with them, something wasn't right.

"I want him alive!" Ulysses shouted.

Nimrod's gun fired.

With a howl the brute slumped against the Master's desk as his right leg gave way beneath him, his kneecap a bloody mess.

Seizing the opportunity, Nimrod and Ulysses moved in together, Ulysses disarming the killer with a flick of his own rapier-blade. With the two of them pinning the thrashing attacker to the ground, Lucy pulled down one of the velvet drapes covering the windows with which to bind the captured killer, as the Master looked on in amazement.

"But I mean, Father Christmas?" Lucy repeated.

"Who else were you expecting?" Ulysses said. "After all, it is Christmas Eve. And from the look of the gift he was bringing you, Master, it looks like you've most definitely been a bad boy this year."

The Master said nothing, but continued to stare into the shadows beneath the obscuring hood of the cloak

"But what kind of a disguise is that?" the reporter persisted.

"One that's kept his identity a secret and allowed him to kill four – possibly five – men," Ulysses stated grimly. "So," he said, approaching the chair to which they had bound the moaning brute with the curtain, "shall we see who it is before we inform Chief Inspector Thaw that we've caught his Christmas Killer for him?"

Taking hold of the hood in one black-gloved hand he threw it back.

Lucy gasped in horror. As did the Master.

"Marley!" was all he could say, his voice a strained whisper.

Ulysses studied the face of the killer with clinical interest, as a lepidopterist might examine a moth pinned beneath a microscope.

The brute appeared to be a similar age to the Master – in his late fifties – but that was where the similarity ended. His head was entirely hairless and where the Master's eyes sparkled with a ferocious intelligence, behind the killer's eyes there resided a brutal and imbecilic child.

The reason for the former Oxford undergraduate's reversion to a state of moronic childishness was clear. It was as if his face had been sliced down the middle, from the top of his head to his cleft palette. A livid sunken scar had pulled the man's features into the middle of his face, pulling his eyes closer together, making him appear almost permanently cross-eyed. Saliva drooled continually from his gaping toothless mouth soaking the collar of the cloak with its stinking residue.

"The gunshot wound," Ulysses said. "The one that you thought had killed him, Master, all those years ago did this to him."

"I-I had n-no idea," Ashton-Griffiths stammered.

"Looks like your 'victim' is not as dead as you thought he was. By the way," he added, "what time of year did this –" Ulysses indicated Marley's face with a waving finger "– happen?"

"A few days before Christmas 1960," the Master replied, a distant look in his eyes.

"Well, Ulysses, you promised me an exclusive," Lucy

said, turning to the dandy, her own shock passing as her reporter's instinct for a good story took over again, "but I never expected anything like this. The Christmas Killer unmasked before my very eyes. Congratulations!" She put out her hand to shake his.

"Oh, it's not case closed yet, my dear," Ulysses remarked, somewhat condescendingly.

"It's not? But you've caught the killer."

"Yes, but look at him," Ulysses said, "he's an imbecile. Severely brain-damaged as a result of his attempt to become a member of the Damocles Club all those years ago. There's no way that he could have masterminded the murders himself, tracking down the perpetrators of something that took place thirty-seven years ago."

Lucy looked again at the pathetic creature bound to the chair before them. Ulysses was right. Marley was a blunt instrument, nothing more.

"No," Ulysses went on, "this poor wretch is merely the puppet. Someone else has been pulling the strings all along. And when we have this puppet-master, then we can consider the case closed."

"So, who's that then?" Lucy was feeling exasperated now. Ulysses flashed her a devilish grin. "You do know, don't you?"

"No – not at all!" he declared gleefully. His devil-may-care attitude was starting to grate on Lucy's nerves.

"But you know where to start looking," the Master suddenly said.

"I do indeed."

"It's the knife-fist, isn't it?" Ashton-Griffiths went on, focusing all his attention on the murder weapon that now lay on the blotting pad on his desk.

It was a rusted metal affair, not unlike a knuckleduster, with a bar that was held in the palm, and four sharp blades that effectively formed claws in place of the wearer's fingers when it was gripped in the hand.

Ulysses nodded. "And I have my old alma mater to thank for that morsel of useful knowledge. After all, it was at those times when I was actually working towards my degree in Social Anthropology that I visited the Pitt Rivers Museum and saw this particular item for the first time."

Ulysses turned on his heel and made for the door. "Miss Gudrun, I would appreciate it if you would wait here for the police with the Master."

"But-" Lucy tried to protest.

"Don't worry, you've still got your exclusive, but you've done enough. Nimrod, you're with me."

As the dandy and his butler exited the Master's study in a whirl of coat tails and well-bred arrogance, Lucy was left mouthing 'O's like a goldfish.

"Quicksilver's wasting his time," the Master said from the other side of the room, teacup and saucer in hand again.

"What do you mean?" Lucy asked intrigued.

"I mean, they won't find the killer's manipulator at the museum. They don't know who they're looking for."

"And you do?"

"I've a pretty good idea," the Master said, the steel back in his voice. Ignoring the curious gaze of the drooling idiot still bound to the chair in the middle of his study, Ashton-Griffiths moved for the door. "Wouldn't you rather come with me, now, and find out if I'm right, rather than wait here for the police with... with that?"

A moment later, Lucy Gudrun ran out of the study on the heels of the darkly determined Master.

VIII – SINS OF THE FATHERS

"This is most irregular," the curator complained as Ulysses barged past him and into the echoing hall that housed the Pitt Rivers collection. Nimrod shot the man a look that silenced him and followed his master into the museum annexe.

Their insistent knocking had alerted a night watchman – saving Nimrod the bother of having to pick the locks – who had then fetched the curator from his attic apartment. The curator answered the night watchman's summons in his pyjamas and slippers. He had not been best pleased.

The cavernous space of the museum rose for three floors above them in the darkness. Ulysses was aware of bizarre shadow-shapes looming out of the darkness all around him. As the curator trotted anxiously after the invaders of this sanctuary, Ulysses and Nimrod turned on their torches.

Ulysses gasped in delight as his sweeping beam illuminated the leering faces of a totem pole, suspended Eskimo kayaks and luridly-painted Balinese ritual masks. The place never failed to evoke a familiar thrill of wonder and joy.

Ulysses had been a regular visitor to the University Museum of Natural History and its Pitt Rivers' extension, when he had been a student at Boriel College, sometimes for purposes of study, at other times simply to luxuriate in the eccentric, jingoistic glory of it all.

It was a magical place, a monument to the attitudes and explorers – like Captain James Cook – who had helped to make Magna Britannia great.

It was rumoured that the collection contained half a million objects, displayed according to type – everything from masks and musical instruments, to fetishes, jewellery and weaponry. And it was the last of those things that had brought him back here on this dark Christmas Eve.

His own collection of esoteric and exotic pieces from around the world were almost a homage to this wonderful relic of the nineteenth century, but it couldn't compare to this collection gathered during Cook's expedition to the South Pacific and since donated by Lieutenant General Augustus Henry Lane Fox Pitt Rivers.

"Most irregular, you say," Ulysses announced, suddenly turning on the thin-faced curator, shining his torch beam directly into the startled man's face. The curator threw up a hand to save himself from being blinded.

"So is murder, Mr...?"

"It's Doctor, actually," the curator bit back. "Doctor Brierley."

"Would you happen to know if there was such a thing as a Hootoo Clan fighting-fist in the museum collection?" Ulysses asked, turning his torch back onto the display cases full of shrunken heads and flint axes that surrounded him.

"Wh-What? W-Well, yes," the flustered curator flapped, "as it happens."

"Ah, I knew it! I was sure there was." He turned back to the curator who was still trying to knot the belt of his dressing gown about his waist. "Can I see it?"

"Er, yes... I-I mean no."

"Ah! And why not?" Ulysses pressed, leaning towards the curator, breaking the invisible barrier of Doctor Brierley's own personal space. Brierley took a nervous step backwards, only to find Nimrod there, looming over his shoulder, watching him with eagle-intensity. "Lost it, have you?

"Oh, no. It's out on loan."

"On loan?"

"Yes, along with a number of other items, to the college."

"Which one?" Ulysses said, his voice low and intense.

"Christ Church."

Ulysses' look of diffident arrogance began to weaken and his face began to pale. Things were not working out quite as he had expected them to.

"And in whose name was the agreement made?" he asked, his throat suddenly tight.

"The Reverend Havelock of the cathedral."

IX – MURDER IN THE CATHEDRAL

"This is hardly the time, or the place," the old priest chided, keeping his voice low as the lilting strains of the choir soared into the vaulted roof of the cathedral. "Can't you see that we are in the middle of celebrating Midnight Mass?"

"Tell me then, Reverend," Virgil Ashton-Griffiths rallied, "when *would* be a good time to discuss your son?"

Lucy looked from the Master to the old priest and back again, her mouth agape in appalled amazement.

The old man hesitated before answering the Master's challenge. "What are you talking about? What is this talk of a son? I have no son!"

But he had hesitated too long before responding to the Master's accusation.

"You and I both know that you do have a son, Reverend, and that he's alive and – although I wouldn't go so far as to say well – abroad in Oxford!"

"This is outrageous!" the old man hissed. He had to be in his eighties – his late seventies at least – Lucy thought as she studied the quivering wattles of the old man's neck and the liver-spotted scalp visible beneath the few wisps of white hair. He was turning an extraordinary shade of purple. "How dare you come in here, on today of all days, making such wild claims!" he fumed.

"I dare because it's the truth!" the Master snarled. His steely gaze locked with the rheumy eyes of the old man. "We all knew even when we were at University, the first time we met Marley – the priest's bastard!"

Fire leapt in the Reverend's eyes at that but it seemed that the Master's brow-beating persistence had paid off; the old man was no longer able to avoid the younger man's glaring gaze.

"I feel like I have the blood of enough men on my hands as it is," Ashton-Griffiths went on. "I need absolution, I'm fully aware of that, but your need is greater than mine."

The Reverend seemed to visibly shrink before Lucy's eyes, his shoulders sagging, his stick-thin scarecrow frame shrouded by his plain black cassock.

"Very well, he said," his voice softer now. "Come with me."

The old man turned and led them back towards the entrance of the cathedral, away from the candle-lit nave and the host of the Christmas faithful.

Oxford's cathedral was packed. The building was small by the standards of other cathedrals, no bigger in reality than many ordinary churches, and it was never fuller than at Midnight Mass. It was only a matter of minutes now until Great Tom tolled twelve and welcomed in Christmas Day.

Her heart thumping in her chest, Lucy followed the Master as the Reverend Lemuel Havelock led them with faltering steps towards the shadows beneath the raised organ loft.

The choir concluded its anthem and there was the rustle of carol sheets as the congregation rose to their feet, with an accompaniment of coughs and throat-clearing. Then the strident tones of the organ began to sing out, breaking into the tune of 'O Come All Ye Faithful'.

"Here, there's something I should show you," the old man said, still with his back to them. Lucy couldn't be certain in the gloom at the back of the church but it looked like the priest was fumbling for something within the sleeve of his cassock.

He spun round with surprising speed, the carved wooden blowpipe already to his lips and gave one short sharp puff.

The tiny thorn lodged in the Master's neck. Ashton-Griffiths gave a brief cry of surprise and fell to his knees, one hand to where the thorn had entered his flesh. A second later, he fell face first onto the cold stone-flagged floor.

Lucy froze, a stifled scream caught in her throat, as the old man turned to her, a second thorn ready between his lips.

Some of those at the back of the congregation turned and looked back, peering over their shoulders into the shadows beneath the organ loft, uncertain as to what they had heard over the stirring refrain of the carol.

The west door banged opened, the resounding crash reverberating throughout the cathedral. The organist played on, but by now many among the congregation had stopped singing and were exchanging comments and glances instead, as they craned their necks to see who had invaded the sanctity of their Christmas celebration.

"Reverend Havelock! Stop right there!" Ulysses Quicksilver bellowed.

The old man darted a glance the dandy's way, caught completely off-guard by his arrival. The blowpipe still to his lips, the old man puffed again and Ulysses – reacting to the sudden lightning burst of his heightened sixth sense – ducked in time to avoid the dart that came propelled by the breath. He fancied he felt, or heard, the thorn-dart whistle past his ear before being stopped by the door of the church swinging shut behind him.

And then, as Lucy stood rooted to the spot in terror, standing over the body of the Master of Boriel College, with a surprising turn of speed, the priest was away, up the cast-iron spiral staircase to the organ loft.

Ulysses followed, scaling the twisting staircase as

quickly as he could. He reached the loft only a moment after the old man and came face-to-face with the priest's puff-cheeked face.

The merry playing of the organ broke off in a cacophonous crash of registers and pedals as Ulysses threw himself sideways onto the startled man, barely avoiding a second poison-tipped missile.

By now, even the choir had realised that something was wrong. All had ceased their singing and were craning their heads to follow the progress of the two combatants above them.

Having untangled himself from the shrieking organist, Ulysses turned to find the old man gone.

"He went that way, sir!" Nimrod called from below, pointing to a narrow stone archway and the tight spiral stair that lay beyond it.

"Give yourself up, man!" Ulysses shouted across the void of the tower. "There's nowhere for you to run!"

He glanced from the withered form of the Reverend Havelock, scrambling unsteadily between the arches of the colonnade beneath the high stained glass windows of the cathedral tower, to the body of the church far below them. He could see pale faces peering up at them from between the myriad nimbuses of candlelight that formed their own constellation of Christmas stars below.

"Never!" Havelock shrieked back at him. "You really think I'm going to give myself up now?"

Distracted, the old man lost his footing. The congregation below them gasped in horror as one. The Reverend Havelock lurched forwards, making a grab for the next stone column as his right foot slipped off the precarious ledge he was attempting to negotiate. Ulysses' breath caught in his throat.

"But you're going to get yourself killed!"

"What do I care? I'm an old man. I might die in my sleep this very night! And my son's life ended thirty-seven years ago. What have I to live for?"

Deciding that actions, in this case were definitely going to speak louder than words, Ulysses gave up attempting to talk the old man down and instead set off in pursuit, swinging from one columned archway to the next, using his unnaturally strong left arm to aid him in his gymnastic endeavour.

Havelock might think he had nothing to live for, but Ulysses wasn't going to let him get off that lightly; he wanted to see him brought to book for what he had engineered. He wanted to see justice served.

With one last death-defying swing, Ulysses cut the last corner of the tower and threw himself into the colonnade opposite the spot from where he had commenced his approach on the old man.

Preternatural senses flared and Ulysses doubled up as the warning bolt of prescience shot right into the middle of his brain. The old man was ready for him. A vicious kick to the shin brought Ulysses down hard and he almost lost his grip on the stone pillar he was still holding with his primate hand. The priest bore down on him, blowpipe to his lips once more, and this time, if he threw himself out of the way Ulysses would be throwing himself to his death on the stone-flagged floor at the bottom of the tower.

Grabbing the other open end of the carved wooden blowpipe, Ulysses tugged it forwards and put it to his own lips – and blew.

The old man dropped the primitive weapon immediately.

He stumbled backwards, palsied hands reaching for his throat, a choking rasp escaping his gaping mouth, his failing eyes wide with the shock of it. As Ulysses pulled himself to safety between the arches, the priest's faltering steps carried him to the edge of the ledge – and beyond.

Screams rose from the appalled watchers below, but the old man made no sound as he plummeted to his death. He was dead even before his skull cracked like an egg on the stones below.

X – IT'S A WONDERFUL LIFE

"So, you're done here, are you?" Lucy asked Ulysses as he walked out of the police station. His shoes crunched on the ice-crusted snow covering the ground.

"Yes, we're done here," he said, pulling up the collar of his coat against the cold and adjusting the scarf at his neck. He had a wide-brimmed hat pulled down firmly over his ears as well.

The Silver Phantom was pulled up next to the kerb, Nimrod at the wheel, the engine ticking over to warm the interior of the car.

"So, what's the story? Why did this all come to pass at this moment in time?"

"You mean, when the wrong done to the Reverend Havelock and his son occurred thirty-seven years ago?"

"Yes."

"It was all down to Doctor Lacey."

"Really?"

"Yes. It all started when he took up a new post at the Saint Ophelia Sanatorium for the Mentally Infirm. Marley was one of the residents there."

"That's something else, I don't understand," Lucy said, interrupting Ulysses' explanation of the events surrounding the Christmas Killings. "Why did Reverend Havelock let everyone think that his son was dead?"

"I would have thought that was obvious."

"Humour me," she said, nudging Ulysses in the ribs.

"Embarrassment. Marley had been a scholar, accepted to study at Boriel College, Oxford. It was all about intelligence, as far as the old man was concerned. And then his boy went and shot himself. He didn't know it had been part of some ridiculous college club initiation. The

Damocles Club members covered that bit up, remember?

"Havelock thought his son had attempted suicide, and suicide is a sin against God. As if that wasn't embarrassing enough he didn't have the common decency to die but instead survived, with the mental state of an idiot child, and with a Father Christmas fixation to boot. As far as the Reverend was concerned it was better that he kept his son hidden from the world, and let the world think his son was dead."

"But that's terrible."

"That's as maybe but then of course the Reverend didn't know that his son's condition wasn't a direct consequence of a suicide attempt."

"Yes, how did he find out?"

"Lacey wrote to him. The police found the letter at the Reverend's place. It was effectively a confession and suicide note all rolled into one. Lacey was manic depressive, you see, which meant that he understood what it was like to be mentally ill and so wanted to help others in a similar condition. But when he discovered that his one-time paramour was a dribbling infantile retard he was overcome with guilt and remorse, and started on a downward spiral of depression from which he never recovered.

"Somehow, the letter came to be posted after Lacey's death and when Havelock read it, it brought back all the memories – the hurt, the guilt – which soon turned to anger. And so he planned his revenge more for his own benefit than for his wretched son. But he was old, he couldn't accomplish what he wanted to himself and so we come to his crowning achievement; he used his own brain-damaged son as the instrument of his vengeance.

"He checked Marley out of the asylum, equipping him to fulfil his own dark designs, while he tracked down the surviving members of the Damocles Club, who Lacey had so helpfully listed in his confession. Chief Inspector Thaw and Sergeant Whately found evidence that Marley had been living with the Reverend Havelock in his quarters at the cathedral."

"Incredible," Lucy said, dumbfounded by the immensity of the reverend's plan. "So what will happen to Marley now?"

"I believe he's been returned to the asylum where he has spent the last thirty-seven years of his life, to live out the rest of it, in the maximum security wing."

Ulysses looked thoughtful for a moment as he studied the patterns the snow had made on the toecaps of his shoes. "It's ironic really."

"What is?"

"This all began because Marley wanted to join the Damocles Club but failed the initiation. And in the end, all the Damocles Club members are dead, and Marley's the only one left alive."

Ulysses turned from his musings to his waiting car.

"I can't tempt you to spend what's left of Christmas Day here, in Oxford?" the young woman asked, looking up at him from beneath the brim of her beret.

"Aren't you spending Christmas with friends or family already? Surely your life isn't all work, work, work. It's not good for you. You must have plans."

"Nothing that couldn't be changed," she said, her cheeks reddening in embarrassment. "I don't know about you but I could quite happily spend the rest of the day in bed, catching up, having not slept at all last night."

Ulysses grinned.

"Thank you for the invitation, my dear," he said, smiling wryly, "but Mrs Prufrock's coming in especially and will doubtless already have the turkey on the go. And besides, my brother Barty would cut a very pathetic figure if I wasn't there. You can't pull a cracker by yourself, can you?"

"You've managed," the young woman smiled coyly.

Ulysses took a deep breath. He gazed up at the clear cerulean sky, savouring the honeyed sunlight and the crisp cold air on his face. And then he turned from the car and returned to Lucy's side.

"Tempting as your offer is, and I may well live to regret this, but if I have learnt anything from the Case of the Christmas Killer it is that the rash actions of your youth will inevitably come back to haunt you one day, so, Merry Christmas, Miss Gudrun."

He lent forward and kissed her on her heat-flushed cheek.

"Well, you can't blame a girl for trying," she said, returning the kiss. "Merry Christmas, Mr Quicksilver."

Back in the security of his own cushion-walled room, he opened the jotter on the table in front of him and creased it flat at a clean page.

For the first time in as long as he could remember, he hadn't written a letter this year, but he hoped it wouldn't matter. Father Christmas would understand.

Pulling a bright red crayon from the box beside the jotter, clenching it tightly in the fist of his right hand, the tip of his tongue protruding from between his lips, he began to write.

Dear Farthr Krissmus,

I'm sorry I not wrote my letter in time this year but I was

on holiday with my Dad. It was a lot of fun. I haven't seen my Dad in ages. And I was a good boy, like he said I had to be. I always did as I was told and ate up all my greens, even though I don't like greens.

So now you know I bin good this year and said sorry for not writin in time can I have my present anyway?

I really liked seeing my Dad again so this year for Krissmus I dont want any more crayons or a puppy or nothin like that. I would like to go and stay with my Dad again. Do you think I could do that? I hope so.

Happy Krissmus

Love Marley

THE END

Cruickshank's
CABINET OF CURIOSITIES

Featuring the astonishing aquatic marvel
that is the **Whitby Mermaid**.

Presented by the
distinguished Curator
of the Grotesque and
Collector of the Macabre,
*Mr. Mycroft
Cruickshank, Esq.*
See it for yourself at The
Holbrook Museum now!

(It is recommended
that ladies of uncertain
constitutions be
accompanied by gentlemen
of resolute fortitude, due
to the wholly unseating
nature of some of the
exhibits therein.)